True Stories

Also by John Fraser and published by
AESOP Modern Fiction:

Animal Tales
Behaving Well
Best Friends
Black Masks
Blue Light / Starting Over
The Beach
The Case
Confessions
The Cure
Down from the Stars
The Ends of the Earth
Enterprising Women
Exploring the Clouds
Fake Fur
The Future's Coming Everywhere
Happy Always
Hard Places
An Illusion of Sun
The Magnificent Wurlitzer
Medusa
Mercenaries
Military Roads
The Observatory
The Other Shore
People You Will Never Meet
The Red Bird
The Red Tank
Runners
'S'
Short Lives
Sisters
Soft Landing
The Storm
Strangers and Refugees
The Test
Thinking Scientifically
Thirty Years
Three Beauties
Tomorrow the Victory
Unsteady States, Vol. I
Wayfaring
Wisdom

True Stories

John Fraser

AESOP Modern Fiction
Oxford

AESOP Modern Fiction
An imprint of AESOP Publications
Martin Noble Editorial / AESOP
28a Abberbury Road, Oxford OX4 4ES, UK
www.aesopbooks.com

First edition published by AESOP Publications

www.johnfraserfiction.com

A catalogue record of this book is available from the British Library.

First edition 2023. revised 2024

ISBN: 978-1-914938-04-7

Contents

True Stories

BIRDS. Always watching us. Songs and calls – incomprehensible and constant. They fly like our souls might. They do it casual. If there is a purpose – they know it, probably are part of it.

What might it be?

'Hi,' I say.

She doesn't look at me. Stands up, not looking at me through the window of the *guichet*, takes a beige coat from a chair, a cigarette, lights up and goes outside to smoke, not looking at me. *Guichet* comes to me unasked, the word ... *sportello: window.*

The hole in the stone, darkness, the oracle. Window: where you ask the question. The same, in all the universe, every language and none.

I'm a lumière, perhaps, looking for imperatives, reason. A dark light, not kindly.

Working conditions must be terrible here, I imagine, though the long room is bright and ventilated. There are clouds all round, and soporific music. I ask her colleague –

'Death statistics, I'm looking for them, to see how worried we should be.'

'Oh,' she says. 'We don't have those.'

'You're public health,' I say. 'There's been trouble here – shifting around: the water, the lake draining and the landslips, those clouds. The virus, naturally. It all adds up to where we're heading. And the heat....'

'I'm sure,' she says, 'those figures aren't kept here. Everyone who is alive will die – that's all you need to know. Be careful, read the instructions.'

*

Some places, if there's luck, the very poor and very rich – they live in mansions. Both types need gardeners. You never finish being poor. It's quick, stopping being rich. The big houses – exist for everyone.

If you're unlucky, the very rich need bodyguards and advocates, the very poor – don't last at all.

I lived in mansions – there were lots and lots of us. Jacob – my friend, must have grown up in a line of gardeners.

Each relished scents – the mock-orange, the wistaria. In everything else, we were competitive.

*

Horses will come back. Pulling, being ridden, whipped and spurred. I'm provident – I sow wild oats: in gardens, on unused ground – my old smock is full of seeds; a long brown coat like cellarmen used to wear.

'They put you on a list. It's the only explanation for your life, how people treat you, how you react. When, I wonder, have they put you on? There's no interest in you personally, what you think or might do. You won't do anything, once you're on a list. You start quite young – associating with a tired bunch, old militants, people of some distinction past, they devour you, sweet young thing. They've been cast down: publicists, resisters, objectors, conscientious or not, who do some time and then you get let out to labour – building what you might have wanted to destroy. They want new cages – and you don't, you want great plains to gallop in, but cages are what there is. Down the mine, in the foundry, into the camp. You must accept – you're fodder.

Or are you just not much good? You live a life where ladders are quite short, the snakes are everywhere and very long, and you fall down, and keep on falling, people avoid you, or they take your cash, they cry, they blame, and life gets really tough: the list must be to blame.... Humanity keeps the record, and your name.

Then your work is sabotaged, you're called in to where you don't belong and asked no questions – just to see you, so's you know you're on a list: and then your mates and colleagues – they know better than you – you're on a list, or ought to be, and ought to have known, and kept your distance, but the distance is already there. It's being close to dodgy people, knowing them or not, who somehow might have trained you. If you needed training.

There is no training – it's just being close to certain people, wrong ones, the rest is what everybody knows, it doesn't matter if in theory you were for, against, the cops, the robbers. You might be born that way, or simply strayed. The list, recording the training you might have had, even without recognising it, it doesn't matter, and besides, you're not an idiot, you are not innocent, you'd every right and indelible mark to be put on. That's the only way of knowing who you are and how your life will go, has gone, and everything you know, the people and the things, are on the list for ever, and it explains what you are, and all that happens to you. You don't need think, or have a brain. Being trained to be a person on the wrong side, or predisposed, because from the beginning you were a person predisposed, to be on the wrong side: potentially.

An error: people make them, you make lots.

*

'You can't be serious,' says Jacob, over my shoulder. 'This is trivial, a banal piece of life-in-the-world – the mousery, the beetlescape, novel without characters, lamentation. Anything worthwhile that you try to do and fail in – gets you on the list. If ever you succeed – it seems there was no list. Today, for you – life bets against you. Too bad. Go back to the big critique – the Kritik of pure bad, pure awful: ask "what is worse" than bad? Reason, and its effects? Pain: pain with its intensities, and times. Pain is worse than badness, harder to bear than living according to Reason.

'What is less preferable? – soldier in a short war, or being bombed in a longer one? ... the *lager* and its types, against the *gulag* and its sentences; the post-colonial or the colonial, the wars for communism and those against ... slavery for short, long periods ... the size of jail-cells: little food against rotting food: life in the mines or unemployment: forced sex or no sex ... deportation, dispossession, occupation, invasion...?

'You have the picture. If you ever can, what's to be preferred, what's to avoid? Absolutely. The pure bad? This is life, it's not ideas, it's situations – situations where power is rampant, you can't bring in ideas, beliefs, all that.... You made yourself impersonal – whoever you might be, succumbed, imprisoned, hunted – so, what's the calculus? Avoiding something means choosing something else – if we have the choice. This is what rules, this is the new philosophy.

'What's worse than bad, and worse than worse ...'

'I know,' I say, 'mine was a provocation, nothing more. My experience, everybody's fears – how can you classify? Everybody wants to win, or not to lose – so, there's no kudos in classifying what is worse, who you lose out to, get caught by, get caught up in the ramp of some repression.... It isn't trivial – it's beyond classification, beyond usefulness or expectation. Pointless.

'You're right – philosophy's no guide, it tells you what fates you should avoid, but when you're caught, it doesn't tell you if you might be lucky, escape the worse, or if you're dropping down – the darkness doesn't let you see the bottom....'

*

We were tired of words. We knew we were hypocrites, spinners of tales, twisters of tails. War. We all deserve what's coming to us, everyone has had a kick at the ball. No one set out to make what is happening ...There'll be nothing for a million years, hot as hell, no seasons. Don't worry – it'll pass in a flash – a metaphor .... you won't feel a thing. We deserve it, those who do and those who have it done .... If I had my time, I'd go seriously into flamenco. It suits my finger-picking skills, and makes up for being a poor shot and bad at sex. Music – the food of love, and you don't need line up for it outside the store, it comes straight in your ears.

'There's Zélie,' Jacob says. 'She's to choose between us two. It seems uncertainty, doubt, choice – it causes suffering. I'd say she has some luck – a choice between us is a choice between a pumice-stone and chocolate cake. Me and you. It's quite unique – she should rejoice, choose both or neither....'

'Anyway,' I say, 'I don't go in for contests of that kind.'

'You're not in contention,' Jacob says: 'It's all between her and her. No rules, no times.'

'Then there are new planets somewhere ... visible but insubstantial. Who knows,' I say, 'if there is life, there may be Zélies galore, who don't know choice, or forms of coupling, communication, we've not thought of. They could be brothers, sisters, nymphs and fauns that sit by streams of life, of water that provide long enjoyment, healthy nutrients....'

'You like simplicity,' he says. 'Two sexes, families of pick'n mix ... and yet, our planet rock is various. It's not just one and one that often make a kind of two. It boils and frosts. Another planet – probably made uninhabitable by things like us, re-peopled by things that exist, sort of, in controlled systems of complexity – let's imagine how their lives proceed through their centuries ... in flashes from a metaphorical trip that knows not only us, our details and our destinies. They'll know the lives of other distant creatures etched on sponges, stones, and swirls of gas whose sort-of lives grind on like lichens or like mayflies....

'So much for Zélie. Our destiny is trivial. We humans somehow made the choice to have gross gobbling lives, short and obese ... sex and friendship.'

'I think it in another way,' I say. 'Those elements that make a life – the hydrogen, the iron – that speed around in explosions that are supernova.... You might think of them as gods. No monotheism, none at all – just elements, equal, each indispensable, and I forget the third. Nitrogen? Or does that only make cucumbers grow? Helium?

'And Zélie – who is she? A routine life – would make a routine personality. And, if she is on the trail of novelties, what time for either of us would she have? And for herself?'

'And yet,' says Jacob, 'though no one knows her, if she exists and how – imagination gives her life, the odds are evens, you or me will win ... a what? Clearly, imagination can't distinguish between ghosts and us – we two, who walk and leap, and never will walk along by them, or anyone they know, or take a drink, or have us carry them to bed when they are drunk or stricken down by illnesses so rare – they're history! The people we shall never know, and can't pronounce on our reality, yours and mine....'

'I always say,' I say, 'distance and scepticism. We lived for multitudes of years in a reality of which we saw the utility and the threats for us. And lo! That reality was the frock of science! and Who knows – beyond science, what might lie? A carapace? Prickles, a thorny hedge – and revelation. Beyond revelation, what is there, I wonder ... the banality of being God who starts a chain of fissions, and sees it spark – uselessly and darkly, on and on; one in a million bits of dust that hosts a slime is you and me....'

*

Everybody knows – Creation was a trial, a boss shot, like Koreans firing rockets in the sea. A waste. Should we love them, rocket-builders, if they are democrats? We pretend there is democracy in America. Maybe there is. There's route 66 for sure, that's what they enthuse about. Creation was spoiled, but – the mayflies? Us. What do you do with us? Hats and caps, blues and greens: let them fight it out. Democrats and what – the bossed? The dispossessed, their chiefs? And who will win and shall we all be rich? Jacob doesn't care – he has a salary, and his obsession. Go far, far back, and plan it different, and wait and wait – maybe his eye is in a jar – watching the millennia clock up – the trees, each worth a thousand years, a life – beyond all measurement. On and on – nothing wasted, gutted out, all re-created, cycling round, the parts re-usable, eternally machined.... 'Yes, Jacob,' I think, reluctantly, to praise him. That'*s a Creation we can all applaud. Duration, the perfection – not of some ideal – just nothing thrown away, nothing that dies, nothing accumulates beyond the room available, nothing degrades, destroys another being, be the being tree or mushroom, ant-eater or feral horse ....*

'It's theatre,' Jacob says. 'Those guys who talk of things invisible and distances unthinkable – the bangs, the holes, the decompositions – the hells and ice-pits ... make you feel nauseous ... The frozen astronauts – they have the porthole to look through ... but they have icy eyeballs. The rest of us – until we are conscripted, the voyages are without profit, without sense. Three generations needed to exit a galaxy – two are expended, and the third which lands – has no way back.

'Back to nowhere – only the grandchild lives, with no water and no food, for fifty years. The planned survivor will stagger for ten metres, pay a tax and see a flower.'

'The systems, power systems – they converge,' I say. 'The structures and the promises, the punishments, indifference. The big power interprets everything – your rights and interests, its own; the culture, its strategy against the others ... how many might they be? Two or three, plus candidates? ... Better for you if you acquiesce. Your tiny power has gone – attach, if you want, to middling powers, the intermediaries: to charities, to media – they mitigate. Subscribe!'

'That's how it's always been,' he says. 'War, preparations, reparations, recovery, submission: and who wins, gets to commit the errors and the massacres – and gets off free. Is there a big winner? Do you know, my friend? The winner interim gets absolution, a pardon not requested. Maybe it's a scam, with no big win, just dust and ashes in a pot, the winner a famished shadow crouching on the heap of bones.'

Jacob is an evolutionary biologist. An anthropological geneticist. He wants to make us better. Starting with mixing the same colour, for everyone, a shady pale. Making us anonymous, sharing gods and stories. Giving us all the goal, ideals – all of us being kind and obedient. Forgiving and innocent.

It's a dangerous sport.

I look through my photos and postcards. I was in a dangerous thicket – lettuce-pickers.... Chavez; the comrade shot in a canoe in the dirty river, lots of soldiers, jingles, pizzas and grass – the silences and being thrown out of a tolerant country and not feeling a thing, the dislike, hatred, abandonment by friends – all coming later, like a hot wind on a husk; a scorpion's shell, and the scorpion moving on, stung out, naked, vulnerable flesh: no one afraid or able to identify, no alarm, just imminent of death.... The end's so near, you can be objective, calm, resigned.

'Your trouble is,' says Jacob, 'you had reservations – the toy battalions you joined were a joke, and you were stupid, questioning the joke. What a fool! You waved a white flag so the snipers could shoot you through the eye! Your side!

'They had your number – they kept their distance ... No! They didn't see you. You were mostly invisible, mostly not there....'

'I had postcards from all over,' I say. 'Loving, sensitive people, all on my side.'

'Ghosts,' says Jacob, 'suffering, suffering and martyred before you. The last martyr is no goddam use at all, everyone is dead, gone home, on a list, "NLS" – no longer sought. That was you – too slow.'

Jacob controls everything he does, small distant hypotheses for amateurs to mull over, cool. Or – swelling up, in nuptial plumes, he brings forth theories of humours for the planet – futures of species, wars, end of supplies and destinies. From counsellor to prophet – he plays every part. He is a guide, a shepherd, poet, divinity – the horrors find him prepared, a guardian, bursting with metaphors of catastrophe. Humanity – on the verge of total failure, disappearance, final chapter. He leaves his prophecy, written, probably unread – no matter. He's a celebrity, brought on to tranquillise.

As public voice – he's comforting. 'It might not happen....' 'If it does, here's what we do....'

With me, with individuals, he's a devil, persecuting, taunting, his fantasising that rots the brain, occupying the skull with poison coils, pushing the thoughtful porridge to one side.

I – have no hook that holds me to my neighbours, my survivor friends. I see the war, the blocks burnt out that reach the clouds, horizons packed with tents and sand. It's hell, I'm its inventor and its victim, there is no escape, nothing to avoid that is not real, grotesque. Jacob is the bully, showing me the print developed – his concoction, his vision: 'This is real! Get used to it.'

Jacob gives me his curse, his mischief. I'll fall down, collapse without an end, blundering with speech and thought – and he will ride me, bear me faster down, and pulp me.

'Listen,' says Jacob. 'Avoid the pop scene. Avoid success, avoid failure. Avoid characters, intimacy, being chosen, being fired: all the arts. Everywhere there's acting: so business and war are out.'

'What will that make me?' I ask. 'No one will know enough to write my obituary.'

'It'll come out,' he says. 'Long long after, but out it will come, you can be certain.'

*

This is a safe room. More like a corridor – and on the wall, two glass containers, on a brass wheel – cogs galore. A clepsydra, a water clock, with a machine to turn it when the lower case is full – but no one to use it, look at it. A strangeness, and I ask Jacob – 'Are you moving somewhere safer?'

He says, 'To quite another country, but I can't confirm or tell you where, because it may not after all be safer, but it's all arranged.'

'We're short of water,' Jacob says. 'Our research – it's taken most of what there is.'

'We could use what's in the clock,' I think, but do not say. Keep it to myself. He's the expert, I'm the genius.

'The water clocks are accurate,' he says. 'More than any other human thing.'

'I should have thought....' I say, and stop. Everything, if you think about it, is accurate.

'You're so close to Jacob,' Blandine, Zélie's mother, says to me. 'Are you sure he likes you? You plus him – you make a whole. Otherwise – you're a zephyr, he's a rock. Uninteresting – you fly away, he's a stodge.'

'Liking's different for everyone,' I say. 'He knows me as a degenerate. We were foreigners in the school, orphans, kind of, the only non-natives, non-Arabs. We weren't a bloc. We sheltered one another, sometimes – each was weak – Jacob provoked and lost, I gave in.'

'He seems to despise you,' Blandine says.

'I insulted him. I had hopes for humankind – no evidence. He thinks he is methodical, working on a plan. I gave up – he's a professional.'

She laughs: 'Nothing methodical, no method, convinces you? A scientist may be a rogue, and so you throw overboard all science?'

'Maybe I'm looking for some reality I might survive,' I say. Stupid. 'The illnesses, the wars – they disturb me greatly. Or – what disturbs me is what they told – the fear of death. It is disturbing, more than death. The death of others, all around, like in a game of spillikins, or bowling. A split, a spare – you're out there on your own – can't be touched unless....'

'An expert ... says....' she prompts.

'Maybe it's the choice,' I say. 'Some choices, they might signify, and others – merely trivial, ephemeral, sweet or sour – Zélie, choosing between me and Jacob, how is it possible? Two unlike entities.'

'Choice is that,' she says. 'And if you're unlike, you shouldn't care that Zélie doesn't choose you....'

'Yes,' I say. 'It would be meaningless. Not worth a pondering. But....'

'It's good that fortune wounds you,' Blandine says. 'It wounds us all. You're one of us.'

'It's the war. I feel it is a set-up,' I say, despairing. 'Either the provocation, the just cause, expanded, flew out of kilter, of control ... or there's a big plan.... There's big plans everywhere, the schools of war, academies, produce them each semester – a mass of them. But to persuade so many to take great risks, ally with infidels and mountebanks ... obtain finance, fix the accounts, the lobbies that have always disagreed.... And someone who can square the media, expose the suffering but draw no accounts of who and why goes down and down, thinks what.... And who agrees with me? Make war, commit atrocities and dare them to do unto you – worse and worse – it matters only to spectators, people you will never see in places you don't recognise – *they* need to feel the outrage – the belligerents don't. What happens, happens, it's all natural – who cares if prisoners are shot, if there is genocide – it's all a genocide....

'It's all a plan, devised and executed – that one day we shall know, and how it changes as realities unwind, and how our side may lose, and I unstick from our side that we ought to cheer, whatever it might do and stand for – and adhere – to *my side*, which in the past has got me on that list ... my side that won't participate, investigate, give credence, not to anything....'

'Distance,' she says. 'That's where you must stand. Stand on a hill, a knoll, and turn away. You don't know, don't know enough to have a view. The bad guys – they may be the victims. They started it because they were tricked in, and being bad guys, they didn't suspect the other guys of being bad or worse, more devious, more thoroughly thought through, less opportunist, or even more....'

'Or just consistent, Blandine,' I say. 'Following their genes, or what the preacher said or grannie, or the oracle ... their banker or their paramour....'

'Your goal is martyrdom, my dear,' she says, quite kindly. 'I'm sure you'll find what you suspect – if a country wants to rule the world, it'll have to beat the rest. By arms or influence, by deals – dirty, dingy, duplicitous.... Everybody knows it. Bad guys, good guys doesn't enter in, and everybody knows – but you're a martyr. It's good you didn't want to be a saint, but bad you've chosen martyrdom.

'You'll be proved right, one day, long after – when there's been an overturning, world revolution, an empire ended, another being formed. You'll maybe even get to be a saint, a hero. The new order welcomes, celebrates you, but you are dead; and would you care?'

'I want certainty,' I say. 'Proof. I don't like being wrong, and being fooled, though it is true – I'm exactly the kind of doubting guy smart people like to fool.'

'Any story,' Blandine says, 'must convince some of the clever ones.'

'If you could go back,' Jacob asks, 'how many years? Thirty? Not a happy time. You hope to find someone who would accompany you. It was in Dante – it's a recurring dream: the authority who loves you – and cannot break with you because it has no substance, it exists as long as you can want it. A thousand years? You'll be live and dead for generations. Do you want uncertainty? Or a second chance. They're just the same. You never wish for qualities that make your life a happy and successful one – they don't exist. Stupidity or genius? There's no reason to choose one or other.... I go back a million years. That's where we're heading to – even a billion, even to the moment when there was no light, and then there was. That's where we're at. Rocks and dust.

'That's where I can begin – the scum of life. And then – there's Zélie. Too bad, my friend. It's me she wants, not you....'

*

They make you run: they make you hunker down because the hunger makes you ache, and that will pass, but running, the escape, that's a need that never will.

'Zélie's gone on,' says Blandine. 'A house-party. Like they used to have – it seems, they still do. college boys and millionaires, benefactors and guys who run the wars – it's by the sea.'

'It's much beyond me, Blandine,' I say. 'You might ask Jacob if he's a democrat. As for Zélie – I think I'll pass....'

'Oh,' says Blandine. 'She isn't rich, she has her looks, is all.' And Jacob – is he a democrat? A funny question. I'd have my doubts about you – but him? He wouldn't have anybody tell him what to do, if that's the test. You? You're thinner than a paperleaf, you'd slip in anywhere. No one would fight for you, I think. They'll fight for Zélie, but that's a different thing – you couldn't call it principle....'

'I'm glad not to be a principle,' I say, 'I thought *that* was the test, not having one.'

*

Zélie writes, '*As you must suspect, everybody here's a playboy. Even the slaves – if they can't learn the emancipation codes they think exist – they would be playboys too. It's like the Frenchman said – the regime calls itself democracy, but everyone's the same, rats in a barrel, striving and equal, to reach the top.*

So, Jacob, you are right. Evolution could go different, though you don't know which way. It'll take you years, millions, before you see where the chain kinked, distorted. Where was it going? You won't know, and it's irrelevant. Being right – has no significance. It's a gamble – that nobody accepts.

And, Kochi – at last you reason out what everyone knows instinctively. By reason, argument, you make enemies, you're the cleverest, but any truth you find is trivial. Too late. Too obvious. Discarded. Where next? Don't start another trek: all your excursions end the same – back at the start or so slightly forward – the hare wins every time in every race, and you, the tortoise, confirm how slow a beast you are.

I'm happy here. I see as far as anyone can see. I'll seek my fortune, and have done with it – this is the best there is, and just for now – they're better at it here than the vainglorious warriors or the scrabbling mass. They're still tops, dictating to everyone, and as for altruism ... no one suffers for their neighbour, for their own sufferings there are cures....'

'Well,' says Jacob, 'She has chosen. Neither one of us – I'm glad. What would I do with her? What is her choice – treasure or sex? Neither of us two has both. She couldn't choose between us – she's unlikeable, we were rivals, not for her ... with each other. She can't be evaluated, she is not a prize. You can't go back to Bloomsbury, or the Secession, for someone like. She has no value stamped on her – she is not a *fiche.*

'She's in the maelstrom, flailing. We pretend domination is no more, that wars are aberrations, the world is filled with brothers, sisters.... The pretence holds good for those who are our masters – not for us.

'Why does she call you Kochi, by the way?'

'She thinks I'm like the Kochis – nomads and landlords, persecuted, powerful: mysterious and well-documented. It doesn't fit me absolutely right, but the incongruity's what makes the joke,' I say. 'No one knows whether to sympathise with them or keep well clear.

'And you're right – what do we do, with them, why do we seek them, pledge to them, struggle to keep them – friends and lovers? What are they for – our gratification? To complete us? We want the cuddles and the praise – but much much more. We want slaves to serve us, unseen plantations, serviced by lines of ragged toilers to pay our luxuries. Otherwise – it's all ephemeral. Zélie's right – we want good players on our team while the game's on.... Then – enough! it's over. The rest's misogyny and bullying. That's you, Jacob, my best friend ... I love you, naturally, hate you – and I'm wary of you – still my friend....'

'Your best and only, Kochi,' Jacob says.

*

That was long ago, not so long, but when 'misogyny and ephemeral' had some significance, some pejorative connotation. Then there was convergence, 'the one-world'; and soon after, autocracy, combat – the long perilous wrassle. Many were reassured. The time was tough, determined, solid, even as everything tumbled down and rotted.

Long ago we were young enough to want a job for life, to have a life for life – explore it, cosset it, that same one. Evolution came slow back then, in years, not weeks: we shaped existence like shaping clay. The persecutions – you could count them, they seemed throwbacks, aberrations.

Zélie is a benefactor, a collector, and her partner is the same, he buys people and collects money, so doing good. She collects art, does no good – or maybe they are more alike and are the same, just as she said. Collecting and investing....

'I know so much, so many things,' says Jacob. 'But it doesn't seem to fit into a salary. I'll have to ask you for a bridge, Kochi – as they say: "today it's you who lends, tomorrow, it may well be me".'

'You go too far back, Jacob,' I tell him. 'People don't want to know "why" things have happened so – still less, "how'll we put it right". They want solutions, survival – any cost: that's enough.'

'Everything has goals,' he says. 'Maybe dreams don't have goals, but goals have dreams. I'm a crank. We're all cranks. Ruling the world's a bore – I want something more interesting, with more power.'

'In my case,' I say, 'they don't want a reason for decisions, they want to see a weight of opinion. Perhaps there's reasons, probably not. What matters is the weight, and not the process.'

It may all be true.

'The army would take you, Jacob,' I say. 'The psychological side. The resentment everyone who enters there – helps their aggressiveness. It's probably essential. It's that which interests you: – why people fight for imponderables you can't eat or fuck.'

'Oh,' he says. 'We both feel we've been fished in – a bad deal. We seethe. At present, everything is shifting, nothing's consistent. The same people believe the opposite of their beliefs. When there were more species, it was more complex, and more simple. You knew your place. You were taught principles – they were your bones. Animals – the same. Armies upset everything. You have no limits, and no haven. It ought to be the ultimate challenge. Where do you stand? With the winners, obviously – do you want them, do you like them?

'Why join them? They don't want you....'

'I'm very short of cash, Jacob,' I say. 'It hits us both – the spend, the lend.'

THE OBSERVERS

'You'll pay us, Claude, to pry and report?' asks Jacob. 'It's all too true....'

We're an awkward couple, needing the cash, but sceptical.

'What's the end?' asks Jacob.

I think, 'What's the beginning, why does it lead to such penury? Such repetition. Cities and huts – the earliest ones, the latest – they haven't moved, they haven't changed. The great illusion is that they were primitive, a ghost of an idea. It isn't so. They've stayed the same. We've lost, along the way – certainly, protecting deities, the sacrifices, the games, festivities, processions with the living god ... Maybe we're fantastic like we think, but we reached our limits very soon....'

'The start showed how the solutions were limited,' says Jacob. 'Or rather – the limitations were with us from the start. The resources, the seasons, hours that circulate, bodies wearing out.'

'You two,' says Claude, 'Could be the perfect team.'

He puts on a movie. Stick men, like Maasai, run and run, maybe they attack, maybe they flee.

Claude, the guy who manages the charity, the spy-hole, human rights ... says, 'You can't see them, but there's observers – just like you – over the hill, where you can't see. Everyone is always everywhere, nothing goes unnoticed. People from all over, representing no power but truth and conscience – volunteers, taking notes in every tongue....'

A tall guy, racing on, a boombox on his shoulder.... 'That's genius,' Claude says, chuckling. 'The music – God amongst us –

Dieu parmi nous. I expect you recognise ... Messaien. A great ecologist, a man of faith.'

Then we see – the red wall of – sludge? It can't be water, unless there is a bloom – of algae, krill....

'A holding pond,' says Claude, 'It burst. Used for tinning, I believe. It ought to stand there in the sun, solidify. Then you can bury it. But no! and there it comes. An accident? Or sabotage. Covering the land, a red sea, fatal if it catches you, a heel....'

We're fascinated. 'Can you observe that?' Claude asks. 'The deaths, the struggles?'

There's no right answer.

'Don't worry,' Claude says, laughing. 'They're actors. Suppose it's real....'

'I think it's real,' says Jacob. 'And – I don't feel a thing.'

'Ah, sentiment,' says Claude, switching off the scene. 'You lost the same woman? How archaic it sounds! It makes you brothers, inseparable, all your life, as brothers are, with no escape, and lets you find the missing sister ... but the incest taboo cuts in. That's a limitation too – you'd think some intercourse would set things right – but no. Paws off!'

'We'd be observers, Claude,' I say, 'at the peep-hole, the primal scene, perhaps. Sentiment – does that come in?'

'Oh, you'll find soon enough,' he says. 'It all falls. Be used to it. Rates of exchange, the credit ratings – you ride high, but you must know – it falls, the city empties, empire drains away, the people wander off, into the forest or the desert, and they leave no trace at all. Nothing. What ever could you expect? That you observe the scene and it is real, and you go on for ever, like the scene, and like the movie, like the story, like the sentiment, the truth, humanity?'

'You make the job sound very hard,' says Jacob. 'Observing's what we've all been trained to do.

It's good, it's better that than acting, even than making movies about why we're what we are; or running from the sludge ....

'And we'd be being paid—'

'—a pittance,' Claude cuts in. 'But you get to set it up – the story. The participants. Hypotheses – they're yours. Yours is the genius – you're Scheherazade, you see faces in the fire, the trees that speak, the vixen with her fable, the trucker with the parable – observe, report, conclude. You, Kochi, have an open mind, and Jacob resents what he can see, but sees it in 4D ... a perfect foil for you, I'd say....'

He's keen to sign us up, for sure.

'Where does this lead, Claude?' Jacob asks.

'The judgement is humanity's,' says Claude, pompously. 'All judgement is. We hope – something will be done. Emotion stirred. Blame. Remedies. A swift reaction. Maybe nothing, nothing at all. Report, describe – you can't do more.'

'I'm already working,' says Jacob: 'All my life – observe, you can't avoid....

'You refer to men of faith.... Is that where our money comes from?'

'It comes from hope,' says Claude. 'Our ultimate aim – is making things go better....'

'Well,' says Jacob, quite aggressive, 'If the universe wasn't designed for us humanity – it's all a printer's pie. Us – stuck here: no goal, no rules.'

'It may be so,' says Claude. 'It isn't relevant.'

'It's clear,' Jacob goes on. 'That God could not design an arsehole. Maybe he hadn't one, or hadn't looked. It is grotesque. A mess. That's where hope lies? I can't imagine your "going better...." And that is fundamental....'

'You've been proved wrong, Jacob,' Claude replies, turning as red as sludge. 'You're there to tell the truth of what you see. That's the first step. Then, sometimes, comes the remedy. You're a cold eye. Others may act – you don't.'

'So,' Jacob says, quite satisfied. 'That is the limit. Now, I see.'

'Everybody knows;' says Claude: he ponders – '.... I wonder if you're right for me...?'

'We are,' I insist. 'It's just that truth's a provocation. What we see is not the truth....'

'Yes,' says Claude. 'It is.'

We leave it there. We need the cash. Jacob and I – we're far beyond philosophy, and tussling over words.

'You *must* doubt us, Claude,' says Jacob. 'We're amongst you, amongst everyone, but we don't know what will happen to us, to what we see, to the story that we make of it....'

It's a mistake, to tell the boss too much. I elbow Jacob, to shut him up.

We get sent to somewhere where there's bodies in the streets.

'They've been dug up and shot, for sure,' says Jacob. 'Natural deaths. And in a war, death by shooting's natural. It could be, of course, they are not dead. Just acting. Anticipating what's inevitable.'

'No,' I say. 'To me, they're dead. They do not contradict, they have no tale, no soldier's tale: quite mute. No after-life, no sadness, and no mourning. Do not speculate further – what we can't know, we can't just guess....'

It isn't what we want, neither of us. Puzzles abound, we don't need showcase more of them. We have no sister, we're not brothers.

'You haven't understood,' Claude said. 'The scene, the picture you have made – that is your creation. You can't do more than that. Nothing more than that is possible.'

'Banal and sentimental,' Jacob says. 'If all's creation, nothing is. It's grind and process....'

We're casting round. We don't make sense and no one listens. We observe, and mostly nothing comes of it. The reality of there and here – all goes in the archive, into the catacomb.

'You'll try ecology,' says Claude. 'You were good on breaking dams, the flight, the tragedy – less so with the militias. Nature is an emptying field, but studying it – a crowded one. I'm not sure you and Jacob have the thrust....' He laughs, puts on a quizzical smile.

*

'Zélie,' Jacob says: 'Introduce her and her cash to Claude. He'll have to give us work for ever.

*

And that's what starts to happen.

'While you two tough guys are in transition,' says Claude, the boss. 'You can doss down in the park.... It's warm at night – the hay is made, it is your madeleines, like summers long ago – your Hodge-like ancestors left you destitute, no doubt, but ah! – the scents of nature.... Hedgerows, jack-in-the-pulpit, cuckoo-spit, love-lies-bleeding, fox gloves, wolf's tongue – those were imprinted in your nose....'

'It isn't so,' says Jacob. 'My ancestors were mariners – for me, the past is fish and waves.'

The hay is full of life – there's stinging hoppers.... 'Nature!' shouts Jacob, slapping his skin. 'What can we do with it?'

'I'm educating you,' says Claude. 'You've seen that observing bears no rules, there's no reaction guaranteed, and you've no powers.... You meet with secrecy, procedures infinite – and really, that's all the response.... It's always been that way – the massacres bring glee or sorrow – or nothing, absolutely nought at all....

'My plan is this – forget the general indifference, don't expect that there'll be a popular response. Everybody knows disaster stalks the world – what's to be done? Not anything that anybody knows.

'You see – the arming of the world, the militarisation of our lands, the spying universal, security, and torture pens – that is not enough ... disaster comes, and grows! Despite variety – what we call 'the freedoms' which arise from difference, the lack of uniformity – the world is ruined, and inequality the rule.

'I set you two to see what happens; how disaster continues, on and on, and gathers strength. Then, consider nature – our resources shrink – smaller and smaller, under siege.... The universe sails on, sterile and inhospitable ... what's to do? Who shares stuff out, and how?

'I have a remedy! Not that I invoke or re-create a dream of past and never-happened ease.... I have in mind another script. Rules, and order – those bring happiness.

'You two prepare the ground that's all.'

'You're not a philosopher, Claude,' says Jacob, scratching, 'You don't understand the world. As for changing it: it changes willy-nilly – do you want the credit? Or more understanding?'

'Let me explain,' says Claude, thinking fast. 'Observing is a tribute to – what? Not the truth – no one can observe that, it must be constructed from the abstract and the concrete.... Nature? You're already in a conflict, Jacob. You must become your itch, and not your scratch. Caress the sting. You're food! – it tingles, naturally.

Accept! You are the cow – the bishop saw it in the field, now there, now not, now a two-pounder on your plate....

'As for the people, who are actors, naturally, and yet – they're not, they tumble into roles and can't get out.... I'm troubled by existence: ethically? Not quite so. Aesthetically? – seeing the deaths, inevitable and premature, deserved or legal, our business and someone' else's – war crimes or condoned under the rules of war – I feel. It doesn't last, the feeling – maybe because there's always something more to feel. Maybe they're guilty victims, traitors from our side, or cancelled out by poison leaks, or hot or cold ... anonymous, fortuitous ... there's fever and your itch, Jacob my friend. There's sentiment, for sure – and reason tempers that and drives it off; and then there's health, that in the end breaks down.... Or maybe health demands that we forget, don't suffer for, or as, an other; other than ourself....'

'You want to change the world, Claude? You too?' asks Jacob, arms and legs scratched raw....

'Poor Jacob,' Claude says, trying to cuddle him, without transferring blood. 'Observing your similars, alikes, your brothers, with sympathy, perhaps, or just cold-eye – that was your first exercise. Then you pass on, to the measurement of nature that we live off and destroy: you might suspect there is a contradiction there. Development as suicide.... Is that too strong? Can we live together, feed the black fly and grow avocadoes too?'

'That's the question that we started from,' I say. 'Now you have Zélie on your side. What strings has she fastened to her cash?'

*

'To make the world seem very very small,' Zélie says, 'you must be very very rich. And you two – all excited, covered in pustules.... I remember, each of you had a wing to offer me. It's not seemly to take one wing from each, but how I'd fly with one; small, grey? And a sparrow's flight! – birth to death, blind and scared ... frightened of the light....

'I had to find a person with two wings on offer – long and spotted ones – who'd fix them on with golden glue, and still have credit in the bank. You guys – you've talent for yourselves, for me there'd only be some sex. I want much more, much less.'

'Beware the sun, Zélie,' says Jacob, 'the glue – it isn't fast ... those ponderous wings....'

'Oh,' she says, 'I'm flightless. I seek out blue males who live in bowers. I'll give a touch to twigs and such, trust in designer's luck, and scuttle off....'

'Poor Zélie,' I tell her, 'we know you are an abomination, and now we're much much older than you are....'

'Oh,' she says, 'that's an effect of coin. We rich – we burnish. But tell me – how is Claude? I wouldn't give my wealth to someone poor.... Claude has sponsors, so his story's sound.... But you two – first observers, then nurturers of the sward ... now Jacob, your mate – is love-lies-a-bleeding, furrowing like an ape ... his nails no longer up to scratch....'

'We saw some pain, Zélie, some caused by fate and much intentionally,' I say. 'We ... reported it, and so moved on. Claude watches movies – "end-of-days"....'

'Oh,' Zélie says, 'I saw one – it happened in a train. The poor – wanting an upgrade – I'm on their side. I've always been. The trains, though, don't have classes in them now. There was a book about the end – fire and blood, when I was young ... but I don't do religion now, and anyway, there won't be people then. Good and bad will have no sense – you'd need to settle that right now. Forget the angels too – they might be albatross, of course ... a metaphor....'

'Claude wants you to make the speech,' says Jacob. 'He says we won't get anywhere unless they involve the rich. There's no resentment, no one must be shamed.... He's rich, of course, but by donations – that's all he wants from you.'

'I'd like to see the circus bring back animals,' says Zélie. 'Those ostriches! The way they danced!'

'I think you'd need another face, Zélie,' I say. 'Maybe the one we used to love ... soft and young, before you got the cash....'

'I do have another face,' she says. 'You'd have to take this old one off. It's underneath. You realise, it would take me further, away from you, and possibly you wouldn't even recognise me.... And the old face would need to be preserved, an icon, as they say....'

'There's no risk now,' I say. 'I don't judge by appearances, experience is duff, reality shifts like the clouds. Plans, blame, and change? I've quite grown out of that. We don't believe in judgement now, it doesn't change a thing.... If you insist, people resist....'

'Zélie'll have to learn the speech,' says Jacob. 'I doubt she has the mind right now. As for the face – it's not a thing that Gucci sells, with buckles or a zip – going right back is painful, I suspect, you might feel stupid or naive.... We'll have to snip the old face off, the new one needs to dry....'

GHOSTS

'Massacres and nature,' Zélie reflects aloud, to us. 'I see all the land animals, the only ones we've left – raised and loved and killed and eaten by us. Then, they say – we could switch – we'll eat the fish. Maybe there's no impact ... except on me. The sadness ... the old clubmen, the groupers: knights in armour – crabs and lobsters: ... and the soft intelligent blushing octopus, the artist....'

'They're not like us,' Zélie,' Jacob says, quite gently. 'That's why we love them. Maybe they are like us. Let's think they're not.'

'They're ghosts,' I say. 'We suffocate them, throw them in a bin to die, strangled by the richness of the air. Unfinished lives – they are the unseen ghosts, they indicate there'll be suffering, ever and ever, never less and never stopping – the faces ... yours, discarded, ours – bitten and inflamed....'

'The armour,' Zélie says. 'Who wears it? Who are the lords? Who do they fight for?'

'Turtles,' says Jacob. 'And their children, the salmon ... the nostalgic ones, the exiles – who come home from the wilds to die....'

It doesn't fit, but Jacob, Zélie, – they are satisfied. I say, 'This isn't it at all. The society we make – spied, controlled, enrolled, a military bloc, like the Roman tortoise – shielded from the sides and from above ... we need it to have an enemy. Hunger hurts, so make our enemy nature: all that we thought we're not.... We have no nature, we're on the move, we transmogrify, and so we're free to kill whatever we are not.... Our aggressiveness comes from the search for food and hunting it – satisfy the hunger, we can confront the abstracts – pride and fear. Values appear when we have eaten nature, ours and everyone's....'

They laugh.

Claude listens in. He's not impressed. 'Free food and heating? The guy who thought that civilisation changed the form of our hostility, that culture could take symbolic forms that calmed our savageness – he saw that he was wrong. Or, at least, not right. Neighbours persecute their nearest, like hates like, and gangs together in a hatred of unlike....

'Zélie has a fine, a rare intelligence and sensibility. I need her help, her money. But not her. She doesn't grasp what's wanted, what I want. I can't use her, can't have her speak for me.... The massacres of humans by their brothers, the military turn, the destruction of the means to satisfy our needs ... that's the connection that I want ... we want, have always wanted, to live in regiments – our order creates destruction and disorder, that is the dialectic of totality....

'I don't wish to soften what is hard.'

There is a pause. 'That's my conclusion, Claude – it is incurable,' says Jacob. 'Chaos, defeat, self-murder. And inevitable.'

DESIRE

'Where do you live, Zélie?' Jacob asks.

'Where a river bends.' she says, 'Indians lived there – not that it's in India. You could pretend it's anywhere, but what good would that do?'

'Do you always think of what good things do?' I ask. 'It's a trick I've never learned.'

'You want to ask, "the person I live with, who is that?", and for me to say, "I don't know,"' she says. 'That would mean I have so little I'm hankering for your desire. It isn't so. What I don't know, it doesn't disturb me, not a bit.'

'We wanted you to toughen up the talk,' says Claude. 'None of the "study, inform yourself, live a better life, the destruction will be less...." Humans will put an end to themselves very quick – forget the slow burn, the hot, the cold – a few months and it will all be done. By the sword.

'Fish won't come into it. Nor gasoline. Just finish.

'Stopping that would be a big test, whether you think it's worth it, or you don't care. Ending death, and not empowering birth: just stop! Stasis. Silence.

'Perhaps you're on the other side. Try the trickery, the shell game, the three cards – re-start the engine, fly the balloon. Save the world, and everything within. You may think the risk of the catastrophe is worth it: or that there's no risk. End it, no last day. That takes desire.

'Mere continuity – it's a cop-out, bland. Let the injustice be done and may the heavens fall. Eternal life is the unearned reward. That's justice? If you think that way.... Thinking?

'That's desire. Can you do that, Zélie? Can you stand on the edge, look down and jump; the depth is illusion. Is that in your power? I don't think so. Is it worth doing? I'd need to hear you try, before I'd know.'

'I've your fish in my head, Zélie: circling round – my skull's an empty bowl,' says Jacob, losing all our threads.

'Your mother, Blandine, said you're poison, Zélie,' I shout out, surprising everyone. 'You mislead, but as we follow you – we lose ourselves, you too. I think your self-assertion is your goal ... the rest, the truth, the justice ... hot air for a mongolfier.'

'Did you find those, Kochi?' Zélie asks. 'The values? Put them on the map, even if you don't go there. Share the info with us, if you did.

'For me – the fish are emblematic, but they're also there, all-sorts stretched out upon the slab: those mouths – the last words clenched between grey lips, the last twitch of the tail ... it's you, Kochi, you lie there in the street, a husk, no one to cover you .... dropped off the stall, your eyes cods' eyes, as dim as cabuchons – you've no enemies now, so who's to dig them out, your eyes and what they've seen, and value them, and everything they've gazed on...?'

'It's always rhetoric, Zélie,' says Jacob. 'Time has our number – all of us, the hake, the flounders and the dabs. Just realise – that's all you're wanted for, a speech. Already written, every pause in pencil – unruffling your sweet face – those fighting words come out unarmed and scented ... ah! if only there could be desire, for me, for Kochi, Claude. I'm an angry bitch, and Kochi – is water, strolling by, just gravity the force: no story there. We are not innocent, Claude is a postulant, Kochi and me are destitute. Lean down and pick us up, and hug us, cosset us, and pardon us when we scratch out dream-lines in your cheeks and run away. You're poison, Zélie....'

'I can't agree,' says Claude, much put out. 'She's exactly the mouthpiece that I sought. Welds together all catastrophe that's made by man on man, and by mankind on what surrounds....'

'You want a saviour, Claude,' says Jacob. 'It's an angel of death you've found. In our myth – they are the same. The accounting, the summary of what we made, and now move on....'

'That's crap,' says Claude, though not convinced. 'You mean – they'll love her and discount her tale? A true Scheherazade? You guys,' he starts to shout, pushing me and Jacob to one side, 'You're glib! You have self-interest. You've an agenda that excludes the rest – moreover, you've no capital...'

'You haven't understood,' says Jacob. 'Zélie is like us, she's one of us. A human, beautified and framed – but still a mortal, human. She's co-responsible. People who do what she condemns – are us. You'd need someone else from somewhere else to criticise, to spur us down another track.... We, locked in our brittling bones, we maybe deviate – but we cannot change our destination and our shape....'

'Someone else, you mean?' asks Claude. 'We need an external arbiter? From space, maybe, or green smudges crawling on a leaf?'

'Certainly not,' Jacob says. 'But Blandine wanted something new – and Zélie isn't it.'

'She's right about the fish,' I say. 'We underplay their sentiments.'

'That river bend,' says Jacob. 'One day the whiskery carp will crawl ashore and start another dynasty. Till then – we have our memories. Oh! How we wanted, longed, to be desired.

'That's all gone by a while ago, of course....'

'I'll take the cash and put her on the stage,' says Claude, decisively. 'She'll get her "likes", and till the verdict comes – "don't like, don't trust", or probably "don't care", I'll have her spin my tale.'

THE SOLDIERS' TALE

'The army didn't get to set up every supreme chief, the potence, the emperor,' Jacob says. 'It was the system didn't hold ... all the rest of it: the corruption. The line went crazy – mass-produced emperors. And the rich weren't taxed. Most people went to the track most days, and watched TV.... But it was salutary: when they lost their armies, on bad days: Syria, Germany – they forgot, did it all again. Then, in the capital, some saw how people outside were really civilised, had plans, were warlike every bit as they, the sceptics, the unappeased.

'The soldiers? – when they were beaten, if they survived the chop, I bet they went off and opened burger joints, or made fine baklava. I would have been one of those....

'You, Kochi, would have been barbarian. Finding a weak spot, infiltrating. Not knowing what to do – assimilate, or copy what you found: more modest than invasion, but original – the most, the first, original that had been seen for years.... Set up a private tabernacle for a private god? Free animals from the free steppe, *repoussé* in gold, wear on your finger as a ring?'

'You're right on one point, Jacob,' I tell him. 'The system didn't work. The only thing that did – was soldiers. Not the generals, not strategy T– but numbers and discipline, cash and standard tools. Weapons that don't break, explosives that go bang.'

'The people must feel that their existence counts,' he says. 'Now, and after they have built the tower.

'They need the soldiers. Soldiers – don't need *them*. Don't make the draft? That means you're dross....'

'No one needs to sell their soul,' I go on, playing his hand. 'They're on the index, and the price goes up or down – for ever, or until there is a merger or a bankruptcy. It all accumulates somewhere: the value. For us – it's all ephemeral – the time is fixed, against us ... We don't see where things will end up, and what they're for: life is "pass the parcel", Jacob.'

And I find I'm full of tears....

'Desire,' he says. 'Wanting something, something you can do, and others too. That is your squeaky violin, you fiddle-faddle, and the tunes streak up and down the mountains, and you hear the sing-along ... "Left. Left, left right left."'

'You're spoofing me, I know,' I say. 'And I don't care. Zélie's just another siren – seat her on the rock, people will sail near to see – "my! she's naked, beckoning" – and then they'll spot the reefs, the sharks, and steer away.... Some will be wrecked at once, and the rest ... warned, titillated, and away, away...!'

'Say what you like, Zélie,' says Claude. 'None of us thinks hard of what we're going to say.'

She makes an embracing gesture. 'Drought,' she says, and pauses, then – 'The big land animals assemble, trek down to find new streams, and some grown rabid – a first-time gathering of the species, all the bugs: there follows – the funeral of all, unmourned. The big ones – marshalled and corralled, most moribund Then, there's followers – the bats, the worms, the pathogens ... ancient poxes, new horrors from the labs....

'My! How they die ... the buboes and the parched insides ... the huge, the tiny, the invisible – erasure, cancellation: a rout. And on to us – diseases camel-borne; plagues and pimples, "don't eat the fruit or stroke the dog, the coyote, or the cat".... What then? A war against the animals? There's one eternally. A cordon sanitaire? Don't say "let's share the water" – that's not on offer....

'We've won! Let's say: the rest are dead, infected – and infectious.... What's to become of us ... the crops? ... the blight, the ergot, locust armies.... And....'

A wider gesture....

'Consider what's the consequence if we go on to eat all that's in the sea. If it has a consequence?'

She swivels round to where we stand. 'See,' she says. 'More massacres, more famine, less time and patience for us to walk a path. Everybody fevered, shaking: diseased hands clutching at the healthy, bringing them down ... "Let's take it out on nature – the big enemy. Home-grow your stuff ... shoot and poison what prowls and brawls in, salivating.... Wash leeks in bleach, bury your sweat...."'

'Yes,' says Claude, amazed. 'Zélie can do it! Get them listening!'

*

'Add me to Kochi,' Jacob says. 'We'd make a human being. As we are, separate, we're not a single whole. Zélie is wild and rich, she'll have an audience. Enough! I'm tired of these disaster scripts. The movie's just the same each time. Let's do something different....

'If you don't change the system, you won't change the consequences that have made the present, and will make the future. We don't know how to change the system, what new kind of revolution – which we can't make – would be required to save our lives, nature, our nature.... Anyway – what do we care? Who charged us to save the world?

'So, let's try something different that's something we *can* do, not what we think is necessary.'

We are the fish. We are the consequence. We came crawling on to land. We can't go back.

'Let me confess,' says Jacob. 'I've no birthright, I can't paint memories, my recollections are trivial. I'd love to afford my life in big cities with shows that would be atom-bombed if somebody decides – I'm a free citizen of a big tormented place that doesn't exist, and is mostly sand and salt. I don't fancy you, Kochi, and if you fall down, I can't lift you. But – we must find something new that fits these absences, gaps we haven't decided where they are, anomalies ... *aporie* they're called....'

'And keep it to ourselves,' I say.

'That should be easy,' Jacob says. 'Whatever we have, we've learnt to hide.'

What use are hidden things? I wonder, ask myself.

'Two hundred years ago,' Jacob goes on. 'They wrote about these heroines – they sought a place to leave their eggs where all their suitors might discover them, and fertilise, and have the little ones – the elvers, slipping like leaves – of birch, the willow – never heard of, never again distinguished as belonging to a family, a tree – even a weed, to seem not so anomalous – like Zélie left her eggs where we would find them, and the little ones swim off, anonymous as we all are until, perhaps, a bear has sport with us, or else some guy will snag us in the mouth and play us up and down until they tire and we are moribund, and fish us out and thrown us back, the wound ... you have one, just like me, Kochi, we can't say certain words, the names of distant chiefs don't come free and easy – like when they throw grenades into our pond and we're all gutted out, imploded, torn apart .... what is the word that charms us out and crawling on the land and wearing pants and carrying our little telephones, and whispering "hi – the world...."! I'm sure, the word's "You will be gods, lords of all you see!"'

'You're eloquent,' I say. 'It doesn't help. When did reality help when we are in a fix – that's when you need forget and go on by yourself as if the universe does not exist....'

'I know,' he says, 'that suitors look the same. They *are* the same, like small fry ... then they wrote about the murders and the gambling and the poor – as if we couldn't walk down any street and find them all, and then the wars...! They must have seen that you can kill many many more without declaring war. I guess it was the uniforms, the noise, the flags, and then the horses. Everybody who was anyone must ride a horse, of course, the poets too – who hasn't seen Goethe, on his way to Italy, crossing the Alps like Hannibal – on a horse, or maybe he'd have used a palanquin, but surely not an elephant – those African models they were small, could maybe carry princes, dauphins, or a princess ... not the gravity, the bottom, of a philosopher ...'

'The point, Jacob, the point!' I shout. 'What's to be done?'

'We're freaks, Kochi,' he says. 'But mostly we get rooked – in circuses, in theatres, robbed on the street – a freak show brings the crooks, believe me! And there's the competition.'

'That isn't so,' I tell him. 'Evolution's adaptation – until you can't. Freaks would be irrelevant – we aren't, or we don't want to be. And yet – apply the motor, evolution, to ourselves, our species. We can become extinct – but not because we can't adapt, but because we made the machine that lets us die by our own calculation. We make our circumstances – up to a point, and they make us – but only to a point. The revolution comes because we *can* – and yet, and yet.... What drives our change of circumstance – it's fashion! A shade of pantaloons they only make in Senegal, the boss on cassowaries' heads determining the shape of hats ... taste, my dear Jacob! Jacob, my pedestrian, my mechanical, my Engels!'

'Imagination, Kochi, takes you just so far. Desire!' says Jacob. 'It's not enough. You need the army and the colonists to take the colour out of Africa, the animals from the South Seas....'

'Yes, Jacob,' I tell him, in great excitement. 'It happens so, when so it happens... But my imaginings and yours – we have no army and no colonists. Our fashion, taste – is in our heads, it swarms, it multiplies in there ... and Africa is safe, untouched, imagined, unviolated – at least by you and I....'

'Indeed,' he says. 'But here we are back in our fantasies. Sterile and dull....'

FLOUNCES, GRENADES, ASPARAGUS AND ROUNDELAYS

'Let's experiment, Kochi,' Jacob says. 'You're not brilliant, but you've sketched a hypothesis. Food, armies, osprey plumes, and ebony for clarinets ... you might say it's the thrust of civility – even of civilisations. *Accidie;* what we have, have loved – exasperates, disables us ... boredom smoking his hookah, the death-wish. Then – there arises the tickle, itch – desire to impress ... the big, the final gesture – the sweep of the hat, the sweep of the scythe.... Change, change without end, without scope, without reflection... Build a bothy, an activity, set back from the road: fossils and reptiles, says the weathered sign....'

'The curiosities are put together many times,' I say. 'Route 66 is full of them – gun stores where you can eat a cow, buy golfing slippers, hear Leadbelly discs....'

'They don't know what they're doing,' Jacob says. 'They don't have the cosmological eye.'

'We can observe, restore, do gardening. Grow the pomegranate,' I say, quite enthused. 'We're ready for surprises – world's end, or much more of the same imbalance: the teeter....'

'The tent – that's genius,' Jacob says, making a pyramid with his hands. 'You need one for a battle. For an expedition. A party, a wedding.... And a circus. You, Kochi, you make a new one, a domed shelter, a quasi-yurt each night: protecting the animals in their suffering, anxiety and terror, the danger of wolves and precipice, tempests and drought – then coolly ushering them to their fate. Cuddling, reassuring.... The market, Eid. The pot.' He laughs. 'Where shall we set ours up, Kochi? It must be gossamer ... the stall....

'America's too easy – we'd be shopkeepers all our lives, bombs and ballads, beards and bombast. It should be ... Italy? France? Or somewhere apart – Abkhazia? Or Badakhshan? A place where we are watched, but given rope...?'

'Where we find the right tent,' I say. 'That is the spot.'

And so it is.

*

We had planned the end – the tent blazing, the revelation rising in the flames.

It isn't so. We hired two riggers, Dama and Trig. They're efficient, and they run the show. It's all a show – the circus, the gunfire, the exploration and the celebrations. It's all one – novelties and conscience. There are crowds. It doesn't mean a thing. The riggers cheat us, take the takings that they made – it's right. It's a fraud, a scam. They're welcome to it, they deserve all that they make....

'Once, a tent prompted responses – it was vulnerable, the wind, the misplaced guys....' says Jacob, much disappointed. 'Now, it's a revolving stage.... All under contract, scripted. Each day is different, but the actors are the same, their schtick identical.'

'We were too ambitious, Jacob,' I say. 'Thought it all too easy. To the workers the spoils. It's just.'

He's not convinced.

What went on in the tent?

'The truth,' says Jacob. 'Without a doubt.'

'Images,' I say. 'Mirages. But certainly, the truth.'

'And you aren't satisfied?' asks Dama. 'I did the course, at the academy of circuses. I'm equipped to show the truth. Trig broke his joints – but he can use the hammer, set the tension on the ropes – that keep the tent standing, the tight-ropes tense.... We set it up, the show. There's rope and staves and stitches, the cannon has its lanyard, the clown his barrel, the beauties ... speak for themselves – and afterwards you find your urine scented when you pee on the grass: wonders worth every cent....'

'It isn't what I wanted, or expected, Dama,' I tell her. 'But all you say is undoubtedly the case.'

'Yes,' says Jacob, disillusioned. 'The truth is a great tautology.'

She's strong, Dama is – she could take Jacob and me and weave us, plait us together like a hawser, and let us go and whirl, round and round until we're separate again, and single threads of wire – strong and weak, at the same time. It's all invention on her part. It's all invention on our part.

'I'm not so sure,' says Jacob. 'But I'll go along with that for now – a kind of prevention, or precaution. It's her trade, you can see – she's supple and inventive – her body does what it wants and ours comply. We are a part of her invention, so, yes, it must mean it's also ours.'

'It's the variety of the world,' says Dama. 'Not what you want. You can't keep your dignity, or stroll away. Variety – it's there, indifferent to you, piled up, if you care or if you don't.'

'We're used to seeing you from far off, where we sit – we're the impresarios, we don't know in advance what you'll do, amazing us – you're made up to look quite young, maybe a bit brassy, quite a tart, in fact,' I say. 'And yet – sex doesn't come in. It must, of course, come in somewhere, but not here. Quite unthinkable. Those flounces on a short skirt – they finish off a tunic, quite military. Roman, I mean.'

She's quite original, and quite familiar, like everyone who's strutted up and down a wire, way way up above our heads....

'I'm much younger than that,' she says, 'Not white at all. It's convention, that I never fall, I never slip, you know it's always me, under the fard ... every time it's different, but I am always the same, always more precise, stronger – and Trig, I fear, is not. He suffers terribly, the pain – arthritis, trapped in his skeleton, and holds him like his bones are iron – every day it's worse. Round and round we go, a clock, round the ring, like horses do.'

'This doesn't at all go where I'd want,' says Jacob. 'It doesn't fit with my conclusions, not at all. It's more and more familiar, every day – it closes in, the scene is smaller, tighter ... we're all shut up together in this cell, this shrinking jail, some watch, some tumble, some climb the walls and fall, some scale the heights, jump down, and someone shoots them when they end up in the grass, out in the open, free.... This isn't what we had in mind at all.'

'I'm the best there is,' says Dama, quite angry. 'You must put up with me. I bring in the crowds.'

'I can attest to that,' I say. 'You steal the show.'

'It isn't what I want,' she says. 'This is a cage. I wanted sails – fear and salvation. My island – in the distance, it seems a ship on the horizon, blurred, scudding off, and then, as you approach, it's larger, frightening – and then you land, it's undefended, stuck to the sea-floor, and you seize us all, and take us off. Your little ship – you cram us in; the island is abandoned, rests, deserted, green. This tent – it holds us for ever and we spin and fly ... it isn't what you want, and you, you and Jacob, you have nothing, nothing of what you hoped....'

'It's true,' I say. 'This tent is made from sails, you tumble in the walls, the little space invented – cling to the ropes, the rigging – it isn't what we want, it's true .... yet, it's a true story. It must be, I've heard it many times. You're brilliant, Dama, Trig is blocked, a dead stick. That's what the truth, true stories, do to you.'

And there it rests.

OF TIME

Jacob and I – each is incomplete. So – no one will give us tasks requiring trust. Zélie has shown, for us, sex will not bud in love. Neither of us has received a kind or sympathetic word – not since our parents read the book that said that kindness spoils. The rest has followed from acquaintance with the world.

The search for solid bases for belief – in anything at all – means you must question the best authorities there are. And if you're average bright – that's where you stick. You're smarter than the prophets and the mathematic guys – but sceptical, fearing that improvement on them may replicate the pathway to dead ends.

Trig soaped the rope that Dama uses to come down from the sky – forgot, he says, to rinse it off. She came down like a meteorite. Her knees ended in her bum, he says.

'And did you give her a kind word?' I ask Jacob.

'Oh, much much more,' he says. 'The Fall is liberating. Revealing – a message – the lark descending....'

‘And did it transform...?’ I begin.

‘Certainly,’ he says. ‘And kind words don’t come in. She keeps the *bordereau*. She has a throne with wheels.... I could have told her, she and Trig were ready to perform a freak show – I mean it as a compliment – she might not take it so. That’s another paradox – my meaning, and how you take it.... There’s something in between of course – hidden from science but visible to everyone alive ... the sense of self that culture gives us, or does not....

‘And, Kochi, on the topic of kind words – it’s not quite so that both of us were snubbed by Zélie, long ago. I was a favourite of Blandine – the mothers love me, always – my acidity....

‘I had a fling with Zélie – though she dislikes the physical, the body and its tailings, the by-products, all that stuff. Desire – is always better unfulfilled, unrealised, and left to smoulder on the hearth. It would be a paradox, if desire’s end were always its extinction....’

‘It makes no difference, of course,’ I say. ‘But you concealed the facts, and on that basis – I’d set up my sentiments ... I can’t forgive....’

‘Then silly you,’ he says, and laughs. ‘Writing. That destroyed the basis of our sentiments. Nothing is solid when we can distance it, and put it on a glyph. The truth is in the tent, not on the ticket.... But – without the ticket, or a forgery, you won’t get in.

‘Magic, Kochi – the word, the thing, the sound – who tied these together? To what end? It’s charms and invocations, but the guy who set the meanings – undoubtedly an accountant. Some guy who added up a patrimony. Kind words? Not in the pyramids, my friend! – you won’t find them there. You think that writing clarifies, gives time, a sort of permanence, that you reflect on and interpret.... But, Kochi, time deceives. It passes, everything is not the same. The truth there once was, fixed in time; and writing – doesn’t give it life, doesn’t take you back – it takes you to a wholly different place – the stick-men make a sound, the sounds go silent on the page – in faces, or in ones and noughts.... The truth, you understand, is what I’ve told you. You’re not an idiot – don’t write it down, remember it and have it gnaw your guts.... You’ll know that I had Zélie, she had me, the having doesn’t leave a trace, it doesn’t mean a thing to you, your innocence and ignorance – but should I write it down? I think you’re stupid, envious, jealous and cast down, defeated you will think – "you're stupid, Kochi". Written down, you can go back, and back, to my opinion, your stupidity, and you know you're stupid, you read it here! Best leave it lodged in time, not alphabet: time is a vacuum, that sweeps up everything that once was concrete, true – leaves nothing, not even a clean sweep....'

He laughs, and pulls a downcast face.

Jacob is intolerable – I'm better on my own.

'It's all true,' he says. 'All the stories. You've only to look at Dama. Of course, time keeps no register – leaves things, memories that aren't often trustworthy, but leaves no trace, nothing of itself. If there was no time, there be stuff left, and shifting memories – but time itself would not have been .... But even if time was, had been – would it make a difference to what's true? Is there a time that's true? – I'd say not, it all depends.... It might all be, of course – true. Everything might be – is....'

I let my mouth open in wonderment, ready to dispute.

'What *we* call time,' says Jacob, 'is a snippet, a milliner's sample – to suit our terribly short lives, to hold what we know of our abbreviated history. Real time – is oceanic. Ours ... take your granddad, Kochi, who surely was a peddler, strolled the earth – would cut you off a length of liquorice bootlace. Scoff too much – your heart would go in overdrive! That's our time....'

'Sherbet, bags of sherbet,' I remember, 'bull's-eyes and gobstoppers ... humbugs.'

'Hmmm,' Jacob says. 'So much for his past in Herat – unless he was a refugee.'

'Oh,' I say, offhand, 'Zélie makes things up, like everyone. Before our grandfathers, it's a fog, you can claim anyone, lament the fortunes lost. All families trekked around – the ones who travelled furthest were the explorers, discoverers, the pioneers. The cavemen were the dullards.

'Now, of course ... we search for them, their scribbles and graffiti....'

'It disappoints me,' Jacob says. 'That you had all these orderly things – mother, father, probably somewhere to leave each morning, ancestors, invented, borrowed – and you threw them all away, back on the heap, to become something quite other – yourself. A free particle ... a radical, in a way. Denying them, all those pale folks in sepia tones who might acknowledge you. Hiding your non-existence....'

'You have to be light,' I say. 'Light to run, to pass, to leave your bullies and invidious rivals, run under the bombs, into the woods, down in the cellars.... What I lack is what you need as well – enthusiasm. I can't cheer, can't flatter, can't laugh along. Most people can, for something or someone, even from fear. I can do fear, but it shuts me up. It's evident, I see through sociality to the bare rocks below....'

'You're right,' says Jacob. 'People here aren't nearly frightened as they should be. You have to travel, not too far, and then you'll find it: huge reserves – of fear.'

'I'm already there,' I say. 'Waiting for you: but I don't greet with smiles, or grins.'

FINDING PEOPLE

'When the world was one,' says Jacob. 'Being lost was an anomaly. Now, we're back into small anxious groupings – there's many lost who do not want to be, and many who would find them, not for a vendetta but for loving care – completion of a pack, at least.'

'The idea is good,' I say. 'But no one pays for being found. And as for those who're lost, we feel location is enough. They know exactly where you are, they think. And where they are. The link – is missing. Even – the cash nexus.

'Where is the profit, Jacob?' I ask him, and he says –

'You must rely on sentiment. On gratitude. On selling tall stories – possibly they're true – for cash. For entertainment. Curiosities on when and how some guy has ended up, maybe with more wives and kids, and even debts ...

'Of course, we'll need a protocol. Remember, many people don't know where to start to look for someone – all the cameras, the lists, the black books – they don't know....'

'Language, in Africa,' I say, 'is a clue. But big countries spread out on archipelagoes – that's tough. Thousands of hermits on a rock, lost there, but found themselves – being hunted or being bored by company.... Of course, there's cemeteries. You find someone with similar name and similar birth – snap the stone, and you've brought peace of mind. And, maybe, mourning. Rejoicing, too.'

'Identity,' says Jacob. 'You might want to renew, rejoin your lookalikes – or find you are quite different. Being lost is being found. Found somewhere new, as someone else.'

'Or you could say that being found is being lost,' I say. 'You're different from what you'd be if you had never left.'

'It's true,' says Jacob, 'but not relevant for us.'

'Those islands,' I reflect. 'If I decide to build a hut – I'd not be lost for you, but no one else would have ideas of where I was.'

'You'd live on fish that Zélie says will not last long. And then ... watch out!' says Jacob, laughing. 'But follow up your logic – most people don't know who other people are, or where they live or where they're running to – and nor do they – and so you'd say that almost everyone is lost, and almost no one ever found. Most people hunker down in families, mostly supposed to be exogamous – and in that sense their lives are quite unknown except to those they live with who don't know they're lost....'

'There's tax, of course,' I say. 'It follows you, if you're in funds. But with no work, or with no pay, you don't exist ... I'm not sure if not existing is the same as being lost. In a sense....'

'The armies,' Jacob says. 'They find you, but they lose you quick. They don't dig up the casualties.'

We put our ad inside the baker's shop, where almost everybody, lost or found, will find it – and a woman ... from Tigray, asks us about her family.... Lost, every one of them.

'I've no idea,' says Jacob, 'how you might be helped ... what "finding" them entails. Your fortune is – your kids and all your relatives have disappeared. Now, look at it this way – to you, they're lost. But look at it from their experience. Whereas to you all of them are lost, to them – it's you that's lost! Or can't be found! Except, in a way, all of you are in between! Not lost or found. They guess exactly where you are. In fact – you're here, and not exactly lost because you're looking for them, you know where you are, and for you, it's them are lost.... Yet – they don't feel lost! Maybe, like me, they don't want being where they are. But that's not being lost....

'We might say, there's a confusion – one that holds good for the universe – that here and there are relative. Think of the stars – we know exactly where they are – relative to lots of other stuff ... and they're not lost. But are they found? They never have been lost, and being lost, in your excruciating case, is a condition that determines if you can be found.'

'I know,' I say. 'Quiet, Jacob! You must contextualise. Not impose meanings on the others.'

'That's what meaning must be,' Jacob says. 'If it means, it can be imposed, or else we're all insane. Contexts are not natural to me. "It moves" – that's what the ancients said: *there* is the principle.'

'Why do people say they've lost someone?' I ask: 'That must be the point – *a* point. The big events, the wars, the famines, the wanderings – are tied in with the more personal – the flights from home, from persecution, from desperation, poverty and violence, masters and mistresses, creditors – flight from the police, from lovers, from bosses, crooks.... Individual, not personal – a small part of the big events ...'

'I know all that,' says Jacob: 'I wish I didn't. It doesn't let you find anyone, not at all. If anything – you want to let things lie....'

'It's true,' I say. 'It's difficult, it takes more history than we have got, more time. In comparison, Zélie's fish and how we manage if they're gone – is simple. And yet she struggles in her net.... Maybe the fish rejoice, not to be anywhere, not hunted, not suffocated ... extinct.'

'Exactly,' Jacob says. 'If you admit complexity, or what seems simple – you never end. You have to find a method that gets you somewhere without you running out of time, examining a pebble rather than the mountain that it's from, which threatens to fall down on you....'

'Is it the patience we don't have that limits us, doing little things because there is no time for more? Or just – we don't have the guts?' I ask.

Jacob embraces me. 'Save me, Kochi,' he implores. 'My questions.... My family threw me out for asking questions, I was a street kid till a predator fancied me, sent me for finishing – the Ivy League, of course....' He makes to shrug a gaudy gown, adjust the mortarboard, and then his knees bend, features sag. ‘Guide me, Kochi, point me towards “up”....’

‘Oh,’ I say, ‘I was much the same. My parents – sent me to the madrasa, and there I found I could remember everything, all that had ever happened, except, alas, to my shame and to my people’s dread – the Qur’an. Not a word, I didn’t have the knack of repetition: my memory was blocked. Instead – I found I was inventing everything, I composed a new, more rigorous manuscript, with deep devotions, small rewards, the fables coloured brighter, miracles that shook the world....

‘Disgrace! Mine was a kind of tribute to divinity, but wasn’t taken so. My family made me trek the world – the rite of passage, East to West, the mountains, fires, the waves, the camps, the prisons – the temptations and the punishments – my hair turned white, and then turned black as pitch, with tints of hell-fire red.... Then to the straw shade – conformity – where it stands now....

‘When I came to rest – the fear remained. Had I stopped the whirl, the tests, the metamorphoses? Was I a butterfly or a grub, or just a set of tattered wings? – and is the process that transformed me an everlasting chain of fusions that never stop until I am consumed, released as homicidal dust throughout the universe...?’

‘Yes,’ Jacob says, releasing me. ‘Yours is an altogether better tale than mine.’

‘We give up too easily,’ I say, ‘Because we see how big the challenge is, and how individuals are crushed, dwarfed, by it.... But you’re an academic. Yours is a small corrupt country. You could run for president – have others do the work of getting votes for you. Then – at least you’d get to know the bosses, ’phone them, get their confidences, give them asylum if they want....’

‘It would be so,’ says Jacob. ‘But you might have known – my character means I never keep a job. I join the *frondes*, seduce the wives, debauch the students, get caught smoking grass with gardeners – I’m out! – and so, I’m nobody.’

‘For me,’ I say. ‘It’s different. I’m timid, and being last in, I’m first out. I never last a month.’

‘Well,’ he says, ‘we may not work as academics, but we’re qualified....’

'So's almost everyone,' I say, 'but maybe we're extinct – we might be intellectuals. People who went to libraries to read the books....'

'Yes,' he says, 'but literate hoboes aren't elected president. No. We could go back, and join our roots ....'

THE STREET

I remember – 'We collect the empty coke bottles, refill them with stuff – water, caramel and fizz, and sell them on. It's better than originals.... And we put caramel in cleaning alcohol, in the right bottles – it's "old brandy". It's been so for centuries.

'And then there's paintings – naive artists ... we take the tourists to a secret place, and they will buy the stuff, and love the crusts and frame them, they're the emblems of the tourist gaze....'

'I'm no good at chemistry,' says Jacob, 'and worse at selling. Dispossessed, I'm a Blackfoot. Now I'm landless. Everything I've lost is always in my eyes ... my lands, limitless....'

'Oh, I could be the same,' I say. 'But maybe it's just a system. A relic. A "mythico-ritual system entirely dominated by male values". No space, no time, is empty; you can't carry a space and time around as if they're empty skins. Lose them, Jacob, so you can take them back, recover them: and they'll be new and clean.'

We make the brandy. If you don't drink it neat, but dress it up – it's assertive, but won't blind you.

It doesn't blind us, and we keep our lost lands in full sight, in our eyes.

'We trade,' says Jacob, 'so we're paid to spy. Don't fight it, Kochi. Be circumspect....'

'We're all poor and most of us aren't active in the light hours,' I say. 'What is there to spy that you can't see by walking down the street?'

'It's how it works,' says Jacob. 'Don't squawk, or you'll be on the list....'

'I used to be,' I say, 'But that was when they saw I was a threat.'

'You've fallen off that branch,' he says. 'Now, you don't look like you turn things upside down.'

'The suffering,' I say. 'It can't be real because it isn't permanent.'

'That's nonsense,' Jacob says. 'You feel like that because you hold those coke leaves, the powder, in your mouth – until it makes a soup. Then – you feel confident, enthusiastic. It won't last, the penury, you think. If it wasn't so, if it endured without relief, or hope – you'd feel the heat, the tiredness, the boredom; and the schemes, the scams, would wear you down.... Everybody knows, now, you're not a threat. That's why they can treat you any way, and you will do the worst things so you can be caught. So they can catch you.'

'We'll have short lives. That's mostly good,' I say. 'My family should be proud, I can be tied up and hung face-down, survive, and be out in years, and wondering why there is the bother with the feeding us and guarding people, maintaining prisons for people who don't have anywhere to go, except back to their business ... and the competition's taken over all the spots and recipes and every chemist and importer of the stuff you can't find here.'

'You're right,' says Jacob. 'We're willing, but not serious. We've forgotten how to make our living on the street and to do so well. We shall be missed, not loved, but leave a tale, as if we're mice. Stuck in a hole and can't turn round. Our bottoms sticking out.'

'No, it's clear, we're not up to street-work,' I say: 'Like we weren't up to arguing with Zélie about us all being safe and happy, the clouds rolling back to give more light after dropping their pure rain....

'But we're not right for war-work either – war and work – when we don't know what will give us respite, let alone freedom from something ... something the provocateurs sent us long ago; the FBI or a sister group, clumsy stuff, pamphlets on cheap paper as if we must be cheapskates or else they were – you'd need be twelve or under to take the bait, take that shotgun and shoot up the empty tanks – going by rail through Canada to Vietnam because there was no security where they were coming from.'

'That time's gone by,' says Jacob. 'And it was before your time. They play the songs, that's it.'

'These days, you don't know enough to be a child,' I say. 'Still less how to defend your country, change jobs when the machine changes: lose substance, be a ghost and chat....'

'You do all that so as to die,' says Jacob. 'That's where the mercy comes in.'

'Help me,' Jacob,' I say, 'and explain. Not to understand is solitude....'

'The owl that flies at dusk, and gives you all the explanation you can have or want,' he says, 'follows the tales – the mice, their tails. And being dark – they can see nothing, can't see him come and strike, although they've always had their fear. And *there's* the mercy, Kochi.'

ZELIE

'You two look glum,' she says. 'I'm happy and fulfilled. Campaigning. That's what we're made for – all the inventions – flints, the wheel – they needed a promotion, often lasting years.... Fluent advocacy. And poetry.'

Blandine says, 'That's a religious country, where you were. Weren't we at war with you? With them?'

'No,' Jacob says. 'That was next door, and you did it all by mail.'

'That's what I say,' says Zélie. 'People die all over.'

'My advice,' says Blandine, taking the centre. 'Is don't be in bed with someone when they get shot dead. You'll never forget the mess.'

'It was terrible,' says Zélie. 'Mommy was in bed with this guy and people got in and shot him.'

'The cops tried to pin it on me,' says Blandine. 'Just to look at the scene shows it wasn't me, not my picture minimally. I'm clean and organised. Not to mention how deep in love....'

'A bump in the road,' says Zélie. 'Forget it and look up, see how tall the mountains are.'

'This is drama,' says Jacob, eyes starting out. 'It could be your father, Zélie.'

'Fathers father before you're born,' she says, quite cold. 'Not when you're grown. It could be the guy come to fix the air-conditioning. If you're straight, by definition, you pair off with people absolutely different. Unrelated.'

'We all must rise above things,' I say. I find I rather fancy Blandine. Believing she's promiscuous is quite a help, and – by definition – she'll be more experienced, imaginative in sexual tricks, than Zélie, but still she'd be derivative, a denizen of the same tree, perched on a different branch....

'Don't leer,' says Zélie, pinching me above the elbow. 'It's best you be moralistic, if you must be anything; not just colouring in the homicidal scene.'

'I don't think you understand, Zélie,' Jacob says, shoring me up and hugging the arm that's not been pinched. 'We've had some tough experiences on the street, cops, crack houses, dawn raids and vigilantes – your mother might be innocent, for all I know or care. We're used to situations – to you, they seem extreme, but still they happen every watch....'

'Oh,' says Zélie, well stoked up with rancour now, 'when you campaign, it's not just diplomatic guys you lecture and exhort – you go to rendering plants, you bathe in scum that gives you *pox*, you can't use soap because it washes off your natural hum....'

'Let's not compete,' I say. 'Aspiring to the higher life – of course, you hunker down with low-lifes, scams and scums. You pick up stuff you don't know its origins....'

My shin: there's an extrusion – like a mussel-shell, a quern maybe – 'Don't pick at stuff you don't know what they are,' my mother said ... I could cry – to think of doctors, razors, crutches and machines that throb and you can't twitch inside or else you have to start again....

'I could be sick,' I say. 'It's like there's more inside me to come out than could have gotten in....'

They laugh.

'Keep your distance,' Blandine says. 'If it's an infestation, keep it to yourself,' and there's more jollity.

'It's the Americans,' says Jacob. 'Dictators, wars – poor people fighting to be free of strangulation, then staying poor, oppressed: – what next? New strategies to keep America on top. Why, the wretched of the earth will be induced to vote the corporations in. They won't know, but they've voted soldiers in as well. The bases and the offices – they swell like pustules, and you'll scratch them till they burst and multiply, the world is covered in them, it's the *pox*

Americana, if you buck them, you'll find you're faced with blowing up the world.'

'What's this to do with who came in the bedroom?' Blandine asks.

'Oh,' Jacob says. 'It's all intimidation. Look for the plotters. Zélie's the wind, invokes it – and maybe the oil, gas, and fire would like to take it out on her .... "Blandine's an embarrassment", and so there's blood that needs to spill....'

'The hell with you,' Blandine says. 'I'm quiet, discreet. And I was well asleep.'

'It's all a pattern: there must be,' I say. 'Or else there's nihilism, randomness. Whim.'

'And so?' asks Zélie. 'Is that how you calm my mother? Does it take cosmology?'

'I remember, long ago,' I say. 'There was this solemn guy – quite bright, who sometimes twinkled – a group of us, we went to ask his views.... Remember, his big house.... We were all young, very young, and flattened by the fear: the great terror hanging on us. Now, we know that when we contemplate mortality, it should give us peace, and even moderation.... Then, we were young and vigorous – life terrorised us.

'There was a long salon – like a Versailles, with silver-gilt and crystal, *strass*, panels of fret-work mirror-glass, lacquer and spangles – little birds, flying free, miniatures: thrushes, blackbirds – though I think they didn't sing or make a sound. A world of wonders; the future coming, though when it was the past – we see we never had it; not the world, and not the wonders.

'"Uses of terror": I remember we discussed it, a pamphlet, essay: who does it serve, what is the wall it builds? Terror's an effect, to make you sweat....'

'None of you's oppressed,' the Master, guru, says. 'You don't have loyalty or faith. Why be afraid? You have your distance now – just use it: think! Use your independence....'

'We're afraid of thinking certain things,' I say. 'Certain themes – you risk. Can't think, can't talk about them – and certainly can't associate with guys who might be....'

'Making you afraid,' he interrupts. 'That is the point. And when you fear, you lose the little power you have.'

Next day, I went back to ask for something deeper, less allusive, and the long salon was calm, still wonderful, but tranquil and antique – 'Where...?' I ask.

'The birds are all behind the glass,' he says.

It didn't mean a thing.

It wasn't terrorism that drove me on, but the fear: at the time, being quite young, it was – uncertainty. I didn't know who threatened me – I had no side to trust....

I mumble '... The night before I'd said to Zélie, how I was in love with her. 'I know,' she said. And that was it, we two, we never went close to that precarious place again.'

'I wasn't there, I'm sure,' says Zélie. 'This is the first I've heard of all of that.'

'I'm sure I didn't know you then,' says Jacob. 'I didn't know you, Kochi, till our troubles had begun.

'And besides – there were the empires then, their emperors' heads on coins and stamps. The opposition – they were "terrorists". Now the bosses make apologies, quite imprecise, for the bad place we all were in. They stress how, in person, they were clean, but I remember, at the time, that there was their terror, their terrorism, that kept the fetters on the dispossessed. And there was terror, terrorists that fought to throw off the manacles....

'And now, we're with those liberating terrorists! We, our side, the *bienpensants*, liberals, traders and entertainers, footballers and fashionables – all networking to make our buck ... all implanted in our hot aggressive cultures ... called on to deplore what we eat and breathe.... Acting as bosses while decrying power ... financing soldiers.... We're post-colonials, and behold! We've become the neo-colonials....

'The world of wonders that we hoped for, that we thought was promised – it didn't come; and we shall die without it being there or anywhere.'

'I remember well that pamphlet – "uses of terrorism", that described how the terror made a space where we were not to go or contemplate.... We were constrained, our mouths padlocked ... What you don't know and can't defeat – we should not speak of it.

'But that fine house, the guy, the birds – locked in the glass.... I can't imagine I, or even less that you, Kochi, were there....'

We leave it so, but Blandine hopes it was the terrorists broke in and killed the guy, and so would make her seem respectable, or at least mysterious.

*

Claude, and the Master – there are many such, giving advice, analysis, and mock tranquillity. Living in barns, barns splendid, and barns cheap and draughty.

'I was innocent, like you, Kochi,' Jacob says. 'I thought that if I understood, I could write an ending. It wasn't so. Zélie wasn't there, she never is, she's innocent on quite a higher plane. Claude and the Master, they knew it all, but didn't know a thing, didn't understand the tale. Paint me out of your memory – I'm only where I say I was....'

'Anyway,' says Zélie, 'Blandine's was a bad experience. And maybe I'm the target now – or maybe I'm to blame. I don't believe it, that I have some guilt....'

'There was much love, those days: available, and I must say, not appreciated,' I say, still riled by my own history, being a screw of paprika, of density, intensity ... mostly forgotten, the context misremembered, not remembered minimally or – traduced and lied about. I'm sure Zélie must remember....

She's suddenly angry – 'Most of what happens is risible,' she says, shouting at the three of us in turn – 'Creation makes you laugh, creation is a freak show – look what comes out! – like scrolls and scraps of potter's rejects, clay worms, dropped off the wheel – the aardvarks, sloths, the frogs enamelled, poisonous, the insects on tall and brittle legs, superabundant – living in the dark, the bark – a wriggly food in waiting....

'Elephants! What a joke! Giraffes, poor things! ... all of us struggling with our single-jointed arms and legs and dripping snouts and hidden penises – sex tools without an edge and boxing feet that don't fold or prick, fingers you can't snap and r's that will not roll.... What fun! What stupidity, what a joke – except you do not laugh.... You swim so slow, run like a barrel on a slope, your breasts you'll hardly use and yet – they're there, each day you package them and hide them, sport with them – all a magnificent box of blundered toys and fallen gargoyle heads and tails…. And – you don't laugh. How can we – we're part of it, the routine, the comedy....'

There's silence. 'You don't tell your public this?' Jacob asks at last, quite set aback.

'You're perverse, Zélie my dear,' says Blandine in a huff. 'That guy who I shan't name – bled out all over me, the pig! No titters there!'

'Creators like a laugh,' I say. 'Their purpose is not understood. That vexes them. For all the audience cares, they might as well desist – it's all too complicated and difficult to grasp – all bits and pieces, no story and too many ends. Ends that snuff us out like wisps of marsh-gas.... So "laugh clown, laugh" the creators think. Why bother to set it up, the crazy parade, if no one sees the point, or even smiles.... Creators crave the company they will not get – "o, leap up to me!" they think. You can't.'

'It's your fish, Zélie,' says Blandine. 'All maladapted. They take over your pity and commitment. Whales that eat the tiny krill with those cathedral maws! – pink dolphins who sing and play the fiddle, gasping Zelenka ornaments, unheard, on the monger's slab ... the blushing octopus who ends chopped up and unidentifiable ... her beauty and her delicacy betrayed in cartoon caricatures as a monstrosity....

'For what? ... A Labrador has better smell and taste than any one of us – she is a fishes' connoisseur if ever there was one – and she can't tie a fly or tote a creel.... Blunt paws....'

'History is past,' says Jacob, 'Done. Sniffed, quaffed and vomited after hours and after years. Anyone over twelve has already had everything sung to them, or seen it on a clip. Nothing shocks, and nothing perks. And you, Zélie, with a dismal past of "she loves me – maybe not: or ho-hum...." – you pretend survival matters, massacre is important, extinction is a tragedy....

'No one cares! Massacre, extinction – it's the norm! If anybody says they care, it's a phase, a sickness, fever.

'I thought of a production, a graffito – it could be stencilled on a frock, on walls and scenery, labelled on a can of aubergines. It starts as if it was a book: with Revelation, the burning of the world; identification of the corpses.... And it would finish, climax, with the flood, new sin; the creation of a repeat world in quick-quick time. A week to bodge it up, the universe, this time around. Not years, not millennia. And just one planet, the only one we'll know, this muddy smudge we're on. My epic – it would end in reality – a pop-up, holograph, cold call – all that.... Us, exhumed, fumbling round, just as we were, have always been.'

'That's pitiful,' says Zélie. 'You've missed a lot of life while you've been trying to be poor, trying to be hunted, trying to suffer. You haven't got the spirit, Jacob.'

'You missed the *grand macabre*,' Blandine says. 'It's been done. Everybody went to war, got mutilated, ran to America, to Brazil, or was executed in the cellar. Or went on trial, humiliated – forgotten. Depending where you were – your trafficker or your lawyer knew your hidey-hole.

'You didn't, Jacob, haven't known where anybody was. Nor afterwards, when our minds were blown and the big blond guys were storming into Asia once again.... You hadn't listened to the music, worn the clothes – and still you think you're one of us, showing the way, waving your lantern, blowing your slug-horn. You thought it was all over, neutralised, and in the movies. You bought the culture California parcelled up and sold in slabs. It was all settled, so you thought.

'No, it's on and on, the threats, the wars, the penury, the dwindling space to stand on.... It's going on and on, the re-makes – even violating my bed....'

'Whoa, Blandine,' Zélie shouts. 'The message is – bring everyone together!'

'Tell that to the sardines, my love,' Blandine shouts back. 'We humans, the favoured ones, we're all in one big can already....'

We laugh.

'Lots keeps happening,' I say, bringing peace, I think. 'It's all different, even if the words and pictures look like they were before.'

THE PROJECT

'What are you waiting for?' Blandine shouts. 'Go, free some slaves, right some injustices!'

'You, Kochi and Jacob, you've had full lives,' says Zélie. 'You'll complain it wasn't fun, you want to do it all again, better, with more compliant extras, music, and a prize. That's not the contract that you have. Maybe you thought the contract was a social one, gave you the right to be a rebel or a boss, some rules to follow, compensation.... You thought you could expect your mates to help, a doctor there to set your bones.... No. It wasn't so, it never is. The contract was between your life – and Death. Death has no time, it's eternal, it has no dates for when it's over, there is no follow-up, no re-make, not for anyone. What you have, the only thing, an absolute, not to be bargained with – is life.

'You'll say it's hard. It isn't so: even an hour of life – you'll struggle for it; five seconds: you will beg for them, for one last time to sniff the rose; one second to escape the fall, the crazy driver, the axeman or the bomb.... Life is the only good you have, will ever have, a good you'll fight for, to get another minute, second ... recall a memory, a scent, a taste ... another whirl upon the roundabout. And you've had lots of life, but slept abundantly, been often drunk or stoned ... and now you whine that no one cares.

'You've had what was available....'

'It's true,' says Jacob. 'At any rate, we don't want life like Blandine's had, with cops and forms to be filled in....'

'We know the contract can be ended any time,' I say. 'There are no clauses, and no signatures. Death has no X, no thumb-print and no thumb.... But, if you know yourself ... you will have asked, are you a lion or a gazelle? What matters more to you, escape or hunt? Maybe knowing what your nature is can stretch your time....'

'Oh no!' says Zélie. 'Toffee-time? Can you spin it out like chewing-gum and park it underneath your chair?

'That's why those guys get suited-up and spend their years in journeying to places in the universe where time might be elastic....' And she laughs. 'They'll only know a metre up and down within their capsule, and their bones, lost with their souls ... unlikely to be found....'

'I never knew you knew all this,' says Blandine, mystified. 'I didn't teach you,' and I say,

'What can you offer, if there is no plan, no destiny?'

'Well,' Zélie says. 'There is my project. "Don't eat fish". It might be laughable, but then – it's full of sentiment, desire to take control, to take our nature, modify....'

'We know it will not happen,' Jacob says. 'And so ... what else?'

'There's politics,' she says, lightly. 'I imagine you think that's tops. Maybe you graduated in it and the idea has never left. There's hospitality. And politics *and* hospitality. When you reach a certain level, platform, of grandness, you seem to work less and maybe *do* more, though you might not feel you're doing anything at all except ok'ing other people's work....'

'We'd be working for you, Zélie,' I say. 'And you'd need to show us how, and do it for us too.'

It's exciting and humiliating, and there'd be pay, or expenses, as if all pay's not about expenses, unless the birds feed you and you live up a tree.

'All work is work for humanity,' she says, primly. 'You might have funny ideas – that some is art or gambling or breaking legs.... It isn't so. The idea is infantile.'

'I'm of the left,' I say, primly, 'Jacob isn't, but he's extreme in everything. Nothing either of us wants, believes in, will ever come to pass, so which of us is moderate and who's a zealot – it doesn't matter, not a bit. We're like people cooped up on the beach, bombed and robbed by aliens – it doesn't matter if you think reforms will do your trick or if it's rockets will. You aren't allowed to swim away, and when you tunnel in the sand, it all falls on your head.'

'You can forget all that,' says Zélie. 'The thing is, both of you is clean. Not like Blandine, a target for the crooks – who anyway thinks giving birth to me was her supreme feat – sawing a woman in half –' and she laughs, 'But you can profess any religion that you want; just don't drink or smoke stuff while you have clocked in. Otherwise – Liberty Hall! Left-footer, Prod, be what you want.... Myself, I feel that shamanism and the ghosts is closer to our common sense – but argument for or against is useless. No good at all. Belief is like a worm inside the cabbage – it eats and eats and then it dies of surfeit or one day it eats its way right out and there's the sky and earth, reality....'

'And all the ghosts.' I say.

'Exactly,' Zélie says. 'You don't need be a worm to understand, that it is so.'

'What can we be?' Jacob asks. 'What life do you have available?'

'There's dinners,' Zélie says. 'You'll be elected, and you'll have to stay up late and talk to guys who'll try to have you give them stuff that isn't yours. But – the menu will be good, you can be sure. Just don't give too many things away.'

'The People. Yes!' I say. 'My favourite poetry. It sounds like we'll start popular and end quite quick.'

'Forget the fish,' says Zélie. 'They're my pet theme. People: they'll be yours. The people know things are getting tough, they probably will not survive. They've tried processions, and enthusiasm, big bosses and the flags. You'll come in with modesty, and common sense and honesty. You'll do four years, and quit.

'Think of the people as a flock, but not of sheep – of monks. Asceticism, and the rule. Just choose the continent, the country, that you'd like to boss.

'There'll be some fasting, and much prayer. The dress will be informal. Tell the people what they know, and by telling them, they'll see you're honest, unassuming, selfless possibly....'

'All this, Zélie, is in your gift?' I ask, amazed.

'I watch the sea, Kochi, and all the life that struggles there,' she says. 'I understand the tide. I know what happens when an ocean dies, and the regret, the sobering up, the promise to do better if there is another time....'

It's worth expenses, not much more.

'And you can tell them, clear and plainly, what you think,' she says. 'It's not done to gratify myself, although I get the buzz from being perspicacious....

'You and Jacob – there's millions like you, desperate, ambitious, wishing they could sort things out....'

We leave it there. We read the papers, watch the news, know what a statesman says. We're naturals.

I'm sure that when the Master told us how to live our lives, Jacob and Zélie were both there, though it was long ago, and we were young, our faces fresh and clean ... no cash for anyone was on the table ... the long room, like an engine shed, a military hospital – had been, would be, adapted for other purposes, the spotted mirrors, base metal swags anomalous – descended from a past once grubby ... grimy now .... the little birds, too scared to sing, just twittering; wanting to escape but for the moment safe from predators....

'The middle level,' Zélie says. 'They are the imaginative ones. They spy and pry, and work both sides – but they have the initiatives....'

'This scheme,' I say, 'I'm sure, although it's a humiliation, is meant from love, affection probably, and calculation – but for me – it is humiliation.'

'Suppose,' she says, 'there is a mine you want – perhaps to close, to clean – who can surmise? – but in between your wish and its fulfilment – there's a boundary. Drawn in red crayon, then patrolled, and fortified ... to get the hole, deep rooted in the ground, filled in – what do you do? Steal? Buy? Or send the troops...? Your middle layer person knows – how far you'll go, how far you'll be allowed ... knows what they all think, the sides – where it will all play out.... The big ones know what they will do, but only that – your middle person knows all sides, and what the papers say....'

'I know all that,' I say. 'Everyone does. It's tawdry. For a story to be true, you need to know where it begins, and where it ends. Otherwise – you'll never know what's true....'

'I told you, Kochi,' Zélie says. 'Your story starts by the calendar, ends when your time is up, if not before.'

'Then it's humiliation, Zélie,' I tell her. But of course, she knows.

'It's evident,' she says. 'I make you happen, so you're on my string. Some people like humiliation – giant steps are made of them. They might take you to Parnassus.'

That evening, while the Master spoke, I had 'love' in mind. Zélie and Jacob must have heard the genius say, 'Think'. They listened, I did not. I shan't make that mistake again. I want to know what happens – not to me – but to the mine. Who decides and how often they will change their mind.

'I'm not sure, Kochi, you have grasped quite how things are ...' she says. 'Where "knowing about things" fits in.'

I'd leave it there, but she says, 'On reflection, maybe Jacob is my better bet. He has a taste for living certain stressing times – and he knows that in our design, everyone's design, there is a flaw. It makes anomalies – as if there is an urge to tell the truth, *another* truth – that contradicts and voids all that you seem to seem.... You have to watch out, and expect – the truthful spasm, the misplaced fart ... not just from everyman, but from yourself as well.... The gesture, the word ... where it will do most harm and reveal ... "coward and charlatan" you tell the Chief, you tell your child, yourself ... unforgivable and lucid... Jacob knows it – it is the basis of the shamans' art ... the true and secret underworld, the dare, the challenge, the true story no one tells but everybody knows, awaits....'

I am relieved not to be president. It's true that Jacob would enjoy the view: and pick his team and push them one by one over the cliff, like the Hun king – sovereign of sovereigns – who pushed his war elephants, one by one, off the mountain, to hear their squeal as down they went....

JACOB

When his term is done, would be done, I say, 'You had the power. It didn't stick.'

He shrugs. I say, 'When I visited, I remember the mountains. There were always people in the way. There was no panorama.'

'The people didn't stick,' he says: he's mostly quiet – tired, I suppose.

'You could have tried flirtations,' I say. 'To excite the press.'

'Not in South America,' he says. 'Nothing flippant. The characters are all baroque. The cities – they were invisible, under the undergrowth, on mountain sides – civilisations, like we shall be when all disappears, and we must learn to read about ourselves in ancient books. If we're still there – as we were, then disappeared, then, somehow – here again. Otherwise – we'd be obliterated – or maybe like small pebbles surfacing a long long road.'

'The mine?' I ask. 'I'm obsessed by them, as if someone knows that if you dig down deep enough you'll find something that there's not up here.... And no one ever has gone deep enough. So far, what you find you make into spoons and forks.... If there are marvels, they lie much deeper yet – or else they don't. Zélie is right – you trawl the sea, but there is nothing there, nothing to find but fish. And if there are no fish – there's nothing there at all, just land submerged....'

'You must have learnt a lot,' I say. 'I'm envious, Jacob. I watched you, but on the stage – do you act or is it you? You're better than the actors, the professionals – your speeches – they really do convince, you shame the villains, your contempt bristles – and then the smile....'

'There are no characters,' he says. 'Just situations. But you're right – there comes the smile, not scripted, at the end. You won't find that on stage: it closes down the restaurant, empties the boulevards ... we hear the threats and promises; terrified, we all go home, turn off the light, and try to figure out the smile – is it for us? For me, for everyone? – or, for the special ones, a secret message, order, project? Or "traitors beware, opponents too....'"

'You never found the project, Jacob,' I say.

'I knew that from the start,' he says.

'Imagine!' Jacob says. 'If someone took up what Zélie says. If everybody did! All running – what a race, all to be boss, popular and obedient.

'It's not for you, Kochi, but you'd accept the offer. Four years. She offered it to me because I'm strong enough that I refuse. At least – I'd not accept.'

'If you'd been president,' I say. 'I doubt you'd tell us – people like me – the truth.'

'You're nobody, Kochi, so why should I?' he asks. We laugh.

'People aspire,' he says. 'They're candidates, they have convictions, and they lose, they win, they're in the stable, in the race. Everybody else must follow them, somehow, no matter what they think or do ... you have to place a bet....'

'I know, Jacob,' I say. 'It's happening all over, but to run, you need to have the right passport for the place. And the language. Then there's the parades, saluting. Burying the unknown warriors ... not all fun....

'You put guys on the list, and end on it yourself.'

'Zélie's the ruler of the world,' he says, 'or part of it. Whatever happens, she's not responsible; of course, she wants the good things.'

'You're acid, Jacob,' I say. 'No one wants their plane to crash. You're up there, higher than a lark or eagle – you know, coming down fast won't get you breakfast. You see it going down, and naturally, you're up there in the cockpit, reasoning with the crazy pilots....'

We laugh some more. I say, 'I know you recognise the bad, Jacob, but you were sceptical about the plane. And your destination, all our destinations ... landing in the good ... you weren't convinced....'

'I know it all,' he says, 'I could have been the president – I might as well have been. Inside – I was, have always been. But, as you say – I'm strong. And I refused.'

'One could be weak, and refuse,' I say. 'The result would be the same.'

'Oh,' he says, 'Zélie and I – we were close. Lovers, as I might have said.'

'You did,' I say. 'And what did you love? In each other, or – well, in the *enjeu* as they say, the scenery. How does it disappear, the love, if it is of concrete things...? Or does it wane, "go off", a fashion – like people might come to dislike Mallarmé, or even Arcimboldo....

'Loving – it's been pictured as a talent, a quality ... but the physical act ... I'm not sure. It's not recorded, usually. There's gender, and body – those have become obstacles, like orientalism, which you can like but must apologise for....

'I always saw you, Jacob, as a masturbator. I mean it as a compliment – who knows why there is this sense that it's pejorative to applaud what – like intercourse, often, maybe usually – is difficult to document and to assess....'

'Perhaps,' says Jacob. 'It's because it's hard to pin on you, to legislate about, or tax. There's no market, I would say, for that ... no products necessarily associated ... although I'm sure I am a dinosaur in this, not knowing about shops and messages, accessories, those sites – all that.'

We leave it there.

His relationship with Zélie – is it, was it, true or false? What might a truth mean, involve, and why should it interest me? It's shadow-play, compared with a romance invented, set down on the page ... full of details otherwise quite inaccessible....

'A Proust, without friends and acquaintances,' Jacob says. 'Fantasising. It could be you, Kochi, or what you'd like to be.'

'I'm not afraid of action, Jacob,' I tell him. 'Not in civilian life. It's the military – obedience – that I can't countenance. It's crawled in everywhere ... And as for Proust – "the longest ghost story ever cogitated". Not for either of us: no bedtime stories! Do, don't tell!... "Make the world work for you": "*l'imagination au pouvoir...*" that's what they say. *L'Imaginaire*. No regiments, no regimentation. No forming fours and fives!'

'I agree,' he says. 'What's thought is thought, what's done is done. The past is not germane. It's inexistent, like your interest. No rules, no models – and no repeats! When something's done, even done memorably, repetition is a bore. Remember how kids used to copy copperplate? Now, there's a useless exercise, that's taken time to shunt into obsolescence: came the Olivetti 22 for Hemingway, and now the tablet – taken by anyone for anything at all.... Lines and the cane – that was discipline and obedience. What an epic, to be free of that, liberated!'

'Neither of us wanted Zélie's way,' I say. 'Not that she's wrong. But we want something more immediate. Service, service before anything....'

'You're wrong, Kochi,' Jacob says, quite sympathetically. 'We need what suits, not what is more important. Something that keeps us free....'

Neither of us can modify the causes. That's what Zélie does. She has, personifies, a cause. We might change consequences – though that's more modest....

*

'You choked, Jacob,' I say. 'Zélie offered you a commitment you'd have found demanding and dull. Too many details and elephant traps.'

'If someone makes you be an elephant,' he says, 'They already prepared the traps. Elephants are in it for the long haul – but not many make it, and only women. Why should I eat grass for four years and have my teeth end up on someone's desk?'

'The offer wasn't big enough?' I ask. 'You'd have been the biggest animal....'

'We all love animals,' he says. 'Animals are dumb. Some can kill you, but you can kill all of them, and all their relatives, and eat their food.'

'You could have been tempted....' I hazard.

'I'd have done the States or China,' he says. 'But Americans are so loud. Russians make me cry – I'd not have touched that one. That leaves China. Does Zélie have it in her gift? And it's more than four years, it's limitless, eternal, and you have to win and win.'

'So,' I say, 'there'd be disadvantages in the big ones, but nothing less is worth your time?'

'You've often said, each has a private length of time, just for you and only yours, and be very very careful with it,' Jacob says. 'Besides – Zélie would do the big tasks if she could. And so – she couldn't, so, she'd nothing she could offer ... except some remote, precarious place, and lots of hungry guys contesting it. No. Not for me.'

'So, it rests,' I say. 'There's no story. Put it in your memoirs. Write "do not believe" on it.'

'You're a paradox, Jacob,' I say. 'You want power, but are never offered enough. You refuse power because...'

'... because it perpetuates the problem of power, of itself, causes new catastrophes, never eliminates, reverses, what you hope it will accomplish,' he says. 'And you, Kochi, you complain because power destroys all you have and want, and yet if offered, you refuse it....'

'That's because you don't know what it is,' Zélie interrupts. 'You don't have it, so you don't know what you might do with it, and if you have it, you know you'd use it wrong. I have the answer – and you don't understand what you're being offered. You think "four years – too little, not enough". Cowards! Both of you!'

'You may have it to give away, but you don't have it, Zélie,' Jacob says. 'You don't exercise it except by not having it – giving it to others on a whim ... not achieving what you say you want ...'

'It's like Claude,' says Blandine. 'He has money and buys people to use his power for themselves. And me? I'm lying in bed, someone shoots my bed-fellow. That's power! And where am I left? With nothing, no one.'

'Oh, Blandine,' says Jacob. 'You try to excite pity to sort things for you – but you've nothing to sort out. The guy in the bed who got shot – they're the sufferer, not you. And for them, it's just too late for anything. You're not a candidate for justice, Blandine. Nor for pity. Workers for the corporation, the universal mafia, get shot, not fired....

'If they are clients, death is the equivalent of paying tax. Choose your associates more carefully, Blandine, if you don't like simple solutions.

'Find someone else and lock the bedroom door.'

I feel Jacob is right, but I don't say.

'Power,' he concludes – and we're exhausted, 'is not what brings truth, or justice. Of those, it is the antidote. The destroyer. I know – I am a witness. I have suffered – but I shan't whine....'

We're confused, don't pursue him, and Zélie says, 'Survival is more important than truth or justice,' and no one says she's wrong.

MANY MORE PEOPLE

'You never get to say exactly what you think, what your position is,' says Jacob. 'They have their questions, your answers wouldn't fit.'

'If you're interviewed,' I say. 'Don't be exact. Leave that for the next, another, time. There usually isn't one....'

'We're getting stale,' he says. 'We need more input, more voices and more songs. For all the years since the invention of paper and students, Masters have been discussing what is good or bad. But no one ever established what following the good entails, what are the rewards, the consequences. I don't want to waste my life going back over all that – it's inconclusive, evidently. Let's get some congenial company together – have a good time. Or – maybe "good time" takes us back to where we started from: let's think of fun. That has been parsed, thrashed out, under and over, much much less.'

We laugh, Jacob and I, Blandine is understandably aloof, and Zélie's not been following.

*

'You two,' says Delia, a new friend from way back, 'have had a bad press, almost a bludgeoning. But to me, your discussions and their dead ends – have been indicative. You are the persons of the new order. You are the alphas, following the big zero, the omega, where the old order finished up.'

'So,' says Jacob, much amused, 'we survived. Despite us, despite Zélie. And for sure Blandine never received justice nor forgetfulness. She's for ever in that room, that bed.'

'You know, Jacob,' I say. 'There's survival always. If there's not, there's silence. Evolution takes the fallen lumps and moulds new creatures from their plasticine. The new creatures eat the rubbish and the ancient bones, compromise again with death and limitations: no building taller than two metres, no decoration except in metallised sea-green, everything hovering close to silence absolute, or already there ... corks made of lint, bombardons blocked with plugs of lead, donkeys' voice-boxes removed, pickled in demijohns of Benedictine....'

The purpose? We spend our lives wondering: the purpose is reproduction. Nothing more.

'Of course,' Delia says. 'It was an evening where it all came to a halt, and then we – you – left, and it all started up again, the lights, fire-crackers.... Then, we knew, that something more must come....'

'The message ...' I say, tears beginning; the nostalgia sucks your blood ... regret, that is....

'"Think",' she says, dreamily. 'That's what it means. Silence.'

'Think "why?" and "and after?"' I say.

'That's you,' she says. 'It wasn't said. Those aren't part of "think".'

'It was a very long evening,' Jacob says. 'Not much was said.'

'Zélie got to start her business, her commitment, her vocation, campaign – which she didn't want,' I say. 'She found she was – a publicist, in fact. If she was there, following the lesson, I'm sure she'd have wanted to come out as more radiant. But – celebrity means travel, over and over ... gigs ... groupies and coke....'

'It was long ago, and we were very young,' says Jacob. 'Now, you're very young, Delia, and if you survive, you'll run and run while we are history, unwritten history.'

'It's true,' says Delia. 'I'm very young, and Fabrice, my lover from Senegal – well, you'll see for yourselves. You must have somewhere you'd invite us two to stay, sleep over, all that ... we two, clean as the dawn....'

'We move on, Delia,' I say. 'If you buy and sell, you don't add value, just buy and sell yourself. All will be stripped and binned, and if you rent or squat – things go wrong. Buying property – as if it's possible! Like buying dahlias or marmosets.... It can't be binding, and what's more, things run at their own speed.... Infestations. Lino and Bakelite at their last breath.... But just for a night, just two of you, no followers, no creditors.... That's probably a possibility ...'

'We spent our lives so far,' says Jacob. 'Spinning nothing out of nothing. We picked our own bones dry, so we're not even carrion. You two are surely plump, well-furred – you'll scamper further and more joyfully....'

'We've tried a lot,' says Delia, 'and were not prejudiced. We made cash and lost it, or else – it got spent. But, you seem people who thought trading alienated your souls, and so you didn't do it. You were against performance, and the applause. Squeamish. In the end – nothing but guesses. No price, no value.'

'That's right,' I say, 'selling ourselves for work seemed like getting to the end too quick. We opted to be something in a box, hidden away, too expensive to throw out, but an unused product all the same. We kept ourselves unsold ... we deteriorated....'

'Zélie has had a life, with audiences: Blandine has had excitement,' Delia says. 'You, Jacob and Kochi – wandered off, into the sand and wind....'

She's just beginning. Maybe she doesn't know the script. I say, 'Try for success, you're bound to break the law. Criminals – they're so loud. They dig holes in the floor during the night to hide the stash. It's pernicious, keeps you awake....'

I expected Fabrice to be young as Delia, maybe flashy, a toyboy, maybe angry, an entrepreneur, a scholar.... No! – he's old, and palsied. He has a beard, white and black, a black face like a low volcanic hill with thin sheep scattered, the green nibbled to the cinders, a stick to carry him, his thin legs, all bone, no veins – a stick with a carved head – Socrates, Dionysius? – on the handle, the lightly curving shaft much longer than you'd need, hip-high, more like a crutch, a colour between mangrove orange, rhino-hide.

'Bed,' he says. 'Where is the bed?'

'I'll settle him,' says Delia. 'He needs the rest, and I shall sing to him.'

And that she does.

'You two,' says Delia later. 'Should concentrate more on getting cash. There's a smell of scrabble in these rooms.... "Rich" isn't hard. It's crass. Look at the idiots who have huge sums. They stick to gold, but you – you must be elegant, and lose and win again. That is the mathematics, the wheel of fortune, the cycle that you pedal. And peddling is what we've done. We met when searching for the Great Principle – we've had stalls, emporia, camel trains. Done street ballet, played the electric *ehu* – a marvel after midnight ... had menageries; alpacas, mitred swans – and never thought of eating one....'

'It's exciting,' I say. 'I'd have enjoyed finding the Great Principle, and doing all the rest....'

'Fabrice is ailing,' Delia says. 'I'm devoted to him, naturally.'

'I hope he makes it through the night,' I say. 'Sickness is a complication here.'

In the morning, Delia's gone. Fabrice is out of breath. 'Guys, pump me up,' he says, and that is all.

He's dying in good form. There's nothing to be done, it's all been done. 'Delia,' he asks, 'she got away, safely?'

'Oh,' Jacob says to me. 'Forget the Great Principle. Forget shopkeeping and dancing in the street. I hope he leaves me that fine stick. What a fine figure one would cut...'

'There may be a ceremony....' I say. 'We need to know the words, the tune ... death must be done right, or everyone is left in limbo....'

'The angel? The mystic peacock?' Jacob asks. 'Ascent, descent? It isn't up to us at all.'

'Wash me, orient me. Dig. Wait. Have a good time, like I have,' says Fabrice, with great difficulty.

We do exactly what he says.

*

'We messed up the new way,' I say. 'We're too picayune. Wherever we are, we turn the leaves with our feet, the smell arises, and we think – "This is not it, not the place", we must move on.'

'None of this is up to you, to us,' says Jacob. 'Though it is natural. Time is a slippery thing. Think of a city, and its boss – swaying from left to right, drifting, to tolerant to authoritarian, controlling everything, then steering without a chart.... Moscow, Beijing, New York. Through time, you'll feel you are the same yourself, a little feebler, but the mind! – the mind will travel, will see wonderful scenes you couldn't get a ticket for when you had legs ... but – the view, the place, its meaning, its significance – has changed. Not by your will or effort, that's for sure.'

'The point, Jacob,' I complain.

'We run, we race, we overtake, anticipate. But never fast enough, and never in tune to what is happening beyond our effort and our will....' he says. 'And yet – we have no tune. We're silent – or at most, we make a squeal or purr. Delia was right – travel with your muse, your guru, god or doctor, and when they're finished – leave them. Where they drop. And leave.'

'It's trivial,' I say. 'You mean, being in a species ought to have us feel the beat, the rhythm – the theme of the whole organism, knowing what's to be done – and yet there is a point where all's confusion, and we see the drop, the rocks below ...'

'That's what religions say,' he says. 'You reach the limit, all of you, you want to live and don't know how. It can't be so: there's no lesson, no resolution, no "end": in the end we disappear. I've told you – the confusion's there at the start. They always have, they always will – any agglomeration that can leave a trace – it falls, collapses, turns into a site, holes in the ground.'

'Well,' I say, 'we can't get stuck in that mud – that knothole, paper fold, the casting bubble, flaw.... The knap, the surface – it must be absolutely flat and true. Think – table bowls, think castrated sages. In the desert sand, playing *boules:* winner takes all, writes the book with the hand of God. The handwriting, though looks profane....'

We're talking on quite different tracks.

*

'Fabrice's stick is wonderful,' says Jacob. 'But look! It's broken and been glued. It won't take my weight.'

'I have some marvellous diets,' says Melissa.

'I know you,' Jacob says, squinting up at her. 'You've been a featured thinker, founder of living styles. You live in fabulous places, but sell up, for no reason, move on, dump your lovers and your small pets. You could try a horse, or eagles – they tie you down.'

'Yes,' she says. 'I could try you out, you two. See what you lack and miss – make myself cash to sell up, move on....'

We can't refuse. It's the call of civilisation – we three run through the woods, perfumed and silvery – already our blood's perked up, the dross on our teeth melts off. Her villa, high above the sea....

'It's rented,' says Melissa, 'and they're strict about the inventory. Don't break cups and steal the pictures – nothing is worth much, but it's designed to look as if it's been accumulated over yonks of time....'

The house, the gardens with their ha-has and statues, the bowers and flowers, the brakes – the follies and the wallows, the grebes sailing on the ponds – all promises a resolution. 'A revelation!' Jacob shouts – and we run whooping from room to room, bouncing on the beds, pounding each other with cushions, closing the brocaded curtains, swigging retsina, and....

We realise we're not the only guests with Melissa. There's a gathering on the patio. Fishermen and smugglers, collectors of songs, connoisseurs of marble, satyrs and gigolos, publicists and recluses.

'These two,' Melissa proclaims, as we giggle to a halt. 'Are my experiment. Serious and over-eaters, skimpers and sceptics – they are, have been, everything that makes one sad and discontented, and they're here to try out my new lifestyles. "How shall we live now?" I ask. How should we devote ourselves to life, and when concern ourselves with other people? Do we seek to change, or leave things, carelessly disordered, chaos well-organised – exactly as they were ... except.

'Except....' she goes on slowly. 'They'll be old. Things, relics and relicts. Old as you, and even older. In some way – mortal. Things break, they disappear, are loaned, grow mould, the leather cracks, the brass corrodes....'

A guy, Dimitri, in a suit of yellow corduroy – interrupts: 'Time being infinite, allows an infinity of possibilities,' he says.

Jacob's thesis, through Dimitri's phrase – explodes, sinks.

'No, no,' Jacob objects, feebly, sobering. 'It cannot be. The past holds the future, and the present, in its bondage. Though, of course, it does not exist.'

Dimitri stares at me: 'In order to proceed, we must hypothesise: – one indissoluble reality, that can be universal, and universally shared. Otherwise, all speech, all efforts physical or mental, are untranslatable. Meaningless or inexistent. It's a hypothesis that we can test – it's never been negated, not by anyone or anything. I am, therefore I think. I think not? I am not. Reality is a starting and an ending point for you, Kochi, and for us all. It has a wall that you'll not breach or leap. Time goes on – you won't survive it, or outlast it. That's reality!'

'I'm not convinced,' I say. 'Your argument is slippery....' but after all, it's my hypothesis....

'You guys,' Jacob says, turning to the fishermen. 'When you have emptied out the ocean – what then? When there are no fish....'

'Oh,' one says. 'There's red beets and there's white beets. No deaths a-gasp, no bones, no goggle eyes, no life truncated in the trawl. We'll cultivate our gardens, you can bet – in safety, without cruelty, no storms, no waterspouts, no whales with prophets in their gut ... no sea-legs and no sea-sick....'

'Exactly,' says Melissa. 'That's the first step. Listen to the beets. 'Dinner is that; coming up – red beets, white beets. Life at its most discrete. Calm, forever re-creatable: tranquil and controlled. They soothe the mind....' and on she goes, weaving a tale of beetles foiled, soils aerated, and moles re-routed....

Red, white and green – a plateful each. 'The retsina kills the taste,' Melissa says, taking our bottles. 'Forget the booze – think "Italian flag". Salute, if it makes you feel heroic.'

There's a rumbling. 'It's the *mouflons,*' Melissa says. 'Hooves. They scamper, bolt above the tree-line at this hour. They show off. Dancing on the crests.'

There's smoke. 'Oh no!' Melissa shouts. 'What a disaster. Burnt beets... It's the help – we inherited them. One speaks English, eats foufou and speaks wolof: Aish. The other, Kadi, no one understands her, she speaks French: a Bété, ran for her life.... Now they're here, we'd say they're rich by proximity....'

'Jacob speaks wolof, Melissa,' I say, anxious to intervene. 'He's a resource. Africa is full of them, resources of all kinds, that move or don't, above or under-ground ... though everyone is desperate to leave ...'

'"No, Kochi," Jacob says, annoyed. 'I speak a few words – enough to get a ride to somewhere else, if – by chance – I meet another wolof speaker, ask directions, though one hopes they all speak English. At a pinch, some French.'

The smoke.

'The smoke,' Dimitri shouts. 'It's here, and thick!'

The smoke is bristly, a doormat over your face.

We run out. Down below – a red lake. We feel the heat, no sign it will part for us: – the flames – no hope they'll let us scramble down, down to the sea.... The fire sucks the air out of us.

Black.

'The paddock,' shouts Melissa. 'On the stones – we'll huddle there ... see, all the little animals have taken refuge....' And so we guess they have. Only the littlest – black beetles predominate, and rats – a carpet of them. We mind our feet and tread on them, but we are terrified. The trees go up like roman candles –

'Lie down,' Dimitri says, and so we do.

'Aish and Kadi – did they make it down?' I ask.

'It's not a paddock,' Jacob says. 'It's a stone floor and walls – people like me lived here once....'

'They were small then,' Melissa says. 'They could hide, heads down below the smoke ... we're crowded here, our legs and heads stick out....'

'When it's hot,' says Jacob. 'All creatures become small. Tiny. But it takes some time....'

'It's true,' the fisherman says. 'The fish are spratlings now, sardines fit like minnows in the can, a hundred at a time ...'

'We need go so small,' Dimitri says. 'So all the ten of us could fit into a hand....'

The stones are heating up – the tree roots carry fire beneath the stone. The *mouflons* cough, far above us, as the smoke goes surging up –

'It's like a tide,' I say, but no one hears. If it is so, it will recede. But there's no sign....

Aish and Kadi – where are they? Perhaps they ran up to the crest ... disaster if they tried to follow us and fell....

'They come with the house,' Melissa says. 'To help. If the house is burnt – they do not help.'

'And us?' asks Jacob. 'Our lifestyles? Melissa, what's your thought?'

'Aha!' Dimitri says. 'We've all been thinking hard: but the smoke, the flames – they have the upper hand. Reality, you see. Our thought – inadequate; it hasn't saved us, not a bit.... Reality wins each time: *au pouvoir!*'

'There's always lessons to be learnt, my dear,' Melissa says, quite irritated. 'Everyone can start to learn right now – no need to wait to watch my interview ... my piece in the culture section, "blazing lifestyles".'

We lie, we turn, like scotch pancakes on the griddle.

THE BIRDS

I fly, just for a moment. Through the burning trees. High above, a nightingale – I hear it sing, incomprehensible, unchanged, as if the villa burns each day, the *mouflons* escape as they have done for years ... and the birds go high, higher, leave us to fry – even if it's burnt their homes, their eggs, their food.... Against nature. I thought nightingales sang from the ground....

Jacob comes tumbling after me, laughing, as we go, heads over tails, down the broken terraces. '*O nein, es lebt ... es war erlebt, drum ist's, wenn es auch war. Hinab den, ach, ich hab' gelebt,*' he shouts – 'Be thankful, Kochi – what would they have done to us?

Lifestyles? Why, we're the most stylish.... Remember! – we fly! The moment of flight? 'O no! It lives on, I have lived it so it exists, even if it's gone. Down, then! I have really lived....'

'Flying! That's what we've done – we flew, just for a moment – and escaped....'

'No, Jacob,' I say. 'Flight hasn't saved the birds. Their wings are scorched. The heat is suffocating, and they fall. The end.

'All dead.... Except Melissa ... she has contracts to fulfil....'

In bounds, flying, flapping, like storks, we leap down, through and at last – past the burn, down the crumbling abandoned terraces, the soil powdery, weedy: and reach the shore. With some other survivors we cluster – our fingers burnt, our toes, our knees, scraped; our hair gone to cinders – soot moustaches, black crania, our t-shirts smouldering, their bold mottoes blasted, tatters: down, mustered to the sea, back to where we came from, desperate to return.

'There goes Melissa,' Jacob says, pointing.

There's a small galley, on the meniscus, oars like the feet on water-boatmen, rowing her away, into the night, into the dawn....

'So much for fantasy of sex with the queen bee,' says Jacob. 'The hive – smoked out. The workers die – us drones live on.'

So, despite the fire, the burnt offerings – we're independent, walking. Is this an island, or a continent? We'll find out. Does Melissa send rescue for us – or is she escaping?

It's true. We are the singles, the heels well-heeled, the quick, the swift – the rest are dead. Guarding their kids, their homes, the pets, the animals – protecting what could not be saved and choking in the smoke.

'You're quite indecent, Jacob,' I say. 'Think of the deaths. The trees, if nothing else can move you – taller, older, more mysterious than you or I – they weren't our ancestors, their language, their inhabitants, a bark without a bite – as far from us as possible – and then ... catastrophe ... We flew for seconds – they ... they are the pillars of our world thrown down, a hecatomb ... feet rooted in the soil – illusion!'

'Wood. No more than wood. It's wardrobes and it's chairs,' he says. 'Everything and everybody dies. If you survive – rejoice! Survive one day – it's wonderful, a marvel. Tomorrow – the boat sinks, the plane goes down. Today – this is your miracle! Don't be a grump, Kochi. You've no way to praise the dead, pretend you knew them, loved them, feel regret, you have no kadish, they have no grave – people are a bundle of charred sticks among the rest ... and we, you and I – we feel, we listen, we can see the ruins and the roots that sprout, despite....'

DESPITE ...

'Melissa didn't like us,' I say, saddened.

'People don't like people,' Jacob says: 'At most, they use the word, but it's more variegated. Zélie clawed me, and spat me out. Blandine's guy – did she like him? I don't like you, Kochi, and it's mutual, but we work together – like the rubber tire is bound to the aluminium wheel.'

Disliked, respected, despised, tolerated, ignored, desired.... The same person – maybe wanting to be liked, is usually all these things and more.... 'So', Jacob says, 'What's the point of wanting to be any of these, anything at all? People – those envelopes so full of emotions, scraps snipped off other envelopes ... stamps from countries falling into other countries.... How do you deploy them, emotions and their people? How to hand them on, have them circulate and signify? Are they tidbits, hooks, or poison treats? What is appearance, and is there substance?'

'What will happen?' I ask, not rising to the argument: 'Everything still smoulders. Will a boat take us away? We don't want to go to sea, to somewhere else. I want something else entirely,' and I laugh. How ridiculous! Walk round the island to see if perhaps it is a continent? Find out who sets the fires, arms the warriors, hides the food and drives out populations?

'You're a visionary, Kochi,' Jacob says. 'If you found out – what good would it do, even if someone else believed you?'

WALKING

'We're amateurs, Jacob,' I say. 'We don't have a side. Or rather – the side we have isn't real. We make it up. We don't have publicity.

We live by what we hope is reason, which almost no one else does or thinks worthwhile....'

He doesn't answer. He must think I'm trivial. I say, 'Melissa, and Zélie – they are opportunists. We're looking for an opportunity to become opportunists ourselves. We have to avoid it, you must realise. Everyone thinks their species has a flaw, even lots of them. It's true, and every species does have flaws – it's evolution. All together, would they make a whole, a perfect combination? One half eats the other half ... you'd need be altruistic to think that being eaten was your perfect destiny. The crudeness of evolution: you must get used to it.... Our species hunts and eats like giants. There is a flaw, though: when you can do anything, you screw things up. In your head, there is a messenger, special to us. Of course: the death wish. We're the only one that's turned out that way ... by chance and by design – our face is set to suicide.'

Jacob doesn't answer. He can't. I don't see him.

I run back a little way. It's all cinders.

It can't be possible – but it is of course. A hole, black in the black, barely half a metre wide. A well that goes down indefinitely, unmarked, a bore hole.... He'll just have fitted. Before you could formulate a scream, or stick your elbows out – you'd be thirty metres down, accelerating – like a projectile in a cannon – down and down, with no target, no aim – except to reach a bottom, if there is one.

I call down, 'Jacob?' Almost never do people live, even get rescued, falling down wells. Who'd go down after them? So snug, so dark. Such a good fit. The science of mechanics tells you – sixty metres, accelerating – would you live when you hit? Better not....

There might be water – you might drown. Further down – the everlasting flame – you'll burn. A pointless kind of death, whatever way it happens – but after all ... only operas get it right, the death, but there, the music stops, you rise, and as you take your bow, your good times await you....

Jacob was all potential, as they say. That must be when you've done nothing in your life but cast around, question the optimists, the orthodox – and can't prove your case, are arrogant, bad-looking, extreme and dangerous in every other way, even seduction.... All your beliefs are hard to catch, disfiguring like leprosy. You need be set apart – no one should listen to your yowls – like a cat in heat....

'All potential' – means you may succeed or lose – but not by being what you are.

So many people die by disappearing. It's a sort of pleonasm – you disappear when you die, some die by disappearing....

There's no one around, alive, but me. I'm peering down the well, embarrassed to be shouting down; and what good, if he replies? He's finished, holding me up, spoiling my walk ... and how I loved him, but I didn't know and didn't say. He was my complement, my opposite, a contradiction that's supposed to activate the human glue – joining fast the unstickables, the loners, epoxying the discontented together; and now it's over and it's time to start forgetting, and remembering the anecdotes that didn't happen, quite, in the way they're told.... Memories – can't be transmitted, shared, everyone has their archive of Rashomons, uses them to stalk, deride, or just – forget.

I could be in shock. Walk on – and it's a crime: abandoning. Every uniform you see, ever, all your life – they've found you.

Walk on – and you've lost your moral patina: you are indifferent. Guilty of not being human.

*

He drones on, our heads droop, like dahlias unwatered. 'Partitions – first and second.... Grand and Holy Alliances. The Schleswig-Holstein question, Abidjan, Danzig, corridors and passages, secessions, unifications. Incidents, Sykes-Picot, "the fuzzi-wuzzis".'

The Boxers, the Philippines, the Maine ... Tonkin, Pigs ... it's like watching someone weigh out pokes of semolina; cabbage leaves, salted herrings; glazed cherries. Or games of draughts – huffing and puffing ... the lines swelling and shrinking, names changing, colours too.

'And so,' the speaker says. 'Who's been winning, how much, and who has not? And what will happen next?'

There's silence. To say it's sad – that might be you, your indifference chiming in. You think so much is futile, maybe you don't have values, interests; maybe telegraphs and cables undersea don't thrill.... After the address, think – Samozas and piroshky, steamboat, nasi-goreng ... will there be dinner?

Did Zélie shift discussion to a different plane? I think of her, I think of Jacob – I think of anything except what this speaker says. That's how we miss the answers....

How amused Jacob would have been, and angry, and vindicated, triumphant. How dull wisdom is, how tedious an information, how tawdry your opinions are, how worn your conclusions. And yet.... You're here to follow orders....

'This is Rhodes – this is the test', if you're an athlete there's no choice – you jump as you are told.

'There's a lizard in Namibia,' he said. 'Always breaks and runs left. Everybody knows it, the lizards get eaten every time.'

'You must ask a question,' the guy next to me says. 'It's your turn, your right. Then if it's good, you can be recruited.'

'I'm always up for that,' I say. 'A job. But doing what?'

He pulls a face. I stand and say, 'Power is next to divinity: it has been – *is,* divinity. In fact, the rulers in the best, the longest empires – they were gods. The people, slaves and plasterers, scored well in science, especially building and astronomy. When the gods – the rulers – failed, or just fell out among themselves, the people suffered, empires fell, the jungles hid the ruins for a thousand years – or else the deserts swallowed them.... Strange tales, and the people lived and suffered more, the languages survived....'

'Ah,' says the speaker. 'Power comes from the gods! I see you're a believer – unloved and credulous....'

'Oh no,' I say, confused. 'I'm quite a sceptic, and an atheist. Of course – if there are gods, and given that the power can make you do quite anything at all, or take the consequence of death ... being a sceptic and an atheist – is no help at all. I don't believe in all that stuff, but since it's there, who do I avail...? No prize for being right, nor one for being wrong.'

There's laughter and applause. Quite inconsequential, naturally: and I go on,

'Suppose a physicist should say – the world we stand on, and the universe – are tiny tiny particles, frozen in a frozen pattern of super-universes that shimmer, blush and shake – and once perhaps soft-shoe through an infinite of nothingness, like a medusa; not that position without reference to anything is meaningful and ... not that we can know all this by observation, only by a computation that we don't have access to unless we're maybe spies – fake passports, American, Chinese – from somewhere alien to us, at all events, known only from its games and telephones ... strange, strange, get used to it....' And I sit down. It's obvious, I could believe all this – it doesn't change a thing, poor Jacob, never got to throw his stone at an authority, ending as a pussyfooter in the well – and now I know that knowledge dies with you when your brain is slime, and as the Master told us – only 'Think': and as we later found, it doesn't change a thing.

'Power is divinity, belief is infinite,' I say. 'What's to be said in answer to my observations...?'

'That your time is up,' the speaker says. 'We put a limit on your time and on the relevance of what you say. I must move on – and moving on, you'll find, is what is left to humans in the current times....'

I go on, and no one listens. 'The divine powers, I stress, are not miraculous. You can't make gold, create babies, stop people having sex with who they fancy ... but you can lock opponents up in gruesome cells for life, conscript them, send them out in losing wars, let them be taken prisoner and dispossessed, invoke free will as an excuse for your mistakes – you're in a competition with the gods next door – whether they've been elected, or chosen by divination or descent, education, wealth....'

'It's useless,' the guy beside me says. 'I'm Amos, this,' he pushes his partner forward, 'is Charlotte.

'No one is listening – either because it's true, or false. Or somewhere in between – there's lots to listen to – long ago, there was stuff you could collect, so's not to listen – stamps and discs and coloured stones....'

'That's trite, Amos,' Charlotte says. 'We all descend from roots made many many years ago. We are the latest of the very old – the very very old, who all died young, but nonetheless left us all recognisable, the brains and bodies, jumping so, and running so, imagining just like the earliest ones.... Collecting soldiers made of lead is trivial, my dear, when you can go and be one when the postcard comes....'

'Human sacrifices,' Amos says. 'The powerful really get off on those. The smoke – better than pot.... Blood ... fires you up. Those pyramids, where you wait for heaven – are shaped like tents, as if you're on a camping holiday....'

'You sound quite close to a conclusion, Amos,' I say, drawing back. Jacob knew much that made me nervous, we had a pact that knowledge should seem open-ended, though that seems to spoil it from the start....

'Your friend – he sounds like he had a theory,' he says.

'He fell down a hole,' I say. 'It was invisible – but he found it.'

'And, Kochi,' Amos asks. 'Did you protect him? Did being nice protect him? But then – you wouldn't know. I don't think you're nice. Nor him! You're sceptical – that shuts you out. He was dogmatic – it didn't help a bit.'

'I think that's so,' I say. 'No one said there was a prize for being nice. So – no one I knew was attracted to it....'

'I tell you, Kochi, what I've often said to Charlotte,' Amos says. 'I believe in not suffering for what I don't believe in.'

'When I was young, we had a Master – he said "Think". What you say sounds much like "Think" – then "run". It doesn't seem to work,' I say.

'I give you "think",' he says. 'But not the "run". You turn your back – that's an alert. No, you find a place where you escape, avoid – but do not run,' he says, and Charlotte nods.

'The gods,' he says, 'are stupid. Very powerful, knowledgeable – but they're idiots, because they hope, expect, you will believe in them.'

'That makes you sound ambitious,' I say. 'It makes for complications. Anyway, I'm going up to see what job I've got ... I don't have ambition, but I want a job that I can do....'

As I go up, Charlotte pinches me, very lightly, on the bottom: 'You have airman's eyes,' she says. 'Don't lose the distances they promise ....'

*

Charlotte says, 'You're a true Odysseus, Kochi. You don't want to go, you don't want to come back, but when you must, you keep quiet. Everyone around you has adventures – you don't. You're timid. They think you're lucky – you stay out of things. You kill the monsters, but don't fuck the witches.

'You're the lover we see on the train while we are waiting for ours, late, and we stay on the platform while your train pulls out – and we love and want you for ever....'

I laugh: 'You seem close to Amos,' I say.

'Yes,' she says. 'Amos is good to me, to everybody, and himself. But you're duplicitous. You have a home. You hate it. But you're stuck there....'

I don't grasp any of this. I go up to the speaker, Doctor Herbst. 'I want you on my team,' he says. 'You're the right sort. But I'm not assigning roles just yet. You're in, Kochi. If you have capital you're wanting to invest....'

'Oh,' I say. 'Absolutely not. I just escaped a fire....'

'I know long wars are coming,' Herbst says, brushing aside what's just been said. 'They thought the big bangs meant wars would be short, diplomacy – would be long. The reverse is true. You can forget diplomacy. The end of the world – did you think it would be quick and clean, painless and radical? Not at all. We – those like you, who follow what I say – we know to change the lines, the boundaries – you need people to stand and – be on all sides. Restoration or revolution? It's too soon to tell. Probably it's both: unholy alliances....'

'There's masses working in intelligence,' I say. 'It doesn't seem a winning ploy.'

'No, no,' he says. 'We know the history. We know how and where things change, how long it takes, and how impermanent the settlements are. Deals last for centuries – or minutes – the same dead souls change hands.... Not intelligence, Kochi – that's done and verified in a day, and after a day – it's absolutely wrong. No – I ask you – where are the Kipchaks now? Who remembers Courland? Livonia? Who identifies with the Zaporizhian Cossacks? Don't tell me there is no one! No one left, all gone down into the ravine, the quicklime, and no one who remembers what they were? Their houses, that you stole...?

'They say the Bolshevik soldiers, whole regiments, deserted, changed sides, when they went to fight the Makhno army, the anarchist, his peasant levies – maybe being godless gives that sense, that you could choose and choose again ... choose not to choose. Not join, not go anywhere, be "as you are".

'You think we've got rid of rulers who are gods, because we vote them in and out. You saw through that, Kochi, that's why you're in my squad. We vote for gods, we vote for ruler gods and vote them in and out, just like we've always done. Better gods, more intimate – gods of love and gods of war – gods who drink blood, gods who drink milk. Gods on a cross and gods like balls of silken cloud. Known and unknown, gods who dictate rules, do Swedish drill, and gods who eat your kids.... Gods who take your money, show you where the gold is hidden, send you down the mine for life....'

'I know,' I say. 'I told you.'

'And that's why you're on my team,' he says. 'You know how long it takes to change the lines, the frontiers, to shift the peoples round, to change the capitals, the languages – to dispossess the neighbours who were liked, to pacify the hated ones, to accept the boyars who give the vanquished work as slaves and skivvies ...

'Long wars. Those change the lines, the boundaries. I'm sure you know the tiny spaces that are usually changed – look at the South Slavs, pirouetting, fencing, on a scrubby plot – it never stops and they are all alike! Imagine, if they had real differences!'

We laugh some more, like colleagues should. He goes on, as if he reads my text: 'You change your gods, your rulers, and your sufferings ... some pain increases, some grows less. But – on you go, you defer, you kneel: you build a pyramid, wear a tall hat, die for your king, your president – your country, if you know approximately where it is, and where it ends and what it signifies....'

'You think, dear Doktor, knowing this, and all the underpinnings of why what it should be – that this can make us form a team, and play, take sides, avoid the worst and profit from the best?' I ask.

'Absolutely so,' he says. 'Dear Kochi – I knew from the start – your question was my answer. Exactly what I think.'

'The system's terrible....' I say.

'Of course,' he says. 'Who doesn't think that way? But you'll find – maybe you already have – the flaw's in the design.'

I've found another Jacob. But I don't trust or like the Doktor, and he isn't fun.

I tell Charlotte, 'I may not have thought this through.'

'You're very bright,' she says: there's a stickiness to her that I can't accommodate. I don't want it, not to be stuck to her – with her; I try not to bring it out. 'Maybe it's the details that disturb, and not the whole. Herbst plays the soccer game by being on both teams,' I say.

Details? Always the same, obscuring the whole anyone needs to know. They don't matter. The whole: that's always the all-devouring ignorant divinity, thirsty and fearful.

'Zélie had other people to help her think things through,' I say. 'Though, it doesn't seem to have convinced the world.'

I ask, 'What does Amos think?'

'Amos avoids what he's unsure of,' Charlotte says, offhand. 'He might work on the railroads. That would be power without divinity, he says. But he knows no one who would place him there. He thinks Herbst is a fake, but you're courageous in getting close to him.'

'What does Amos give, then, Charlotte?' I ask her, much attracted....

'I'm with Amos for my life, I fear,' she says. 'Don't trust impulse, Kochi. That's what he had, and I reacted to it. Impulse: she's an iron maiden that nails you round her. Impulse condemns us, and when we're in touch with genius, like I am with you, we wonder, and are unsatisfied.... What do we lack, and hope we find in you? What do you lack? Are you lonely? Does power attract because you have none? Or not enough? There's reprisals waiting for what you want to do....'

'Well,' I say, 'we're trains passing in the night, Charlotte. Maybe Amos could schedule them so they linger longer in the station.' I laugh, Charlotte stares at me. 'Amos is in the signal box,' I say. That's rash.

'You don't believe in anything, Kochi, in anything you say,' she says. 'That's smart and cool. A little ordinary... It's common coin – the goats say they will lead the sheep to grass, the sheep say baaa. I guess you want to be a goat. Amos believes in compromise – he'll survive, but it's not my way, nor yours.'

She keeps on staring at me, as if to fix my image in her head. If this is how love or dislike work, I prefer the indifference Zélie showed. The stream of life is swift and cold, and I can't swim, I'd sooner watch the flow, walk along the bank....

Herbst takes money from all sides. He mediates by promising something for everyone. Everybody tries that trick. He doesn't assign the roles, the 'team' doesn't win a match. But – we've nowhere else to go. We're loyal, we stick by him, and Charlotte thinks that is a grand mistake.

'This is the beginning, where we learn,' Herbst says.

There's a great appetite for war. For competition, for winning, being top. For being on the right side. For being good, better than the rivals: being better than you are.

'Herbst's idea is great,' says Charlotte. 'You should be safe and sought by everyone. But ... be careful. Very very. Being between all sides means you're accomplices to all, traitors and confidants. You're renegades. You share the worst of everyone. The idea may be fine, but, Kochi – you are vulnerable. You are not liked. Jacob was worse, I hear ... and now you two went for a walk, and only you came back.... Now, you are him.

'Talking with the enemy – is spying. That's why dear Amos takes another, blander route. We two – we shall be safe, whatever comes.'

'And me?' I ask. It sounds quite querulous: 'And you and me?' I contradict myself: I'm no sure thing – I hedge my bet.

'Oh, love?' she says. 'Fixation? You mean the fantasy, what might have been, with me – making your career and earning gratitude, fidelity? It was all that, and more, and it will be – forever more. That's it. Thought. Memory. It's found a category – the love that's unrequited, will never be fulfilled. It grows, a world of mushrooms. Dislike – just the same.

'Remember. Careful. That's why Herbst seeks your capital, your stake. He needs insurance.'

'You're a martyr, Kochi,' Amos says. 'How will they pin you to the board? A Catherine wheel or Sebastian against his tree? All the praise you'll get is for playing off the Russians, the Chinese, and the Americans. Each against all. You'll be accounted as a tricky sort, although you aren't.

'What will get you is the value thing. No one's supposed to be fighting, killing, for their country or themselves: it's values. Everyone on your side must have them, no one else comes near.

'Not to accept that – is unforgivable. Fatal. You, Kochi, the disbeliever – you'll be left to dangle. Having values is believing in the rules – if they aren't sure you follow them, they'll never let you play.'

'I agree, Amos,' I say. 'It's plausible. I should have gone with Zélie and the fish....'

'Beware,' says Amos. 'Zélie's predicting disaster if we fish up all the fish. So – it will happen, that's for sure. She'll be right – probably it's calamitous. Except – she's just a prophet. Books are full of them, their previsions, lamentations, sufferings and disappointments. That isn't you. You have the innocence of someone who can't think things through. Can't get free of messes that you're in and haven't caused.... Zélie says "Don't eat the fish – it's bad for them, and you." When the fish have gone, a blessing probably for them – the oceans will go too. Then what? People are hungry – they don't listen. She's right – there may be a disaster. That is prophecy – but nothing more.'

I'm contrite. 'Maybe it's so,' I say. 'She can't do more. She can't steer the galley off the rocks. I drifted into places where the stakes are high, but I hadn't thought things through. And didn't have the capital....'

'Your cause,' says Amos. 'Might be noble, if you're not. The motto is – don't ask a question if you're not entirely certain what the answer is ...'

'I'm not interested in Charlotte,' I assure him: 'She's my adviser, nothing more. I'm quite certain.'

'That's quite intimate,' he says. 'Be very careful, what you say. Relationships can last a minute or a century, two people never have the same time-scale in their heads. Their emotions can't coincide. The finale – different in each performance.... It's slippery....'

'My work – it's sensitive,' I say. 'We advise all sides....'

'The value that's supposed to be the top,' he says, 'Is voting for the bosses. Then jailing them or having them replaced. It's like a polytheism – you're always bringing in new deities and throwing out the old ones that have lost their power, or got too much.'

'The ones you vote for aren't like that,' I say. 'They have real power over you, and so do their replacements. That rests on experience, not belief....'

'Well,' he says, 'There is a catch. The myth of equal power and worth: that, for each – is the supreme value. But there's another one – that the supreme value can itself be substituted. You vote for a boss who never leaves. Or a boss comes in that you can never vote for. You choose the supreme value, but once chosen, you can't change; but it can change or disappear! You may prefer it so....'

'I'm confused,' I say. 'You're making something simple seem complex. Nothing is predictable, save unpredictability? Once you know that, you can stack the deck, make provision for not knowing what will happen, but be prepared for anything....'

'That's childish,' Amos says. 'Though it's the case. No – what your Herbst understands, is that humans have three choices now: – murder, suicide, or rehab. Your team rides the options – murder and suicide – both ever-present, either a catastrophe.... Murder always tried, but suicide – perhaps the novelty....

'Destruction, destitution – the aim in poker games, but not in life. So, you're into rehab. Abandon murder, suicide, find something else that spares the species. Something that alters destiny: successful rehabilitation. Love life, tread carefully.

'But rehab's inexistent. You don't have it, it's not invented. Rehab would be great. What you offer, Kochi, is quite different: delay and compromise. Postponement ... merely more intelligence.'

*

'You don't want a woman,' Charlotte says. 'You want a friend. You had one, he disappeared. Now, that's it. No more friends.'

COURAGE

We see lots of soldiers, young soldiers, from all over, everywhere in the world. Doing the rounds with Herbst, we see them drawn up in squares, in oblongs – like Zélie's fish, faces identical in their cans. Their fathers have shaped them in these simple shapes: the old ones. Those know how not to get caught!

The young are silver, fairly uniform, like *coregoni*, fresh water types, tranquil on the lakes, lively in the torrents ... The majors, generals, do they protect the littler ones, the fry, the sprats? Do they marshal them, try to lead them off, a swarm, away from the nets? Do they deliver them, whole regiments, battalions – pushing them forward? Is it a battle, contest, sort of? Or a massacre? The leaders – the young ones out of Sandhursts, West Points, trained in sight of the beaches ... trained to deliver the miraculous catch.

Those are skirmishes: but ah! The sea! The sea unfathomable ... Campaigns, continents mobilised, atrocities recorded – the *mattanze* ... the trawls. Uncounted masses – dead, all dead, dead souls all sold.

When they're fished up by a caring sort of guy – they're stiff, resigned. Some twist, make a last struggle in the net – it takes some courage to face the situation, stark, but there's no escape, it's habit, almost ritual, the world's like that, will always be ... it's what the young ones must expect. The kindly ones, the fishers, respectfully, just tap them on the head before they drop them in the ice. The more experienced, those who catch the most, don't bother with a blow to finish them – just let them flap and gasp, expire.

'They're fish, Herbst,' I say. 'Except you can't eat them. They die and they are thrown away. You can't do anything with them – even those who don't get caught – they're useless after. It's the stress.'

'Once they're caught,' he says. 'And mustered – there is nothing to be done with them. They're fodder. Our task is to see there's no excess. Some will be sacrificed – and others hide. The best – is moderation. Sustainability. Don't kill the mothers, respect the mating season, protect the rarities. That's all you can expect.'

I know nothing of fish and fishing. It's not a metaphor, it's something that comes into your head. Zélie, I know. Her obsessions. And Herbst. Never committing, always untrustworthy. Together – an alliance, leading nowhere, nowhere at all.

'Everything we deal with,' Herbst says, 'is corrupt. And violent. Everything that moves in our world, remember, is violent and corrupt. Violent or corrupt. What's not in our world is also violent and corrupt, but there's also money and sex and gambling. The last ones – those you can exclude – they don't come into our world, our calculation. They're accessories, for when you've lost, like pills and stuff. Don't ever think that after us, still less because of us, the world will be moved, turn, except by violence and corruption. Do you understand that, Kochi?'

I play him along. 'You mean,' I say, 'that all the benevolence, the hospitals, the schools, the movies and the festivals, the sing-alongs, artistic skating – is all to guarantee that there'll be rockets, petards, bought, and that the whole effort of all civilisation is to produce a supply of soldiers – fish – so that we can go forward, seated and strapped in our countries as if we're ready to be fired to paradise, eating fish at times, and martyred flesh at other times, and being proud of battles won and heroes on the plinth?'

We laugh.

'You need courage,' Herbst says, suddenly serious. 'It's wet and cold, your stomach gives you hell, the other boats are swifter, they trawl deeper, make more cash ... but if you are courageous, it compensates, it won't seem such a crapful job.'

We laugh some more.

My role has still not been assigned. I doubt I'll ever have one. Herbst likes having me along, irreverent and deferential, but doesn't trust me with the talk, the raising funds, the pushing up the price. In the last and first resort, we are facilitators: selling arms. What the clients have and what they need, then what they have to counter what in theory they or someone else might need. That's our business, our lubricant, our trade.

'Sweeteners,' Herbst says. 'Sweets for the sour. Pushing up the stakes, and evening things out. Losing here, but winning there – diplomacy. Taking stock of what you have and what they have, and guessing if the guys are serious....'

THE WORKS

'Listen, Kochi,' says Herbst one day. 'Of course, we can't sell anything, material – no *matériel* – to big guys. But we can play upon the differences....

'Americans – their soldiers have many ranks and many offices. All over. Hundreds of centres all over the planet and in space. No one takes responsibility – it's a society that goes ahead by being – a society. Of course, some guy exaggerates, and is thrown out – but is tossed back into the society, the other one, the subterranean – where people don't wear uniforms, unless they're working in a restaurant. And some guys have to do the gardening, get dirty – squashing the bugs, weeding the ground. But the structure stays as it was: success or failure – no accounting, no responsibility. Immense.

'The Russians – it's all "who whom". Who bosses who. That's all you need to know – who gives the orders – then, it's up to somebody below to say that they obey, and do what they are told or simulate.... There's those who give the order, and those who know they are expected to obey. Or make a show. If they're found out, there's a chance of punishment, so it's best to look alert....

'The Chinese – maybe they're more subtle. Guys in the middle – by sharp practice or because they're good at organising – they're held responsible; they do the toughest work. They don't make the policy, but the guys at the top are very prudent: they don't throw people like them at the top out of the club, not openly, if they can help. The top – is in the clouds. The middle takes the strain, but after all – the top decides what's to be done. The middle organises, does its best. It takes the rap, but can enjoy what rewards there are. A lot, if that is how you think.

'The bottom – it is sacred. It counts – for everything, and nothing. It's for the middling guys to make a settlement. They enforce consensus – between grumbling and indifference, they aim at – being resigned.

'But – if you follow the money – the military might be quite different. It's my weak area, I confess....

'These are the fields we have to cultivate....'

'Agriculture, Herbst?' I say. 'I'm really not into that. It sounds quite simple, but so complex – the beetles and the rain.... I'd not know where to start.'

'And that, if you were wondering, my friend,' Herbst says, unamused, 'is why your role is not assigned. Or not to you, at least.'

Coordination, command, mediation. It's never quite like that – though I don't insist with Herbst.

For coordination, there must be coherence at the top – and when there's not, and there can't ever be – the system goes ahead, makes its own roads and destinations.

Command? – orders can be obeyed, but – who knows if they really are? Or really can be?

Mediation – sounds most reasonable, when one is starting out. But at a certain point ... you've made a system: or a hierarchy. An elite. An elite that does it all.

Stability? Or teeter…? The same for everyone – try anything....

What does Herbst want? Respect and long life.

Is that what everybody wants?

Outcomes are problematic – like Zélie's. A different world from Herbst's. His seems quite an inconclusive plan. What if he's ineffective? What conclusion will be worse? Whose failure, Zélie's or Herbst's? No fish at all, or everyone a fish?

Why do we think 'worse'? Who's counting, who's assessing? All those people in those situations – remember: 'not characters, but situations' ... playing their assigned roles....

What can Herbst hope to gain from them, and what does he make of all the tasks and destinies they all, willingly or unconsciously, pursue? Best not to ask!

'You're right, Herbst,' I say. 'I lack focus. When I was young, I did something my father would never do. Crossing a line. He was angry, disappointed. I was finished, without hope. Clever and weak – what a combination: disaster!'

I oughtn't say this to Herbst – but it sets me free from him. He can drop me off ...

What's worse – the solitude of never being what you are? Or the solitude of always being what you are, and suffering identically?

*

'There,' says Amos. 'You got there, Kochi. Dirty money to see who's top. Spying for all sides.

'Or – save the world ... save the fish, at least. Which way will you go? I wonder. Don't look at me. Don't look at Charlotte. Zélie has no time for you. Don't bed down with Blandine, or you may not rise again....'

'Maybe Blandine will tell them about the shooting,' I say. 'She must suspect....'

'You're ingenuous, I fear,' says Amos. 'What intruder? If your bed-mate's shot, it's obviously you, become intolerant ... with an iron.'

'You should watch Charlotte, Amos,' I tell him. 'She's too clear-sighted for my taste. Check under the mattress for a piece: – or you could sleep with body armour, like an armadillo....'

And we laugh.

'You have your troubles too,' says Amos, slapping me on the shoulder. 'I saw Zélie. At once she said – "where's Jacob?" I told her, if anybody knows, it must be Kochi....'

'When the fire came,' I say, quite discountenanced, 'I had a momentary flight – it's like the nightingale had wafted me.... Did Jacob fly as well? You might say, that once you have experienced it – flying has eliminated boundaries between the species. What that entails – who knows?'

'It's quite unclear,' Amos agrees. 'With Herbst you know the strategy. Be content with that – it isn't much.... But flying ... even a metre, that's how it began with those machines. Now, almost everyone goes up in them.... Then, there's some life-time flyers who don't do it well ... the butterfly, the ladybird.... We could end up there, a backwater, you might say....

'Don't drift, Kochi. We need some fish to eat. Those fucking birds – getting up so early, before we do – they eat the insects that sting and eat the gooseberries. And the fish.

'You must draw conclusions. Can birds be dumped somewhere: Africa, New Zealand? You decide, my friend – make the campaign. It'll fill your life. It doesn't mean a thing. Your flight has been a one-off, and the nightingales have all been killed by ravens.

'Read a book. Think! – like that old guy, maybe a teacher, do what he said, then *do* something, accept the zero consequences and die a burden on the world ... shut your eyes, play dead, drop in the hole – quiet; peace. The struggle – forget it. Finished, done.'

'You're lucky to have Charlotte's love,' I say. 'At least, her clarity.'

'Think: and add – "listen"!' Amos says, pink with frustration.

'Cherish your hopelessness,' says Charlotte. 'Find a religion where inadequacy is the norm, pleases a divinity, lets you and them off the performance hook. Let human sacrifice be intermittent:

maybe a lottery? Some birds, some fish? Right! Be content with what you have, with what you don't.'

'Time and friends,' I say. 'There are other things. But people like to hear about those. What do the stories tell? That love will come? Maybe Zélie likes me more – especially now that Jacob can't be found...'

'... doesn't exist,' Chalotte adds. 'No, Kochi, it's not like that at all. Zélie has competition. Politicians deal with what you call the other things, though they espouse poor Zélie's cause. She struggles! Her mother! Those bed habits! Cast a gloom....'

IN BETWEEN

'I need a place,' I say, 'where I can decide where my next move lies. And where I can be found, recruited, prepared....

'I'm in a warehouse,' Zélie says. 'Above, there's Charlotte. The guy she's with, Amos – can't find his spot. They're deep in need. I'm on the middle floor. I told you – I've been taken up by politicos. It isn't good. They pick and choose – an animal here, a weather forecast there – and it's all subject to their bigger game – relations with the even bigger powers, flirtation with the little ones....

'Down below, there's cellars – but don't fantasise. That's where the squatters are – the wine was drunk long since.... It's best for you; to find a place, a little one, where you can wait until you can decide, or maybe you'll be called and found. Keep very quiet, and don't have company. I know your family's all dead....'

'I'd no idea,' I say. 'I didn't know I had a family, and now you say I don't. We were discreet, there were some coups, secessions, ambassadors recalled and not replaced, births unrecorded, deaths extolled....' I laugh, but it would be an awful thing – except it's not a thing, a circumstance, at all, to lose a family you never sought, or had certificates; without a memory, and photographs of nameless ones or maybe who are not them at all ... the custom being in my country that when a neighbour died, the photos went next door – the servants if they'd had them, cats, babies, dogs, all passed on, as if one day when only one was left alive, they'd have an archive of unknowns, and documented dead without a face to fit the name, without a memory of situations or of disappearances, people too young to have fallen prey to situations....

'Yes, a corner would do fine,' I say: 'I've no cash, of course, and so....'

Zélie doesn't rise to this, of course her world is fish who don't pay rent, who go wherever they are swept, preyed on in whoever's patch they wander to.... Besides, she lives from charity, like the politicians who decide how much they're paid, and she can use likewise the cash available, dependent on her schedule ... saving the world comes through expenses and an honorarium, she says, and so I'm fixed up; under Amos, but above the squat, only my food is left for me to find, just like any common haddock or a sole.... I can curate, she says, a tank of fish, of Silver Dollars. They flock and flip, about-turn their heads and tails. Can't be spent, nor converted.

I laugh.

'The empty floor,' says Zélie, 'is kept for Jacob, naturally. The ground.'

It all feels glum.

'It's good you're happy, Kochi,' Zélie says. 'I'm marginal, it seems. The suffering, stagnation, death – those were my themes – they didn't stick.... No one alive fears an extinction – sad but true....'

'I know,' I say. 'You try to think things through, but always there are consequences of one-off situations, of novel sensibilities and laws of physics and of appetite no one is qualified to know....'

'Those are phrases, Kochi,' Zélie says. 'We are friends, and there is time. Time's all that interests we humans, if there's also food. Time is all around us. Friends – may come, others may show themselves more abundant. More passionate, more intimate, as the time unrolls.'

'There's maintenance,' I say. 'The building ... suppose floors one and two fall into the underground?'

'You've only just been given space,' says Zélie, irritated. 'The building's fine, and purposeful.'

We leave it there. Rain is the accelerator, it seems – it softens structures: here, it hardly rains at all.

'Most things are accidents,' Zélie says. 'You can't blame anyone at all for them.'

'I thought we were talking about stopping one: disaster,' I say. 'The top floor collapsing into those below.'

'I've been through all this with Blandine,' she says. 'I found that concentrating on what is not an accident is exactly what we're not cut out to do.'

*

Amos is sad, depressed – no one employs him, despite his eagerness to compromise, or ... because of his eagerness to compromise. Charlotte supports him. She gets bored with his sadness, his failure, and the unrewarding pain of supporting him. She withdraws support, although he doesn't notice that, or anything at all.

'Can it be the spirit of the warehouse?' Zélie asks, in general. 'I'm not getting anywhere. I'm dropping reference to the oceans. They can take their place, somewhere in the background, down below and deep. That's me. Me, irrelevant and deep.' She sighs, and shudders. 'Oh horror! The octopus! I hate the feeling – fishy fingers over me, and everywhere, in the shower ... in the rain ... under the waterfall….'

'You're the only one of us who's been successful, Kochi,' Amos says, quite nastily. 'You've done everything you set out to do. No one knew what that might be.'

'You're right, Amos,' I say. 'Though few people recognise my success. It doesn't give me satisfaction – though I guess it stops depression. It's my accident.

'But I insist – the building is a risk, you feel it wavering. Zélie's people – they stamp and sway. The ceiling is the floor, remember that! It is the rule of civilised existence – a complication, the storey, we should get used to. Floor on floor, higher, higher.... There's rumbling – Herbst's people. Heavy crates....

'Zélie boarding her survivors: us! And all the species we resemble or we eat – spliced into other issues. Might we be useful, might we be saviours, bodyguards.... That's politics – the pecking order, chicken hierarchies, the how we live and what we are....

'It's clear, the noise their boots make up above...! Marching. They want to bring her in to *their* campaign, survival matters equally to everyone....

'"*If* we survive", is Zélie's line. For how long? – the conditional's a sentence offered by the law....'

'Yes, yes,' says Amos. 'You must accept, Kochi, that everything is multiple, that all is various, we link from tooth to tail, connect, they used to say, but now – connection's broken, and we move like in those dancing marathons, automata, asleep on our partner's shoulder – and everything in the world is moved along with us in waltzing time. The beat goes on: if it stops here, with you or I, the drums in space don't pause, that is the only time they know. In the beginning, "let there be time" – or else there's no beginning! And no end determined: hypothesis, of course, unless it ended long ago, but, as I said, the beat goes on, in everybody's head....

'You can compound it, jazz with it – but in the end, your end is in that time, in lengths of string already measured out and when you hear your music end – so do you too....'

'Oh Amos,' I josh with him. 'Those are old spy stories! That's what they say Herbst did – someone makes threats, he gives them cash and guns to do it, and he says "my condition is, that what you can, you won't. Not now. Wait. Calm down, cool off, and then there'll be more stuff..." and so he says to everyone the same, and everything remains the same.'

'It doesn't sound the same,' says Amos, scornful and puzzled. 'Shift the pegs upwards all the time, and when it all falls down, it will hit hard, much harder...' and I realise he really needs that job – on roads or railways, anywhere that he can get away from Charlotte, and Charlotte tells me there's no heat upstairs, and can she warm herself on me, and "yes', I say, although it's cold down here, even – especially – in bed, and in a little while she goes back up, and Amos shouts at her about the work he hasn't got. We're all quite poor, except for Zélie, but she pays for Blandine's lawyers and they cost a lot....

Amos always wants something outside himself, like a turtle's shell which really is himself. First – work, then, tired of that, a hobby. Gym. Then flight. An illness. A charity.

Zélie wants something not Blandine. If it helps save mankind, it's incidental, but good, naturally – lots of recognition. A statue, even. Without her mother, though.

Charlotte wants sex, because after a certain age, everybody does it, then you stop, when it is time. And you organise people, more and more, so you can forget the face of each one, and they're a crowd like Ensor's – rotten-apple-cheeks, demons and cretins. Christ in procession, not noticing anyone at all except Himself. Concentrating on resisting pain and dying well – inflicting pain and death on those around her.

All those, my incidental reflections, naturally.

Zélie must re-design her whole campaign. There's more competition, people competent with facts, much spontaneity, and guys who tell her to think of something realistic to be done. All that is what she'd not imagined for, and probably she never will.

We all chip in with some ideas, but she's been queen bee too long and pissed us off, she's not a winner, and her mother's story pulls her down. We all want to get away; or stay on, but being richer.

'True fantasies,' says Amos, and we laugh. Being poor's a fantasy until you are, and then you don't want to be, want more than anything to invent some way of managing not to be poor, but the something else, you can't imagine.

Amos is a good old stick, beneath the anger and the jealousy. 'We should try to put something together for the two of us,' I say. 'Some activity.'

'A gym?' he suggests. 'Small animals. Sea acquaria: or tropical. Exotics – parrots smuggled, with false documents.'

'A bright parrot could forge its own,' I say. 'They'd not be economic migrants. That's what you mustn't be, or you'll be deported somewhere not economical. Migrate where there's a big economy, where anybody would want to be. Some birds still migrate – for food, and singing, having kids. They used to pass over, high up, excited, courageous too. How we envy them in retrospect – no one stopped them trying to be natural. We were all for them, in favour – all of us stuck here.'

'You have to live somewhere,' Amos says. 'And it must have an economy. Stay or go: it's basic.'

That's it – that's in the nutshell everybody's looking for. I tell him that, and how we laugh!

*

Someone shoots Blandine in the bath – someone from the dead guy's family? Zélie's dismayed:

'A shotgun,' Amos says. 'Lucky not to have holed the tub – and Blandine, the saucer-wound plugged with a loofah. She's between life and death, they say – an interesting zone, with interesting people showing you around, though spaces are for rent and by the hour....'

'Another scandal,' Zélie shouts – 'a Titanic! A gash beneath the plimsoll line.... Not Russians, I'll swear – a mafia....'

A tragedy, of course, that only the spectators can appreciate – without the suffering, the scenario, and its peephole to the lighter side.... Those, the subject knows, but no one else.

'The tub,' says Charlotte. 'Is a way of approaching the body and the self – laying it out. Most people shower, because that way you don't see much – the body's stretched, ready for walk or run.
No defects visible. The tub, instead: you are dismasted. Creatures, invisible and not, engage in sub- and circum-navigations, even to your orefices. Your timbers scraped. There's seasons as the ocean cools and warms. You blanch and steep, wallow, and above is wrack and jetsam, bubble and splosh – life abounding – confetti lives of krill and plastic....

'Then – the blast. The tempest, the intruder, l'homme armé. The woman – with the hunting rifle, the elephant gun, the sawn-off piece.... That's it! The end.'

'A parable?' I wonder. 'Leviathan – we've all had one – a parent, companion, an idea, a goal. Now, is it us? As usual, we're alone. Us and the waves. It's only us, trying to get clean: the booze, the dope: all in the tub.... action-reaction – test your reserve: soak, drink some manhattans, smoke Montecristos, dirty-up.... As for Blandine –

'The scrubber scrubbed....

'And only Zélie could have set it up so neat.... Carried it through, carried it out. Blandine's scandal's over, quite resolved ... and Zélie, well – she knows more than the rest of us, sees how dramas are set out....

'Just think,' I say. 'If we negotiate this well, we'd expose Zélie, replace her, and if we want – take over her campaign ... Circumstances, Charlotte – those run on. Corals, fish, the heat, the water and the sand – we can't change all that ... the food, the bloodshot skies.... But – we can take Zélie's place, be big figures on the screens....'

'Exactly so,' says Charlotte. 'That is what it takes to be transformed, re-made, re-figured, utterly transformed ... magnified and cleaned....'

'But,' I say, 'it really doesn't interest me. I'm not cut out ... You are, maybe....'

'Justice, Kochi,' Charlotte says. 'Must be done. Blandine did it to the guy, now Zélie does it to Blandine. Then, it's our turn. Justice – is an obligation – like giving food and water if a person asks: in the Qur'an....'

'It's what they say,' I say. 'It's another of those chains – the chains of being. You fear disaster if they break. And yet – those chains are all you have. They say – nothing's left to lose except your chains....'

'No,' says Charlotte. 'You can't say that. You must reformulate. Justice must be sought: always. When found – it must be done. There's no way out, no alternative. No "wait", no "half and half" – it's to be done. We all have a right to it – wherever and whenever: you can't duck out....'

I think of Jacob, but without a thought of being just. What would "just" mean, and mean to him? A right you never use, because of accident and circumstance. Then there's myself ... am I owed justice? For what? What must I do to deserve my justice, what do I do with it, where does it belong – by the hearth or at the door...? Have I ever been unjust? Or just? Can I get justice for something that's been done to me?...

'No!' she says. 'I see you wriggling – you're the puma with the cute baby fox gripped tight in its jaws ... you're both of them, the prey, the kill. Justice must be for both? No!... You can't get stuck like that. That's lawyering: a pleading that justice should be just. Forget that – you'll get nowhere. It's a compromise – like Amos makes. You'd be a trimmer, a walker of the line – no one condemned, no one found out, the guilty pardoned or excused, the innocent – given a medal or a tip.... No! Justice – quite unconditionally assigned. Whether it seems just or not. It never finishes, the trail of justice, its trial – the culpable become the victims, history is paved with them ... No matter. Onward! On to the next.'

There's anger around. Everybody feels it – the shooter and the shot, Zélie and Blandine. I feel it too, but don't know where it leads.

*

'Listen, Charlotte,' I say. 'We are old dogs, with lots of the original wolf inside. What we've lost is instinct for life lived in the pack. We know that talk about subjectivity, the dark days, the white nights – matters to no one but yourself. It's all been written down. It's on your shelves if shelves you have, and if you don't – you can't avoid it, it's in your head.

'We're much too wise to want to modify the world. We've travelled it. It shimmers – like the gauze curtain they drop down in transformation scenes, when they need time to place the scenery for the final act.

'The point is, Zélie must be innocent. No one punishes their mother when the world is at an end. Rather, think of cosseting the children. Spare them the fear, the trembling....'

'Zélie doesn't have children,' Charlotte says. 'I don't think Jacob....'

'No, certainly, that was not his thing,' I say. 'As for Blandine, there was no justice done, no punishment. An intruder did it all. More injustice – or just vendetta...? Our life is infinitely sad, the good part is that life in general is indifferent to individuals. That is the message – search the books, the sacred, the profane ... there's no conclusion. Nothing at all for you, specifically. There are ends – but that's the law of everything. The last judgement is provisional – jail time or not proven. Another start... We have an end, but no conclusion ... no answer....'

'I know all that,' says Charlotte. 'It's absolutely out of place. We can do Zélie's work: campaigning is interesting, at the top.... You'll do what I don't want to do – that's what being vice entails: – still, you can take your shower in peace....'

'Yes,' I say. 'I don't underestimate it. If the water's off – we can do like sparrows do, and ruffle in the dust, to shed the bugs and exercise our wings....'

We laugh.

*

'I love your superficiality, Kochi,' Charlotte says. 'It's useful, when we campaign. Those guys, big cheeses, chiefs – they never wondered why there were those floods and droughts, and when they told them how their island was submerged, the rivers turned to dust – how full of wonder they all were, and doubts as well, and difficulty with envisaging the numbers, and the times. They were no good at figuring out. Why, Mayas had it calculated, and carved it too – and that's why people knew their bosses were divine, experts in time and universe.... But nowadays, instead....'

She tells the cops how Zélie did her crime. 'Well, well,' the head cop says, 'we never thought of that....'

'Forget the why,' Charlotte says. 'Think of the how. There's never clues that tell you why – why one thing or another happens, why you decide to act and do or don't: stick to the how, and that is where the finger points....'

And so we get to take responsibility for nature: Zélie's story ... what will happen without fish. And all the other consequences.

'Poor dear,' says Charlotte. 'The cop – he has a boss, a swelling, right central on his brow. They need it, to remind you of the unicorn, of innocence – but it's a giveaway when you are stalking somebody.... All honest cops have one, that's why you or I can never join the force....'

'For our dishonesty?' I ask. 'Or because we don't have the horn? "I hear the horn, sounding in the depth of the wood...." But they were all around, hunters encircling the stag, the deer ... musicians and butchers.'

'That's it,' says Charlotte. 'Be reassured – we didn't hunt down Zélie. We were just. There's nothing comparable to chasing stags. Nature! We must bring it back – the sound, the forest....'

CLARITY

'We must defend her,' Charlotte says. Clear Zélie's name. Our denunciation – must have been a misunderstanding – we wanted clarity, the cops messed up, arrested her.... We did our duty, it misfired as usual....'

'It worries me,' I say. 'What we did; now, what we propose to do, the opposite.

'Blandine's waiting on the river bank, part shade, part wounded flesh ... nascent or moribund.... Nothing to do until she can decide to call the boatman, pay the fare... I don't go along with our intrigue – the tales of guilt and innocence: they're plaited, tangled.... I can't remember all the past, her devotions and enthusiasms ... the pillow talk, shooting her P38. Her rage, and then her silence.'

There's more. 'I'm not so sure,' I say. 'The cause is just, of course. Life, death, and where Blandine is – the in-between. But – it doesn't snag on me, it doesn't catch. Survival – it must be good, but I can't handle the procedures and the tests ... the lobbies and the interests; those pouting pigeons – the politicos. The eagerness, the hope, and even worse – apocalypse and revelation – I'm sure it's right for everyone, for everyone but me. Then – there's the physics. The quantities, the times. The string, the knots. Where we are, where we must be, how late we run, where we have stopped ... it's like Amos and his trains.... I don't want to make a journey, not through the universe – not just to stay alive....'

'It's not just you,' says Charlotte, quite surprised. 'It's everyone.'

'I know,' I say. 'It's terrible. A burden of sadness – infinite, far beyond me and my telling.'

'You don't make sense,' she says. 'There's obligation.'

'I agree,' I say. 'The book is right. When someone asks. Food and drink. And now, it's everyone who asks. And me – I ask as well. I am unique, it's true: I flew – but into smoke and ash – I think about it all the time, could I have taken off and gone – who knows? Like Icarus. Learnt some humility. Distrust of the technology. What ecstasy – and what a trip! into the sun....'

'What, then?' she asks. 'What is the theme that powers your symphony? I knew you were a leaky barrel – but don't make yourself a void. Everybody fails – your duty is to fail, get up and run, and not regret.'

'Oh,' I say, 'I'm sure everything I do is done for everyone, in their name, and mine. Philosophy has said as much....'

'We have moved on from that,' she says. 'It exaggerates, then falls back into an 'as if ...' As though we *think*. As if we want the good, as if you are the specimen who stands for everyone, their thought and deeds. It can't be so – you're rudderless, adrift ... a nasty guy at heart.'

We take a breath. Ah yes. The oceans. Here they come again, the sadness of the fishy eye.

I say, 'It's where we came from, Charlotte: those guys, even the enormous ones, we were in shoals and clusters with them – we're their offspring. Was it to escape we went on shore? No more the gaze of shark and whale – those sad fatalistic eyes.

'We never can escape. Our eyes are theirs. They are our relatives, our forefathers – we come from them, they are our bloodless flesh....

'What then?' she asks. 'Sobriety. Survival: – realism. Those don't seem to be your creed. And so...?'

We look out: the scene, it brings to mind – 'the living world'. It's too weak, too late, to mention it ... the world where everything was living and everyone was part of everything; there was a soul that each one had....

It never was. It would have meant acceptance of a destiny unfathomed, unavoidable, that made us all accept extinction – the price for being part of an enormous whole ... the centre of the universe, the earth where there is a paradise, a hell, an in-between where our life passed. Has almost passed. Shot in the water, our destiny – like Blandine's.

And left us sad, horrible, spaced out. Space! Leaving the earth, our vessel broke the bowl, the blue and black: the sky ... the great illusion. We are alone, we know it, but we seek a company that is not us ... not our kind? We cannot stand us ourselves, can't love, converse with our alikes – and so – away! Away, away – the whole is broken, there's an infinity of emptiness and useless nothingness out there, and on we go, guiding the spaceship which we don't drive ... it's really being aimed from desert bases, a spectral galleon that ploughs ahead through rocks and dust, long after we the crew are dead, white-suited virgins, clutching dummy steering-wheels and scrutinising frozen dials ...

Charlotte stands by me – shoulder to shoulder, hers a span taller than my own.

'That talk of hunts and horns, the music – leaves me quite horny,' Charlotte jokes. 'Maybe, Kochi, it affects you too....'

'It must be all those cops, the bosses on their brows ...' I say, and move away, not to offend, but breaking off where we had touched.

'Don't tell me, Kochi,' Charlotte says, amused. 'You're in the dream! The living world. You want to leave the human lot, go on the eternal trip, life inexhaustible – the illusion that comforts, even as you slow and start to fall and stagger....'

'No, no,' I say. 'That's immature. The living world is where we disappear. We're unobservant, homicidal ... we spent a million years without the wheel, though the round world itself should give a clue.... Jebel Irhoud: there, they found we'd been around millions of years not grasping anything at all – the calendar, flush toilet, resurrection – anything! And then more millions of years, somewhere way down South, another somewhat *sapiens*, as if protracted ignorance counts as a success....'

She insists. 'Maybe you think that other species fornicate and propagate quite tenderly. You would be wrong.

'Sex, my dear, is central but quite rare; timed, programmed, violent. Unwanted but essential. Maybe you have been seduced by pictures of the lambs and hares ... it isn't so. Courtship is rough in beasty land....'

And she laughs: 'Take toads, for instance. Herbst would like me as his mate – in body, and in politics ... and yes, he's toadlike, in a way, but fascinating too ... he and his mates, all piling on....'

I'm roused by this. 'Herbst is gross – he has a cleavage. Toads are leggy, muscular – antithesis to him....'

She doesn't hesitate: 'There's the horned toad. We discovered him at school.

'Now, I am assigning roles. Don't quaver, don't object. You must accommodate.

'Zélie is spent, even if we intercede for her. We'll denounce her, retract, take over from her.

'I'm uncertain what I can have you do. You don't react, your thoughts....'

'You know,' I say. 'I had a thing for Zélie, not reciprocal. But it is true – the case for nature's got too complicated. It used to be for naturalness – now it's machines and retorts of bubbling stuff.

'I can't face down the chemists and the climate guys, designers of the rockets and the ships that trek to Mars, the gas men, ice men – the carrots from the snows a kilometre long ... the crowds – their posters and their shouts ... it isn't me.... And then, deserted villages, salt flats ... their only inhabitants, undertakers of their world: the secretary birds, accounting lizards....'

'No, Kochi – that is not the word for them,' she says. 'The name has flitted out my head as soon as I could picture them – although I know ... they're not as big as those amphibians, their flesh – tastes like a chicken nugget, but their name escapes me too ... Iguanas, possibly?... No! – *Monitors*. That's it,' she says, triumphantly.

'My role, Charlotte?' I ask. It all depends on Herbst, of course – avoiding war by stoking up capacities, so no one thinks they'd win a war, and so they ponder other ways to save themselves.

And sex with Charlotte – nothing personal, but if I am to join the living world, I must....

For mating, usually, it's an assault: rarely a dance ... uniquely there's a bower, but not for a cohabitation. A frolic – that's the best preliminary ... my totem is the hare: long legs, long ears, but often fatally abstracted by a captivating thought....

'Oh Kochi,' Charlotte says, 'you're so slow, abstracted. Alas, I fear, while you moon on, my mood has passed.'

Moods mostly happen once a year, five minutes flat: and I might eat the cubs, make room in the lair for mine....

THE BOOK

I tell Amos, 'It's late, it's very late, to look for a solution. Herbst is temporising, risking. Zélie was late, a populariser among the many, and Charlotte's following her: all much too late, irrelevant.

'We act like innocents, free to tramp the world, drink in its airs. None of us, our thought, seems to be constrained by culture or tradition. We act as if we're free to take up causes as we wish, discuss and argue with whatever terms we want. But are we free, or freer, better, more aware? It's late, it's very late. The bird of wisdom – here it comes, carrying a poison load....

'Of course, I don't know really if it's late. The last chapter? There's always been another volume.... Suppose it is too late....'

'You dropped out, Kochi,' Amos says. 'You fell. We all did, went down the cliff face, some got stuck, halfway or so, fixed like flies in glass; some went right down, like you.'

'What we should do,' I say. 'When we have cash, is get someone to write a book about us, us being unconstrained, but being constrained also – not only by mortality, but by the walls we find, that seem to rise out of our arguments. Many walls we didn't make, but – we really, we add to them. Like Ur; they don't know if there was a palace, or if the palace had a maze, or if there only was a maze.... What was in the centre? Maybe nothing, just a way out....'

'No use,' says Amos. 'That book would be our book – the book we're writing as we go along. There isn't anybody outside us who sees more clearly than we do. They'd only find another wall. Or else repeat our book, every word the same....'

MAPS

Amos is watching the TV with me. He responds, jiggers up and down, argues and contests. It's useless, and in life, he takes great care not to provoke. To quiet him down, I say,

'As for constraints – you'd say that we are relatively free. We've no activity, of course, no income, what you'd call identity in our society. But still – Zélie's in custody because of family, Charlotte is vulnerable to sex....'

'I wouldn't generalise, Kochi,' he says. 'Things could turn out well for them. Right now, they're confined, but we are struggling for ever.'

'The maps they put out on the screen,' I say. 'They're flat. They should be full of the dynamic thrusts – who has more troops, which way they face ... instead, it's full of victims, as if a game of chess involves the pawns that's taken by the bigger guys, *hors de combat*.... What counts is queens and knights....'

'We put constraints on Zélie and Charlotte,' he says. 'Maybe it's not so bad. They can remove them – it's up to them.'

We walk up to the woods, behind the town. There's war, but we feel safe. What Amos says is right. Most bombs and missiles fall quite short – 'They're out of date,' he says. 'Like the whole enterprise. We're in the mixer – of one world, one people, all free and all constrained.... We chat, we pay, we work, we fester too....'

Maybe they're targeting the warehouse – and Amos says, 'You see – they strike all round. You never hit exactly what you want – we could have stayed and watched the movie that comes on later....'

'It's always Doktor Caligari, Amos,' I say. 'It means, you can't go somewhere else, but if you follow the instructions, you can *become* another person, much more powerful – and spooky too.'

'In theory,' Amos says, 'if we, we two, became more powerful and qualified – we'd be a better prize as prisoners, as if we're rocket scientists, who're taken off and given light teaching loads....'

'It's reassuring, Amos, to be with you, with your military past, and courses taken in the natural sciences,' I say.

The lights confuse the owls. The wood sways, bristles with the wind, the heat.

I remember.... '"The king, with his whole army wanders the plains summer and winter alike..." Not a king, really, a nomadic emperor. Shall we see that again? War – expunged whole peoples, the name forgotten, the cities devastated many times. Languages expunged, libraries on birch-bark on the pyre.... Bukhara ... a feisty place, center of the world where you would like to be, emptied completely many times....'

'Of course,' says Amos. 'This is an exercise. A skirmish. Better always hope for regulars – the militias want to leave their mark on you. And you, Kochi – not a warlike type, I'd say.'

'Oh,' I say, thinking of the schemes we've had, the futures to avoid – extinction, crowding into one cool space, the cows upended like card tables, the green grass side down, legs waving most unladylike – dried out, the milk on sale – chalk and dirty water ... gives you body, as they say.... 'I'm too individualistic. Maybe I'm stuck on nomads and peoples with a language that just disappears, their kids speak many languages badly, grannies tell no tales, no hush hush little baby.... The Kitans, Eastern Hu – gone, gone utterly, the decorative styles, the instruments, the epics, all of us becoming something else, moving restlessly as if in dreams and waking to be something other....'

'I must confess,' says Amos, embarrassed, giggling slightly, 'I've sworn allegiance to many flags.'

'Well done,' I say. 'Most of us have. I wonder if the species has a flag....'

'Maybe it needs one when the soldier ants campaign,' he says. We laugh, not much.

'War ought not to carry hocus pocus,' he goes on. 'Yet almost everything has much of that....

'Magical escapes. Evil on the ramp. Invocations, spells, nameless heroes with all-conquering swords. "Walls have ears", "your country needs you" – a touch of the outré ... surreal, untrue....

'You see transition, disappearance: I see instead a layering of schemes, an artichoke of plots and plans, "a second capital in Deogit" ... "The Tokharians taught The Book of Filial Piety in schools, not in Chinese, but in their own tongue...."

'Such endeavour. Discipline and order. Marshalling survivors: giving them documents, killing them. Exchanging prisoners. Killing them. After the wars, the migrations and displacements – you must have peace ... summer palaces and winter capitals, the "man with the iron bow" ... every army has one ...'

'Several,' I say. 'It sounds ridiculous, but your big guy, your hero, needs something special: more than an Armani suit....'

'Plunder,' says Amos. 'Remember the temple with the lingam of the moon god – ten million dinars stolen. Mercenaries, volunteers who are the dispossessed, the dispossessors in their turn, campaigns long forgotten, incursions, expeditions, leaky boundaries, rivers diverted, armies swallowed in the night by bogs, the massacres, the towns besieged, oases poisoned, yaks purloined, people driven – into the desert, the forest, and the sea....'

'Oh,' I say. 'It will come to us, it always has. Remember history, memorise it all, the books get burnt....'

'Well,' he says. 'I'm unemployed. You need rich people, millions of millionaires, to fight, especially to win, a war. The side with most millionaires will win.'

'And us?' I say. 'We're easy enough to stigmatise. We've been, we are, most things and none....'

'It's our side that doesn't like us,' Amos says. 'The other side will not discriminate.'

'We're as likely to be heroes as anyone,' I say. 'Especially as we think about what heroism might mean.'

'Heroes come in two sizes, shapes,' says Amos. 'Heroes strong and heroes weak. You can't be both, but everyone is one or other.'

'It's bad to lose. Bad to be conquered. Indifferent, if you win,' I say. 'Normality. It's banal, but that's the war aim most will fight for.'

'It's the postcard,' Amos says. 'Best not to have a fixed address. The draft. Conscription – makes a nonsense of what we've just been saying....'

The night is quiet now: black. No one navigates by stars.

'See?' says Amos. 'The warehouse. The target – missed again.'

'You realise, Kochi,' Amos goes on. 'We talk about movements, causes – and their effects. But I'm not interested, not at all, in being part of a group, any group, that wants to fight another bunch of guys. That's my opinion, my conviction, my high value.'

'That's just not a position, Amos,' I say, irritated. 'None of the things you say it is, even for you.' He says,

'All I'm interested in is finding where I can be with Charlotte – I don't care if she wants to get away....'

'She does,' I say. 'You know it. It may be part of what interests you, but it happens and it isn't up to you.'

'She's a group,' he says. 'She goes on tour, she sings a song or two, and mostly it's a bore and technical, lights and smoke, but she's content, that she's asserting the right point of view.... It's travel – when you travel, travel's all you think about. She's not too bright, she doesn't moil about the main idea, one's as good as any other.'

'They'd take us off to camps, Amos,' I say. 'It doesn't matter who you are, or if you want to organise and make a side. We'll go. It comes nearer, every day.'

The camps – you won't find them on the maps.

We did badly about Zélie. I'm an expert in betraying: there was Jacob. It runs through everything, the future, but anyway, Zélie wasn't much of a friend to me.

ASSEZ VU

Amos is selfish. I'm subjective. Much hangs on subjectivity, each one of us: reality, its colours and its depth ... cognition, experience – and loyalty, belief.... You'd need to add – illusion, hallucination, double and triple vision, beauty and ugliness, style and fashion, charlatans and gurus.

So, there's lots to do, and though here they're only exercises, best to be off, leaving the warehouse ... still the target.

Zélie hates us. Her organisation falls apart. Herbst supplies a little war – it's that which targeted the place I live.... I leave them all, and Amos too. It's not a scene where I would choose to fit....

'Experience,' the guy asks.

'Yes,' I say. 'Lots. From lifting stones to rolling news. Publicity, data analysis. TV – finding people who will talk about themselves in public, quizzing them, getting them ready to expose themselves, ironing out confusions, shouting them down. Curating animals. Interior design. Fancy gardening.'

'Impressive,' the guy, Marcus, says, not showing how impressed he is. 'Campaigns,' I add. 'Ecology, and geo-politics. Then there's my experience abroad: migration, law, and refugees.'

'I prefer,' the guy says, heavily, 'to have them viva voce. I can judge, and be responsible. If they write down a curriculum – people lie. Writing should be outlawed.' And we laugh.

'You'll do a digest of the news,' he says. 'Of course, it's a digest already, but you'll regurgitate. Make it slip down. The people here – they don't study, don't know much. They're curious, opinionated. They don't want raw stuff. Oh....'

Crickets: owl pellets: clots of larvae – how prickly it must all seem as it goes down; contested too – the siblings are homicidal. I say, 'It's wrong to underestimate the people, Marcus.'

'Of course. It's out of the question – you'd be fired. Jail in some places – places where they watch us,' he says. 'But there it is. Say no more, it's obvious. Mum. Mum's the word.'

Mum feeds you, after all, till your arms and legs grow and you can fly away. Anyway, the helpless aren't the problem – it's the crows, the falcons. The eagles, specially.

'Look,' says Marcus. 'You need to back the winning side. You know which that is – if you don't, I won't hire you. The winning side – even if it's lost a leg, an eye ... both eyes. People know it, which it is – they need it to be confirmed – at all events, it wins.'

'That's quite banal,' I say. 'Simplistic.' Maybe I don't say out loud – but Marcus is the only one who thinks like he thinks everybody does.

I can't do it.

'Of course you can,' says Marcus. 'Anybody can. It's not principle on your part – it's perversity.'

'Oh no,' I say. 'I need the cash now so's to leave, go somewhere else.'

'It's being awkward,' Marcus says. 'Not liking the material, not working it. Not liking what there is. Existence. Not giving an interpretation, taking another side – instead, rejecting all the evidence. Starting from a place that hasn't yet been found, or found but not put on a map.'

'Yes,' I say. 'That's the problem with a map – it ought to be articulate, dynamic, but it falls within the limitations of the territory, the ground, staticity.'

'Think', the Master said. 'It'll stop you doing anything else.' He didn't say, but saying 'think' gave him a power, a handle on an infinite nothingness no merely powerful person ever had. 'Well,' I remember saying, 'Way back, the gift of free will made powerlessness seem the proof of an almighty power.'

There's something fishy in this tale – but people recall it. It seemed evidence of something we now know did not exist. The reason, purpose ... what they had sought in chickens' entrails.

'It's like I'm a spectator at a poker game,' I tell Marcus, almost apologising. 'I've funded the best player – he has colours in his hand, there's others who will fold, they've rubbish and they are loungers of no account ... but there's another guy who has the makings of a winning hand, no colours, but played mundanely – not well, but by the book – it seems sure to win. The players – are big guys, big countries – continents.

'I can't shout out – "the wrong guy wins, get used to it, adjust yourselves accordingly". It's not the wrong guy: it's poker, that's all. Nothing special, a nine-high straight, but, enough....'

It's not like that, of course, there's no table, no anything, but Marcus surely grasps the sense....

I think of Zélie. I think of Charlotte.

'Saving the world, Marcus, means saving the bad guys,' I say. 'Saving everybody, including the horrors, the indefensible ... does it mean just saving the starving and the persecuted? In theory, all is for the best, it always is.... So, saving and survival means everyone. No judgement and no criticism.'

'If it's the news, Kochi,' he says, 'you set it out. That's all.'

'I realise that,' I say. 'Mine – is just not a position. The big solution, would be brought in by the biggest cheeses.... We – they – would survive, live on, like before: or worse, as what's left and saved fragments, degrades ... up to the top they float....

'But, if I can't change anything, why should I care? And do I care? Suppose I do, it may be good for me, but so what? Everything is hybridised, compromised – Charlotte needs Herbst. Dealing with the devils, does she expect to win? Without him, she's a flop, and with him – she's a renegade, accomplice.'

'You're right,' he says. 'You're not right for the job. Your opinion on anything, it isn't sought – besides, it's rhetoric....'

'You're right, Marcus,' I say. 'Rhetoric, hypothesis. The flaw in the design, Jacob, my friend, has said. 'Do we destroy ourselves by ignorance and self-absorption, inventing life unlivable and creating stuff that runs away with us? By naive fantasising. Or by the competition for advantage, pillage, domination, between the peoples organised behind their chiefs...? Taking account of power....'

'We're dualists, Manichaeans,' Marcus says. 'The prince of darkness, maiden of light – all that. But that's philosophy. Really – from experience, we know, evil is stronger, overall, it's evil wins.

'Your friends, of course, are good, like you.'

He laughs.

'No, no,' I say. 'Friends ended bad. Or did the deal with presidents.' We laugh.

'So, given that the evil wins – maybe we should let it do just that,' he says. 'It's better so. Stand aside. Grow up. Our evil nature finishes Nature off.... Nature too – the "beast eat beast" – maybe it's evil too. Our Creator? Blind. They say it may self-regulate – maybe it's instinct, leading on to nowhere ... ashes or dust: chance.'

'I follow you,' I say. 'The flaw is in the universe; creation self-destructs – by accident or as it's stamped in the design.'

'That's how I read you, Kochi,' Marcus says. 'That's why I was in error when I gave you work. What disturbs you is how we are. How what is, is.

'Human sacrifice is our particularity ... the Celts are nowadays much admired – the Aztecs too ... our way with land, with territory, disputes and battles, wars, invasions – is "kill a lot of people – first the weak, and then the powerful". Did it take so long to figure out the appetite – not for the necessary, but – when we reached the top, the golden link, the peak of the great chain of being and of eating – sacrifice. It's how we settle things – direct and indirect: by dynamite and famine ... by guns, fired by states or individuals....'

'Well, yes,' I say. 'Maybe evil's not the word. No, not at all. Evil without intention ... but on principle....'

'I like you, Kochi,' Marcus says. 'You have a tender soul. That doesn't matter, not at all. All I wanted was a chronicle, the truth....'

'You make me feel quite stupid, Marcus,' I tell him. 'I know that what you say is all around us, visible – the peat men, kings and claimants killed in rituals....'

'Populations, Kochi,' Marcus says. 'History. Surely you were aware of what goes on – that would have been your work. On and on, today the massacre, extermination – tomorrow it's forgotten – tomorrow there's another....

'Armies: resource management: scarcity, recession, floods and droughts – all planned, engineered ... by the strong, by consent and underhand, oiled along by assassinations, genocides....

'... fags and booze does for the rest of us....'

'Yes, yes, that's Jacob's "flaw",' I say. '"Survival" is perpetuation of our natural being, our humanism, if you like.... Survival of the worst.... The species that lives and prospers by perpetually consuming, indiscriminately, itself; its members ... Those spaceships, carrying it all over....'

*

'Poor Pierrot,' says the lady in the fluffy blouse, cradling my head between her breasts. 'That fascist Marcus! He hires people, then he fires then when they can't produce the news he wants....

'There you were, all crumpled up, lying in the corridor, near death. Welcome to our cosmos. You must be terrified. Do not fear – we shall overcome, quite soon.'

'I didn't sleep,' I say. 'Just exercises, but noisy. Not a real war, just probing....'

The dark wood, the warehouse splintered – I don't mention them. If I do – they want to know your country, language, preferences. Stand you up to knock you down, said Amos.

'I pick the best bits, Lakmé,' I tell her later. 'Countries, sides: only the best ... who wouldn't, who doesn't? Language that lets you say what you want. But in a crisis, and there's always one – you have to lie or suffer pointlessly. Can't like art deco, can't mention dead souls or Ubu Roi. If you do, it's jail, or insults, then the worst.'

'Oh, Kochi,' she says. 'You have to take a stand, and that means being identified. Otherwise – you'd be a kind of albatross – forever in the air, high up, all over everywhere....'

'You're wrong,' I say. 'Those are at sea except to sit on eggs – absolutely not the life for me ... probably not for anyone.'

*

'We can protect you,' Lakmé says. 'But you must tell us who you are, where you last came from – then we'll put you on the list....'

'Oh,' I say. 'I'm on some lists already, but another one ... what might it mean?'

I must give an account. Some background....

'Where I was living, way down South, the spicy part....' I start. 'It's like, in the world, we're a fine hunting dog that can do anything, and does, without responsibility – except he cannot wag his tail. That's us. Southerners. Maybe it makes him feel ashamed. He can't, in fact, do anything with it, his tail – show pleasure or excitement, say thank you, or would like a walk to somewhere else.... This is how they think down there, and I'm convinced; I'm with them –

'A poor situation is preferred to dictatorship, stasis is better than adventure. We can say anything we like, it has no consequence. Is that political freedom? Probably. What is there to gain by defining terms? It's all done for us – we're indifferent.

'The bosses – they pretend the area is rich and normal, a partner of the richest and most determined powers, big armies and big profits ... but – all we see, all we are, is crabbed people, caught in webs of circumstance, of obligation and fraud. To be honest is to be poor: the tolerant, the wealthy, the experts, the pros and politicos – all fakes and chancers. We're half the world and growing....

'We're the folklore in a sphere of influence where otherwise we're seen as criminals and beggars – picturesque freaks pounding out traditional food – in fact, no longer eaten here. That's our reputation. All is decided for us, by the sphere of plenty ... its wars, its cash, decisions and who bosses ... there is no other sphere of influence that we could join, so we don't fantasise, we submit ... laughing and singing like monkeys, sometimes.'

'Oh no!' says Lakmé, dismayed but hopeful, 'what a lament! I'm sure you move around, forget all that, make efforts, take a course....'

'It stays with you, Lakmé,' I say. 'Experience is set up for that. There's no solution, so I push them back, the memories – mean streets, and shoddiness.... Buses leaving for ever, full of adolescents.'

'Our view is different,' Lakmé says. 'The future. We must anticipate, and live in it.'

It's a group. What do they do? When they're not here, they leave a hologram or an avatar, and you can message them, their understudy will respond.

'We cook for each other,' Lakmé says. 'Collect funds. There's lots of self-parody, that is a spur.... "Think" is the first message. Being together, but not touching.'

'I'm impressed,' I say: it's true. Not touching is a good first principle.

'Rich associates,' she says. 'Give money – and feel good. Poor people take it – and feel good.'

'I see that,' I say. 'And is that all?'

'No, Kochi. You will see. The path is long....' she says.

'And stony....' I conclude for her. 'But the first step – excellent!' I mean – feeling good is good. Even if the reason's infantile.

'Don't patronise, Kochi,' she says. 'You're not the brightest in the room, and besides – what do you offer us?'

'Oh,' I say, lightly, 'I can cast my net. My net upon the Net. Into the Net.'

'Obviously,' says Lakmé. 'You'll have to expose yourself – messages, opinions. Commitment. Not your face – a symbol; not a name – a twirl....'

'It sounds easy. I've never done it before. Maybe I shan't be able,' I tell her.

'If you don't appear, Kochi, how do we know that you exist?' she asks.

We laugh.

'You'll need to come to the studio, first thing, so we can try you out,' she says.

'Why is it so far away?' I ask. 'It should be central.'

'It doesn't matter where it is,' she says. 'You can't tell. It could be underground – in the metro, under the sea. No one knows, cares, or can find out.'

You have to take the bus. A wonderful clean bus, that passes by where the sea has come, stranded the little boats, and retreated. The guy beside me points them out – strakes green-grey, ribs flattening out, like herrings' skeletons. There's wonders – castles of pink coral, dolmens like stale cakes.

'Look at all the people,' says the guy. 'The music brings them out.' It might. There's a constant chuff-chuff of drums beating to different musics – salsa, afrociberdelia, metallica....

'Who's left, who's here? There's lots of blacks,' he says. 'Not many Jews – remember the singing, "four, the four mothers of Israel"? Not here, that's certain. Three – "Moses, Jacob and Abraham ..." and I forget the rest....'

Jacob. It's a shock, my friend's name in this context, this guy who's forgotten who's the next sacrifice ... Isaac...? Victim or Patriarch?

He says, digging in to his prophecy,

'There's guys like you, without guarantees, always off to auditions. You've got protection, so the dark wing passes over, and so who'll it be? Not drifters, losers.... Who's next? Sex? Is anyone explicit? Anybody out of line? Politics? Too feisty? I'll bet it'll be protesters. They'll get beat and shut up. Truncheons on the legs and thighs – months that you can't walk. So, it starts, it must, it does.'

I don't respond.

I know I don't want to make exposures, send messages. I renounce all that. I think of Lakmé, her embrace, and wriggling out of it. Her wanting to be good. And safe. Offering that to me – just hopes.... That's no favour!

This guy, met casually, not needed. Perhaps not casually – but not wanted: feared.

He's called Erhan – the driver shouts after him 'Erhan' – he never pays the fare.

The bus glides on – passes walls built by titans, enclosing nothing, trolls' bridges, trolls galore ... empty plinths.

It's late. What are we doing here? What are we here to do? Whatever it was, we didn't do it. Self-destruct? Certainly, we just evolved, and on and on we go until we don't. My questions wasted, unanswerable, baseless.

It's not time to get off the bus, I've not yet decided where to go. We do the route, five, six times, end to end, sometimes the guy gets on, we pass the market, he buys salt fish, I see their tails poke out – you buy those if you live alone and always have and always will.

The sea is close, it seems to prowl around.

The bus takes a different route – maybe there's a manif, or the driver wants a change. There are tents – it's like the desert. Maybe there are dancers. I read 'Pavilion of Friendship.'

The guy with the fish is beside me. 'You don't want to go in there,' he says. 'You don't need friends. They can't stand you. They slip away. Besides – it's about the world order. Which do you prefer – Americans, Russians, or Chinese. That's it, that's all. You don't want any of them. There's your usual cop-out! You have a life, perhaps, but not a model of life. You might want parts of others, Ladakh, say – but just to pass through. To get to the future – which you won't – means plague pits and route marches. A vale of fears and desponds. Besides, once you go in, to get a refund on your ticket you have to choose the winning way of life you'd like.'

The place looks deserted.

'You wander,' he says, 'That's fatal.'

'I'm looking,' I tell him. 'Anything else is trivial.'

He must say all he says to everyone. It's a kind of Kantian substitute, an echo. What you do and say – should tend to towards the universal. It makes you think, and want to get away.

Don't talk to them – that is the rule. The crazies! This guy – what a fate! He's fantasising, and it's like my sane interior deciding to tell me what's been what.... To do him justice – I might ask, 'is the truth a test of sanity?'

'Don't get off the bus,' the guy says, getting off. 'The bosses – they are happy that there's war. It's their element, they have good possibilities – that they'll survive. But they've been told – this is the end.... This is it – the big bang, the light that started it all off, and now....'

'There always is the end,' I respond, breaking my rule. 'What starts must finish. But – I'm not to be recruited – not for a statement of enthusiasm, still less for standard issue kit....'

In that war, you don't fight, so you can't surrender – you look on your aiming-screen, and shoot into the air. Then you drive off, and sometimes your truck and its gun are blown to smash.

*

When I was with Lakmé, before I took the bus, she said, 'And did you have a childhood, Kochi? Parents? Teachers? Filling a pail with coal fragments off the tip? Down the shaft into the goldmine, or rocking to and fro in the madrasa, a pendulum? Filling your head with fragments, like filling a bucket; a shift lasting ten years....

'I'd open you like an oyster. I've always wanted a love story that goes way back – to horse-time, slow, with white clothes in a suitcase, worn once and stowed under the iron bedstead, every morning the cockerel comes to wake me, there being no glass, no window frame, he stands, crows, in the opening in the wall, at the bed's head, where I'm dreaming of prison or of rowing a boat to an island that's dropped below the horizon....'

'I know,' I said. 'I'm not up to you. I'm in bad situations, make a bad decision – then I have to choose between a bad situation and the bad remedy....'

She took off the fluffy blouse. 'See,' she said. 'Skin. It frightens some of us, and some – we are in awe. It joins us to the rest – skin, feathers, scales....'

'It's too much,' I said. 'Humans often turn off the light, and go by touch. The animals – they can't.'

'See,' she said. 'I'm civilised. My life aims – are written on my skin, indelibly.'

'And what for?' I asked. She's covered in bold scripts – the hands and feet, then you see, all over everywhere – mostly with hieroglyphs, 'god's words', the rest in alphabetic – you'd need to have been prone or a masseur, with a dictionary, to read them all, reflections, invocations, bills, Sumerian, Akkadian....

What should I have said?

'Script and speech – contradictions in terms,' I said. 'Oppositions. Most of these languages are unspoken for millennia. Unread, the readers dead: they say Sumerian has three thousand years of literature. Zapotec – a long tradition, most – inscriptions. Who publishes the stuff? Where is it reviewed?'

'Love,' she said. 'Can only be where there is skin and skin. Where there is discourse – it's ephemeral. If you want, Kochi, you could have war aims and treaties written on. Or else – you're wanting to be one of us. It means there's presence, and you'd need to fuck with everyone, just like in life.'

'I think that's so,' I said. 'Of course, your friends would be mine, but I foresee bad situations....'

She smiled, she sat, naked except for all the writing, hieroglyphs and cuneiform.

'"They shall give as an offering",' she said. 'Look here – it's Urartian. "Offerings", occurred much more then than now, from respect, not something in return when almost everything's transactional. I'm not. I am an offering, but one that no one keeps – that too is how it was....'

'I think you're right,' I said. 'The skin ... the messages ... I can't match up to you, Lakmé.'

'Why ever should you want to? Why should I ask you to? What do I match up to?' she asked.

'Your world is not one I've encountered,' I said.

'It's not a world,' she said. 'It's me.'

I couldn't match up to that, no, absolutely not....

'I'd be afraid the writing would rub off,' I said.

'The literatures,' she said, putting back her clothes, 'they might. They're all the same – epics and lyrics, hope and regrets, monsters and maidens. They persist, and then the language is forgotten, the poets lose their memories, the written goes archaic. Dialects branch out. Wait a few centuries – new languages, and here they come again, the names are changed, the monsters don't....'

'To me, this is fripperies,' I said. 'Plots, campaigns, the putsch, incursion, culverins and bugs – you may ignore them, but they won't escape you.'

'That's an odd turn,' she said. 'You don't look for each other ... you and the mishaps....'

'But they're all that matters,' I said.

*

'I know it's cool at night,' says the lady with the goats. 'But the waterhole doesn't fill up again till morning. No use going early, they won't let you near – there'll be some water left at midday.

'Mind the neighbours don't drive off my goats. Anyway, if you don't go for water, they won't live.'

We're not related, but she looks out for me.

The bus came after. After Lakmé. Away, away: permanence – I'm not cut out for that. No one is. The guy with the authorial voice – he helped put me right. The goats, the water – they come in somewhere. Mostly likely, a story, item, maybe I thought it up myself. You wouldn't choose that life.

THE PROJECT

'No, it mustn't end for you in anti-climax. You must be there – the rifts in the baked earth, the troopers riding in on half-tracks through the city's marble gate, the animals all scampering, humans staring upwards at the swollen moon, green – corrosion or florescence ... the birds....'

'Oh yes, the birds,' I say to Erhan, standing beside him and looking up.

'See it all, don't miss anything. Don't eat or sleep, and don't take notes....' he says. 'Don't remember anyone – it's too late to make appointments. They'll all be in bed with people loved or managed....'

'Was it you stalking me, on the bus?' I ask. 'It's true you're ordinary – to a fault. I could be mistaken....'

'There isn't time to chase that hare,' he says. 'People you've known well – you'd recognise them, possibly; even on a bus, in a strange city. Caution, though! Then what? Their campaigns? Join them?

'Wonderful escapes – re-set your necrology – and what's so wonderful? Accidents are accidents, so they attract more accidents. You should presume it's all an accident....'

'I do,' I say. 'That's what you said too.'

Zélie, Jacob – she might have fled from her campaign, the commonplaces: fallen down a well – one of Carroll's sisters, possibly a sticky end.... Jacob has walked out of the pit, campaigned for trophy hunting, or against it....

Erhan is right. There isn't time, to foretell and then to tell, to plot, make an account ... all those old lions that ended up in Berlin zoo, got bombed or eaten. Who could predict...? Their world most monstrously transformed and finished off....

'Ah, Africa,' I say. There's much to be said – I can't begin.

'There isn't time,' he repeats. 'Look – if you want to go down in legend, not in history – this here's a bottle-shop. We go in, get drunk, then on the sidewalk, have a *zuffata* – a d-and-d, and gouge an I – an eye – mine, yours, or someone's. And you'll be remembered: for the exploit, in the very short time that's left. No, it's not my thing, of course. I'll tell you what you didn't know – I was espoused to a real *infanta;* not paedophilia; the royal line. They roam, you understand, the royals: they've nothing we don't have and maybe less.... She came from an arid land, Iraq, I think. I was a smuggler there. I smuggled till I could afford someone to smuggle me.'

'I know,' I say exasperated. 'You worked, you had a filthy life, here was your hope and now you find it's worse. I'll justify it, some of it. I'll do justice to what happens next or last.'

He can't be stopped. 'You leave nothing, Kochi,' he says. 'You accomplished nothing. You've been a passenger, while we slaves rowed and held the plank for you to go on shore. I accomplished much, moved matter, gave orders, went on strike, stole my food – stale bread, alas. And now I've less than you.'

'I come from an upper crust, Erhan,' I say – he doesn't smile.

'People remember people who travel, bring nothing back – Candide, Gilgamesh, Simplicius – wisdom, a happy end? Not quite!

'I bring wisdom at quite a higher level, having heard of those inexistent guys, and many more. And now you say I'll see the cataclysm ... a revelation of some sort.

'False questions, false laments, Erhan – there's nothing to bring back, nothing to bring the nothing in, nor where to put it.'

'They say that,' Erhan says. 'But act quite different and treat you so.

'And you may be coming to understand, or be already there – whatever there is to see, we all can see it. Everybody will, especially if it's large, magnificent or terrible – it doesn't matter who you are or what you've done, where you've been: everyone. Not specially you, Kochi, however much you'd enjoy being singled out.'

'You're right, of course,' I say. 'I fight back my arrogance. Reality requires that if it's there – yes, everyone can see it, maybe already has....'

'No,' Erhan says, 'don't run ahead. Wait! When it is visible – there it will be for all of us. If not, not: for everyone. Every country, every regime and everybody's place in it, their opinion ... universal, real! That's quite something.'

'Absolutely!' I say, forcefully. 'This is something quite new and progressing – I won't give a date – most dates will do – 1917, 1945, 1953, 1956 – yet much bigger, more significant. Quite different from the *longueurs* of Jacob, Zélie, and the others ... what bores: the

Master! What procrastination. Only Blandine had a quick draw, but it did bad for her. This is definite! It will happen, and soon.'

'We could buy a bottle of something pure, sit on this low wall and wait,' says Erhan, pleased to have changed my life.

We sit on the wall, drink, sharing the bottle. After a while, I say to Erhan, 'You're taking more than your share.'

'We're not here for shares,' he says. 'We went through that. Everybody sees the same, if it is real. It's shared, but indivisible. The drink is incidental.'

The *zuffa* becomes a possibility – not the reality we're waiting for, but Erhan's a nobody, pushing me around. We struggle for the bottle – it's nearly empty, but I want to use it, as a threat ... I try to break it, to give me something to hold – the neck: and quite in moderation, hold it to his face, his throat, just to show, I'll not be pushed around some more.

The bottle's tough, or I can't find a surface hard enough – at first it doesn't break, and then – it shatters, leaving a neck too small and short to do the job – the job of threatening. We struggle, rolling in the bushes – they planted tropical stuff, abandoning the grass, then laying down grit there's only need to rake.

It's very hot, and in a while, we give this up. We must have slept.

'Don't tell me, Erhan – have we missed it?' I ask, quite sober, though my mouth is foul. 'You bastard idiot – how can we ask now? Who would say, and think us other than two drunks – if it has happened, everybody knows, if not, then not. You cannot ask!

'There's been a plague, some wars continuing, famines and massacres – that can't be the big stuff they all talk about. Are we at the point of no return? They say that when a world is ending, someone sends a sign you cannot miss. But – have we missed it? Was there a statement, and we were rolling in the sand?'

BUFFOONERY

After a fight, you recover on a bench – you're a fair target. People come and beg off you, steal a drink, a conversation. You can't move....

'I recognised you,' Adèle says. 'I was with Zélie, but my enthusiasm dropped. She was aware – she was remarkable – the most sensitive person I have known, though light on brains ... And so, she let me go. That's what they say, although I didn't want to go. I remember, you and Jacob – we were all in awe – you knew so much, so probing, such leadership – though maybe less from you. And so – I ended with a youngish guy who took his pension all in cash, it ought to last for forty years, we spent the lot in weeks – and that was it. I felt the urge towards him, but – the conflicts grew ... I was amazed, I'd never read this is where love goes, as if it really is a rose that dries out in the sun, and gradually the petals drop until there's only a brown stub, a fag-end trodden underfoot....'

'Yes,' I say. 'I know all that. You're a bad case, Adèle, but really – joining on to me is not a good idea, and it's a stereotype, of people who don't have another option left....

'But – what I need to know is – is there some decisive news that broke in the last day, when I was quite abstracted, wrapped in my affairs....'

'You mean with Erhan?' Adèle asks. 'He's eternal, the spirit of the stone and sea, the champion of the Hanse, or the Knights....'

'You may be wrong, Adèle,' I say. 'There's some Turk in him, that's for sure.'

'That's what I said,' she says, quite sharp. 'He's always been here, bumming rides and shipping stuff....'

'So,' I press on, 'there's no development, all's as it was?'

'When you've no cash,' she says, 'there's no one gives you more.'

'The malady?' I ask. 'What we are waiting for? Is there a therapy, crisis, or a cure? Just yesterday – the crucial time, and I was out of it....'

'Oh lucky you,' she says. 'To be in coma. What Zélie spoke of – it takes centuries. There's millions, billions, who depend on fish. The sea remains when earth is uninhabitable. I never heard of special news – how could there be...?'

'Except,' I say. 'There will be a day. The feather stirs, the spider drops, comes down her rope and tips the scale and that is it – you're cooked, contagious, roasted, drowned – one day alive, the next day not. Weighed and found wanting, quick – or dead. It happens to us all; to everyone, it's so. The day.'

'Oh well,' she says, 'I've not had mine. There's no more slots where there is cash – no telephones that take a slug, no arcades where the march of pennies works – we tried them all. I shouted at the idiot – there's nothing to be done, this is the end, they found the answer to the casual theft, the snitch, the lift, work in the black, the coins left for the courier underneath the mat: there's nothing left to steal!

'Cash makes cash, and if you've none, you're done, you're sterile.'

'You just don't grasp, Adèle,' I say. 'One day the news can't be ignored. I can't imagine what it is, or when – I only need you to tell me if....'

'No, Kochi,' Adèle says. 'Nothing happened yesterday, nothing at all.'

'I could do a deal with you, Adèle,' I say. 'I don't care much about "the day". It comes, or not. I'm much more interested in myself. And keeping far from Erhan too.'

'But after the fine causes and good people that you've known,' she says. '"Yourself" seems rather trivial.... And Erhan's an obsessive drunk, who must shape comrades to accompany his drunkenness.... He doesn't care who those companions are.'

'The deal is this,' I say. 'My life needs shape, a plot, a start, an end. You give it that, and I'll help out with cash. With looking for it, anyway.'

'That's not a deal,' she says. 'Though I can offer nothing more.'

With that, we pause.

'Death is the cure for madness and ambition,' Adèle says. 'In that, you're right. It's best to keep a look-out for it,' and I don't mention it's a cure for poverty as well.

*

'All these people,' Adèle says. 'You didn't appreciate a single one of them. Some are interesting – Lakmé, with the picture of the Cortés house in ruins, on her back.... Some of your old mates fell, some burned, some murdered and some liberated....'

'Yes,' I say, 'I'm less demanding now. I won't find anything original, not in or for myself. I should have given them more space....'

'My lover, with the stolen money that we spent as if it was red-hot, a stash of Mexican pimentos – he was a commander. He brought his country into war; when he was losing, he changed sides. He brought war in from both directions – and he left. You could have pondered over him,' she says. 'Those who make war – they must make peace. Or else....'

'Eternal war....' I say. 'It must stop some time. Eternity is what you feel when you are six.'

'When the music stops, sometimes there are no chairs left at all,' she says. 'So you put it on a loop. Resist. Accept defeat.'

'You're baroque,' I say. 'A cast-out. Cerberus and serpents all over you. What can you do about it?'

'Sing,' she says. 'That's all. I'm the heroine, whatever I've done. And I've done nothing but get on the wrong ship ... those poor sailors.... I can't help the north wind, how it blows. Lay me down here....' And she points to a bush, thick with pods.

... there's one of Erhan's shoes!

'I feel there's a bond between us,' I say. 'I'd like to know you, before I let you go.'

'You're right, Kochi – when I call our cash a pension – it's true, but it misleads,' she says. 'We scooped a pool.

'I promise you, people don't see things like you. You're an anomaly. Rich influential people care that things won't change too much. The rest don't worry, or they think that whoever has the power, it won't change much for everyone. It could be good, or just the same, and if it's worse – too bad. It's only you, Kochi, who're neither rich nor influential, who thinks that power might be contested and transformed. And disappear.

'It isn't so. It's science: the stronger power prevails. It isn't up to you.'

'Is that me, Adèle?' I ask. 'Defined? The person in your tale?'

'Not many people can be really bad,' she says. 'Those that are – they mostly stay at home. Not many get to put on uniform and do the massacre.'

Adèle is stringy. That comes from sitting on a tank and waving to the crowd – be very very careful not to fall off ... or possibly she's whittled down from sleeping rough, drinking and not eating; the stereotype, for sure, people go soft or stringy when they're penniless....

'Where's the general, Adèle?' I ask.

'We rode high on storm winds,' she says. 'Then we stumbled, lurched, we were unhorsed, and rain swept over us.

'But war: that is the bone of history, nothing else is solid, real. Distrust the blood, the brains – those don't come in. They leak. Anything you try to do, and will not calculate in military goods, is never taken seriously. Zélie didn't want to see this, but it's so....'

'This is all new to me,' I say. 'We were just told to "think" ... not about specifics, necessarily....'

'Rations, Kochi,' Adèle says. 'Who gets what and where you can go to get it. The dispossessed for years were promised a sufficiency that never came. Now, we're all in that position.... The wars go on, but we aren't told about the Zélie part....'

'What I don't understand, Adèle,' I say. 'Is how you calculated badly what you'd need. What did you spend the money on?'

'Old mothy palaces,' she says. 'The fruit machines, those Vegas desert inns, the ravens with deliveries of figs, the Ponzi schemes, the baklava we had flown in.... Options on camels, on statesmen and – women, cliques and frondes: trotting on cinder tracks, ministers in cloth of gold....'

'I understand,' I say. 'It just seeped out. The general must have taken some....'

'Money will come to matter less,' she says. 'Zélie must have known – when the gunpowder has been shot off, we'll go at our enemies with stones and branches.... We killed the bigger animals because we didn't want to fight them for our food: our waterholes can't be full of crocs.... That aspect is resolved.'

'So,' I say, 'there's no room now for scepticism and truce, eternal friendships, rhetoric....'

'Oh, absolutely not,' she says. 'Forget your literary bent – besides, the best will be on Lakmé's skin.... Enough, enough. No more!'

'Tell me,' I say, 'you really don't have bus fare? The little boys hang on the back....'

'Listen,' she says. 'I can be of use. Intelligence. Mostly it doesn't work: guys don't believe it. War's often unpopular, and they may lose. Or, they pre-empt – and there's the trap. The come-on, then the ambuscade.... So, what you might know or guess, it doesn't work.

'Your instinct, Kochi, is to run, a helter-skelter. That is wrong. You have to calculate the winning side, and then go calmly far far off from both – the winner and the loser.'

'How will I know which ones they are?' I ask.

'I'll tell you,' Adèle says.

No one before ever promised so much for me.

'Suppose,' I say, 'a cause attracts. Some sacrifice – might be considered....'

'Don't think of it,' says Adèle, laughing. 'If you want to make a choice, and risk – remember what happens in a war is largely chance or instinct, and what is not will be concealed from you.

'Resist the truly awful side of friends and enemies.

'Remember, now – these conflicts may seem to have a single or a major cause. Rather – they share contributory causes. They compete for similar goods, their peoples are identical ... the philosophies unheard, unread, or quite grotesque. It's not like history, Kochi – we don't fight for our masters and our nationalities; we're cosmopolitan and free.... We choose where our loyalty may lie, but many affective bonds survive....

'Be prudent! Avoid a turmoil, conflicting sentiments.... One rule is constant: deserters will be shot, draft dodgers will be drafted.

'You get one chance to choose your side or sidle to another place: don't expect to change your side.'

'Besides,' I say, 'sides aren't what you want to join.... A side's a last resort....'

'You're mobile, Kochi' Adèle says. 'Most people wait for wars to roll and cover them, or to drive them out to vagabondage. Avoid that if you can....'

'It means I'll go on living by expedients,' I say. 'Moving to higher ground all my life – won't bring a fortune. There's an Erhan in me too – I'll never settle on a position and expound it straight....'

'It's turning stuff out and trading it, and renting hands and buying arms,' she says. 'And rationing the rest. I was with the best. I know, I don't regret bedtime with them – but that is all. Generally, they were not fun....'

'I think this is the way the species will survive,' I say. 'Things go on so long since no one's smart enough to strike decisive blows, corner the water and the soil.

'They used to say, "vote for the stupidest". Now, it's "vote for the mediocre".

'Somewhere the general waits for you, Adèle. You'll make a couple, live in ease....'

'It's not at all like that,' Adèle says.

'Look,' she says. 'This is a little film of how he is, my general....'

And there he is, illuminated, on her telephone.

'Only kill soldiers,' he is saying. 'Mine – and I'll kill yours. Nobody else. But – most soldiers are homosexual – that's why we need more and always more: – they don't self-generate. Prisoners are like that too – there's no solution. There ought to be a way of making them perpetual: soldiers who breed soldiers....

'Wars against soldiers – stick to those. Maybe you forget, that if you use the bombs, it's final curtain for us all....'

'He's quite a bore,' says Adèle, snapping him shut. 'He's sure the key to war is childbirth. How the Chinese managed – all that Wall to man: and woman.... That's why they wanted boys born, until they realised – girls are more determined, more obedient. Now they are tops....

'My general was interested in supply – in going where the soldiers were abundant – finding oases where they'd taken refuge.... Lining them up, have them form squares and fives, and count aloud ... oh yes, and sing.'

'And that's the key?' I ask. 'Soldiers singing, and packing crates with loot.... As your land becomes unusable, you need more soldiers – and more war...?'

'That's it,' she says. 'That's nature's way. We mine the land for noxious stuff – we mine the sea to stop the fishermen from catching food....'

She's quite a wit. We laugh together at her *mot.*

'What can I believe, Adèle?' I ask. 'Soldiers live off what they find and steal. It's not just killing – it's the theft that causes harm to enemies.... Besides, they'd never kill enough. Soldiers take their time. You need the camps – camps for safe-keeping, camps to fester in, camps overnight and camps for years.... Poison of land and water: trees, birds....'

'You're eloquent, Kochi,' Adèle says. 'Say something new, and help me get my cash.'

*

'You could see the future,' says Adèle. 'See if it works. Come with me. You're quite good company, and on the bus, we need some jokes.'

'I'm a person who sits back and weighs the consequences,' I say. 'I don't travel.'

That's absolutely true.

'You're a slug,' she says. 'That's true. Now, look up insurgencies and secessions. Militias. We can track him down. He'll want to see us – but we have to make a move. He can't communicate direct, of course....'

'I'm not so sure,' I say. 'And anyway, we two – we are anomalous. Travel together – we'll be spotted and tracked down. For sure, I'm still on a list. You will be too....'

'Of course,' she says. 'Stay or go. You're who you are. Whatever happens is a risk – and ultimately, we all succumb. Our number's waiting in the urn.... That's the motto of this place, the guarantee: "every number will eventually be drawn...."'

'I was in Zélie's group,' I say. 'Her campaign....'

'That's all explained,' says Adèle. 'Sugar outside and long life: black bile inside and a grenade. You know, we're all already split up into teams, that's why we carry passports and ID. Then, when it's clear survival's under threat – we all must back our champions. Check your document. Get back in line. You're no exception. Swan around in town – they'll catch you, maybe you will have the choice – do time, or wear the uniform....

'Water, food and land.... It once was "peace, land, bread": and how they fought, the leftists; how they battled everyone! Now – each against all ... the animals, the plants, the viruses, and every budding grove.... All struggling to survive.... You hoped, like Zélie, all would cooperate, but from the start, it wasn't so.'

'I know,' I say, 'I'd join a chorus line. It's that I don't hear the cues....'

'People like you, Kochi,' she says, 'have funny fancies. You seem to be a straight timid guy – maybe you've always wanted a hot affair with someone more beautiful than you could ever hope to win.'

'A doll,' I say.

'I'll bring you one back, when I have found the cash,' she says.

I don't know what I don't believe in, that there's cash, or a general, or both.

Zélie's campaign offered salvation if we used our reason. It seemed sweetness – it was force. Force – taking all they had from anyone we could ... driving them like goats, away from food and water, mutilate and scar, bayonet and burn....

'Yes, yes,' says Adèle, 'you must have seen the pics. Didn't you realise there was no scientific chat, not about the climate and the carrots, telescopes and raptors, layers of this and that, and snails that farm the wrack, taste good in pies.... Just pictures of destruction...?

'Money and generals, they enslaved, made empires, left a devastation.

'I'm going now to my general to get my money. Afterwards, what will there be? Hard times, Kochi, in the name of faith. Obedience. Submission. And on and on it goes. Money burnt the world. There's nothing to be done.'

'People did it, Adèle,' I say: it sounds feeble. 'People will suffer – worse than they ever did.'

'Watch what you say,' she says. 'Yours is a shrill theme that wafts up high.... Someone is alert, and listening. You aren't reliable, and you're weak....'

We squabble. She'd be much stronger than me, I'd not consider using force – besides, she's militarily trained.

She takes the bus and leaves alone, promising the driver she will pay the fare when she arrives. She makes her situation work for her: – the general, the cash. Even the phone she leaves with me, so I can check, and pass a message on....

I take stock. Nothing accumulated, but here I am, on the brink, like everyone. Adèle – strong as a galleon's figurehead, but on the bus, into the maelstrom, seeing clearly what 'survival' costs. Zélie said it just required good faith and sense ... the green, survival. It seems, it isn't so....

Memories of strange events – are not strange memories. Myself – constant, the well-wisher. Past it goes, time and its creatures, like a parade. All that is real – it slips away. It does for everyone, of course – and I have nostalgia ... my frozen portrait in the frame, seemingly untouched, unmoved, uninvolved, once more left behind and undisturbed ... the attraction, affection, gratitude I felt – unnoticed at the time, and afterwards quite ineffective, spent; no trace, like one night of waning moon – signifying nothing, leaving and creating naught – mechanical trekking of a one-dimensional body, under the clouds....

FORTUNE AT LAST

The scene arrives.

There's a line of them – the general, with feathers in his hair, a porcupine quill rakish through his nose – a squad of little warriors, they could be kids, with twiggy bows and blowpipes; and Adèle on the end – her stringy arms and legs, but quite a belly too, with dark sun symbols: nipples standing proud like dice, the aureoles picked out with spirals – spinning earths.... She says – "Look!" And there's a box. "We found it in the Cortés house – silver, in ingots. It's a fortune! But – too heavy. We can't carry it ....' Behind her there's a structure – might it be Itaipu? Except she's only been away an hour. Where, then? A theme park, war games on the Plain, a charity show...?

I remember – the ruins of the Cortés house on Lakmé's skin ... coincidences, accidents; how we believe in them, stronger than resurrections, stronger than a shaman's breath....

'Leave it, Adèle,' I say, but don't know how to use the phone. 'You're armed, and so it seems – there's an attack quite near....'

There must be desperation wherever they are. The real Itaipu now is waterless, there's gangs and soldiers roaming round – and yet ...

ebbs and flows unstoppable ... resistance, restoration. But – yes, there is a fortune there, or somewhere, if I could only be in touch ... to tell them to forget the wealth, forget their allies, never risk a fight when you are naked and your line is thin, out of condition, in an uncertain place ... the bows are small, from when there were the trees – you couldn't manoeuvre with a larger arm ... be prudent, never move in line, in file....

Nothing.

No contact There must be some toggle on the phone that lets both persons speak.

As it is, it's all wrong – my gaze humiliates Adèle – humiliates me. Belittles them, the resistance: – they must be a trick, posed in the Potemkin jungle back of them, and they – dressed up like – losers? Like idiots? Like grotesques of themselves. What do I do – let them go to ruin, if they're not already there? Send fresh curare from the stock all civil nations keep ...? Or all the other things we do – send bags of flour, toys for the kids, tranquillisers and anti-aircraft kits...?

She said, 'I remember how you seemed to me ... I saw you sitting at the table, writing, and while you wrote, I saw you looking down, and it seemed ... your body slowly disappeared. As if it was eaten, from inside, or by some parasite, first the shoe and then the foot – not even turning to opaque, but just – disappearing, then the leg, the knee, and there you were, one-legged, one-sided, then you levelled up – the other leg, the shirt and what was in it, all of it ... going, going.... And I knew – it was unstoppable, neither slow not hurried, like a pill in water, sugar dissolved, one moment there, in and of itself, the next – nowhere at all or everywhere, exactly as it was but changed, so utterly it became what it had been sitting in ... like a lizard in a parrot's gut, dissolving, becoming parrot, and yet not, because you'd seen it, running up the wall and panting ... nothing of the parrot in itself until it became – completely parrot.... And so your face, the head – away, inexistent but ever-present, no pain, no grimace, and still one arm to hold the pen, wrote on and on, a dreadful scene, of course, you, I, wouldn't think of looking, asking – what have you written today before you weren't, faded out, were not yourself today nor any day? A lizard in a gut, dissolved, and maybe what we'd never look for, the fæcal residues of what had been ... something you wouldn't want to find, so wouldn't look for....

'It sounds,' I say, 'like you've remade a story read way back – Chekhov, perhaps, or something like Peau de chagrin, without the philosophical bent, such as it is, which made an invention less banal because it's really happening ... because – Kochi, you really are not here, not here to me, not anywhere, not even Itaipu....'

'You see?' she said. 'If you're not there, you've gone into the parrot. Me. If you're not with me, it's because – I have digested you.'

We laugh. 'What makes me disappear?' I ask.

'It was the light,' she said. 'Like light seeping in a camera – they say it's fog, but if there's enough of it, it washes out, dissolves, all other images ... over-exposure, Kochi: that is where you went.'

'That's what they say,' I say. 'People who distrust a sensibility, a reasoning. Who think they're right, and can exact a sacrifice, a martyrdom. They impose their judgement, perhaps it's essential, perhaps just wrong. How do you tell? You must tell. No side is clean, but the space between the sides – what use is it?'

She can't hear. Here she comes again – 'Come, join us. It's the imperative. You can't profess, act, like a human being, then hold back as if we're parasites who owe you nothing when the poison comes on us, and you owe them absolutely nothing except what makes no difference at all – your benevolence, perhaps....'

'I don't know where you are,' I say, quite uselessly – it's my excuse. It wouldn't matter where she is, and if I'm acting wrong ... Reticence, cowardice, honesty. Being afraid – that's honest! Being incongruous – they say wherever and whenever – you must resist....

WHEN WILL THE DAY COME?

> *Everybody is waiting, everybody is hoping, and children are now growing up imbued with hopes....*
>
> N.A. Dobrolyubov (1860)

'Where is Jacob?' an old friend writes to me. Jacob's friend. Full of anxiety and analysis, Jacob, Jacob.... He didn't go for these analyses of why you wanted didn't happen, and how if you change the epistemology and the driving wheel, it all turns out as you had hoped....

'It didn't start in Detroit. There were workers' cities round holes in the ground – Cobalt, Sudbury, Rouyn-Noranda, the paper towns, the auto towns – where it would start instead, however unlikely it might seem from elsewhere, the revolution we'd all wanted – until the stuff was mined, the trees cut down if they'd not been burnt off first ... everybody moving off or staying on to die in their little houses with the shabby yards....

'Red Finns, White Finns – always a bottle of rye to sell in the trunk.... Tough women to be won in all-night games, people coming off the graveyard shift to join in and get lucky when the sun came up.

'You had to take a break, get away, feel sober for a while and calm down enough to earn, signing on and running off, starting over.

'That's what they told me. That generation was quite inconclusive. Nothing to show at all, except more generations.'

It's poetry. Maybe Jacob in his hole is remembering all that's written, passing his time ... poetry is ideal for that.

'Change is coming,' I write back. 'Prepare to resist it. Remember how the German weavers broke the machines....'

'I'll dust off my m'bira,' the guy replies. 'Dump the omnichord. Maybe what was wanted – the great change, the revolution as they called it – maybe it was there at the beginning, and all that was wanted was to resist what was brought in after....'

'Change is consequences, not innovation,' I write back – 'But be very careful, very, very – restrain your donkey! No galloping – you'll end in the ravine....'

And of course – everything I've said is virtual – invention. The friend, his fear – and Jacob too, by now ... inventions. I couldn't use Adèle's phone, I said, nor respond to Jacob's friend. Inventions all – you all are: if you're not present, there's no word to hear, respond to.... You never see the bird of wisdom – you're in bed or dead ... only the blackbird sings for all his existence, never repeating himself, and never understood, not a single note – is it about him? About you? You can't tell, no one can.... Yet there he is, on the roof, unstoppable, if not from the beginning, from before you can remember.

All together – everybody must unite to undo what's been done.... Where do you re-start? 1815 with Metternich, perhaps.

There's been a small war – very small, a contingent of six, all casualties, no one knows quite where – a match unequal, without consequences we can see.

'We were set up to say what's true....' It seems that Jacob, after all, did have a friend – Victor. Who worked with him, or after him....

'Creation and destruction,' Victor says. 'That was the unit's thesis. Civilisations innovate, and wars are the accelerator. Some guy in the States – used the idea to justify what they were doing anyway. The fittest civilisation wins its wars, invents – until it falls to war. It isn't so, of course – Fordism and war – two Janus faces.... Call it civilisation – you can call it destiny.... Or History.

'Only those old racists, supremacists, gave civilisations such a gloss. Those shards left by the Chichimec – the figurines are supposed to make you civilised and warlike – something to kill and die for.... It justifies inventions made to kill, exterminate, procedures that exclude, discriminate – because it fetishises what is called a civilisation.... It *justifies* the working on the line, enslavement, death camps – because done by civilisations, as they're called ...civilisations that in turn will fall until, maybe, there comes one that has won its wars, enslaved the world....'

'Oh,' I say, 'I turn my back on that. Alas, when you do that, you don't see what's coming up behind....'

I think of Adèle and the general – they weren't a civilisation, I would say. And what got rid of them – those guys, they certainly were civilised.... It all fits in. What Zélie didn't say, was that survival needed wars perpetual.... Shall we survive, when we're all civilised, those who are left, and there's no weaker rival to defeat? No war, no innovation?

'Jacob believed that when a guy pays you to work for them – if you are not a slave, you are a partner,' Victor says. 'He objected, and he criticised. That was a threat – and insurrection too. He had this notion of the flaw – the self-destructive practise that will lead to death of the species, not more civilisations....'

'Yes,' I say. 'No boss likes that idea....'

'The bum's rush,' Victor said. 'That was Jacob's end with them.'

'He embodied the thesis – creation leading to destruction. They wanted it the other way around,' I say.

'No, Kochi,' Victor says. 'You have it wrong. You think survival's open to us all. Just find the switch, the mechanism, the daily exercise. Jacob's comrades meant to ensure survival of themselves, the top-dog civilisation, against the rest; civilised or just its copiers, allies – critics even: – by war. War that would turn out to be pre-emptive, or by proxy, any way at all....'

'I'd say I was surprised,' I say, 'But....'

'There are questions you can ask,' says Victor. 'Like – how to get on the good list...? The civilised. You're on lists already, so you might not have a chance. Who could have thought of such a scheme, and sold it as a general hope? Who are the ones who stand to be survivors, on that list? Can I improve my chances, can I help more populations get civilised?

'I asked all this,' he said. 'Quite sneakily, of course. The answer usually is you can't do much, or "that's a secret". You could start from there. But – everything you uncivilised guys do to help you to survive – it won't help you, it only helps the ones who're out in front, and have some tricks to keep them there....'

'These wars,' I say. 'Aren't a surprise....'

'They don't reduce the population,' Victor says. 'Often, the numbers rise. The big reduction's due to what Jacob called the flaw ... in nature, as it reacts to us, as we slash and burn it, eat it, take it to be stuffed.... It's a ploy – nature will win, moreover, it doesn't care, not if or when or how. Enough that we should know it does, it wins....'

'Oh, Victor,' I say, and laugh. 'What banalities! A secret in a plot!'

'You're bright, Kochi,' Victor says. 'Of course, it's comic book! I'm leading you on ... and you won't fall for it.'

'A RANDOM COLLECTION OF SPECKS OF DUST'

Nadezhda Mandelstam

'And yet,' I say, 'I felt Adèle had more substance than I ever will, I felt a coward not to join her in her hopeless stand....'

'Perhaps you hit on Jacob's "flaw",' says Victor. '"Compassion", or irrationality. Self destruction? No matter – the big issues are beyond me, and you, Kochi, never began. Your genius lies in knowing they're beyond you. We should team up, go together, look for Jacob....'

'No,' I say, 'I'm sure it's unavailing. The earth took him. He would have wished it so....'

'I'd come with Juliette,' he says, 'she appreciates me – once, I'd say "it's love"! The three of us – unless there's someone you would like....'

'Oh no,' I interrupt. 'They've all had other things to do – and Adèle had the final chord.... They were right, they didn't want to carry me, although they thought I'm light – as Jacob did....'

Victor's an executive – only blamed for doing what he's told. I have a passion for Juliette. She talks to me, and when we part, she's off to bed with Victor.... I feel I have with her – a true story. Like it really is – or how, with some twist and hop, a jig in the script, how it will be ... will always be. Happy ends are always premature. The moral is – don't risk, enjoy vicariously, watch sport on the TV, see your lover off to bed with someone else....

'You're a voyeur, Kochi,' Juliette says. 'That's rather good. You live to tell the tales. It doesn't bother me a bit.'

We drive aimlessly – very far. We follow Marco Polo, but no one boils us noodles – they piss quite differently here – through straws, or reeds, if they are cultured – just like in the lies they told to little Marco, and we believe them all, like him.

'It's stressful,' I say to Juliette. 'What's it for?'

'Victor doesn't know,' she says: 'He's a stallion for sure, but those are just executives, like him. When they've been broken, they don't know where to go or what to understand....

'We're looking for a place where we'd be safe. Maybe the earth should swallow us, like it did your friend. I tell him – "No, it's not that kind of place we need – it's social place. We need to be bosses with a pass and special clothes."'

On on we drive, and yet, nothing is promising: – 'We know where China is, and that it isn't specially our home....' says Juliette. '– that Polo guy – he didn't understand – the Chinese knew exactly where he was, and may have placed the liars that he met. It was a pointless trip we know he didn't make. Anyone could tell him where those vases came from and the silk ... he was an innocent, probably the only one that Europe knew: until they went and conquered Africa and people thought it was to educate the blacks....'

She laughs. Her teeth are porcelain. I hope they don't break off, for where we are, no one would glue them back.... I am besotted, excited as a toad, a mantis.... 'I'm sure you're right,' I say. 'Seeking survival is like seeking – assurances of our mortality. What's to be done is to be done now and quick.... "Love all you can, spend, spend, listen to the beat and be prepared to run."'

'Wise words, Kochi,' says Victor, who's much amused by my passion for Juliette.

'We should have been here a thousand years ago,' I say. 'Before the Mongols, the Yuan.... Then before the Turks, before people I don't know, no one knows who, what language, beliefs ... people always moving East to West and South to North.... We look for something else, perhaps....'

'A hundred years ago, the physicists stopped understanding why the world, the universe, was as it was or might be,' Victor says. 'Understanding where we're at lies further and further back in time – before the deserts, before all the knots came untied ... when people knew what they could do and what was opportune to believe.... Then we stopped roaming and had to build the ziggurats. It's as if you're given a fixed time to sort things out, grasp the design, master the processes, do the maths – and if you fail, you go into the boiler, the hopper, the mixer, shaker – and something else steps forward to replace you....'

'Hops, crawls, slithers....' Juliette adds.

'Where shall we spend our lives?' I ask. 'That's simple, and immediate. What shall we do, and think? Shall we be sensitive, more receptive, or just like we are now?'

'The animals here,' he says. 'They all die. No food. We've come too late: you're right.'

'Your disillusion makes you quite attractive, Victor,' I tell him. 'Now, you believe that only the bosses make a civilisation, and that a civilisation's the only place worth living in.... Reaction triumphs....'

'The argument is over,' Victor says. 'Outside the strongest civilisation, the strongest bosses – no good life is possible, the threat is constant, there's no life worth contemplating.'

'Specks of dust,' I say. 'Us. Especially where there is most force....'

There's stones, in squares, that look like chimney tops – you sit on the rim, below there's nothing – nothing visible. Victor perches on one, more harangues – all three of us are talking all the time, like macaws; about ourselves, the cultures we passed through, cultural quadrilles and revolutions we endured, and which of us fell out of them by too much dedication to their self-development – pot and acid, fevers unassailable by science.... We've all been dark objects, flying fast and high, and bleeping ... and down he goes! Victor – out of our sight and ken. Over-excitement strikes again! His a dry drop, where Jacob's probably was wet.

No means to hoist him out – 'We'll leave him here,' I say to Juliette. 'Go on, and in Mongolia turn right ... maybe we two should take a pause, on Tahiti beach....'

'No, no,' she says. 'You're sweet, of course, rather a bore, but Victor's been my man – he is extravagant and loud, but all the same ... we couldn't leave him here....'

'Of course we can,' I say.

We argue. I say, 'Let's take off all our clothes and tie them in a rope,' and that we do. She says, 'These chimneys – they are not for fires – there is a house, buried down there in the sand, these are parts of wind-towers,' and I disagree, and while we're arguing, out scrambles Victor, and doesn't grasp why we are standing there quite nude and baffing at each other in the fire of argument – and I've dressed, walked down, into the sand.

I see them in the little jeep, still talking, making gestures, baffing each other in the face....

Two guys turn up – maybe they are border guards, except there is no border here. They've rifles, and I walk down, out of their sight.

A guy is sitting by his shack. It ought to be a yurt – it's not. It's felt sheets tacked on poles, a hut. He greets me. 'I'm Marco,' I tell him, but he doesn't understand. I'm poetry. 'Polo,' I repeat, and 'Pollo, Pollo,' he in turn repeats – just like it was, a thousand years ago.

'I need some cash,' he says. 'The animals are dead – there isn't water here....'

'Oh,' I say, 'I'd have gladly shared your lot, but that would have been generations back, when guys passed through here, smoking weed and buying those embroidered Afghan coats....'

I look up – the jeep has gone, the guards as well ... I jump down, down the hill where the shack stands. Getting away.

To add my poverty to his does not make a plenty, and he's throwing stones....

I jump, I spread my arms out, I remember flying from the fire ... and again I fly, a metre, and then two or three, and hop and fly down like a turkey or a vulture....

I sing, like I am sauced up – 'flip flop and fly....'

I've half-flown down ... and there's a city, cement towers, and automobiles running up and down.... The names on buildings are those I've always known, a continuity I didn't want ... cereals and bleach....

Juliette wires you up. What pepper-juice! – an hour with her, you do the danse macabre and Victory Day parade.... Her fierce and pointy tongue pours out nonsense like you never heard, except it's yours, burnished, returned to sender....

I need tying down.

It's hard to find where toiling people go – there's more of them than anybody else, but they're in the part you don't see as you go through, towards the centre .... then in an unpaved street, the guest-house – the dormitory, 'Chakra' it says, and there's a sign, a joke – 'first-time flyers': from the airport. I don't qualify. Nor, I suspect, do all the guys who'll sleep with you that night, everybody making a separate thing to eat, and afterwards, you all sit and everyone must tell a tale – and mine start well, and swell all right, but what matters here is a bang! An end, the pay-off ending, that makes you laugh, especially you the teller: and the rest join in. I don't think the teller of the tale should step too deeply in their story. There is confusion, between who you are and what you say, where you came from, where you're going. As if the end is in the beginning which is a nonsense and is not a tale at all but the strip of situations which is yours, and being animated, if you can....

It's warm. Everywhere is warm, so I don't need the hot long room, I can avoid the 'Chakra', and sleep outside.

And that I do.

The more you travel, the less you know ... the more you know, the less you know – that's the futility my dream comes up with. I've been stung, the grass is full of them. You should accept the closeness, the heat, the snores, the filching hands – and listen to the stories, laugh with your fellows, feel with them ... coalminers who've dug out the coal, sailors whose sea has run out, monks too poor to live by poverty.... Instead, I scratch.

JAHAN

Animals on strings, and humans – a crowd so dense, so tightly packed, the land in terraces – so many stories to be heard right through. I pass the 'Chakra', rumbling with snores. I'm nearly round the world, there'd be no choice but starting off again, collecting more languages, more strophes, more tall tales and stunted stories. No one would relish that. Avoiding nothingness – that was vain, and long ago, as if you, the atom, you still might be posing the question, whether everything was in vain, or whether vanity was the high card.... And now – there's no question. When we're at the end, no one has doubts – it's better to go on, ignore the evidence, find the trick answer to trick questions. The fly in the whisky – struggles to climb out, not to drink his way down to the bottom.

Dense as flies ... resourceful, but with no resources, except their circlet of eyes. Watching our backs, our fronts and sides – 'Entertainment' says the sign, outside a dun brick building, idle bouncers filing their nails outside – and music! Ouds amplified and rebabs, serpents and the universal metallica.... I sidle in ... and

'Mind!' she says: 'Clumsy!'

A classy lady, kohl, patchouli evident.... Destiny bumps people into you, you into them....

'This could be the one,' you think, but it's a line remembered from a song – 'I'm on a delegation,' I say. 'I'm the counsellor of Princes – but they keep going down like skittles, and I'm the one left holding the wrecking ball....'

We laugh. This place, standard and glitzy, is where the truth and lies have equal weight, you put them in the slot and pull the handle – maybe you lose – you usually do – or win a manifesto, an apocrypha, a fortune left for you in unnamed cities....

I pull up my ghosts – important friends make you seem important, and they've gone down but you are clean, unused ... Claude, the Master, Zélie, Jacob, Amos, Victor ... Victor? I show them off, all of them, to Jahan.

'Curiosity brought me here,' says Jahan. 'You could dance with me – to pass the time. There's not much left.

'I have a charity – you could put an offering in my little box....' and she parts her dress, and down, far down between her breasts, beyond, there is a box, a slot for coins and one for notes....

'Let's dance,' I say. 'And later I can get the cash – it isn't safe to wander anywhere with valuables ...' And again we laugh – we understand each other perfectly....

I try to shuffle round – she says, 'Forget it, Kochi. I'll go up on stage – you shouldn't touch me, till you've donated to my charity....' And up she goes and shimmies through a fierce routine – the guys all bellow and throw coins. 'There,' she says. 'That's what I can do. Now, show me what you do....'

I prepare my speech, but at once she says, 'I know exactly who you are, and so does everybody here – the maitre d's Chinese and they must remember ninety-thousand characters ... faces, that is, characters, not situations. The situation's what we're in.... The faces are all recognised, especially yours. There was the murder case, the disappearances, and not to mention arson. You're a witness, Kochi, but I can hide you: for the rest, saving the world, I'll be your interlocutor, everybody is....'

I remember, far far back – 'Think'.

I try ... to think, and think I've never thought, just asked the questions, and yet there's nothing now I want to know!

Think, think back – that's all we ever do, like we were forever going back to school, and wondering – what's best, the best place – Baalbek or Gomorrah, and I remember 'I am not feeling well here, I would rather go home....' But I have no home except –

'From now, your home is here,' says Jahan. 'Get used to it! If dreadful things should happen – they will happen here. If not – then we are safe, and we're at home.'

'Why me?' I ask. 'Why a performer like you are, a professional ... shows kindness to me...?'

'Oh, Kochi,' Jahan says, and laughs and tickles me. 'Don't underestimate your best performances! Here, you have recognition, genuine – all anyone could ever want.'

'Well, maybe,' I say. 'In a way....'

'Those people you've been with,' she says, 'all your life: you must have wondered, and at last found out: so, you know how it will end.... What will take place, the order it will happen – the conflicts and the sickness, the exhaustion and the wars of all against the rest....'

It's a heavy sentence, and she breaks it off. '... One more turn,' she says, going on stage, 'And then we'll see how we can proceed....'

All these people, so flesh and blood, mostly so poor, or else in funds through dodgy deals, the faithful covered up, the infidels painted over with tattoos and if you read the symbols you'd have travelled through from Maoris to the Celts, from runes to earth mothers – making a thickness, a consistency; all on their feet and rooting for Jahan – 'bring it on, you're a princess' and she is that and more, and much much more, she carries forward the spirit manufactured when we chased gazelles and barbecued the little elephants, and sacrificed our kids and put our enemies in jails with scorpions and spiders....

'Well,' she asks. 'How was I?'

'It's a great talent that you have,' I say. 'Except ... it's perfect of its kind, except ... we know its kind. There's no originality at all. You dance like they have always danced, or tried – except you do it well, supremely well.'

She's not put out. 'Most cultures don't prize invention, they resist it, they survive through their traditions. Change, originality,' she says, 'it comes, like fall and winter. Look around,' she sweeps her arms at the worn depleted people here.... 'You guys, Kochi,' she says, 'have driven us and worn us out and made us use the stuff you sell. Enough!'

That's not original either, I think, but do not say.

'You'll sleep in my room,' Jahan tells me. 'You're stippled red! We eat, we are not eaten! – you put the creation upside down...!'

The room is unlike her – scabby walls, a dirty sink and clothes scumbled like a disused palette, where someone's tried to paint the stormy sunlit clouds.

I like decoration. Jahan wants nothing beautiful but her.

'This is Minu,' Jahan says.

Minu is maybe fifteen, Jahan's servant, I suppose. She looks quite blank. There is no radio, no music to be played.

'God made one sex,' says Jahan. 'You told me. He didn't see the need for breeding – the Adam that he made was perfect, like He thought were all the other things He made....

'I guess there was rebellion, and women got produced – from spare parts of the man, the Adam model. Not well thought out, and of course – the rebellion went on, and they got booted out....'

'No, Jahan,' I say, 'I didn't tell you this. I don't think it's true.'

'Well,' she says, 'Minu believes it. She thinks it's why women get treated bad. Men have known God, pretend they're like Him, but women are rebellious – they want to know, to help each other, not to obey....'

'There's every kind of tale that circulates,' I say. 'Here's one that's true – in the desert, a village trades salt and cows and buys its women – brides – from far down south. That way, they avoid inbreeding. I guess the men are Arabs, and the women, they are black, from far away, over the desert....'

'That's what I mean,' says Jahan. 'There was one sex, and now there's two, it makes no difference – men go with men, women with women – as it was, as it should be.'

'You may be right,' I say. 'It doesn't always seem that way, but really, it sounds plausible. It's as you want. I don't believe in a creator, nor in first things, nor in causes and effects, nor purposes nor destiny. We go on, one commitment after another from curiosity, and if we're asked to ... and that's enough, the asking.'

'I ask you, Kochi,' Jahan says. 'Like you said.'

There's a flaw, an omission, in the story about the trafficked women, though I know it to be true – essentially, at least. There must be children finished up some place....

Jahan is exhausted with the dancing, though we talk after she gets back till very late, about what is certain, secure, objective, and all the rest that's not.

Determinism? It seems you can't avoid it, but in the longer term, we feel – it's been much overrated ...

Jahan: sleeps on a low bed, Minu on the floor, and I lie on a short divan, maybe Minu's – my legs hang over at the end. Jahan snores. I try to sleep, counting the camels swaying on and on, with saddle-bags of salt, and – what kind of cows? Alive or dead, maybe humped bulls, or those thin beasts you see in places waterless, unable to trek through the Sahara, surely...? What does it show – necessity, cooperation, exploitation, trafficking...?

I slink back out – the dance-hall. It's closing, though it's early, only three – 'Where are all the young guys?' I ask the head guy, 'You should be rocking at this time ...'

'There's nothing here,' he says. 'The youth has gone to wars, or on the seas ... I'm looking for a DJ ... we can't afford an orchestra, even a dancer, doing it for nearly free....'

'You don't know me,' I say. 'I could DJ....'

'We know you, Kochi,' says the head guy. 'Everybody knows you through and through. Just move around, take in the scene – there's no danger here, except from cops.... I fired the bouncers – no one makes trouble here, except the cops. They shoot you, or they pick you up. They beat you. If you're not subversive – it's for vagrancy ... they're very twitchy, and they're poor....'

'I have an idea....' I say to the head guy, Maxi.

We watch the flashes high up in the mountains – they sparkle, there are starbursts, silver glitz....

'There's a range,' he says. 'For firing. Sometimes they seed the clouds. It doesn't seem to work. One day – they'll come. We should have done a deal.... They fly over, but there's not much you can do....'

'I'm all for settling in, and seeing what will happen,' I say. 'But of course – if you're rounded up, there's not much you can do.'

I do a deal with Maxi. I'll clear up the venue every night, and he will feed me – 'As long as there are chickens, we will curry them,' he says.

I'll stay close to Jahan until – I can't stand it any more.

'That sounds the best thing you can do,' he says. 'We danced when it all began for us, and we'll get better at it every day.... Jahan will, that is. She needs protection – that's your job. There's a cartel after her, for sure, she says....'

'She can ignore it, then,' I say. 'There's a cartel or intelligence after each of us, but they have millions to sort out before our number's at the top. It's quite irrelevant – what matters is that green toads mate and nightingale thrushes thrive and sing, their eggs should be controlled to see they are not full of lead or radiation, fish too, not loaded with our heavy metals ... you must know, Maxi, that is all that signifies, and maybe take some photos of Jahan's dance for private satisfaction....'

And we laugh.

'You could be anything, Kochi,' Maxi says. 'Or nothing. That's how it is – you've looked at how it's done, the tricks, the rhetoric – the sincere. You know it all, like we all do. Think of the wrestlers, the gladiators, the simple soldiers, who were emperors, the illiterates, the spies, the demented and the unreliable who govern millions – us included. Don't delay too long with Jahan – or take her with you, when you're chosen – fly with her....'

'You give too much weight to my humanity,' I say. 'Of course, anyone is capable of anything, but mostly we don't try, aren't called, we fall down, we're sequestered, denounce our mothers....'

'Of course,' says Maxi. 'But you're none of those. You're hardly used. Your exceptional ordinariness, immaculate past – all that's in your favour....'

'Don't mock,' I say. 'Because the big poppies – they too are mocked. Even the gods are mocked – maybe not when you're selected as a sacrifice ... conscripted, even....'

Each morning, Jahan has the same routine – exercises in the park, and then to watch the cherry blossom by the river ... you never get to eat the cherries, it's not that kind of cherry-tree, but there are plums and bergamots – and three kinds of figs – they grow in silence, unpicked, down the alleyways where the artisans make the bricks and dip the candles.

'Jahan saved Minu,' Maxi says. 'Once, all the big guys had their slaves. Now, they needn't bother. Labour is cheap. Jahan saved Minu from slavery, now Minu is her slave. It's our tradition, Kochi – don't buck that....'

I notice Minu doesn't go outside. 'There's people will sequester you,' says Jahan. 'Just on a whim.'

There's nothing much that Minu does. Jahan and I eat at the dance-hall, and Minu eats what we bring back. I give her the short divan, hers, and sleep badly on the floor. If I've been chosen for some role – it's not a good beginning. 'You're my authority,' says Jahan. 'We've hardly started to excavate the holy books, and holy theories. There's Schumpeter and Schopenhauer, Spengler and Oriental Despotisms, the orgone box, Love Story....'

The Hinayana tradition and the Mahayana, the Vedas. Tantra – the three body system, the Shah-nameh, the placing of *om, ah,* and *hum* – some wooden plaques with themes of sex, a bundle – birch-bark – which we don't unwrap ... ideas profane and sacred, more and more profane and ultimately – transcendental.

Jahan discusses everything, and criticises if I misremember or sell short....

'When we have found the truth,' she says, 'I'll let you go. Then, you will reach your destiny.'

I'm not a slave, I think, but though I seem a teacher, really I am her disciple.

'"Dirty Dancing", Kochi,' she says. 'Were they on to anything?'

I wonder if Minu began as mentor, and was hollowed out – there's precedent for that, it's quite a sought-out state – and is a shell of someone else who knew so much and trickled learning to Jahan, and then became a shadow – one we all have: what we know, revealed and certain – and ignorance. What we don't know, or class as wrong or useless or mistaken. It's clear – we're all made up of knowledge, and of ignorance. Like most of what we study – it's banal. Truth is like that – so drab and evident it's not worth having. Is it worth the slog of finding it? A forest of untruths and decoys to navigate.... Maybe it's what we start with – that's what Jahan says. Of course, truth, if it exists, it must be always there! So, why does she want to keep me till we find it? Different kinds of truth – it's plausible! That too's a theory we have long discussed. She is so curious, so ravenous, I feel like Minu – scooped out, like a mango.

What knowledge can Minu have had, and imparted, lost, I wonder. She looks, as ever, blank. 'What did you know and now have lost?' I ask her.

'Just the same,' she says.

It's what Mafiosi say, when they're introduced to one another.

That this is a conspiracy is no surprise – that's how it's always been. Two or three together – they can't avoid making a plot. But if there's a conspiracy – who else is in it? It can't be just a Mafia – they are men of honour. They live by crime, but don't admit it, don't recognise it so there is no guilt – just membership. Like being human only better at it than the rest. Which of us is honourable? Do I have my slavery lifted, and who's in line for eminence – Jahan or me?

Jahan is filling herself with a future that can't be mine – always in a shabby room, someone sleeping on the floor, like a worn pelouche, outgrown.

'People, Kochi,' Maxi says. 'You don't trust them, you want some substance – and yet they're all around you, have always been, like brambles. Get away from them! Don't think you can corral them, milk them for sustenance, still less for ideas or purposes. Vanity, my dear! Puffing up yourself! You know it, but always you want more of them, people, any people, their clues, their love, their secrets, their devotion.... You won't find it, they haven't got anything and they won't give it to you.'

'Really, I thought,' I say. 'Stuck here, at the end.... I thought there was a plan, that this was a terminus, a destination that unknowingly I'd reached ... and that there would be a prize.'

'You have to win, to get a prize,' says Maxi. 'The competition's always younger, always faster.... I'm in training for the race, of course, but if I must go back, back home, I know they'll venerate my years. Not me, I fear, but age and senility.'

'Then there's the apocalypse,' I say. 'You can't train for that. Maybe you know Zélie.... She thought the oceans matter, cool us off. Probably – she was too quick. Extinction must wait. It would take a century or more until there's just two humans left.

'Jahan thinks the gender's immaterial. Maybe it would be, but I doubt that either one of them is her, or me.

'Then it would begin again – maybe with built-in parasols evolving, always open on our heads, like hoopoes. Toucan beaks to crack the nuts. A range of squawks to get the basics said, no fancy insults. We'll run, but we won't fly. It's frustrating, not to know what happens. But we can guess....'

'No,' Maxi says. 'I never heard of Zélie. The problem is – there's hordes of people left, and all the stuff we eat is eaten.... You know where that problem tends? Watch your fat arse, my friend!'

I wave that thought away: 'The species was around for ages, nothing accomplished – then, a few spectacular feats. And massacres as well,' I say. 'I didn't contribute, but I was around,' and Maxi says. 'Well, there's no opening for bosses here, and Jahan's the local candidate for everything. Dance, dance – that's what she can do.'

*

'We haven't done the sciences,' says Jahan. 'I confess I'm not attracted. They show the fragility of our bodies. Then there's the universe – ridiculous! No one would have invented such a shambles – no artist, anyway. The rocks, the loneliness, the distances, the purposeless speed and age of everything – what ever can it signify?

'The gods, the philosophies, the exercises – there's always someone taking credit for putting an order on the chaos, conjuring a miracle perhaps, demanding sacrifices, but....'

'No one really believes in that, Jahan,' I say.

'I have to,' she says, 'Spirit. It's my job.'

'Talking of order,' I say. 'I thought there might be something I'd commit to here....'

'You want to be a big poppy?' she asks. 'Despite all the theories we have studied? Don't you see, it's all going to disappear, quite soon. Maxi is bankrupt. We'll close in a few days. No one pays for anything.'

'It makes me feel I've not been of much use,' I say.

'Guys speed things up and others slow them down, Kochi,' she says. 'Maybe you are in between.'

*

It's clear – whatever happens, Jahan must stay, see the end, and start afresh, maybe. With faith. Not me, not me at all.

I ask Minu, 'I'm leaving. Do you want to come with me? There's not much for us if we stay –

'It could become worse, harder still – that's how I feel. And you?'

'Just the same,' she says.

We've the routine. Jahan does the dance, there's not so many people now, it's easy to clear up after – she sleeps, exhausted.

I've finished here, instructed Jahan, as much as I can. No one believes it, none of it, but it is spirit, Jahan says. There in the dance.

I am prepared. Purified, stripped of some stupid hopes, rejected and rejecting ... friends generous, friends congealed. I'm ready to begin, experienced and primed.

This is the night. I don't wake Minu, I leave her. I take the birchbark bundle. If I find a monastery, they'll want it, take me in – and then I think again, what if it was stolen? – and I leave it, put it back, under the bed.

It's dark, but there's a sparkle on the mountains far away. There's sounds, but nothing you could place. Birds on the edge of sleep.

Clap Your Hands

CREATURES

THE CAT who's lost her tail – a birthing accident, vandals, or by derring do – watches the grass snake size up diameters, make its choice, and seep to disappearance in a crack between two stones.

A Cheshire snake? As if it's never been, without a name: 'snake'. Sneaky snake.... The cat has many names – runs obedient to each one, as she does her begging round for food in every angle of her territory. She's imperilled; but the snake can manage on its own.

Damage, escape: you're always there but no one sees you, you're at war though nothing belongs to you or ever will, your life lasts seconds, you're tiny but you're stubborn and resist; an ocean drowns you a huge forest burns you up a desert buries you.

Living things – they treat themselves, each other, in complicated ways. You eat some things, seat others on your knee, walk them, ride them.... What happens when you break the chains, tilt the scales ... plan to occupy a territory bigger than you can see or walk? Everybody wants a fresh helping – more green, red, or black. To eat, to mine, to enslave.... More, the same, wherever you end up – finding those colours in rehab, a slaughterhouse, and just cinders. A world for grabs, the only one, sliced thin and meagrely. It really is the only one so far, you can't have more: why do you crave more sand, more expanse? Brittle cities. And all war – is world war. Even to win – you must go very very gingerly. You need to be an expert in consequences, next moves. It was like chess; now it's like *go.*

You're an invader, they'll want to hurt you, you can't apologise for what you want – your claim, your assertion.

I didn't follow all the arguments – nature, apocalypse, freeze or fry: four years, Annemarie instructed me, I did the exercises. I was sent to analyse the disasters she'd anticipated. She knew them all, the subjects: invented them; said I was too stupid to understand. Ecology – her study of everything ... Most studies say they study everything. She says 'everything that matters'. It isn't that, exactly. Living things, the lot, she spoke for them, but humans were to be the winners. Saved at the very last. Turn nature round to scrap for you. Thrown together, all in the deep end, in hot water. As if there's no responsibility for anything – all's volcanoes, earthquakes. We humans are exempt: we suffer, and that's it. Hoist with everybody's petard, but still the tops.

Some humans end by saying they're happy to be what they are, but the people they distrust are the Americans, Russians or Chinese ... Neapolitans or Belgians, Scots or Muslims. It took years to formulate my own dislike: frustrations....

Distrust of my – our – species, past and future.

That's what I can't stand. My species. I divorce myself. We argued, sweet tolerant Annemarie, and one day, we reached the truth. 'You disgust me,' she said.

Live and die by the word. 'Disgust'.

You'll never forget or cancel that.

'The species, Annemarie,' I said. 'Disgusts *me*. I've lost patience with it, with hope for it.

'And what you say – disgust of me – concludes the story of affections, cohabitation, that I thought we have. It's personal, but we can only know things personally, every thing or possibility, rhymed, excogitated. Other people – we cannot be an other, it's a tabu. However hard it is to be yourself, that's it – you are alone, no one else can be inside you. No company, no voice, no one but you to pull your strings. Absolute. No other thing or person. You must keep the boundary. We're like the animals that live alone and mate – quick and resented – once a year; the male trots off, the woman, wife, the mate – digs a deep pit to hide the infant, keep it from the father's rage – and from all the other men who prowl around.'

Nothing more to do with them, I think – the humans: their strategies, the philosophical ploys to hide their violence, their greed, insatiable appetite to consume, destroy, eliminate ... to master and annex.

I resign my membership. I'll dig a hole and die solitary in it – so far down you'll never find me, know which bones are mine, blended with the roots.

A durable economy? A pact with nature? – perpetual existence, species immortality? Space empires? – Ah! The horror!

Dropping out of the species and its plans – I feel free, but freedom, defined in and by the humans – cannot be for me. Not free exactly: fluid.

I flow down to the sea, just water, and so untraceable, indecipherable.

'You think the choices are open for you, like choosing religions or other people....' says Annemarie's brother. 'They are, but you don't want them. The choices are not radical enough. People see you as a non-belonging being ... not interesting. Not interested. They're centred on themselves. The real choice before you, my friend, is for varieties of sex, or kooky politics. And you don't want those. Besides, being disgusted, as Annemarie said – it's her, her about you. Don't take it seriously.... It's so local.'

It confirms where I'd arrived. First, self-disgust. Then all the rest.

Mediocrity the hope – initiatives are destroying us, making us follow peddlers' carts like madmen craving brighter rags....

'There's no affection left,' says Annemarie.

'I'm passing through the looking glass, and I shall watch you from the other side,' I say.

'And to think of all the times I saved you from the firing squad,' she says.

'Sometimes I changed my name. Sometimes they turned pacifist. Sometimes the wrong side won, and they all saluted me,' I say. 'Made me a general.'

'Now you'll have to make your own way, and sign up for the whole war, whichever side they put you on,' she says. 'Yours is a lovely uniform.'

'You can design your own, no one will see it anyway,' I say. 'You sit in the truck, it's fitted like an office. Fire your cannon. If you're a target, you don't feel a thing.'

Some people must be lovable, some – exciting. Some are your guardians, your drivers. There must be some of everything in the box: your favourites, fondants and jellies ... or else it's grim, like cave time. Millions of years, shut in there, nothing to do but drawing on the walls.

Sex, opinions, empathy – those must come in. Much formless, much laid down like clay, unchanging and unchangeable: principles. They're the residue: populations you distrust, opinions unconfessable. It's when you don't know, can't think – that you fall back on principles. Then, disaster. Uniforms ... numbering from the right.

We trained for catastrophes. Many were to come, some were happening. Bring them on, they make us stronger!

We didn't count sheep – we loaded them on trucks and waved as they went on to slaughter. A kindness.... We piled our possessions where the flood didn't reach, the earthquake might jar them but would not destroy. We ate only potatoes for a month. The radiation – we had to suffer that – also the epidemics.

I often went to war – sometimes scouting, sometimes far from a front, sometimes a militiaman – sometimes firing missiles, sometimes marshalling evacuees.

There have always been catastrophes – you know, if you're the anxious, informed type, what they might be. Fire and fleet and candlelight: the tag left by the body – the mnemonic is the colour, green, the colour of corruption. These exercises were the only practices that brought us, Annemarie and I, not together, but in the same boat, refugees, trafficked in the inflatable, sufferers in the same disaster. Nothing in the future would surprise us. It was her work – prevention of catastrophe, but of course – nothing protects. Familiarity's a help. When you've been dispossessed – the second time you know what you must save and carry, what you can hide – in a hole or up a tree or in the pond, in oilcloth in the standpipe, in the hay, the trough....

What you can eat, what must be killed – and what passes its suffering on, muted, as you 'put it down' ... your dog, the pigeon, the horse. It's distressing – you're a victim, but so is everything around you, and this time it's simulation, imagination – nothing happens, the neighbours don't know they won't be saved, that it's easier to die of cold than heat ... and so, and so until the end.

The military part – it's easy to find real wars – they even pay you to take part. Famines are everywhere, bring your own hunger, that is free.

'We know exactly how it feels, and where the unexpected lies,' she said. 'That way – I'm prepared, experienced in the unexpected. As for you, my dear – you are without responsibilities, but also – you've no constraints. You needn't be a hero, follow rules, hold back. Survival! You can hide, lie, steal – that's what people do.'

So, she contemplates, experiences, survives – the future. She pulls me along behind her – the sacrifice at the rehearsal.

'What about you disgusts me, Yannik?' she asks. 'Your tics. Opinions – invented or borrowed. And when you're above me, riding me to nowhere – I think of those little lizards, tiny dinosaurs, eating the eggs of those black birds – the megapods – who lay them on black roasting sand – the chicks, never to be born, because of evolution, hot-spots ... What are you looking for, as you burrow into me? My eggs? You, only you, no destination, no purpose, a tired humanism making architecture from your dreams, and has you whine when the walls fall down on you.... You'll let the bosses boss you while all you want is being boss yourself.... You stand for crass evolution, opportunist humping, and gut-filling – the enemy of reason ... gobbling and slobbering ... You – a midget dragon, a tiny Komodo, a *varano* – a dwarf....'

'I suffer, Annemarie,' I say. 'For your whims, or your benevolence….'

'I suffer for everybody,' Annemarie says. 'Alone.'

'It's my atheism,' I say. 'Fatalism. No happy ends, no good design that keeps us top despite the challenges, the strategies that foretell catastrophes but not whether, at the last, humans will come through … and even prosper. I disbelieve. That is what disgusts you.'

'It's physical,' she says. 'You. A prissy scepticism. Not the cosmos.'

'Four years with you,' she says. 'An eternity. You should be grateful. You'll say – such a short time. Cut it into seconds – it seemed never to finish … and of course a second never does. Too short.

'You never wanted it, none of it. My life…. The preparation, the exercises – meant nothing to you.'

'We could have guessed it all,' I say. 'We knew what was wrong. Instead, done something interesting – even if it didn't please a public. Damage exploration was your job and so I felt obliged …to follow catastrophes, following your band of hopefuls…'

What an idiot! I knew it all – bourgeois culture, bourgeois ideology. If you don't like your work, and the work you make the others do, don't even like capitalism – then pal up with someone who will sympathise, assist you, take out the stings, give sex to take your mind right off…. It isn't so, I'd always said, and acted stupid knowing that it didn't work – and yet I knelt before it… Annemarie and gambling on preparedness – there was no other culture, no ideology on hand, except what she'd decided to perpetuate. Civilisation – the theatre of cruelty, danse macabre, the colonies and TV series, camps and dawn raids. Your life lived to save that?

Quite inadequate…. Some would be saved so as to change utterly how they lived out their precarious abandoned lives. For everybody else – survival was no guarantee of anything except anxiety.

There was China … but there had been Russia. The revolutions. Forget Algérie française and after….

The great change…. A painful birth, then heroism, hope disappointed, and on they went, breaking the horses, whipping them on… These wagons, tumbrels – they go past, laden with unknown manikins that dance, throw kisses to the crowds…. So many – can they all be renegades and idlers? You follow oppositions, even if you need invent them – so, back to the preceding century – to tsars and emperors. Back to the past and try again….

The Jacobins, the anarchists? They'd published pamphlets, then their time was up – the feisty individuals, the secret organizations; enemies, they hoped, of army-states, the cop-countries…. Arrested and condemned on principle. Principles against principles.

Who would live there, in that future, all of us saved from fates like death?

Well, said Annemarie, better there than nowhere – 'let's adapt to hell on earth, then we shall see….'

Except, there will be some with a view who think they can see, and those who've mostly – no view at all, nothing to see!

'You lost!' says Annemarie's brother, Hammond – like the organ. Compact, plug in, you mistake it for anything except an organ. 'Those revolutions were for catching up – not for new worlds. Transformation and transcendence – that's for dupes! Now, the remedies are much much simpler. 'Drop out. Work at home. Go on manifs.' Nothing happens. Screw who you like, say what comes to you. Nothing will transform us. We'll get excited, hop and shout, but we're convinced we're great survivors – explorers who keep discovering what someone already had. The best available is to fight the very bad to get the bad….'

'I envy you, Hammond,' I say. 'I never was a child, you remain one. I need to know how it feels. I study being infantile – yet – your expertise eludes me….'

'They call the lemurs ghosts,' he says. 'You want to be a lemur – but if you were, other lemurs would come and sign you up. The humans, the integrated ones – they'd pet you. No other animal has so many fans. You've none. You're just a ghost.'

'I'm going into cinema,' I say. 'I've always found myself on the screen. It's the dead thing that's closest to life I know.'

It's an impulse, but thank you Hammond. I could have flashed out something more anomalous that I didn't want to do – trawling for cod … bail bonds….

'I lost my life – I mean, my hope, my plan, my work – to accusations of being a utopian,' I say. 'Defending what can't be any way defended.

'I was clear-sighted. To have a world where I could live with satisfaction, there must be purgatories. It's clear that they contain a mixture of the hopeless and the striving, the good who've failed to keep it up, the bad who didn't convince themselves that being good was good. So, when Annemarie says we are all facing a sentence of indeterminate length in hell, I'm sure hell is somewhere where there is no time. That's its only characteristic: a place with no exterior, and no endurance, no lapse, no counting, no judgement of anything because there's no before or after, no deed, no constancy or logic … no tenses, no imperfect or conditional. Extermination without favours, a non-being.

'I'd accept a better situation – purgatory; which has time, and time in long lengths of string or pasta … and it's just like here and now, except, like here and now, it's always getting worse, more extreme in what you do not want, can't tolerate. Will you be released to other purgatories, as if we all decided without speaking that we want to try existing somewhere else – yet since there is time, but no sentence, no release – there's no respite, no improvement.... Your stretch is uncalculated and unmeasured.... And so there's chance. Cracks in one purgatory's floor let you crash down into the one underneath....'

'You mustn't make a movie that says that,' Hammond says, quite upset. 'No one will even give it an opinion. It's bruised and adolescent. People won't know how much you are an atheist – they'll think there's criticism, or good and bad, that it's your parallel account, a metaphor. Wanting a better god. Something about religion, not intended to be serious....'

Death, it seems, is male. Annemarie fancied him – at least, he frequented her circle, her salon, her thoughts – did she seek catastrophe, or danger, I wondered, even risk? Her Dakar rally motorbike – a Monster – tall, much taller than she was, the kind they race on in the desert, too heavy to pick up if it falls, she needs a mounting-block to climb into the saddle, kick it as you would a mule, some beast that accepted its own badness, ill-intent, and so did not resent especially the violence used to make it run ... dare-devilling, cast for her psychology – for her, speed at any cost, the rush like free-fall, death but not decay, the body tossed like junk, stale, uneaten, a bun with ketchup and a pair of eyes, discarded....

'The Rally bike, loved more than I could ever be: – it did for her. And she for it.'

None of this did I contest, nor analyse. I never queried the motives of her death-defying tests – not with Annemarie, nor anyone at all. She was the magician, the conjurer of her destiny – inventing, faking, grandstanding, roaring like a bear.... She was the scientist, the saviour, replacement victim – her message, last cry, indecipherable; the death perverse.

She found the road blocked when there was no choice, and no backtrack. She flew, maybe held out her arms, but hit first with her knees and then her head. No lesson there, but symbols yes! a bodybagful. Quite nothing at all instructive, except to register the spoiling mechanics of the splat, goose-bumping image of the transformation – into the red ... The force, finality, destroying any hope of being generous, of leaving an eye, a lung, a heart – to have it carried by another, others, through life stages – pony express! ... bearing her organs until *their* death, the terminus, a component flipped from hand to hand … the sequence ending in turn maybe in catastrophe, another miscalculated accident.… Her spare part, cannibalized, could have served its hosts – and ended only in infinity ... in the breakers' yard, a hospital incinerator…

Instead, she must be written off: a total wreck. The hope of making a recycling serve as metaphor of survival – absolutely not.…

The motorbike was useless too: and scrapped.

'I regret,' says Hammond, 'that she used that bike – against her principles. And then – the end. What lessons learned, how can we avoid...? Should we inter her? Pollute? And call her friends?'

'Her friends,' I say. 'Are bunkered down in apprehension. As for a burial – I put her in a paper shroud and laid her underneath a tree.… It seemed quite fitting – when she hit the truck manoeuvring in that narrow lane, she flattened out exactly where the logo was – "Animal Treats". The shroud is edible, I think.… As for the rally bike – it was in tune with her and got her quicker where she hoped to go.…'

I don't see Hammond not ever, not again. Events gave us a perfect ending, all the ends were tied. She finished sucked up inside a tree, or maybe into those foxes, wolves, trucked in and living poor in coppices, being fed by volunteers.… She'll test the boundaries of what is natural – enter the great chain of who eats who or what – lower into higher, until it's back down to fire and worms.…

Annemarie believed all threats, and she was right; she lived them through, fought and resisted where she could – a kind of therapy and a benevolence to all.… I'd followed her, but lacked her vision and her courage. I was the sufferer, and survived. She, the messenger who died.

CINEMA

'Make them long,' says Petrov. 'You're my assistant, Yannik – you must have ideas, repetitious ones, and very long. If I let you, you would fill the cinema all day, and tell the same tale in a hundred different ways – your faith, your mistresses, ordeals, a sour portrait that might be me. Art is like that – Mahler only wrote one symphony, but it came out in instalments – so keen was he on what he thought, he repeated it exactly, indefinite times, infinity – using his own and anyone else's words. Opus Unique!

'Webern, instead, said all he ever wanted in a piece that lasted fifteen seconds – very soft and very loud. It was all there. Which should you prefer? Why, both of them – but that's all ancient stuff. I see from your stone face you never heard of either, your bum's not made for concert halls – you're "on your feet and wave your arms and clap your hands". I'll cut your nonsense down, you'll see! You'll disappear, but mustn't cry – you're in an industry as if … you're making Lamborghinis, and what do you care if one goes off the corniche and fragments on the rocks? You don't know what Lamborghinis are, of course: let's say they are a kind of magic cake that makes you very small or very large – like movies. Exactly so: some make you fly, some make you drown – like Lamborghinis. You'll drive around the world, quite aimlessly, belonging everywhere, but disappeared….' And he laughs.

You don't need laugh with him.

He goes on, 'You've had a life of grandiose idiocy. Take the tragedy in your stride – you're on the way to farce, your pilgrim's stave – a yard of sausage: your penitential whip – an octopus of tripe. Don't think of suicide – that's in the script, but there's an oratorio of laughs to come, they've not yet been bellied out….

'A sad clown with pants half-mast? Just improvise! Bring on the Aida trumpeters, let's see the hippos dance – up to the high wire, drink the gin, play the drunk and tumble – aaaah! and glide down on a swan's wide wings…. Amaze, alarm – your audience knows nothing, thinks only of its cancer, dreams of candy floss … but never try to shock! They've done everything, everything abominable that makes you vomit at the thought, each one a star of theatre of cruelty and the absurd, black belt in sadomaso, old hands in eating friends and crucifying foes…. Love them. Love pleasing them.

'Do not be wise. Eschew the beautiful. One day you'll die, it won't be fun, and if you're lucky – all alone; no bell and book, no audience rejoicing that it's you, not them…. Remember! Think of death a lot. Expect nothing but incomprehension, and don't use actors, not for anything, don't let them near your food; lock up your cat and dog, your kids, your lovers, and your car….'

Petrov's a great man, an artist. Already I have learned a lot….

'Are you a democrat?' he asks. 'Do you think that changing ideas as you go along is best? Do you jazz and improvise? Or is it – Vote for the Auguste, put a pistol in his hand.... We're all equal, just our makeup differentiates one from the next....'

'I haven't felt the need,' I say. 'I never asked what worked, or what came next. Annemarie told me what to do, and what to be done was already there – or coming. Or had been.'

'Because,' he says, 'in cinema, you can't change anything, film's an autocracy, except that you can jig the story and the order things might happen in ... but not how they turn out in the end. In this way, it's realistic – futuristic, if you like. It's realistic, but it isn't real, you know. You'll enjoy living there, we all do, those of us who like to make a story up.... Of course, it's mostly horrible, that's realistic too, but sometimes there is sex, or kindness, but you'll find that those won't last. Don't trust the story if it seems they do.... The wars – they never end, but you, you always do....'

'I think I shall enjoy myself,' I say. 'It's really complex – and it takes a squad of you to make a simple tale....'

'I supply philosophy,' he says. 'Then the money comes. I don't know how. Remember to avoid the actors, anyone will do instead, if you need some figures, figurines – there is the janitor, the lady washing floors ... you must be democratic in your attitudes. You did do '68, I hope?'

'Oh,' I say. 'I'd heard of it. Perhaps I inherited, but I am much too young....'

'No way,' he says and laughs, 'No one's too young to do their '68!'

BREUGHELLAND

'If people find their imagination's blocked,' says Petrov, 'sat in the dark, with popcorn in their lap – in real life, they're not so slow in doing what I should not contemplate – the whole, the *grand macabre*. In life, they roast and fry and boil their fellows, long-lost cousins, pen-friends, comrades, co-religionists – they see them stretched, compressed, tossed high and buried live – perhaps they give a shudder, then the image fades. So – I'm not involved in that

– it's all been done in puppet theatres, a hundred years ago, before the studios – and the world – could be organized and built as it is done today….'

He pauses, and it's like there was Annemarie who's addressing me. 'We don't exploit that genre,' he says. 'Horror, the cruel and the absurd. It's mostly adolescents and real tiny ones who get off on the *Macabre….* No. We must be sophisticates. We feel the heat, the mud, the floods and sand … our skins erupt, our humours swirl, we see the soldiers on parade, the missile tubes are trundled past – ready to exterminate us all for reasons bad or excellent … but – remember, we're not into that! No documentary – not like the guys have trekked and measured, been on tv, been framed, denounced, and into court…. So, why repeat?'

'I'm absolutely with you there,' I say. 'I've been a volunteer, slave to some scientists, a measurer of permafrost, guardian of mangrove forests, all that stuff … I've dealt with people too. You're right, sophistication is the key….

'There's action, Petrov. Spies and soldiers, politics, vendetta. It's mostly guns,' I say. 'Then there is uplift – angels – but they're dull. Monsters and ghosts, transmogrification. Real life, a novel – what's your choice?'

'I can't do those,' he says. 'I didn't do the course. You left out sex. But I'm like you, I'm not so keen. It's a bit … peep-showy. Vulgar even. There was one that went six hours, I hear. Me – I have my special tastes, I don't propose to share….'

'That leaves the awful future – the warming – or the warning – mode; apocalypse,' I say.

'You know,' he says. 'Telling the possibilities – they sound so trite. You didn't mention history – I've seen the tin suits that they wore. Straight out the Wizard. You hire the horses, I believe – you get to sell the horse-shit, or if you've mushrooms – it's a boon….'

We look glumly at each other. 'Now,' he says, '*Fitzcarraldo*. That, I'd love to do. Alas – someone got there first. A sequel? I don't think….'

'I heard of it,' I say. 'But I am much too young…. It's like my '68….'

'A movie can cost millions,' Petrov says. 'Even those that have been done – and done again. While we think of which to do, we might raise the money, have a good time?'

'Even stevens, Petrov?' I ask him.

'I never heard of those,' he says. 'You'd get your ten per cent, of course....'

CHINA

'This is the movie,' says Petrov, after much argument, many plans coming undone. He hands me a folder....

Moments of tranquility, of beauty in small movements, in a coordination of effort, practiced so often it becomes a sudden thrust, a twist and retreat – like a fencer's....

'This is what the world is like when it is China's turn,' says Petrov. 'I haven't decided on the music yet.'

'But – it seems this is more of an opera,' I say.

'There's much you can do in opera that you can't in movies,' he says. 'And this is not to be filmed. It's real life.'

'This,' I say, borrowing in the bundle. 'Is a kind of map. But it's only distances, from a central place, a meridian. It doesn't show more.'

'You wouldn't need show more,' says Petrov, impatiently. 'You must know where you'd want to go.'

'The politics is left out,' I say. 'But of course, all the shouting and banging, exhortation wouldn't be part of it....'

'That's right,' he says. 'That's for quite other kinds of hegemony. Many people aren't so proud of how they got what they have. Some just storm their way and have flags and coffins – to me, in this case, it's not germane.'

'I'm not sure if you're inside or outside, Petrov,' I say. 'Are you assimilated, acculturated – or observing?'

'You work that out in rehearsal,' he says. 'There can be different versions. It's like Boris Godunov – you might cut men out of one version entirely – just as an exercise.'

'For the fun of it,' I say. 'So the apocalypse has been postponed?'

'I don't see where I could fit that in,' he says. 'I couldn't do the journey down the river, or the coronation. I think you'd need to show more space, people moved around to where they could survive. They don't like that, of course.... But we agreed – we don't want a movie or an opera, a shadow play – a chart – not about liking anything, or making a big thing of sex and guns.'

'Right,' I say. 'And the theme is great. We should mute the drama and the shouting.'

'You see?' he says. 'It takes hold. It must be absolutely un-American, un-colonial; in the French or English sense – anti-imperial. But spiky, peppery. Even shrill, at times. Not Russian, if you get me....'

'No heroics?' I ask, knowing the answer.

'Absolutely not,' he says.

'We should set out at once, to get backers, and the best producer,' I say. 'And I'll brush up my mandarin.'

'The theme,' he says, 'It's magnificent. Not to be thrown away, or diluted.'

Everyone acknowledges – it's a great theme. Fitzcarraldo, they know, put a toe in the *macabre*.

Petrov was a natural to pull off the re-make. But 'China' was a step – a flight of steps – up higher. It was, alas, too big. Cinema's an industry, stuck in the present – it can't admit the future, the potential, except as caricatures. There's the fixation on the dinosaurs: on love in war: on explosions and the simulating of a violent death. That's it. My idea, the scenario – it was admired, and never breathed.

'What's my best contact?' I ask Erin, an old guy who stacks the pizza tins, the celluloid, and labels them.

'Pedrov is,' he says. 'He lives like that – he pollinates, his assistants blossom, the seeds are poison. He grows dwarf thorn trees, his assistants must carpenter palaces from them. He helps you become a genius – and everything you do is sterile.... Did no one warn you?'

'Oh yes,' I say. 'Maybe that's what the admonitions were. But – who wouldn't want to be a genius?

'I reason – Pedrov has cash, and anyone at all, anywhere – will take his cash. So this is no place, and the best place – Russia. China – is dull. It's not an interesting place to live, it drives you mad with being dull. But Russia – sometimes the dome breaks – because of how it's made, or something falling from outside and cracking it, or someone moves a stone, and others too and then it all falls down and there's a new dome underneath, you never thought it might be there, all shiny, burnished.... The Izmailovskiy! – nearly dead but resurrected ... warehouse to cathedral, forward and back ... a monolingual empire, a cold tongue.... Russia too is dull, unless you know that everything that's permanent is not....'

Erin waits patiently for me to stop what he has heard in bars, shebeens and icy woods – a hundred times.

'You were a slave to science – you thought it was to love,' he says. 'You wanted to invent – but just did experiments. And now – you want to be creative! It will not happen. Find yourself a niche. You're set up to be a walk-on in the *Macabre*. It won't be made, not ever. It's what you, what we all, are. It's not a movie – it's an illusion, the great one. A portrait, self-portrait. So good – it's what exists. But then, you'll say – even a bad portrait exists. Yes, but a *very* good one – you can't tell what is from what is!... It's what we are; what is. If you like – it's what we think we are, what we know we are. I'm sure you've done mescalin. It's you, it's in your head. It's not a heightening, nor distortion – it's your brain, what it wants to see ... what it *does* see. Pedrov didn't create you, you do it all yourself.'

'I don't believe it,' I say. 'Not one bit.'

'That's the genius,' Erin says. 'He invented something that is just the same if you believe it or you don't. It's being – you can't disbelieve in it – but what does believing in being mean? Nothing. Like – nothingness is something you believe in and so – it's there! It means – and so do you. What? Who knows. Go see the movie. It will not be made. You can't find backers.

'You believe in China, though?' he asks. 'That won't be made. It's more likely that it would be, but it's too hot to touch....

'Oh yes,' I say. 'Every China. I believe in all of them, and all to come.'

'That's what I say,' he says. 'No one will ever make the movie – not until it's all gone by, and maybe not even then. You know – maybe there's no need. We are the *Macabre*. A China will come and have its turn. Why make the movies?'

'I must do something,' I say. 'Reality – you tire of it. Today's a bore. This moment – palls. Movies are the best….'

We laugh. 'Exactly!' Erin says. 'Where it says "way out" means – you're in the street. Waiting in line for the next showing.'

'It moves swiftly, this discussion, Erin,' I say. 'I imagine you were Petrov's assistant in your day….'

'Well,' he says, and laughs some more. 'My day is now – a bore. The discussion moves? It may be the only thing that doesn't – but yes, a lot of us end up like me. I am like lots of us … the guy that plays the triangle in the orchestra started as conductor, and he's written fifty symphonies … we all have, but just a few still play an instrument. The rest of us are archivists and stack the scores….'

I feel like crying. Truth is something I have never sought, nor wanted – here it is. Erin.

I have the script of 'China', should I add one original, 'Macabre'? – neither ever will be made … what is plausible, what is – will never find a backer….

'I'm troubled, Erin,' I tell him: 'China's day. It's epoch: free at last…. But suppose … we all fall in a hole. To me, a hole you can fall into – means it isn't full. And yet, the holes you fall in and can't get out or even see where you are at – no bottom and no top…. They're all around us, invisible unless – you fall in….'

'Oh Yannik,' Erin says, and laughs. 'I knew you'd come up with that one! We're simple cinema folk. The movies, and the stars – are not just global – they are universal. I'm in Russia now, but where is Russia? – why – strolling on "Waterloo Bridge"! Veronica Lake! That's the lake, not Baikal – or did I hear Bacall? If we don't grasp an argument, or get it wrong – who cares? No one corrects us. We are not a "thing", an institution: a prof, a sage, a general, that cares if it is right or wrong. We're like the snake that finds a crack and squeezes in – and if it can't get out – who knows? Where did the cat's tail end up? In the universe, does anything get lost? Who knows. If you can't find it – what does that signify...? Has it disappeared, like keys you put down somewhere, and….'

I feel the void, its fullness, its inescapable density, its darkness and I'm trapped. It's like Annemarie had said – that what is inescapable can't just be dodged, or avoided just by planting trees. It's what it says – you can't escape, you die, but other people don't.

You'll never know – are you the only one? Maybe mortality affects just you, and all the rest live on. And on. Perhaps you are the sacrifice that guarantees immortality for all the rest – their conquests, more prisoners to offer up … and so and so….

'It's terrifying, Erin,' I say. 'I understand I'm the *Macabre* – but that is inescapable, for nothing can be other than what it is…. And is that all there is? What we, and telescopes, can see? It doesn't seem so – all changes, all expands, creates … nothing is fixed. There is no time and then there is….'

'Oh,' he says. 'But you forget – the cinema's the *Danse.* Dancing doesn't signify. We cine-folk can weave in and out before and afters, like a needle that knits up … holes in your pants, in space – whatever gets worn out. Holes in your dancing shoes, or bullet holes….'

We laugh.

'It's Petrov, Erin,' I conclude. 'He throws out these scraps of sequences and thinks you'll glue them into sense, coherence … a story that'll keep us in our seat….'

'Fission or fusion?' Erin asks. 'Which makes the bigger bang? The bigger frisson? Remember – we can set things up, but there's an end – and not *the* end. Still the sign glows by the Gents – "Way Out". Be thankful, as my granny said, for little things.'

I carry 'China' everywhere, next to my skin.

*

It's time for some normality.

She's young, Galina, old-fashioned name, blue eyes, black hair, from the Kuban. Cossack. Seventeen, she says. 'I need a partner, Yannik,' she says, straight off. 'We could train, exercise together. You're out of shape, and so's your face….'

Maybe she saw it in a puppet show – on a gallows; as a cop … a scary portrait in a film….

At once, we're like those magnets you can't pull apart, attractions in a fairground, some strong man is planted, he's the challenge, and the hayseeds try to show they're stronger. Nothing pulls them apart, the rings, the current's flowing, but…. In this case, there's no strong man – instead, a rich man. A boss. Not old, he wears a tight white shirt. Does he groom her, monopolise and tend her, or do they make love? Would he be her choice, or does he match her price? He's given her a share, an income, an import–export biz. The kind of cover I'd have worked for, eagerly, and paid off everyone, been modest in my take, and pleased not to go to war, or into a catastrophe....

In this place, it's normal to pay off the woman that you fancy – before a move is made; to tie her in. Work; a place to live: that's the down payment – two addresses and no sweat. It's an arrangement; if you've cash, everybody does it here. If you don't, you might not spend your money before it disappears....

'Yannik,' she says. 'I appoint you cousin. Chaperone. You can be seen with me. Ah! How I love you, you're my treasure, I wear you as a princess would – on my body, on my head, like a princess should.... You are my soul.'

And so it goes. For the place, arrangements like this are the norm. They do not satisfy, but they inspire. No one is free, or thinks to be, nor satisfied, nor thinks to be. Galina is inspired – she has a brain, it's not decided where to turn itself – and as for me, I've been inspired, I carry 'China' with me, even when we run, embrace, and watch the swans, the cormorants, the lake....

'I love you, Galina,' I say, as if she might forget.

'You mustn't touch me there,' she says, pushing my hand. 'It's a disputed spot. Yuri claims it as his own, his future, I say it's mine, and now – you have designs....'

'It seems there is no choice,' I say. 'We couldn't stand America....'

'I'm not into movies,' says Galina. 'They're too risky. Americans can afford to lose – they're used to it. And you have to wait years for one you liked at first to come around again.

'"China" – it's obvious. I can live with that. Put it on. The other – what's *Fitzcarraldo*?

'An old German film,' I say. 'About the damage you do when you escape, and climbing the mountain and finding an empire that you should leave alone.... Actors you kill so's they don't kill you. And opera. A metaphor for life. Or empire. Mainly opera. We can't do that.'

I don't mention *Le grand macabre.*

'Poor people,' she says, not committing, not coming down for wealth or penury. 'You think – easiest to conquer. But poor empires beat the rich. The Westerners are asking for it. Lots of kids in school were called Genghiz – they knew history. The poor are those who sing the most – if you're hungry, or want to be heard without a fuss, cops beating you....'

'It hadn't struck me so,' I say. 'In movies, really everyone is rich, but you can pretend anything you want.'

'But there are soldiers,' she says. 'I bet there are in "China" too. In real China, they used to be scorned, rather. Useful, but – not gentlemen. If you are urging on your soldiers, it's best you don't know them personally. Almost none of them comes back. Do soldiers help, if you want to go beyond? – like "art beyond art"...? That's what I want. Ah, if only there was still expressionism. I can express....'

'You're right about soldiers,' I say. 'There are substitutes, but the trigger finger's built into all of them. You need the uniforms – legal reasons, I believe. Of course, there's warriors – they survive better.'

'Everything you say, Yannik,' she says. 'Sounds trivial. It's cute, but it's wearing. I think I'll go to painting classes.'

And so she does.

We shall always love each other, naturally. It's a fixation, almost. I have to go around, seeing people about 'China'. It's not a great country to try that.

'Earlier,' I tell Galina. 'We explored nature and humanity – me and Annemarie. I concluded nature was done for, and humanity was in no condition to repair it. Not nature, nor itself. As part of nature, humanity was quite disastrous. Omnivorous and indiscriminate.

'As part of humanity – Annemarie on the Rally bike was a disaster.

'I'd visited the catastrophes – nothing led me anywhere.

'The cinema was neither here nor there – for sure, not in humanity, and with all its puff and business – a long way from nature too.

'When you're a little older, you'll decide if I reasoned adequately – and make suggestions – about what is left for me to do.'

It sounded flat. That's the pitch Galina loves.

'You've done everything, Yannik,' she says. 'A conclusion would be too much. A cherry on your bowl of them. No one would be interested. Petrov has had his fun with you, you've broken off with Hammond. Annemarie was broken up. Time to start again. The future! What matters what you think of it?'

'I'm convinced the cinema is not for me,' I say. 'It won't even register that I've left.'

'It's easy to escape from me,' she says. 'That's the straightforward part. But can you escape from love, your love for me? You're whole, not damaged, not a chip.... And as for damaging – that's your problem, you don't know how. None of us can. It's not allowed – not even damaging ourselves – we're valuable in the immaculate state.'

'Well then,' I say. 'That's done for me and my conclusions. Stasis! Talk to me, Galina! Stir the air!'

'I'm late for class,' she says. 'The teacher is a genius – he'll do my portrait, even without my clothes....'

'People will see you as you see yourself,' I say. 'It's rather dumb. Realism without the socialism.'

'I like dumb things,' she says.

Bird cages: imported, exported. Some for wrens, some large as a cathedral. Yuri and guys like poorer Yuris, bring in forms, compiled and signed. All bird cages. In, out.

'Birds come in different sizes,' Galina says. 'So they need houses fit to live in. It's trade, Yannik, not wine-tasting. The birds fly on these paper wings ... bills of lading – that stuff. You don't hear them sing, that's all.'

'I believe you, Galina,' I tell her, my fingers crossed. 'Every belief is water – we drown in some, and some we drink. Every movement of the people, each war, incursion – is fruitful. No one ever dies in vain: every written word resonates, gives life. Khotanese Saka: discloses a tall family tree of tongues. "The Hsien-Pi's horses were swifter and their weapons sharper than those of the Hsiung-nu" ... the fire-worshippers, the *Magi*, turn up when unexpected. Can you say what these people did, were? And that what we have found out is forgotten: better so, not worth the effort? It would mean all that *we* do, unless it obliterates everything, is equally of value.

'What I know is less, much less, valuable, than what I don't. I promise you it's so – and you're the same!'

'Brave words, Yannik,' says Galina, much impressed. 'These way-bills – they really should go lost. It means a failure of your thesis, but too bad! And if we destroy ourselves – you're right, it's interesting, but there'd be no one to read about it, and appreciate. No consequence for us, after the end!'

She sees I'm trying to put the present in its past, to leave something of today that someone might pick up and assign a value to – tomorrow, when we've forgotten each other's name.

Everyone is interested in it – 'China'. No one commits.

'I give up, Galina,' I say.

'You had such insights,' she says, wistfully. 'All these wars, the languages they spoke, the burial and the planting techniques – all useful. Like our wars – they've rolled like wind over the cornfields.... And produced our world – its bad bits and the good. The good, Yannik! What we should celebrate, defend, risk atom bombs! Think of that. Maybe "China" was one of the successes, unacknowledged and unseen. A good. History is piebald, and we must welcome every shade – it produces the agglomerations, the devotion – what we can't accept and what we can identify with.... Bigger and bigger – the empires are called civilizations, the big yield to the bigger – big's admired and documented.... However it got big – go large: that is the winning strategy....'

We stare at one another. Our romance – for sure it's piebald. Could it be a poison fruit – or just a mouldy one – or a pomegranate, a fruit of good and evil...?

'Who gave us all these fables, recipes that disguise foul medicines, to get them down? Can there be some earth mother, a monstrous babushka, primed to have the world accept what botch and smudge produce...?' I ask. 'The larger, with most soldiers, wins: that's what we admire, what we trudge towards....'

'I told you, Yannik,' Galina says. 'You have your feet. I've not yet cut them off. If you want out – just leave....'

And that I do.

*

I'm a buzzard. I'm caged, labelled, on a truck – in my bowl – there are pirozhki.

They send me through to Trabzon. In the book, the towers are memorable, there's even a romance. But here the sea is dirty, shrinking, oily: the city grey, industrial and featureless. The smell is everywhere, ships scuttled, every stinking cargo sent down below, to fester.

I'm unloaded.

'There's a pigeon,' someone says. 'A huge one. Huddled in its cage.'

'Take the message, let it fly away,' a woman says. 'They don't go back to where they came from. The sky is full of necklaces – the circling messengers – the warnings we wouldn't heed.'

Or read. The earthquake that will send down Holy Wisdom, Ayasofya, tumble the walls: at the last, drain out the sea....

'Galina sent me,' I tell her: 'Destroy the paperwork, I'll walk away. I'm just a bird – no papers, no identity.

'Even for me, misnamed, misidentified – hawk, kite, vulture, falcon – there's excess. I'll never eat all the carrion, here, all over – the earth spreads out, a vast sheet of offal, drying like pemmican in the sun. Too much! I don't have the appetite....'

'Too bad,' says Galina's contact, Kismet, tossing my conveyancing in a bin. 'You're not my hawk, my Mehmet. Just a scruffy tripe-eater. What did you think that you could do? Be a Garuda bird? Attain the spiritual – a cleanser, chronicler, friend of the demi-urges, gliding on the spirals ... a peacock? What happened? Lost your tail?'

'I want to show what I have seen. And what it means, and that it is the truth,' I say.

'You want to be Vishnu,' says Kismet, throwing my cage into the lock-up, piled high with containers, perches, aviaries. 'Here, that's not allowed.

'We could have you shipped to Paris, but I doubt you will be Proust. You don't have friends – you're sociable, but quite aloof, elitist and obscure ... exactly all the things not fashionable. You question time, but while you gaze – it's passed, it's gone! No trace – nothing stuck to it, no golden girls, no retreats. You're a black hole, you suck in the light. Your gut's sweet spot – it craves the dear deceased: you have a taste for death, my friend. All round, there is a glut of cadavers and moribund … go north or south, the fields, the woods, the desert sands – a feast, Yannik! Eat, be eaten, be a dervish, a poor man with a vow – I'm indifferent.'

'Am I the first Galina's sent?' I ask Kismet.

'Galina – and Yuri – send me a host,' she says. 'You're the first buzzard, though. She has the eye – not for men, nor women – but for birds. Their spirits, characters. She's right – when there was the flood – the animals were drowned – but not the birds. They found a place to perch – on the ark, on floating stuff.… And here you are. Full of the dead.'

'I know,' I say, blushing. 'It's my strong point. I wish … if only things could be otherwise. But, history's the only thing you can be entirely sure about, although you never are; but that's your problem, after all.'

'Be careful not to know too much,' she says, 'or you'll never learn another song. Leave room for afters.'

'And the dance,' I add. 'You think I'll never do what I set out to do? To find? Invent?'

'I don't feel sorrow,' Kismet says. 'There's too much going on around, we must forget again where we have come from, where we took our names, beliefs, the uniforms.… But if I once was sorry, it would be for you, Yannik, poor man.'

Her desk is yellow, yellow oak. Her hair is hennaed, with a streak of green. The colours of a parrakeet, I think. She's very fragile, legs too thin to bear her skimpy weight, or risk a *fouetté* … and yet.… 'This is where we muster them, and send them on,' she says. 'Galina – Russia – now, only a branch plant. There's nothing there now, just the melt. Of course,' and she stretches out her twiggy legs, lets me see up to her tiny drawers, she lifts her bonelike arms above her head – 'I don't fly, of course. Everything is changed. The ordering of everything, the states, the powers: the small are magnified for a while, the middling – hold the balances.…'

She cries, quite silently. 'Oh,' she says, 'It's so hard, being here not knowing where we stand and if we'll fall – I'm not a monster, Yannik, but I see them all around … And here you are, chased out of the barren forest … your destiny – just rocks and sand.…'

'Oh come!' I say. 'I really never think, take stock – a chapter closes, I don't know what's next! That's the good part of my life – bewilderment. What I should do to be quite different….

'My movie script – "China". It's brilliant, but suppose – things turn out different? Or – exactly like it says. What would be done…. I need advice, not enthusiasm….'

'I'd take you home,' she says, 'and show you passion as it used to be…. But you don't have the faith. You don't know even how to pretend. I should dispatch you, keep you safe, and send you on, find a safe place if there was one….'

'And if you show me passion, Kismet,' I say. 'What will that tell me? It might make me have the faith …. I've been everywhere, I know there's no safe place – not in nature, nor humanity…. Passion and faith – they've been recommended … very hard to find …'

'What will that tell you, Yannik?' Kismet asks, composing her clothes, herself, snapping her pince-nez on her nose, and scribbling notes.

'That's it, then,' I say. 'I'm free to go.'

'That's all you're free to do,' she says. 'We two are done.'

This place has all the soldiers that it needs – more, even. They used to walk around, hand in hand. Now they can't – their arms get in the way!

In Russia, the soldiers were all elsewhere. In America, I'm told, they have their own cities, so you usually don't see them – but they're always overhead – here and there and on the way.

They have a way here, to get results: they made the Kurds escort and kill Armenians. It can turn and turn about, of course. That is what I've learned – the investigators are investigated, the meek are set upon the bold….

A Turkish friend had Armenian neighbours – she climbed a tree and shot at them. She sensed a plot, she says. A woman of great delicacy – she did a picture of the family they'll find on the moon, if they decide to build the rocket big enough … she didn't sell her work – she'd too much character to be an artist, she knew it, would have changed – but … how would you do that? Change yourself, change utterly. And would it work?

I take out 'China', sit and read it over – it calms and reassures. It's like a mother's goodnight kiss.

It's not who you are, or what you want. You've landed in the future, so what matters is where you came from, what you think, what kind of future you propose for living in the future when this future has become the past. All such places have a comfortable past they'll nestle into when they aren't the future. Galina dispatched me – she was loyal. Kismet unlocked me – she could sell me, not for treasure but to gain credit for herself. But – she's contented – in that little body that can't get littler, that's nothing superfluous at all, a brain quite likewise. I'm in the future, quite alone – a soldier of fortune, lover of what's to come, already scripted … 'China'! That's espionage. People are locked up for that, until they forget the past, lose hope in their future and so then you can have them abjure the scenario, the 'China' because it doesn't correspond to what you see – whatever the real seems to be around you – desks, uniforms, the questions you'd enjoy replying to but they don't ever come.

Erin – too knowing. He'd sell me. Petrov – he'd not want me as another of his troubles. No, it's my being in those wars, the dry places and the flooded ones, the empty and the overcrowded … everywhere that doesn't end up in a future that you'd like to have. That is the Holy Wisdom! Coming through – out the other side. Trust in what you don't believe in, there's nothing more sure.…

There's a monkey on a perch, paid to fool around. He pulls your nose, sneaks your wallet, pees on your shirt – and while he's having fun, he takes the side-blow to shell the sack of peanuts his owner sets for him. Work and mischief.… He's a multi-tasker – pain in the neck. Who would follow that dead end? The joker and the clueless worker, bound in one …the ape of God. Father of man, my brother and my son. Forget it!

While I'm there, philosophising, two guys come up. They are selling: dope? A holiday with fake steamer tickets? Twenty minutes in a cat-house?

'Can't pay, won't pay,' I say – the monkey goes on shelling – maybe he's a part of it, the scam. I'm all alone. The first blow's a surprise. That's the one that hurts the most, and goes on working, but the kicks must do more damage – our insides, we have to take on trust, are full of tubing, wiring, that you mustn't touch and no one understands. I fall down; it should mean part of me's protected, lying on the ground. Don't believe me – it isn't so.

It's pointless, so it's worse. You can't defend yourself – you're dazed, too stupid to explain – the cops think the bandits are your mates.

Maybe you were carrying? Selling or propositioning? It is their job, they take hours doing it, and Galina didn't send the documents, because there were no visas anyway … the monkey left, and thinking about evolution and wanting it to stop – it doesn't help. The dinosaurs produced more models than Detroit – the humans settled on the one – an ur-Toyota, or a Chrysler … and you're it.

Why do the cops think I'm from Serbia?

Because they're looking for a person who is, and hope it's me.

They can send me to a camp for deportation, but they can't send me back to Galina. I wasn't really there. I can't ask Kismet – she isn't really there – her slightness, her poise on the edge of being blown down among our feet … so delicate, so nearly not anywhere – I cry a little. For her.

The law is complex. I might go anywhere, Iran, Syria … not back to Galina...? There is a lady lawyer – very harassed, partially informed, with clients dripping through her hands like minestrone.... 'Where do you belong?' she asks. 'Where do you want to go?' 'Your wishes don't count.' 'You must have some back-story and documents, everybody has.'

So, it's good the cops don't come. It hurts, but you stay where you are, propped up, and no one opens up your case. I cry a little for myself.

There's paranoia here – they're right. There always is a plot. It's best to put your feet into modernity – it's learnt a lot about your weaknesses – and put another foot back into history, your paradise, invention – the warm nest beneath the oak.

'Galina sent me here' – that's all I know, and it's catastrophe.

They used to ask, 'What shall I do to be saved?' Too late for that. Rather, what must I do to fit the crisis I live in? Annemarie gave many answers – grow trees, give food: grow what you eat. Don't travel. Travel where there's people dying.

Well – you can find ways to accommodate all that. Join the army – any army, any intelligence; spy and denounce, betray trust – all loyalty is extorted, all is false. Take risks: assassinations. Abstinence and silence: break the system – deeds not speeches.

A catastrophe might suggest different strategies, lots, would be a help. For me, it must always be the biggest single answer, test – that I shall surely fail.

I'm like that. An absolutist.

Then – I remember. I'm neutral, out of it. I don't involve myself – I can do anything I want, or nothing, nothing at all. I have the script: 'China' – I can go East – to China or its sphere. Or elsewhere – its allies and competitors. If you know too much, you can't rest, can't perch. Some people can stay where they want – I'm a consignment, I'm packed up and sent.

*

'I read the script. It's brilliant,' Ruggero says. 'No one will make it. It's possible, might happen, so it's banal – too close.'

'You may be right,' I say. 'I must get out. This place – full of loose ends. A huge empty airport, suburbs full of peasants, nothing to do, everybody scared of jail. If you've not taken sides, it means you are on all of them.'

'It's strange,' he says. 'They knew exactly how to make a revolution, and no one ever did. Now, everyone knows how a future will be made, but no one wants to hear.'

'It's destiny,' I say, and think of Kismet, slight as paper. They don't think like we do,' I say. 'Despatchers and receivers, lawyers and cops – their lives are full of misses … near-misses, wrong addresses, people falling in the cracks, the wrong country invaded, listening to someone else's intelligence.... And yet – all the words like justice and equality, used and misused for centuries – there is the chance of seeing if you could attain them. Maybe not, in all probability … where there are definitions, no one will give you rope, a margin – the rope is always someone else's, and will be used on someone else....'

'Oh come, Yannik,' Ruggero says, and laughs. 'Did you expect you'd drop in, sell your idea, get a destination and find a bower that fitted some vague words that have no real equivalents? Esteem, respect, and recognition? All in an afternoon?'

'Yes,' I say. 'That's what happens, that's what you can do. Some of it, at least. A passport?

'If I went to China, I don't think they would enthuse.

'Would the French buy into movies about their time in the Sahel, the British ruling India, Americans in Iraq, Afghanistan? … anyone can see how those unroll. Take the first step, and the others – all the future, is set out.'

'You're stuck in countries, Yannik,' says Ruggero. 'All capitalist, or aspiring so, all in the web, worldwide. Your China – is different: not a country, it's an idea.…'

'A world,' I say. 'In Petrov's treatment. Not to be liked or not. Without a plot, no human interest, no robots somersaulting and having intercourse, no hero, and no worth. That's why it's brilliant, unsaleable. An Iroquois who made a story about American presidents – when he saw the first caravelles on the horizon – would he, would she, be honoured at the inauguration?'

'Just think,' he says. 'How difficult it is to sort you out. The real is like Pompei –it's there, beneath two kilometres of ash. When you get there, everybody's dead, like playing Statues.…

'And if you're shipped somewhere, you'll simply disappear … hawking your script. No finance, no contacts, no crew and no one interested. If you wonder what death's like, you're well into the experience.…' And he laughs.

'Already I am damaged, that is true,' I say: it quite surprises me. 'I'm no one's dog, and I'm glad, especially as – I'm a special dog, one who sings and dances. You're like me, Ruggero, no one's dog, and you are special too – you collect gnawed bones, and sell them on. Alas, my songs and dance – you don't know what to do with them – besides, the words, any words, and any sense, may cause offence. They're meant to. The dance is pitiful – it's like the shuffle the bears do, the dancing bears whose paws are mutilated so they stand erect. No – it's the words. They speak of vanity, Ruggero, of you, and of your destiny.'

I think of Kismet – it only takes a paper-clip to weigh her down, to stop her being wind-borne – with nothing out of place … And yet – the cages come, the birds step out, and disappear … She's part of it, the great Grey *Armee Fraktion,* chancing those fragile *biscuit* arms, gambling with her double *marramao,* two thumbs flaring from the nose: 'catch me if you can'.… And they will, Kismet, they always do. Quite useless to resist: guilty as charged, of dumb subversion, and even guiltier of what they didn't know, of fiddling documents, transporting shady types, spies and deserters, terrorists, embezzlers, bankers and paedophiles … even me, the innocent, crumbled into the living soup.

How could I get away, Kismet? You freed me, but left that cable of indefinite length tied to my Achilles heel…. Confidences – build affection, unwanted words. Words are designed so there is no end to them….

I take against Ruggero …

'Help me, you bastard,' I shout. 'I'll denounce you – blasphemer, schemer against the president! Kurd! Friend of our enemies, intriguer, Arab, artist of the coup, subversive, plotter….

'Forget my stupid script – what will come will come! Accept!

'Your feeble citations of Marcuse and Heidegger, pretending you were in the trench – a sergeant in Debord's platoon … they condemn you, condemn utterly without appeal … hypocrite and mocker….

'Help me! Or I'll get you fifteen years in solitary, for obscene and treasonable publications, taking kickbacks – milliards of yuan. I'll break you, stomp you – false revolutionary, arms trafficker, fomenter of mutinies…. Corrupter….'

He laughs. 'You're a shadow, Yannik. I'm covered. I have guys who choreograph the big ones. Mostly – they're robots, the autocrats, the elected. So, don't think of assassination, not worth the bother….'

'Don't go on, Ruggero,' I say. 'Into the *grand Macabre.* My speciality.'

'But you've no sense of humour,' Ruggero says. 'You think it's vulgar, frightening – the flames, the masks, the stony wastes. You're stuck in olden times. Remember, "the second time as farce" – we had the tragedies, the fall of empires, collapse of the shamanic worlds. Now, is the farce, the show: Las Vegas, Yannik.'

'The people, Ruggero,' I say. 'All around, they die, are sacrificed….'

'Nothing can make you laugh,' he says. 'If you don't see the funny side – no one can force you to. But – people … they have always died, been sacrificed … rejoice – they live much longer now...!'

'It's not a comic script,' I say.

'It's you who has to see it so,' he says. 'Besides – you did the right thing – for you. You've given up – you're not in any audience now.'

'I see the irony,' I say. 'Everybody does. The rich, the poor, go down together – only the very very rich escape – the rest are damaged, all the invention, the pretension too – goes to set up a funeral pyre.... The civilizations bite their tails, emarginate the working stiffs who run the show.... It's slapstick, *grand guignol* – not to everybody's taste. It's deeds, not gags, make the parade – excess, indifference.... The massacres, and the penury ... They said the end was nigh – and here it is! Don't be surprised – your turn will come, cast an amused eye on other people's deaths....'

'I'm sure you'll find there's lots of hope, and volunteers,' he says. 'If I were you – I'd keep my distance, and appreciate the detail ... the guards of honour, guns that salute – oh, the vanity, Yannik! The festivals, the sporting – their preening, pouting....'

'I underestimated you,' I say. 'You see a frieze, a scroll – design. I think of clan wars in Japan ... the monsters, huge boars, the soldiers exterminated – and on and on.... Chaos, indifference – but you see performances. The slaughterhouse – first come....'

'People are encouraged to be protagonists, some even ask to be,' he says. 'But life does not make everyone a star. You need the numbers – pouring anonymous over the cliffs, into the sea around the ghost ship, lost souls, souls never registered, given numbers ... and, Yannik, to be frank, your script, the "China". It is dull. I don't care if it is true, foresightful – I'll always take the same position as I have today: "No! Forget it!"

'May I be denounced? – it's probable. Then, if my powerful mates desert me, I'll end up like you. Who cares, who cares for you? I hope no one's too interested in me ...' And he laughs some more – and this time, I join in.

'There's time, there's lots of time,' he says, as if to comfort me. 'Things will go on, and on – until they really can't.'

It's bleak. He says, 'And do watch out, Yannik. Your insults show you what you are – banal and prejudiced. You're like the rest – on the slope, wavering on the edge ... proclaiming a personality you don't have....'

'I have whatever personality might suit,' I say. 'But mostly – what you are makes no difference at all.'

'If you're not one of us, and critical to boot,' he says. 'I suppose you've no emotions. You can't recruit, can't be involved, can't love or make an idiot of whatever self you are or aren't.'

'I don't see that,' I say. 'Fear, anxiety, rage and irritation....'

'Of course!' says Ruggero. 'Those are the traveller's pack, the soldier's housewife – without those, you are dead – whether you're an extra-human or a sloth ... But more involving passions – betrayal, jealousy, longing – for booze or dope, the urge to kill, betray....'

'You want me to commit,' I say, 'to what it is to be a human. What might it mean to be outside but still a biological – perhaps a moral – being, with legs and stuff, but mentally outside. At the worst – you're self-condemned. Usually – you're just expelled, locked up, abandoned, unemployed, unwanted. Not in a funny fictional way, not as a loner, oddity, not from Kafka, not in Musil, just "out". Not "in", not responsible, accountable.'

'It sounds an unexciting stance,' he says. 'What is it to be human? Who has the time or interest to know? I'd rather see you as a dissident. Probably jail-bait, with no following – an isolate, from delicacy and from standoffishness: no imitators, and no friends. Yet – everybody knows what you are dissident about. You are the conscience, that says: "the emperor has no clothes, moreover – the emperor is not the emperor, the little father is a butcher, vain and superficial...." And everybody knows it, whatever they may profess....'

'Maybe,' I say.

'You are an innocent,' he goes on. 'So, the bad things that happen to you are necessarily not deserved. They're forced on you by perversity, by malice, and stupidity....'

'That's true,' I say. 'But that's potentially for everyone. I make no case, expect no redress, no sympathy, support.'

'You know,' he says, 'China will bring another form of capitalism. There'll be no use of atom bombs on anyone, because we all know that it's their turn. People will be jailed, impoverished no doubt ... they will be different people from before, but as you've seen – there is no principle worth risking for. A shift, a jiggle, in what you're free to do? People don't read books, and if they write them – no one reads them … same with everything. “One forgets”, as the song says – there’s always other things to fill the memory….’

‘You’re wrong, I think,’ I say. ‘The emperor *is* the emperor, naked, but he has no prick. Having one – apart from everybody sizing up his anaconda! – would mean he acknowledges an other, male or female … a “something else” he seeks, has not. A purpose that requires – perhaps consent, sometimes cooperation – or a crude exercise of power.

‘The emperor has the empire – and that’s it. Unsexed. An empress – that would be a different thing entirely – the emperor walks, the empress – rides. It summons up the childhood we mostly didn’t have. “If wishes were horses….”

‘The rulers who had to move around, inspect and tax their lands, semi-nomads they’ve remained … travelled always with the mint: – largesse, status and power. Of all the institutions – you have to reproduce yourself in gold or silver – your face…. One way to resign your humanity – is to have no face.’

‘A mask?’ Ruggero wonders. ‘A cataphract, sporting a helmet that contains a face. Iron make-up – that leaves your mouth, your voice, exposed. So they can see you eat the children – like ducks consuming frogs, the legs, the croaks….’

‘You want a life of me,’ I say. ‘Exemplary. The life and loves of someone who has resigned from us.’

‘You need cash, Yannik?’ Ruggero asks. ‘That’s the subject for a film – you’d live on that, and not rejoin us, not at all. Sell that, forget the script of “China”.

‘Except – you could live free, and even critical – because you do not matter, not at all. Already we know all about you – that’s what makes people go to movies and remember them. They tell us what we know, but often do not think about….’

‘I’ll work on it,’ I say. ‘My “China”, though, has nothing to do with movies as they’ll be, when there’s a dull and vulgar future…. Besides – we shan’t get there, all will liquefy or turn to powder, we shall eat fingernails – our faces, skins will be burnt until we all resemble one another – scorched and bloated faces, Ruggero. That’s the probability, that’s what I’ve seen….’

‘It’s alarming,’ he says. ‘I understand why anyone would seek a hidey-hole.’

'All I've said,' I say, 'could be seen in a pathetic light. It may be I'm more an expressive type within than sees the company. I'm volatile....'

'Each life is an invention,' Ruggero says, prising the script of 'China' from my arms and closing it in a safe. 'How do you find something unrepeatable, that belongs to an environment uncertain, it too – unrepeated and unrepeatable? It's not like inventing the circulation of the blood – there's no reality to test what you've discovered ... and you don't know what it's for....'

'It could be,' I say, 'like setting out to discover a lake, that may appear quite seasonally, may feed a river – or may pop up in different places, when it rains here, not there ... the name's the same, but every clan calls it by a different one....'

'Yes,' Ruggero says, pushing me towards his door, 'but you've not invented anything, using this analogy. You set out to find a something that's already there ... all you invent is how you set your path, finding lakes or sink-holes – it is all the same.... Inventing light? It's always there ... no one much cares how you knew it was – no. There's something else you need – to capture light, transform it – even in a miniature ... a prism or a bulb.... That's what you invent – not light, and not your life....'

I'm in the grounds of Holy Wisdom. Kismet is my only guide. I rush to see her – 'Send me away!' I say – it's quite ridiculous.

'Hush,' she says. 'You and I – we ought not to be here. We can't just hope for somewhere else. I am from Budapest....'

Of course ... I remember, a line outside a dance-hall there, the women like tiny birds, standing on wet tramlines like swallows on a wire – so – so porcelain, so fragile....

'Only three hundred and fifty years ago,' I say, 'the Turkish artillery ... I saw their plans, the targets, in Vienna – they were cute, personal, with faces ... that's why, I suppose....'

'Yes, it was not their turn,' Kismet says. 'Anyway, I'm taking the opposite direction.... Back where we come from, from the East....'

'Like me,' I say, 'and you – you come from the *puszta*, like Galina.... The steppe – at some time we must all have come that way.... There you thought you'd ended up. Were we really ever all as one? The human kind? Did that dream urge on our departure? Or was it to be the goal?'

There's a dead end. We've no idea, how it all began, and if and when it stopped.

'The *Alföld*,' she says, 'is the great plain, full of life. And Alföldi was the historian of the City – Constantine's; Rom, Rum – Istanbul. An empty airport? Built for the peoples … all of them. Coming and going, forgetting, not recognising who we are, we were … bombarding, and retreating. Some Turks, taking over the cosmopolis, appropriating Greek names…. Leaving you and I to make the sense of it….

'Whoever thought we would be one? Some have land and some have yaks and goats – that makes us different, profoundly, and we're never one until there's communism, and we know now – it won't come. Not ever. Does it matter, concern you, Yannik? It's not part of your plan – that's good. A waste of time … we're fragments, you must accept, make the best of it, rejoice….'

'Get me out, Kismet,' I say, and she takes my face between her hands and straddles me, stares in my eyes; I smell the raki, the paprika, her desk, the mucilage, leaf-mould and mushrooms, her skin, her breath – she's pressed against me like a butterfly … she loosens her long hair so it envelops me, she croons…. I mustn't move, break her, shake the powder off her wings, we are embraced as one….

She opens wide her round black eyes … and….

'No!' she says, and laughs. Climbs off. 'No – I can't magic you somewhere, into something, else. You'll have to find a boat, a horse…. A ticket….'

'I've no papers, to identify me,' I remind her, and we laugh.

'Write down something unforgettable,' she says. 'And hand that in.'

Slowly she climbs off me, like I'm losing an anaesthetised arm or leg.

'I'm drawn to you, Kismet,' I say.

'Of course you are,' she says, patting herself in place. 'Everybody is, we are, we're made like that.'

I try to hold one of her brittle arms.

'Oh no, you naughty boy,' she says, laughing she pulls her arm through my fingers. 'You're nothing to me, just a parcel with no return address…. What can I do with you? You're covered in seals and wax, and customs stamps – why, maybe you even leak a little.... Are you fragile? Perishable? "If not collected by the date, dispose of ... in charity or dump....'"

'I know,' I say. 'The culture rules – say my passion's quite illicit. We two have no destinations, and no plans – you receive, send on, you do not weep for misdirected stuff.... I imagine you – your lodging, down by the sea, you, sitting in the ancient Ottoman veranda that overhangs the alleyway, the tamarind tree – there, the smoking lamp, the tric-trac board ... you waiting, rolling a cheroot, while your lover ... takes off his janissaries' coat, the slippers with the curly toes, and comes silently up the warped stair to your glassed-in world....'

'Oh Yannik,' Kismet says. 'How you romance. I bet they all got caponized....'

I say, 'I'm no one's destiny – I am in transit, I am even – transitory.'

What am I doing, what have I been? Where did I leave my mind, where do I return, where do I start again? What does wasting one's life mean, who knows where they are on the scroll, where I was and will be? No one answers, but everybody can, no doubt.

'Don't panic, Yannik,' Vikram says. 'We'll get you out of here. Try blowing in this paper bag.'

'I don't see any planes,' I say. 'Or steamers. I'm not escaping, have no plans to have a better life – don't tell me you're a trafficker. I can sit here on the concrete, not run any risk at all.'

I guess you'd call my film script 'China' – 'baggage'. It's my asset, under consideration. Potentially worth millions.

'You underestimate your luck, Yannik,' he says. 'You're not an actor, so you've always been exactly who you are, you're not a journalist, so your story is your own – no interpretations and no fumbling after truth.... You won't leave any cash when you are dead – it's good. You'll spend all that you ever get. Reflect on me – I'm my family's second choice. My elder brother wins the prize. Even if I have three wives – each chooses me as second best, and it's reciprocal. The third wife might be the best – but my experience shows her I'm not satisfied ... a bad judge of people ... possibly I'm sterile, or gay, or who knows what?

'You've just been rejected by the woman who parked you here, a label round your neck. You're free, competitive. You can try men, or abstinence, and no one knows. Or cares.

'My case is terrible. I was sent here to organize the planes – but none have come. Your life is lived by seconds, and it's hard, everything registered, resented, and experienced. Mine hasn't started yet – maybe it won't.... Somebody has blundered, and I shan't know who....

'Your movie won't be made, but it won't fail. Your part in it is over – actors would mess it up....'

'That's what the great man, Petrov, said,' I say. 'The subject is the future, not some guys' careers....'

And yet, and yet. I say, 'I may have something I could offer, Vikram. But there's been no takers yet.'

'Yet? The world is coming to an end,' he says. 'Life is unlivable, repetitive and hot. The final empire staggers on the stage – beset by sickness, floods and drought, cults, gurus, business religions, greed – and you will offer ... what?'

I've no reply. We stare at one another, and we weep.

'It isn't about you,' he says. 'Get back on the subject, and forget your gripes.'

The future! Yes!

'Meet my family,' Vikram says. 'It's all here, in this box.'

And so it is – a little office, aluminium, like the rest. A little boy says, 'My daddy is a spy. He writes down everyone who comes. There are no planes, but there is traffic overhead and underfoot....'

'Vikram,' I say, 'no doubt they are delightful – but the children lie. They cheat and steal and fight, and massacre the cats and tease the snakes. If this is innocence – I can't converse with it. There is no point....'

'Oh,' Vikram says, 'sometimes they play at being mute, or scream. That lets you off grown-up response.'

'But it's true,' I say, 'everyone from anywhere – they won't land here, but pass, be visible.'

'This way,' he says, 'I think I won't be killed, Yannik. I know the planes, where they come from, who'll be in them, where they land. Some countries like to kill the spies, and people think it's right. Tell me that I'm safe....'

'Do you know what the guys say?' I ask. 'When they land.... What it's all for?'

'No one knows that,' he says. 'It's all a question of whose turn is next. What matters is that spies should tell the truth. That's quite essential, and it's why we're killed.'

'Who pays you, Vikram?' I ask.

'It's not that, not at all,' he says. 'I told you. We tell the truth, that's what pays us.'

'It's too complicated, I'm afraid,' I say. 'I've been through all this, what is said: the clearances, the hunger – everyone wants peace and justice – but the results....'

'It isn't that,' he says. 'First comes the truth. But no one thinks we're loyal – they assume we tell a truth to one and lie to someone else.... I hadn't spotted you. I bet you came here in a cage....'

'It's true!' I say. 'I was a bird, the cage is only big enough for your intelligence. Mine was quite small ... a buzzard is quite single-minded....'

'Oh yes,' he says. 'There's little women who have their feet bound – they're twisted into bird claws, they could perch – but that is not the point.... I still smell your fear – you huddled, I would bet....'

'Well,' I say, 'there must have been a plane....'

'That's interesting,' Vikram says. 'I must have been asleep....'

'No!' I say, 'it can't go on like that. You must be in charge, Vikram. I sneaked in. By boat, or truck? Kismet found me....'

'You don't know much,' he says. '"Kismet" is destiny.'

'Yes, yes,' I say. 'But it's a woman's name as well. Delicate as wire sculptures, but strong as snares for wolves. Besides, everything is destiny. Like who's turn is next.

'It pains me, that my Russian friend, Galina – she had no future, no hope in one. None of them has, that lives there. It's a fable – like on those lacquer boxes, Palekh ... horses that gallop, princesses, dwarves flying on treasure chests.... It seemed to all vanity – she shipped me out, and I was glad ... but of ourselves, we never spoke ... nothing crossed our minds....'

'You must have been escaping,' he says. 'But you've found – it doesn't work like that. There's nowhere else but "here" to go. The world is very small – the future's sealed, the past is in the library or you can take a spade and dig it up … there's no fast forward, and no "back". Of course, there's destiny, and winners, losers – but that's reality. You can't touch that. Most places where we – voyagers, adventurers – end up, are difficult – snow, sand and mines … all kinds of mine, those that explode and those that sink.… Climate extreme, nothing to eat, cruel bosses – you'll have met all that. A purgatory, a hell, that makes you think of worlds divine – and then you realise – if those exist, they're not for you. You're far too human for all that.…

'The only quality humans might access – is truth. The truth's the only precious thing you can profess and seek. Humankind has access to it, no one else, none that we know, at least. What is a human worth? Not much – reduce one to a powder, he barely fills a vase. Saints or generals – exactly similar. Gods – you can carry them round the town, with garlands on – next year the same. They're made of bronze – they weather, you can clean them: you? You age, you die.

'As for you, Yannik – look at all the time you've wasted here already. Your asset's gone, you didn't score with anyone.…'

'I know,' I say. 'I'm wasting what I am. All I want is to be sent on – but this airport's immense and nothing lands or leaves. An army could leave here, or could land.'

'Oh,' Vikram says, taken aback. 'You'd need customs, and a baggage area – that's obligatory.'

'You know,' I say, 'when I was looking for resources, I found a lot of talk about the obligations, what's obligatory. But in the end – nothing at all was obligatory, nothing and no one was obliged, respected, nothing that should be done was done. And that's the truth.'

He shrugs, there's silence, then he laughs and I laugh with him.

'Smell!' he says. 'Imagine one of my wives has prepared the *nan,* with sultanas – taken with *dal,* the best you'll ever taste.… They're all good cooks: – 'one of my wives' – it's mathematics, not affect. I could do it just as well myself … but I'm engaged in standing firm, and watching.…'

No wife, no child, no *nan* – his cover.…

'I fear,' I say, 'you're right. This is a place where you must stay. I – must be off. But – tell me, Vikram, tell me what you've found, your work here – the truth. Not all, of course. Just a crumb … a taste….'

He laughs. 'You can't expect me to? No, not for real! And you who wrote that script that does the rounds! You know how hard it is to sell the truth. Or even what's not quite….'

'I hadn't seen my "China" so, but yes,' I say. 'It is a kind of truth. At least – it's not a lie, it's not untrue. It could be watched, over and over, like an opera. It's not appropriate to wave your arms, kneel, shoot into the air, when it's all done – but some applause…. Oh yes!

'The truth: you'd need a little something for your pains, Vikram; at least the recognition, though it isn't your invention, naturally, rather, what you've found….'

'Exaltation?' he says, 'or fear…. We should be unmoved by what occurs, or what we find. It's all a bit contrived – like saying you find beauty when you step on Mars, disturb the dust on Saturn, plunge into Jupiter….

'Not that we'll have time for those – adventures: but we can imagine them, the two of us.'

As I turn to leave, he holds my hand, quite tight. 'Remember everything I said,' he says. 'It won't do you any harm, no harm at all. It makes us partners….'

*

It's a small yacht. Just bigger than an inflatable, but all the same, it's small.

'Vikram said you'd need a ride,' the captain says. 'The boss is Russian, but he's never here, he has to find another nationality – and I'm Yakut, the name's Altan. The Turks think I am Russian, but I'm more Turk than they…. It makes no difference at all, but just as Vikram says, you have to tell the truth, whatever is the cost….'

'Ah yes, the cost,' I say. 'I cannot pay….'

'Then there's no cost!' he says. 'That is simplicity!' And that's the pact.

'Now,' he says, 'Where shall we go? I have to sail the world, not stopping in a port, in case…. My boss – is pestilential…. Who can tell where Russians and their ships can dock?'

'I know,' I say. 'My lover, Galina, was the same. A daily impermanence became essential – it broke us up....'

'Hmmmm,' says Altan. 'That doesn't sound complete. I realise, the total truth – is maybe a pleonasm, or concealed: but there it is. You hold things – the truth – back, to guarantee companionship.

'Now, Yannik, hoist the flag – we sail under that of neutrality – maybe of scepticism – a flag that disbelieves in flags, or in their truthfulness, at least.'

There's interesting places we can go, but do we wish to go to them right now? I think of the emperor Zhu Di, the big ships discovering the world, though it was always there – perhaps we could do the same, and drop into the fantasy, of discovering what there was, and ran itself quite bad – or downright ill ... suppose we'd anchored way offshore, and peeked through early telescopes, like ibn Ma'ruf dreamt of, in his 'Light of Truth' – and listened to the activities on land through cunning trumpets shaped from gourds....

And decided not to drop the anchor, not to stay.

'Everyone has given me hope, understanding, and the means to find a destination, Altan,' I say. 'But here we are, sea all around – nowhere to go, no acquaintances in port....

'It seems to me that usually, if things go really bad, there's incomprehension, shouting; you're stuck with someone penniless, like you, who hates you, bad company and debts – top floor of some rackety Auberge, no bus service to get you out, the front desk's lost your document.... But no! None of that. I'm mobile, everyone I've met is made of gold.... and yet, I'm stuck! It's like the other scene, but worse – the cheap room you can't afford, the sloping floor, the window gives out on the refuse bins, the malice.... It's all the same!'

'Yes,' he says. 'With me – the tundra melts, the reindeer have buboes and no food. I've to pretend I have experience of boats, know how to navigate....'

It isn't about us, of course.

Indeed, the sea is all around. When we leave this sea, there's another. The tankers try to run you down, the warships shout at you. The inflatables fold and sink in silence. It's the first day of a new, an old, world: it's an anonymous day, and we're in an anonymous part – all humping slate-blue sea. Indifferent if you skim or sink. It's up to you, everything. Forget the general ending of the world – yours can end in seconds – with no record, no regrets.

'Let's go back,' I say. 'This is no good.'

And so we do.

'You're in the middle, Yannik,' Altan says. 'Of places you might not want to see: there's Syria and Georgia, Baku, Tehran. In each one – even up Mount Elbrus – there's a Kismet, who will perch on you and sing the song of trees and clouds and flying high … no permanence, but she will magick you and part of you will never leave, and you will grow and spread until you are a forest or a desert…. Just as all Yakuts are part of you and you of them…. We know a huge amount of science that doesn't work, but is important for a classifier….'

'No, no, Altan,' I say. 'That's sentimental stuff, it can't be so….'

'Of course it can't,' he says. 'But – you need cheering up. You're like my Russian boss, and me, and all Yakuts – we have no future. It always happens – people lose their names and place, the gods turn into spirits and philosophy, and back and forth … the tundra melts, we all fall in the hole – with Qara Kitay, Khwarezmians, Sarmatians, the Yueh Chi, Tokharians…. We're ghosts – it never was to be our turn, and we – we're dead….'

'I know we'll never leave this sea, the Black,' I say. 'You've dumped me here, like I've dumped you. I don't belong and so I'll work things out myself….'

'You never did, and never will,' he says. 'Remember – big states stay big, even when the faces are no longer on the coins. Autocracy's for ever – when there is a pause – it comes back in, an inexhaustible stream. It's what we're made for, recognize – it's our hope, not our escape. The more we are compact, the more we hope the species has a chance – like ants, we cluster round the queen and serve…. You, Yannik, you're a buzzard. Do they sing? No one's alive to hear it, if they do.'

'Maybe,' I say, 'there's a deserted monastery, where people who can't escape hole up, live by fables as they've always done – or, better still, take vows. Of silence, and of abstinence. No opinions proclaimed, no needs, and when it's time, we curl up and go on – to paradise, or in the camp where everything's renewed, for ever – just the gadgets change.… Those of us who're citizens of everywhere – there must be millions, though we never find another just like us.…'

'And in the end,' he says, 'someone will make your "China" – but when it's too late, when all has come to pass, and yours is just a curiosity, a journey to the moon, a corny classic of non-happening. You were a radical – forget the Leninism, it was Marxism had a hold on you. And now – you're in retreat – more desperate than sad, but sadness waits.…

'Meanwhile – you're brimming with emotions. Those women you have loved, you didn't know them, and they didn't like you. Love is something intense and lasting you should feel: the books say that. They say it so writers can write more books. It isn't so. You're better off with documents, a passport, and a job in Kismet's office, so you can make her Turkish coffee and have pastries flown in from Budapest.…'

'You thought you – and everyone displaced, with feet to travel on, initiative – could have that chance, Altan,' I say. 'Or something like. But then there was the melt, the hole – and you were set to wandering, no port you could approach, pariahs, both of you … you the captain, and your Russian – the boss, of what extraction no one knows. A Cossack or Mongolian, elitist, proletarian, debtor or a moneybags – Armenian, perhaps?

'People with too much affect for where they said they could belong, they're banished from the pack. They can profess new loves, new homelands, deeper cultures – no one believes them, no one cares – they're parvenus. There's only one such place, a home, and when it dies – you wander off – a rogue, a vagabond, lone wolf.…'

'Tribes and clans,' says Altan. 'That's where we humans start and end. Medicine lets us live for longer – but we're tired, through all those extra years – dead tired. In the millennia when there were no pills that worked – what kept us vigorous was wars and dancing. Nothing can replace those – see us! on we go with them! That is the animal we are – the extra-T's, they study us from rocks out there – up, down, so far, they're happy they will never visit us.… We say we'd like to meet them, aliens – but it isn't so. We fear each other … aliens are hassled, they must register.…'

'That's much too philosophical,' I say. 'I've seen how it will end, our stewardship.… The nature – a huge dump, a tip.

'I'm looking for a way to pass my time – the movie biz and shipping stuff, don't promise well….'

He nods.

'Help me, Altan,' I say.

'I could use a mate,' he says, 'but there's no pay. They called the Black Sea black because of the colour of the fogs. Now – it's the water. Black. I've no pay, and so I fish. There's mines down there. And sailors, soldiers too – all sides – they're black, as if they're mercenaries from Africa. You've heard of Black Russians? And Ukrainian caviar? The flesh is perfumed, delicate – dark viscid grey or sooty black … the cause was noble, so they say – it is not mine. If it was ignoble, or just blah – I'm quite indifferent, but as they say, "a man must eat, or end up eaten". That's my motto too.

'You'd prefer a monastery, or an abandoned mosque, where the faithful come and leave some bread – you'll be competing with the cats and dogs. You're still quite whole and vigorous, Yannik. I'd say you're good for seven months.

'I studied Jung, and I agree – you'll maybe find a partner complementary, with faults exactly opposite to yours. Alas, Jung had patients, they came to him … will someone come to you…? I'm not so sure….'

'Oh, Altan,' I say. 'It isn't about loneliness. It's that I've seen the future. We're on our own there, each one of us, but in a crowd of similars! Millions of us foraging, for food, for shade, for people like ourselves who have the clue, how to survive awhile; people, anyone, that we don't fear on sight, our own or not our own, running from them or towards…. Just wait, and you will see what I have seen. It's dangerous. They mistake you for an angel, angelic messenger of death.

'The Brahan seer – they burnt him in a tar-barrel on the sands … what happened to his stone, I wonder – he put it to his blind eye, saw what would happen, naturally a little blurred. For sure it wasn't with him, not in the barrel … someone snitched it … used it to make some cash, I bet…. Even now, movie directors have a thing, a tiny reverse telescope, put to their blind eye to spy the set – but I'll bet, they don't see the future, not as I have….'

'If the end's the tar-barrel,' Altan says. 'They are better so. Unsure.

'Concentrate! Where should we go, my friend? I've seen the past, and you – what is to come. From you and yours I've learned what I don't want to know: we'll end up bad. Remember, if they say "escape and run…" don't move! It is the classic trap … "shot while trying to escape"….

'It's best to lie quite low: not to describe what you believe – the Samoyeds, the Nenets, they were better known than us. They had imagination: cosmology. It was no help.

'The Russians called the Samoyeds "cannibals", self-eaters … maybe that's what I am. The dogs though – are a wonder. Best ever made – closest to us, but more refined. The Samoyeds….'

He prepares to give a lesson….

'Altan,' I say. 'I am a simple type. These are strange, convincing worlds – I feel quite alien, and now – with all that heat…. It's over, all that stuff. Fit for cabinets of curiosities….'

'Ah yes,' he says, a tear not far away. 'The worlds that we have lost. The melt – the digging, all that gas … everything going, if not gone….'

'It's the past, Altan,' I say. 'Useless to have regrets.'

*

The cinema – was my past, Erin, Petrov, Ruggero: my memory of them – almost effaced…. And yet the movie: everybody's future. In the present, the script may be in Ruggero's safe, or "being read". There's much of that "present" to be got through, much more; all familiar and all new. Just be patient.

I may not get a credit.

I need an agent – will they pay in Turkish currency? Or Lebanese? Syrian? Everything is on the slide. They won't use dollars – they're too strong. Like Polish vodka – the best, the only kind you can find here, except … there should be Finnish, and now – everyone's distilling, printing labels. Here, there's Stolichnaya empties too.

For me, it's academic. I'm fed together with the cats. Cats, birds – what do they do? Always active, always thinking of reproducing themselves. We mustn't hurt them, not the cats, nor the snakes, but they end up, all of them, with no purpose, none whatever. Yet – we see when they are damaged, have suffered something they ought not.

We invent a place for them – snakes are eaten so someone prospers and can be eaten in their turn. Every people, every population, should be there *for* something. Russians can't be content with being Russians – if they all disappear, what would they have been here for? Yakuts are asking already – for themselves; what was it for?… Like cats? To fill a space in a design we have invented? To justify us – top dogs? If we all disappear – we should not be missed. We shall all disappear – that's why they resist, Americans, Russians, everybody who can. Most living things would rejoice. There's no one who understands that, not even what "missing" humans means … a cat might, not a snake. Not a bird, for sure. You miss, I guess, your fledglings if you are an eagle or a vulture, the little ones if you're a dingo … when they've died – most do, at once. But a dingo surely doesn't miss a vulture? She should be rather glad. We are the emperors – our subjects are the cats?

It's very hot, there is no shade. On a tree stump, I see a notice – 'Trabzon International Univers….' It's torn…. Maybe they want staff. It could be 'Universal Movers'. Everything must be movable, and moved. One world means if it can't be exported, it's an antique. You'd need a licence for it. Same with people – they need to speak the language and be understood: just arms and legs? Not wanted.

Kismet would be delighted to have me near. Perhaps.

There is an interview. That's bad. 'I thought it might be a university,' I say: 'There can't be many candidates for prof, not here, not alive. Nor students….'

'It's a little joke,' says Julie. 'We're Universal Movers, but we do give lectures. We move everything! We're boosters. Lifters of spirits, doorkeepers of the jobs. It's consonant. We hoped to find a specialist in Buster Keaton – showing his movies wouldn't disturb the other classes.'

It needs some working out. I laugh, from courtesy.

She continues: 'It's all about moving – stuff, or everything else. Intangibles. If you can't stand it here, we'll have to move your stuff, and charge. People – they need lectures, so that they can move. You're not a packer, don't know streets and villages – that's the need. Otherwise – you'll give the doctors courses: future of ethics; rights and wrongs…. They're sceptics, so you'll need invent some argument quite strong.'

'Are they medical doctors?' I ask, confused.

'They're nothing in particular, until they graduate,' she says. 'They carry boxes, when the word is heard. We must be practical, prepare for the real world: can't sit around writing our books.'

'I'm totally in favour,' I say. '"Long live the Bauhaus". Away with the bourgeois universe, its universities – the factory for employment....'

I realise I've fallen in the trap. 'I mean, we'd prepare the proletariat,' I say. 'The revolution, and the aftermath.'

'Exactly,' Julie says. 'It's all about promotion. Social for them, career for you. Publicity for us. The students will pay you what they think you're worth. I've no money for you. You must show initiative, and graft. You're not to be paid for what you've done already in the past. Do something new – and then you'll see.'

Being in this is much like *not* being in. Maybe this way, I shan't be fired, or if I am, it won't be documented.

'Is "China" your only try to do a movie?' Julie asks. 'It's rather slight, as efforts go.'

'It would be serialised,' I say. 'The world....'

'We're not yet sure if it is fantasy or fact. Fact, of course, is dull, and fantasy ephemeral. The inhabitable world would be becoming rather small,' she says. 'And Tabzon's in an awkward space – there's delicate places all around. However, you're well qualified – you're used to moving on.'

'I know the best despatchers, Julie,' I assure her. 'In Trabzon. I have an inside track.'

I start my lectures: the Shang dynasty – the history's been going on by then – I'm cutting corners, but, there it is. 'Be imaginative, inventive, foresightful, if you like. But not too much,' she said.

I get to the Xiongnu, and the class – it's very small – seems troubled. There's Turks, Americans, and people who don't give their names, and no Chinese. Barbarians, all of them....

'It seems to me,' I tell Julie, 'they're all spies and cops. I knew a spy – he seemed puffed up about the status of his trade.'

'Of his craft,' she corrects me. 'Of course – the subject's delicate. The Turks came from what might be described as – early China. Thereabouts. Now, perhaps, China's coming here. They say they're loaded. The dollar's very strong, no doubt they have a sea of those

… but you must be circumspect. When a new prof comes, does geopolitics, they always set some cops on him. You might assert that someone will bring paradise.

'Paradise, if not yet here, is round the corner now. You should be careful – we're movers, and if things don't arrive where they're addressed on time – we have a miserable chore. If labels drop off on the way – who'll re-direct...?'

I know it's metaphor, but she's so serious.

The guys who take the course – they only audit, say they won't do the exam, not that I believe in those, but nonetheless, it seems quite aimless.

'No, for sure it's not,' says Julie. 'But you took a bold approach … dealing with the dynasties, the frontier perilous and porous, usurpations and the long humiliation, occupation, the wars – you leave the impression that it's all been a precarious jaunt – incompetence patched up by the geniuses, who're replaced by more incompetents….'

'That's not my take at all,' I say. 'My pessimism has its glint of optimism. I shall die before the future's run its course, and you will tell if I was right, or wrong. I'll have my shot: predictions are the master science now – and no one remembers if you're wrong….'

Anatol, my student, sidles up to me, when I have said my piece. 'Hey, prof,' he says, 'it must be boring, writing out your notes and then there's no one listens in the class….'

'Oh well,' I say, 'it's something I can do. You can't sit in the monastery drinking vodka all the time.'

'I could give you stuff,' he says. 'Just read it out, and in return – stop asking me for fees and sweeteners. All you say is on the TV, where it's easier to understand….'

He is the first. And one by one, they sidle up with notes they say is secret stuff from states, just give it as a lecture, and in return – no fees and no exams and maybe they'll pay up for grades, if those are good enough … or recommendations, letters of support….

'Julie, it's not that it's corrupt,' I say. 'We're in the world, it's right that we reflect what is … but I wonder, what I am doing here, what I am for….'

'Reflect, Yannik,' says Julie. 'I for sure am not here to suit you, nor to cuddle you. Don't try it on with me, I'm not your saviour, you're a poor dreg, another intellectual manqué – you have your tragedy, your humane sensibilities were aroused when you were in funds and travelled. And now – the leaves have turned, will fall, your time is up. But … it occurs to me. We've a space lab. Maybe you thought the gantry and the rocket was a minaret. We need more spacemen for the crew – it must be ethnically mixed, religions various but not hostile; and omnisex. You'd need to fit the uniform – it's not a suit you snip and fix….'

'The moon?' I ask, amazed. 'I'm not trained in anything like that….'

'You'd need to ask the commander where,' Julie says, quite sharply. 'I don't hold with any of it. God made the moon quite inaccessible – he had a motive, maybe it's His second home. It isn't written in the Book I use…. Maybe it's just to shoot up into space – you look around and choose your rock…. My province is "humanities", that's what I run. "What is man?" I used to ask; my freshman course. "Nothing much," I said. Quite popular, but now I only do admin….'

'I thought the level would be higher, Julie,' I say, and she says, 'The level's level. People won't digest it if it's not. And no banal nostalgia about the ancient times – the past has made the present, the people were exactly us … they didn't wash, died young, wore clunky boots and heavy clothes, were no more educated than us, most less – and otherwise were identical in every way…. That is the point. Otherwise – "what is man?" is meaningless, chaotic, a confabulation of impossibilities….'

'Yes,' I say. 'You're exactly right. This – the life you give me now, all the past lives I have endured, salvaged some memories from – it's Mann, Proust, Tolstoy. *This* is humanity, it's *life* – it can't lead anywhere but to THE END, but they – all sages – have seen totality, the universal, the banality, of our freshman course – the "What is Man" … and from it reaped their reputation and the credit, "A" grade in comprehension.

'"This is humankind": the notice on the tree, the quests, the rebirths, the loves and deaths of all the figures, characters we'd come to know better than the baker, butcher, cashier or lover in what we call real life…. The staid provincial towns, and then the war and deportations, "a survivor" who recalls…. Taste, literature, the brick-sized chronicles of friends and relatives – it is the truth. We need to have it set down to believe in it – truth, normality; we're in the stream, we're the good guys when it suits.... Literature! You live it, even if it doesn't strike you so.... It's the best life, the life we cannot live. How can you save that? No one asks you to. You can't make anyone live well, the good life – they know what it is, they don't try, and you don't try to make them.'

'And now you know why "China" won't be done,' she says. 'Or maybe – someone will copy, plagiarise, make unrecognizable. The script – it isn't true, nor normal. Is it a banal masterpiece? Or genius. You'll never know....'

'I'd almost sign up for the rocket, Julie,' I tell her. 'But I can't digest dried food from packets. I would starve. It's from experience of visiting the famine spots and sneaking charitable rations....'

She laughs. She is a great romancer, but she won't romance with me. Probably, it's rather good.

LOSING THE TREBISONDA

'Yannik, you could worry me,' says Julie. 'There's a phrase, "to lose your Trebisonda"; your Trebizond, your Trabzon: becoming disoriented. Not knowing where you are.

'The truth – you realize, it's only yours to lose, and even if you find it, you're on your own, no one else believes you. What's the attraction anyway?'

Julie files some papers while she talks.

'I followed orders, Julie,' I tell her, wearily. 'My wife, Annemarie, sent me out to see if the predictions of disasters could be true. If I say – I found my Trebisonda, but I am one of few ... it means I know where I am, but no one else knows where....'

'Well,' she says, 'you should get over it. You can't change what everybody knows, not with your truths. Or if you can – don't go to pieces here. This is the place to start from, the magnetic north of travellers.... Start and finish, what happens in between's ephemeral, of no account....'

She has much to do. Filing.

I hope I'm not caged in the rocket and sent up. I fear the up, the down – and don't know which is worse.

'Up or down – you don't know where you'll land. The best advice is "feel discomforted in every place",' says Julie, tying up her hair and settling it on her highest point.

'You're quite profound,' I say, thinking of what she's said before, 'If truth must be considered by everyone, established by and for each one alone … if the truth is individual, what are we doing, lecturing on it? Each has a journey individual. If finding truth is marginal, and not the point or motivation … if each of us has a truth that's incommunicable, or at least not shared – we have a chaos.'

'Exactly so,' she says. 'That's what I think, and why we have a rocket ready to blast some of you awkward guys out of our hair….'

'Then,' I persist, 'my course in humanitarianism is really to train spies?'

'You puff it up, but in a way,' she says. 'That's what happens. You thought nothing was happening … that all was bland, becalmed….'

'I met Vikram,' I say. 'An exquisite personality….'

'They'll kill you if they must,' she says, 'but that's explained in senior years. You need more study before the application of the discipline is clear. But – ah! The regret! They'll hold your hand, if there is time, when yours is up…. Loyalty: that is the word. Obedience – that's a synonym.'

'It seems to me – it's like a map,' I say. 'It's huge – and where you are depends on how you fold. One fold shows where there is salvation, others, the opposite – the terror, subversion, occupation….'

I look to her to reassure….

'My!' she says. 'Where have you been laid and hatched? Under a bush? Or in the sand? Maps don't tell you where you are! Nor where you've been, or where you'll go. One world! – you put whatever happens on a globe, or flattened on a parchment – it's the same. Everything happens all at once, here, there. And everywhere.'

'I've always known,' I say, 'but seemingly – it never quite sank in. If I had thought, I'd not have worked out "China". If it happens like I see, what happens in the other places…? Who knows what people make of that?'

'Listen,' Julie says, taking files off a squared pile, and ripping them before she baskets them. 'The Book they used to put by your hotel bed, before the world got rude and dirty – nothing happened much in that. Spats. Tribes and clans.

'You turned to the last bit to see whodunit and what was done. It was like Cluedo – many hands, and many visions – Rashomon, maybe. There was talk, and family unhappiness, and lecturing – fantastic stuff, and ghosts, community cohesion – but the action, when at last it came, was just one death; judicial murder. The back-story was an anti-colonial plot … but all in all, quite predictable, remote, and intellectual. As if someone had read my notes from 'What is humankind?' Someone with a load of spite, that is.

'There's lots about the universe, though then, it was quite small. Nothing about the world – they didn't know it wasn't small. As far as you could see … the dust from armies fighting, over and over … Time – in long lengths: – it drives you mad. The repetitions – an eternal football season – goals and trainers, buy and sell, slaves and prostitutes….

'But if you turned to the last chapter, the dénouement – it was quite crazy: Berlioz! Or that movie with the devil in it all in flames: 'Burn, baby, Burn!' Now, I admit, the Book I take with me, a different one, can tell you how to make big bucks. That's not the point. It has philosophy: starting small and ending with a lovely home. What I can't see is, in the hotel book, how you get there, to the end; no cops, detectives, even no characters – it's a rough scene, like world's end movies…. Everybody – finishes in bonfires.

'Wow – it ensures insomnia! As if they all had lost their Trebisonda, slipped off the world….'

'Le Grand Macabre?' I ask.

'That would be it,' she says.

'Julie,' I say, 'that file you dumped – it had my name, and ended in the bin….'

'You can't say nothing happens,' Julie says. 'Be thankful I've not put you in another pile.'

That's ominous. Julie faces me. 'If you want to know,' she says, 'they complain. They say your lectures are apocalyptic. There's no subject, no names, no faces; though they know the world is full of bullet holes and missing limbs, you don't talk about those, nor about the cat-houses by the docks … you shimmer.'

'That's good,' I say, 'and bad. I could change the emphasis… We know apocalypse will come, even the prisons will fall down … all will be free and loosed upon each other….'

*

'I'm not a violent person, admitting those exist, in profusion, where the occasion arises, in support of certain situations where they're inducted, or eligible, to be themselves – or unexpectedly, in situations social or domestic…. But when we speak of political, of civil violence, not when – as they say, by legal obligation, by and for a state – I have to say, yes, there's situations where I'm on the side of violence, attack, defence – even if myself I continue to abhor it, would personally resist the idea of using it. "Using it" … massacres, assassinations, sabotage which ends in injury or death – the range of what will, might, even against the odds – is violence against people. The case must be explored – but, on the whole, if we judge all other means are tried or just impossible – since using violence requires not a majority but a democracy in its most elemental forms, in stuations of great difficulty – the *mouchards*, informers, spies, opponents, or a state that uses maxi-violence in return – I feel …

… when there's no other recourse, no redress of oppression and repression – yes, violence; better organized than scattershot. Better a movement than a mob, better a military organization than an individual; better a semblance of limits, rules, lines not to cross, effects to be evaluated in terms of ends envisaged or attained, better imagine reconciliation, justice, than a final settling of accounts, but yes: violence, with all its unforeseen and unforeseeable effects ... victims, increased repression, massacres and pogroms, genocides and deportations…. Better a violent reaction to a violence suffered, with injustice, than none at all, though none is conditional, a tactic, and will also usually be planned and organized with care and years of preparation…. Involve a generation at *least* of horrible unanswered suffering….'

'You see?' says Julie. 'That's you, your talk! Dropping us all in it.'

'It's a decision, using reason, like they mostly aren't,' I say. 'I'm clean. I've already called myself out. Things don't get better, usually – if they might, you're probably about to lose your cause....'

'Stop, stop,' says Julie. 'Worse and worse. Everyone will take it personally. You can't say certain things, not anywhere at any time, and you will feel results of – *this* –' and she holds out a tape – 'for all your life, and mine.'

'Someone must finish the French revolution,' I say, 'and avoid Napoleons.'

'Pandora's vase,' she whispers. 'Can't be dropped twice.'

'This seems to me a pretext,' I say, 'to obliterate what I was doing right.'

'Anyone can please the spies,' she says, pouring fluid in the basket, full of files, seeking a match.... 'They give you the material you don't need invent...'

'Then, Julie, it looks like flight, not fight?' I ask.

She's trashing documents, ripping, burning: does not reply.

'Anywhere, you say,' I ask. 'Will take what I said – personally? React? It seems quite rash. Precipitous.'

Altan – for me, he is the answer.

Julie – there was no bond, no contract. Nothing reasonable. She said, 'Forget at once that either of us has existed.'

I trot on, down from the cliff.... My lecture –

'It doesn't sound like you,' says Altan, pulling up a lump of stone he uses as an anchor.

I say, 'It doesn't have to,' and we're off.

'It's my truth,' I say; the engine wafts my words away. The consequences – not to contemplate, nor even speculate on who will take the most offence and where they'll take revenge ... terror or treason? All of those? Guilty as charged?

'I was cautious, Altan,' I say. 'No names, no principles – a glimmering, that's all.'

'More than enough,' he says. 'Where shall we end? You've taken me on the devil's ride, Yannik....'

It's true. We might land anywhere, we can't settle. Down the coast – after Syria and Palestine, there's many other places we can't land – Egypt and Libya, Tunisia, Morocco … then we turn up to Spain and all the places following – and we're known, not wanted, watched, accused….

This is an uneasy sea, small and stormy, ungenerous. You need to have a cargo everybody wants if you're to land, and then, they don't want you. They've got more than enough of you, unquiet, insatiable, querulous. Criminals and alien.

And we're back in Istanbul – no longer an old city … where they said the founders must have been blind, to build in waterless Europe and not see the sweet waters on the other shore.

We move so slowly, it takes centuries … the sea is sticky sweet, toads squat and watch us, on black crusts of wave.

'Civil war – not much use to me,' says Altan. 'No one to fight. We might go to the Delta. Wild horses. Birds. More in your line, Yannik….'

'Nothing, Altan,' I say. 'I made nothing. I was shipped, throughout my life. I evaluated the odds, on human survival – I wouldn't bet. In fact – I didn't care, not all that much. I was a parcel, having no destination for a shipment is the same as having lots…. It's just – you may not get where you had hoped.

'People want to know how to improve things, and yet they know, it's all before them. You get frustrated with explaining what people know and can't do, won't do. It must be someone's fault. It could be theirs? Tell me, Altan.'

'You know it all, Yannik,' Altan says. 'Give it a break. The engine won't work in this molasses – use the pole…. Everybody here is fighting or getting ready, we must go very softly….'

'That's all you have to say?' I ask: 'It's a bit nothing, you know.'

'So be it,' he says.

They say 'wild horses', but really they're just horses: and no one says 'wild birds', or do they? Yakuts know every kind of homeopathy, natural cures, all that. Most don't work or make things worse – but there you are – that's all they have …

'We could build a hut from reeds, say we're researchers from the Universal University of Trabzon. Movers by request. Farm the horses, eat plovers' eggs….' he says.

'I'm a city person, Altan,' I say. 'People like Kismet and Galina, even Petrov – I try to weave them into my life. My principality – we are all citizens.

'I don't hang around; if it's time to leave, I leave. They pack me, label me, give me something to deliver. I know what's to be done, and I don't expect improvement.... How could I?'

'I'm not the person to ask,' Altan says.

We move slowly up the coast, not feeling safe.

'They never knew why Ovid got sent away,' I say. 'He ended here. He got up Augustus's nose – they say it was the great man's incest trend – he thought Ovid would sneak, or put it in the poetry....'

There's a lot of silence between us, me and Altan. He sacrifices himself for me. So, in a way, did Galina and Kismet. I – for Anne-Marie – saving the world, reconciliation with nature, cooling things down ... Straightforward, but impossible – I didn't make a dent....

'Kismet sounds unusual.' Altan says. 'Galina – much less. Get used to it, Yannik – they worked in transporters offices, you were goods. Not "good" for them or even for yourself. They knew about the customs, getting stuff through, about greasing greasy palms. Customs – you don't seem to have any. All you know about's catastrophe. Everyone has studied that. It got to you, that's all, and sank deep in.'

I think 'China' is lost to the world.

'If they take the yacht, Altan,' I say, 'you must be sure you get a paper from them, to confirm.'

We could be inching towards a newly forming desert. When it's hot, the sea comes up the rivers, with its salt. It's what Anne Marie said, but as we move along, we see the beaches full, at night there's fireworks. There's concerts where you must wave your arms, all that. Clap the poor turns, cheer the better ones.

'All war is civil war,' says Altan, putting on his captain's hat.

'Whatever you choose, you must have a good chance of winning,' I say. 'Start a conflict unprepared – you must back down. Or much much worse.'

We settle on the very edge of Romania – consolidating the foundations, making a watery island. It's where the Romans sent their awkward squad. I don't think much of Ovid, don't know the language, never thought a word of poetry for myself.

When they're in trouble, Galina, Kismet, might come, escaping, I don't know how, but that's my deal, the offer. I can't imagine why they would – you'd think running a courier's was fairly safe, secure. They'd need patching up. Altan's pharmacology ... the insects, herbs, and spit … it worked on his own people, sometimes, he says – it's defining, their treasure: what they'd have.

There's water-snakes, and dogs: the dogs escaped, they're fairly wild, and if there's time, they'll go back to being wolves. That is the project, you might say – waiting for it all to happen for them: for everything.

Kismet – could wait for an East wind, stand on the ledge, be blown here. Could be any time.

Smoke

THE LOCAL mafia's harassing me.

I'd leave, but I am here through force of will – mostly my own. To leave would need big efforts, too big to make right now.

Where am I? you will ask. I'll tell you in due course.

I could draw a map, but I'm not an artist. Many countries have other countries, authentic but occluded, encysted, in them – Iran, Turkey, Romania, the continent called 'Russia' – on and on. Africa. Asia. The further you go, the more a country is a rooming house, tenants from all over, living together for centuries. Where I'm in the forest, here's like that, a witches' hut, but it's not made of cake, but of fruit on vines. It's covered in berries, poison if you eat them, but smoked – you'll get a trip, no fare, no customs.

We stand out, Denise and I, but you need to know where to look before you'd recognise us. And not want to go further, not for our company. We're preserved, like pears in syrup or in cognac: or like apples in the grass under the tree.

The birds. They're fragile, even more than us; frost, cats and poison – does for them, they don't last long, although they have an art – of flying – a skill and a perspective we don't have.

Not a single one of us, however many other species fall beneath our spread, has the gift of flight. Who gives them that, the gift? A misnomer, probably: it's time and practice. It gives them wisdom. How does anyone acquire a wisdom, what's it made of? No one knows: they guess. The birds – they might have pity on us, but we have none for them, just curiosity, and so they shrug, and call to one another. Reassuring; for company, reducing distances.

I met Denise when both of us had given up. She'd found her freedom much too late, it came to mean being gaga; no one would eat her food or listen to her nonsense.

We'd gone, before we knew each other, to a lecture.

'Everything you can reach by land,' I intervene, I interrupt. 'We've used. The other two-thirds is under water. It's untouched.

Maybe we should be accustomed to living down, not up – a smoky-green perspective; still masked but possibly with gills acquired.'

'That isn't necessary,' says the big speaker – from a corporation, or a state: 'I've read you, Osman, what you wrote. "Biologically engineer" a few of us. Create a fishy working class, that lives not down the hole or in the sweat-shop – but underneath our keel. They're the miners. Is survival worth all this? You thought not, I think....

'Quite unnecessary. Yours is a flight of fancy feathers: or a scud of fins.'

The public, mostly young, laughs, quite nervously. They're happy with their bodies, most of them, don't want goggle-eyes, a waggly tail, anonymity, eating the pink invisibles.... Being sucked in by whales, blown out through a domed head....

At the end, a scatty woman – Denise – is interested, blocks my path. 'You're an explorer, then, not for the money,' she says. 'That's quite rare.'

'Well,' I say. 'There's explorers and explorers. Some are prepared, they know for certain what they're going to find. Others – it's a cast of mind. Exploring, not discovery, is what they crave.'

It's simple, but she puzzles over it.

I say – 'In the tropical forest, at night – there is a sound – at first you take it for aeroplanes, hovering above, up to no good.

'It's the monkeys snoring. It's as if we hear ourselves before we wake, before we can prepare our own reality. Unless, of course – we're always dreamt. The monkeys dream us, we are future for them ... theirs, an expansive imagination, stronger than their crude experience.'

We're the only two without a car. The roads are iced, the autos go wiggle-wobble down the slope. We cling together, plant our treacherous legs like twisted sticks in what looks stable....

'I thought I knew everyone,' Denise says: 'You slipped through my net, haha....'

'I'm in my room a lot,' I say. 'The local police are corrupt. They persecute me, fine and arrest me at the call of a small boss, who doesn't like that I exist. Doesn't know me, doesn't want to, and it's mutual. When the cops die, I take responsibility, silently – for my own satisfaction. They don't die in service, but through ignorance: – car crash, smoking, overdose.'

'I'm sure it's true,' she says. 'It sounds paranoid, but most things lend themselves that way.... You have an innocent's gaze. It's very irritating.'

I go on: 'I am detested – and hadn't thought how common a situation that can be. In the community – it takes a something to be shunned. You need to be a murderer, a paedophile. But in the family – it's common. In marriage, in couples – it is usual. Silence. How does it come to this, when alternatives are close at hand – tolerance or flight, understanding, cordiality ... an undercover lover...?

'That's why I live alone, apart. You can escape your companions detesting you, but not your enemies.... The fear persists: of being unloved, of being intolerable.'

'If you let them out, your thoughts,' she says. 'Life is impossible. You'll want war, with everyone.'

'Oh,' I say. 'I'm a moderate. Exaggeration, fantasy – it's old hat. And now, keeping too quiet brings you under public gaze, suspicion....

'Humankind raises its problems, advertises them, in samples, bit by little bit. One century – the theme is slavery. Another – genocidal wars. It's up to you to recognise what torment's dominant. Too many brain-twisters at once – and everyone despairs; there's stasis. The solutions come with the puzzles; like in the algebra class. The answers are at the back of the book. You needn't look; it's quicker, though, than work it through yourself.'

'You're inventive,' she says, looking hard at me, my face, as I turn it from her: 'That's a great inconvenience. You'll not be liked. I know that doesn't bother you, but in these wild depressed parts – people think of getting rid of you.'

It's very cold. Her house – is a tunnel, a cylinder, you reach it through a tunnel, a cylinder, of brambles. It's dark. I see fringes of straw, like skirts worn high on long white legs, and white-painted globes hung up high where there should be lights....

'You'll find here's refreshing,' she says. 'In the metropolis – the problem's time. All representation takes it into account – will a city last, will it peter out, does it remind you, evoke a memory, a form, a structure, fried-egg sandwich? Think differently here: the country, nature: before the cities, before the civilisations – think of a contemplation and a fear that has no time, and no development, that's always identical, static....'

'That's banal,' I say.

I recognise the relics of the south-east Congo, stolen and piled up, in a corner nearly out of sight... She'll be a traveller, or have known one....

'So true,' she says, 'Your remark. And so true – your perception. Mine too.'

'The Congolese,' I say. 'Are artists free of taste and criticism ... the Luba of Katanga ... anticipated everything, and reached the limits. Everybody else will get there in the end.'

'I know nothing,' she says. 'They're beyond me. I found them on a dump.'

There's a long silence. Then, 'I have these seeds,' she says. 'It's not good, where they take you. I wouldn't journey with them on my own....'

'Oh no, Denise,' I say. 'Not drugs?' I laugh. 'Someone sold you the bad stuff?'

'That's what I thought,' she says. 'It's so, you're right. It's absolutely not my thing. Enjoyment, self-exploration – that does not exist. The trick would be to get there, wherever, if it is really there, without taking anything. I think there needs be two of you, in case there's help to call. But – I don't believe you go to anywhere with anyone. Have no fear. You'll be always on your own. All of us.'

'I'll watch you,' I say. 'As for the art, they say you ought to give it back.'

'Oh no,' she says. 'It's stolen. The cops are always buzzing round. They don't appreciate us. They want to scare, that's all. Behind their post, they have a still. Their livers – wizened like prunes. I wouldn't trust the fuzz. Some of them – have pistols....' and she stares at me, to catch my expression. I try to have none. 'Who will they have pracised on?' she asks.

Those fetishes – it's wrong to call them art. That is a put-down. The fetish is about the wings that we don't have and never will, but that birds do, and will, as long as they exist, and we don't kill them all. It's about existences spent watching one another: existence.

It's worth telling someone, my illumination ...

'It's not Time,' I say. 'That's a secondary effect. You start somewhere, and it lasts: – time doesn't explain beginnings. Nor existence, the concrete. We live slow through time – then to find meaning, we look back, and speed it up. When we find a meaning – there's nothing concrete there, no chairs or tables, nor a pen....

'You ask, what's this place stuck in, and us too? It's nature, evolution: not time. Everywhere has time, the same: but each of us, us animals, we also have our own. We're stubborn, independent: we die in our own time. Here, what's defined the centre and periphery – is integration and conquest. One follows the other, but you'd think them contradictory. Instead, it's first conquest, then integration. Then – integration that permits fresh conquest. Here, there's been a hitch: people conquered and not integrated, not integrated in the plot. Forever conquered and apart.

'That speaker, lecturer – he shows you how our history works. Nothing to do with time, or meaning, or inventions. How do we postpone the death of all, the consequence of all we've strived to build, to enjoy, and to exploit? Ending our history, soon, as one day anyway we must. We prefer murder to suicide, but murder produces suicide, since we are the killers and the killed. That's what conquest entails, our victories, our knowing what was there already, waiting to be known. The science of our potentiality ... is knowing when we'll die.

'That speaker – he wants integration, keep us together while we try to find a way, another path. Then – more conquest – new culture, new stuff, new shortening of time and distance....

'And yet we still, each in our own unconscious unavailing way – die in our own time: of our own hand, in our own body.

'We must make the leap, from individual end to the collective one. The needle swings, that is, between the I, the we. My time: *our* cause. Same dial. Same delicate distinction.... All of us, loaded in the same farm cart lumbering through the mud.'

'What a disappointment,' says Denise. 'You're awfully confused and limited. We sit *in* time, we can't sit *on* time – that's for chairs. Now – watch me while I trip, and if you see me start to disappear – hold on my ankles, don't let me slide to where you can't pull me back.'

She lies down beside me on the chesterfield, puts her legs over my knees. 'Hold tight,' she says.

Her veins, I see, have leaked; the dusty feet are flecked with bluey-black.

It's very dark in here, the kerosene lamp smells strong.... I don't notice whether she has snorted, smoked or chewed: – there is a vase with teasels, maybe she's trying out their seeds. Or she's gathered berries from my walls. It's dull. No: there's more. It's boring, boring as the grave.

She lies very still. I hope she hasn't died – I'd be in deep shit. At last, she stirs, and says, 'It's very dark in here. That kerosene – the smell is awful.'

'Yes,' I say. 'I thought that.'

'I hope it wasn't you my head leached in to,' she says. 'A dark corridor, full of painted wooden shapes.'

'That sounds like me,' I say, amused.

*

The bar is fifty years old. 'I find you in the Mens' side,' says Denise, 'And transport you. Ladies and Escorts. You're an escort. Here, I'm a lady, and it's grotesque. What you've lived through, no one knows, but it wasn't serious. Equality, inequality – it matters nothing to you. You've never had anything stick to you.'

The lights in the Mens' side are yellow: I look like a dried apple. We men are very old, look comic. In the mixed part, it's twilight. You don't sit next to strangers – and it's mutual.

'I'm sure the bank robs me. My money never comes,' she says.

The more we drink, the more she blames the bank. I'm a rock. I'll make no loans, no presents.

'The birds – they are my pets. Anything that can't fly – the neighbours poison,' I say.

My way of saying – my cash is mine, it doesn't leave my side. It's in my cage and on my perch.

'When I was in Tunisia,' I say, 'there was fun. It's very hard and tense, but almost everyone is very young, they sing – better than the birds round here.'

'You should have stayed,' she says, not meaning it, not having any sort of picture of me there.

'You end up sick or teaching a language you wish you could forget,' I say. 'A mother tongue? – that's a kiss from someone you don't want, down into your throat, a long thin snake. Insinuating: opiate, dreamt.'

Dreamlands, I think: best keep them there, in sleep. Don't wake up in one – you might find you've landed somewhere once exotic, now a slum, you in the lowest caste.... Better smoke the seeds, Denise, don't travel, don't trust the boats, the planes, the safety drills – they will not save you, down you'll go, the little whistle won't call anyone except the grey boatman, the overburdened raft tilting on grey waters, the reasonable fare – under your tongue.... No winds here, once he had a skiff, now there's scores, hundreds of clients, passengers, him poling, blaspheming to everybody's gods....

'Don't trust what is inevitable,' says Denise. 'You're charmed, it's true. Believe in the charm – we all do – about ourselves. Otherwise we're damned....'

'You're out of time, Denise,' I say. 'Where I live – the creeper took over years ago. Those berries – give you a trip – just boil them up, and let them dry right out. The building's covered in them. The house – built as a jail. If you traded all the drugs it's covered with, it would mean jail for life- and the house itself a pen for lifers. Condemned, with no reprieve ... an infinity of lifetimes: concurrent.'

'Maybe historic houses are all made of drugs,' she says. 'Perhaps that's what history is made of. And so, you didn't buy a crack house, you bought....' she pauses.... 'A stash, and live in it....'

'I bought nothing. It's a rooming house, but I'm the only tenant. I'm an explorer, I don't do drugs,' I say.

'You explorers – you aren't trustworthy,' Denise ploughs on. 'There was a movie – some guy tied a camera on to an eagle: "that's what the eagles see", it said. It isn't so. Birds see laterally, two realities, two brain halves process each one – and ... do they put the realities together? We see in depth because of our eyes and nose – flat faces see ahead ... but we have one brain, though it's also in two halves. One half for concrete, one for fantasy. The eagle has two concrete scenes – the mice in both, at different times.

'God has a special brain which sees in time, not colour. A brain like the universe, the universe's mind. So, finity, the everything, has only light and dark. God's brain is not like ours – it must convert space and motion into time. Black time, white time – what's here and you can't see it, what isn't here and is invisible. We human animals, we have a half that's practical and solves our problems, the other half's fantastical, exotic: orientalist. That's why we see just one reality, but it makes no sense. We see a context, a future – but it's hypothetical. We concoct a meaning for the concrete – but it's just mirage. Meaning must have future, or it's instinct. Those halves.... We are unique, our brains are – but they're no use at all to us, the halves. They beguile, deceive. We have a brain that can perceive what isn't. So what? It's not! In every other way, we're just like everyone, the other brother beasts – so when we die, it's all wiped out.'

'You are exceptional, Denise,' I say, in admiration. 'You're weird, and more than that, a specialist in weirdness. You talk to you, and maybe in your life, you will find other yous. That will be horrible, disturbing, too. But you are right there, at the start – prying the life project open, the mollusc. One in a billion has a pearl. The designer must be you, at God's elbow. You realise matter isn't difficult to make. Not just rocks and fossils, space bangs and volcanoes – the hard part's seeing and giving meaning. That's where the difficulty began, always begins. How to record it, and have us think: – and not just us, but rats and bats and crocodiles – each seeing different colours: what to eat, and what eats us and them....'

'You make me sound an idiot, Osman,' Denise says, quite irritated. 'I smoke the berries to relax – to bring me down. Living makes you overheat. Try it some time. Sleeper, awake!' She shouts, kicks me on the thigh, and prepares a fanfare with both hands – a trumpet flaring from her nose.

'Many people have found the answer, Denise,' I say. 'Reality is dual, not singular. Like experience. You and it. You and the observer. You and all the other objects. Eagles know. You can't put the two realities together because they keep coming apart and making different shapes. Get used to it! It's why you're a genius, and so am I. It's a banality of the banal.... All that's there, that can be known – it is banal. Discover that the earth is round? Flat? How dull and evident. And so it goes. The smaller you are born, the quicker you react, the brighter coloured is the world. Experience is multiple, it signifies – well, suppose the eagle had flies' eyes ... would it see more...?'

'Well, certainly, you can't have it seeing less,' Denise says, concluding.

She doesn't hold the pace, she spurts, then falls away: 'All of us – we're on the stage, we wear our eyes, our wings: our brains go sparking on and off.....'

I say: 'What is the play, the scene? Variety? Just being different? No plot, and over-production of some scripts no one has learnt, no one remembers them – it's all an improvisation, adults only – over the lights, into the pit we go – the biggest ones are taking bows, a step forward into the lights – and down we go, a row of stars and divas in lace and paint, into the dark....'

'You have no wife, no children, Osman,' Denise says, taking a step back. 'I could be those for you. It makes me sad, to think not having people saves you all the trouble.'

'You could be a child, Denise,' I say. 'The same age as me. My child. Or me....'

We laugh. We're not serious. I say, 'I miss the Altai. Everything there is unused, it's like a storehouse of things too big to fit in where there's people – mountains, plains, the cold. It's like there was another Russia, waiting, immense, an empty history, without the tragedy you've left behind. There's a train, even ... The Altai makes sense of the trip you've taken: – the camels look at you, great flocks of them, and keep on staring – it takes hours for you to pass out of their sight. Who knows what there is for them to look at afterwards?'

'Each other?' Denise guesses.

I go on, 'The shaman will take your soul, put in for safe keeping – in a bird. An eagle. A swan. And send it off. The swans go to Bangladesh. You have to pay him. Of course.'

'That you sold your soul, I can believe,' she says: 'Not that you know the Altai. In pictures, possibly.'

'I'm an explorer, Denise,' I say. 'We come back, we have the pictures, and the memories. There's nothing more.'

I have the pictures, you could make a book of them. Nothing that I found could I have taken back, back to here. When voyaging, you mustn't think of coming back, of a return.... Try another voyage, maybe, an exploration, unplanned? – terrain sticky like spider's silk ... my legs stuck in a parcel that's waiting to be wound around the rest of me.

Denise – she sees the humour – or at least she laughs a lot. We humans – climbed the ladder of existence, invented the big Ego who is calling us: up the steps we toiled, pushing down the disbelievers and the pastel shades, down among the snakes they go....

At the top – you can eat anyone you want! Ants or aardvarks, whales or weasels. But you have to work hard, being a busy bee, a beetle that eats shit ... prelate or postman, gopher or ghost, and then you die and make a shadow that a tree can cast, a spray of foam tossed by a leaping fish. Absolutely born with nothing: leaving nothing, your unworn nothingness's new pair of shoes passed to the doctor who ignored you.... Laugh! Denise, laugh! The vanity, the humiliation, your voice the noise the skin makes on the empty drum....

Is it worth it – take a few other bastards with you, launch the grenade, and all of us – we go together...?

You're sensible, Denise: live by your bong and do no harm.

*

'The village kids,' Denise says. 'I knew exactly what they'd do. I thought of it myself, but in a fantastic, innocent way. Here, the people haven't started yet to humanise, detach from the landscape, the other animals. And when they start – they're still in families, in swarms, like killer wasps. They've far to go before they start to suffer individually....'

The lads had always thought they'd burn the house, the berries all over it, a creeper, roasting like coffee beans, take them on a trip and all would settle back again.... And me inside – the explorer who never found a thing, nor brought it back – a stranger, strange and foreign, negligible, and if he left or boiled, that would be insignificant.

It was.

They burned the house. Not me.

It's like the cops, who'd burn a ton of cannabis, before it started to be worth big cash in stores: – no one got high, it was the law, no more than that. They didn't have a network, couldn't sell, and feared the competition. The smoke did nothing for you but obscure the light; a smell of poisoned hay.

'My friend was clean,' Denise would say of me. 'He didn't use, not anything. It was too late. He'd lost the memories along the way, but had the photos left.'

'Kids' stuff, Denise,' I say. 'Pot! Not serious – "going to pot": – they nailed you with a phrase. The giggle of an idiot – that's all.

'The house has gone, my cash as well. Do I leave, or just move in with you?' I ask: '*My* accomplishments – gone to sepia. Bones of cuttle-fish. *Your* aspirations, never taking off. Just swirls of fiction in your head.'

'I don't want you any nearer to me, Osman,' Denise says. 'For myself – I crave more depth, more excavations, hidden profundities. Not yours. You're a traveller, a passenger, a renter, carried by your cash. Those dreary brown scenes from the Ottomans, your eye-spy under the camera's mackintosh, the scenes inverted – what a pain! – the camel and your slave, upside-down – they make me puke. Postcards. The language you never spoke, the clan you never joined and wouldn't want you. The journey back to where you came from – never finished, useless anyway. You come from wherever you are now, promiscuous. No one knows the beginning, who you were, if you were anything, why the Manchurians, the Han, the Mongols – didn't want you nor did you want them.... Futility! The damage done, the empire built on scores of others, the plaster hides what came before, layer on layer, covering the angels' wings, until all's effaced. You don't exist! Each second, you live, you die. You're you, not someone else's past.'

'I don't identify, Denise,' I say. 'Not with that, nor you, nor where I am. Time is not a desert you can cross, and reach rivers, or a sea.'

'No more smoke for me, Osman,' she says. 'I see how we seem: – we're desperate. You could cut us out, stick us on paper; in a book. Sell us. Make a cutesy movie of us. It could end in blood or tenderness. I am indifferent. I stick it out here, where I lie. Tomorrows don't attract.

'Those arsonists – they should have warned me – I'd have given you a ticket out – but as it is, we're classically, and for eternity – damned and desperate.'

'If we're extreme,' I say. 'We might get a something out of it. A screenplay. A hillwalk named after me....'

'You're a clown, Osman,' she says. 'But at least – a tragic one.'

I don't say what kind of clown I find in her ... maybe those rough-and-tumble ones, with pails of ice water down inside their pants, a challenge to convention, to good taste. No pretence of gymnastic excellence.

She's slummocky like the rest here – no eccentricity, except the holey slippers and the henna *mèche.*

'The cops – aren't looking for the arsonists,' she says. 'You can be reassured ... an accident ... there'll be no vendettas. Stay here, with me, until....'

'Until I don't, Denise,' I say. 'It's you, with a safe line that fixes cops! You're in cahoots. Your pact's with them, no legal charges are worthwhile. You want me here with you just now: it's temporary. Maybe the fire was started while you were an innocent – an innocent who told them just to harvest, not to burn....'

'If it were so,' Denise complains, starting to cry, 'so what? Nothing will change. The crop, besides, is done; the sheaves – you might say – all brought in. And useless too.'

'Yours is the departure lounge, Denise,' I say. 'Farewell eternal. For me, each door leads to a different continent.'

'We'll fight them off, the gangs,' Denise says – 'I'll let you use my gun.'

'No, nothing doing,' I say. 'I've lost my fight. My story's finished.'

'What fight?' she asks. 'You served on pirate ships ... this is a pleasure boat. Relax and drift.'

'I admit,' I say, 'most states are pirate ships. Pirates steal, throw prisoners overboard: it is their job. What matters is the treatment of their crew. The Bolshevik state was, is – a pirate ship. It had the blessing that the sailors got their due.... All welcome; just take the risks.'

'Are you sure?' she asks. 'Those matelots don't seem to mind they've lost their privileges. And if Russia was a galleon, an antique, what of the battleship America? Each broadside blessed by God, on target too, or close....'

'The lower decks are full of guys in chains,' I say. 'They can't be released while they're at sea....'

*

'What I would like,' I say, 'is to be a petrel, migrate for three years across the sea – the waves like rolling music staves – maybe we petrels hum, compose an oratorio of storms, since our voices don't stretch to song. Land in a place unvisited, and build ... who knows for what? Like nothing seen before, or never seen at all. Then fly back against the wind – five years, and have another lay an egg for me, identical to me, the chick, and when I die I'm him or her, and three years voyaging, under the moon, in lockstep with the sun. And on a beach forlorn where no one's been, to build a structure no one's seen and no one will – there comes the wagging finger critical: the prompt erasure by the waves....'

'I am amazed, I'd never thought of that, not any of it,' says Denise. She finds my tale a revelation: 'I can't imagine why you'd want to be ... a lonely bird....'

'Well, there you are,' I say. 'That's you, and me. There's petrels, and there's old crows. They don't have much to talk about together.'

'It isn't good,' she says. 'You have to slow it down, or else it's all over, finished in a thrash of wings ... hurrying, creating – it will be a death. Happy are those expecting nothing in their lives, and nothing expected from them.'

'You're free, Denise, involved and even in control,' I say. 'I'm not. I know. I'm in the trap – I'm light, so it's not the pit, for elephants – it's for the lighter ones ... impala, peccories. A woven trap, that whisks you up and up, up to the canopy. You see a vast expanse. It's useless, all is unattainable – struggle tires you, acquiescence is your death.'

*

'I accept, Denise,' I say. 'We cannot walk in step – but, I am desperate. The gangs here, the cops and the accusations ... they weigh on me. My sad condition.... Are you indifferent? Don't care, don't want to be involved, don't understand? Maybe you're on the other side – so, you exclude me, suspect the worst of me – or is it that you have to find a reason for disliking me, not wanting to be involved, or is it that you see in me the essence of your own frustrated hope...?

'And yet,' I persist, when no answer comes, 'You are a friendly type, a busybody in the mildest way. I appeal to you....'

'No,' she says, 'I really do not understand. What do you ask of me? You've lived a life – have you learnt nothing, no wise saying.... If you end up as ash and smoke, what am I supposed to know...?'

'You are a rubber-tree, Denise,' I say. 'What you extrude – it bounces off, a ball, a wheel, a tire – away, away! The words, the deeds – ephemeral.... The tree itself…? Voiceless, tall and unyielding....'

'Yes,' she says, 'that is a tree. But me...?'

'The lads, the cowboys – they shoot at us, at the bushes round your house, when they pass by....' I say.

'They're just trying out the guns,' she says. 'Accept, Osman, that everything but you is cast in a normality. You are the exception – enjoy it if you can. Think what you might want, what satisfies ... wish it....'

'I want? A lady admiral from Belize, us drinking kosher wine, cat's cradle with a ball of goats' wool, and Gil Evans on the gramophone,' I say. 'Or something like, or something not like that at all....'

'You never get what you have wished,' she says. 'A proverb, but it's true.'

This can't be called a village – it's a scattered settlement, the people guard their boundaries and hate the newcomers till they leave, and hate the people living here for centuries, steal their sheep, kidnap the women and cut their faces with iron knives....

I'm a hunter by a lake. I have a spear, and must go into the mud and reeds ... I go in, deeper and deeper. It's hard to swim. I don't even know if I can, or if what I'm doing is 'swimming'. I need help and instruction. But the water's deep and I am frightened. There's fish here, they're all around, they flirt under me, I clutch at them, the spear floats away, useless – I make a basket with my hands –

there's so many fish, catfish, torpedoes, I have twenty, thirty, big ones – they can't flap away, there's too many, they're all hemmed in, but I've no way of holding them, they weigh me down. If I grab them, kill them – there's too many, and I can't eat them or take them to shore. If I let them go, they're gone for ever....

'You're not that hunter, Osman,' Denise says. 'The wrong height, the wrong colour. Do you have a family? A clan? A tribe? Maybe you're enslaved, or maybe those fish aren't for you but for your master.... Riddles, my dear – they show you aren't part of the scene. You're none of what you might imagine – empathy is for the guilty, the privileged. Those who suffer don't feel empathy. You need to change many things before you're equipped to wet your toes, Osman. Or you could drown: have flashbacks, hallucinations. Transmit an emotion. Scandalise.

'See? You can't; none of that. You're not in our century. You just see going after all those fish leads to bad times. Death for you. We began threading through the maze, and it has led us – humans – to the centre, the monster, the minotaur. But not yet: it hurts, hurts everyone – you're not a desperate case that somebody might help. Until you're past salvation, you must be a brave soldier. That's the contract.'

'People still drown, Denise,' I say, 'trying to get out of bad places. Then there is fear – fear of leaving, fear of starting it all over.'

'Strange,' says Denise. 'People get locked up for being bad, or imprudent, having the wrong friends. You don't have friends, are prudent – and beside, bad people seem to circulate a lot outside the jails.... You weren't confined – only constrained....'

'No, I was penned in,' I say. 'You didn't know if it was for life, and if that life was very very short....'

'Oh well,' she says. 'That was your politics. Meddle in that, what do you expect?'

'Keeping me,' I say. 'It doesn't cost. Re-use my clothes, have me chop wood for winter. Give me salted food, cheap and won't spoil – herrings, cheese, salt pork – like a sailor, down among the chained men, a castaway, tossed up on the beach. You could live like that for ever, no one has bothered fixing you a date of death.'

She laughs. 'It's living with your fear. It drives us mad; and then, if someone comes for you....'

'I've done nothing,' I say. 'Almost nothing. They only come for you if you've accomplished what you're set on. Losing it – it should destroy you. And mostly – your accomplishment is making kids, having a secret lover, blackmailing the boss, buying false documents. Or not needing to do any of that at all.'

'What did you set out to do, Osman?' she asks. She laughs.

'Like children, Denise,' I tell her. 'They get a cardboard theatre when they are six or so, with paper actors. All your life, when the gift has long since been destroyed, you listen to what they say, the characters. String it together, dialogues, make a drama. Get some good acting from them. It should be good, that play, it's bits of what you've seen and want – the figures have their rules, their personalities....'

'That's you,' she says. 'Not me at all. It's fey and whimsical. The point about the play is you ought not be part of it. It should communicate. I sit there in the audience. Your stuff is silent and untitled – shadows. Someone behind the cloth manipulating rods and strings. Always you, and about you.'

'Yes,' I say. 'That's it. Exactly it.'

'Oh,' she says. 'Your difficulty's with everyone. We've all had that. Some had a lot of cardboard theatres. You cut them out of milk cartons and cereal boxes. It used to be for boys, then girls developed it, and now it's gone, gone totally. Dead. When theatre ends, no one looks at themselves.'

'I'm desperate, Denise. Help me,' I say.

'Ask me anything but that, Osman. Not help. No obligations,' Denise says. 'Maybe if I'd met you earlier, followed your stories, seen you put on the makeup – every clown chooses and it's theirs indelible until their death.... Seen you make the pratfalls, stand you up again.... As it is, I've gotten so I can't bear you. You won't change. You go on and on. Space is infinite, you can keep falling for ever, but it's always you falling and waving, shouting, grasping....'

'They're not pratfalls, Denise,' I say. 'Somersaults, perhaps. It was my French Revolution. The first one went on for centuries. Then there was the next – in Russia, and it went all over – Africa, China, and I was in it, and its victim and its fan, its mother and its critic, judge, survivor.... Why do these people here chase me? They know exactly who I am....'

'They don't care, Osman,' Denise says. 'You know why they chase you? Because they know you'll run. And your run is laughable. That's all. Nothing personal.'

'Shelter me, Denise,' I say: 'If I have space, I can devise a message....'

'You are an insect full of legs and sticky stuff,' she says. 'You cling. Perhaps you sting. Your values are a nonsense.... Liberty? – without power it's trivial, and power destroys your liberty. Equality threatens the difference we want to be assured: and no one concedes it anyway. Solidarity – it takes a state to make it real: laws, uniforms, Osman! States, laws and uniforms – they cancel solidarity when an interest is under threat. I'm free because I compromise, make deals, make friends and allies, and I have nothing other people want – no cash, no body and no voice. Live with your mistakes, Osman! Start from another place and end up differently.... Try to seem complicated, not just assertive. Say, do, things, but all the while, think others. Marry a girl from Maryland, divorce her because you're not good enough for her.'

'I understand that,' I say. 'The paradoxes. You free yourself, I understand, and then you find you are the only free person in your town, and spend your life trying to defend your life....

'Everything would need to change, before I felt safe here. I would need to transform almost everything. I've no way of making a debt for you that you would need to pay me back. I've no hold on anyone, no obligation, moral or financial.... No appeal, no attractiveness.

'I need somewhere....'

'To change it all,' she finishes. 'And here, nothing will change. If it can improvise, it will go on. If not – there will be no one, nothing, left. We are the next in line to be the world of poor: the wretched ones. Here, you see the start: – they're used to being always poor, precarious and marginal. When they're not needed any more, when they've exhausted nature and themselves – once, they could be bandits. Now, the clans and families collapse and fade away. The young ones go to cities, into jails, or maybe just like you, in rooming houses where they'll never pay the rent.

'You were given an itinerary, and you followed it, and here you are. If you were clever, you'd have refused, gone somewhere else.

'So, the great change. Where'll you start?'

*

'*Je n'ai jamais vu la Chine*....'

'I have to study,' I tell Wu. 'To see if I could live there. I'm set on Tianjin, but I must understand what people say....'

Wu: the Takeaway they call her – 'Just racism: ignore them!'

'Why shouldn't you live there?' she asks. 'And understand? Everyone who goes to school is able to....'

'I'm not sure,' I say. 'I can't do the tones, can't differentiate between them. Then there are the words: I understand the oracle bones, but if I want to say "a flight of owls..." there is an obstacle. There's the distinction between long and short-tailed birds, and I'm not sure about the owls ... though I could do the sounds and flap my hands....'

'Stop reading and listen to me,' says Wu. 'Forget the characters while you learn the sounds....'

'Things don't decline,' I say. 'I feel I'm stuck where there's no roads or sun ... no gender, time – all these made up what I called home.... My native tongue, running foxy on my teeth....'

'A child can draw a picture, write a poem,' she says, exasperated, 'Forget the tenses. You're not so different, even if you're not a child.'

'I may have left it late to understand,' I say. 'I can read the signs out in the streets, the stores and the directions, but not relationships....'

'You know what they say,' she says, and laughs. 'China has no friends, just interests. Your interest is living there and finding friends – how can you get over this, surmount the contradiction...?'

... '*mais je l'imagine* ...' (Georges Dor)

*

'You've no persistence,' says Denise, 'and China is the worst place for you. You'd be safe, but under suspicion – of what you'd done, where you had come, what were you doing there. Questions that here you'd love to have been asked. And no one will. But there – what would you do, without language, without reading, without a conversation?'

'I could watch the little screen,' I say. 'Most do.'

'Who are you on that screen? You aren't!' she says. 'Nothing personal. You are anonymous, exactly what you wouldn't want to be – a breeze, a scurry of a leaf, dead or alive, real or an invention – it's irrelevant.

'First, as animals go – we're different. That's the idea – first you imagine, then you build. The others don't, they say. That is creation – not the imagining alone, but the consequences too. Bees build – they don't need imagine. We do. I wonder why. Because only imagining do you build a complex thing, that's not the *pueblo* where you live and die? I don't believe it – not for a moment. It's a fraud. Bees are like us – they're clever, but they're limited. Dupes: – they make the honey that we steal. That's it.'

'I could have another life,' I say.

'It's dangerous here,' she says. 'And you provoke. I'm safe, as safe as you can be in nature, with all the animals around – the imaginative ones, they burned your house. It wasn't yours – and that was wise of you .... We'll get old, and shaky, we'll forget, and down we'll go. That is the best.... You lose your edge.'

'Of course,' I say. 'I could go without language. Who would know, or care? China is getting back where it was two centuries ago, before it slipped and the dogs of war and punishment chewed it up. Stuff. China has been good at that, for ever. Screens and poetry, brushwork, singing metal birds, like an infinity of Charlie Parkers....'

'It's true,' says Denise, indifferent as usual. 'If you don't speak, no one will know you can't. Or can.'

'I'd want to see those pots,' I say. 'With hollow legs, where you can make millet soup while in the pan itself, there's healthy food a-seething.... And once you recognise the character for pot, or maybe plough – you see them everywhere, the roots that lie within, or have procreated, given birth to other characters and concepts, contexts, sideways slips ... so, writing makes the telephones and graders, tanks and spaceships. It's an imagining that attracts, but I wouldn't expect it to be the basis of a civilisation. It's not the way I'd set up shapes and usages but....

'How can we have lived without it – "pot". Quite meaningless – a case of words and things not corresponding, not at all. They rarely do. Why should they? A word is not a sound – the same with sinigrams – a character is not the base – it maybe follows eye, not tongue, you study from a principle, the principle is not the start.... I think when I was that first person with a spear, a pointer – you see the tree ... not sound, for sure. And what is tree? A perch, a nest, a chair, a fruit, a shade. What sound, what sounds, can correspond to these? The same with pots – the special kind with cavity legs that boils and steams – that's home and hearth, reward and taste and being where you live and farm the millet.... It's many things, and not a sound, and many characters are born from it, with sisterly resemblances, no doubt.... But see the character – and then the shape – a marquee, a woman in a long skirt, a dog with thin legs and shaggy fur but all in place like fir-cones on a pine – quite like a chow.... No wonder the Chinese are so much cleverer and write their poetry and see how matter and cognition form a unity, a plastic installation that always opens out to broader and to broader views....'

'You can stay here, imagine China, don't let it take up room, though it will be pervasive, enormous, filling all the empty lands before you reach Kokand....' she says. 'But then, Osman, you've set a limit to us who live here: you've imagined the death and flight of everyone. The place, the continent, is dying; we'll have somehow to leave. We stole the global wealth, and now we've nothing left, nothing to envy, no resource: no loot.

'Who will take us in? We're demanding and bigoted, pushy and arrogant. If I don't want you near me, Osman, imagine how they'll feel about you on Sumatra or in Windhoek.... Maybe we should choose a sample; warriors and ballerinas, let the rest of us wither: halms.... Or like poisoned bugs....

'So, if you're chosen, Osman, are you going to pack books and dictionaries? They're no use for bartering....'

'No one can say you're complicit or corrupt, Denise,' I say. 'If there's time for tombstones, I'll write that on yours. You face the front. You go along with doom, it doesn't shake you, you don't take your destiny seriously.'

'It isn't easy, Osman,' says Denise. 'Being simple is as hard as travelling your shifting boundaries, the complex infinity of origami worlds.... You are much diminished. All you hope is that your catastrophe comes not from some kid's whim, but from recognition of your greatness never realised. Now, you won't change your place, your possibilities – you've only folding realities, over and over back to the clean sheet....

'The Jacobins and Bolsheviks – those who lived by their imagining, imagined they were in a world unrolling, a path star-specked with galaxies: the unseen and unbelievable becoming real as on and up they flew.... Imagined worlds, Osman. For them, it ended bad. The rest, the others – they are modulation: accidentals. As for the capitalists – the poetic ones imagined that the riches that ended in their bank, and only theirs, enriched the world. Instead – the wretched toilers stayed just that – wretched. If they were fortunate, the toilers kept their toil, and made more wealth for someone else.

'So, be careful what you are imagining – it can turn out bad....'

'Mistaken? In bad faith? Bad in that sense?' I ask.

'Oh,' she says, 'you know it all, much more than me.'

Mount a mirror on a truck and blast if off – see the universe almost at the start. Next time – try to see it almost at the end. The second journey may not take so long.

Change the climate, save us all, save the pigs, the sheep, the worms, the monkeys ... *pli selon pli*.... 'may you live ten thousand years' – and indeed you shall. Why not? Depends on how you fold the sheet. And how you count. The square of paper holds all shapes, but is only ever its own, unchanging dimensions, its original square.

It doesn't satisfy? If not, it must be because – there is no satisfaction. Satisfaction is a condition inexistent. A category error. Infinity precludes satisfaction. It's too bad, but there it is.

Not all roads lead to the sea, the world turns, but you don't move. You've had the choice, the chance – you're stuck. The future comes – resolving nothing. The chicken that you counted turns back into the egg.

'The cops won't have you,' says Denise. 'You might try a gang. It's banal – but anyway, you're wrong. I'm satisfied, here in my space-ship, digesting space and time. If that star-trekking cat's immortal, even a small bit, maybe its tail, I could get there too, where it is lurking – hungry, probably wants a cuddling by now....'

'It's true,' I say. 'A gang attracts. Usually, it survives, there's order for the warriors and if they don't obey, they end real bad. You, if you're the boss, you rule your roost. You don't do all you'd want, but then, the guys who aren't with you, they go hungry. Just the foot soldiers – they don't count for much. You aren't in business, don't lay bricks, what you do's a mystery, but if you fail, can't pay your way – the pattern's set. A new bunch comes in, greedy, rotten, tries to follow what you did. It is a tribute, in a way....'

'Let others have their say,' she says. 'Even if they're ignorant. Let them protest....'

'You can't do that,' I say. 'You will stagnate, or others take you over and you'll lose the way....'

'What way is that, Osman?' she asks. 'If you're not boss, who'll you obey?'

'You make it sound naive,' I say. 'The aim's survival for the world....'

'Oh well,' she says. 'If I were you, I wouldn't start from here, this place.... Even those who've never been elsewhere don't wish survival on this space, this grounded boat and all its crew....'

'I've been disappointed, Denise,' I say. 'I spin the wheel – so far, it turns and turns and all the numbers – they are blank.'

'It's quite too much,' she says. 'You are insatiable, Osman. Failure is your vindication, it confirms your belief that life is so. Yet you seek a lucky break. Suckers don't get that, never – it's the point. And now I've this Anna making claims on me. How they progress, demands: a room, a house, a home – a garden "if I can". A loan, a gift, a capital, a fortune – investment in a movie. She's here because she lost the cash, everybody makes these slender films about the tenderness, the rage, in marriage and cohabitation. She's Polish, and she found that Poles aren't interested in sentimental tales about themselves.'

'I have a theme,' I say. 'Would do for her. Tough, political – it shoots itself....'

'You two,' Denise says. 'Two failures. That's coincidence, and coincidence is rare. Another failure, that's not rare at all.'

*

'The Workers' Opposition. Dramatic, women heroes, tragedy – the saga going on....' I say.

'Oh no!' says Anna. 'History! How people hate that. Russians! How I hate them.... Women heroes failing ... who would want to know?'

'The right actors, Anna,' I say. 'They make the history. Forget about the script. The Russians – they have interests, they don't have friends but they have relatives – some by marriage. The money....'

'Yes, the money,' Anna says, stretching out and up her stringy neck. 'Had you thought.... Surely, Osman, it's not you who'd go around and ask for it? The pebble glasses, muddy clothes, dark as a mole's.... What a picture! Turning over those gouged-out gravestones....'

'If you bring cash in,' I say. 'The people here will give their love quite indiscriminately. For sure, we need them – love and cash.'

Our brains – are pockets. We turn over our thoughts as if they're cents.

'Workers' control of everything,' I say. 'A free opposition, principled, political; and free elections – it's explosive, Anna. It challenges the world ... the universe, no less.'

'We're unemployed,' says Anna. 'There's nothing we might control. We should think of fashion, taste. People like to see themselves, dragged in their street clothes, reticent, on to the stage, to play out dramas that they're living through, hope will end well but fear they won't.... "Where is the humanity, the nature we should trust...?" they ask.'

'Your question's answered, Anna: over and over. It's grown stale,' I say.

'Those ancient visionaries,' she says. 'Your founding grandfathers. We'd have to show they're idiots, as well as dead. Our movie'd have to show the idea fails. It is the law of art, aesthetics, and raising of cash. Ideas are crazy, and the more they grow, the more they threaten the believers.... Creating more nostalgics – that is your consolation. Making a film about ideas – you have to show the possibilities, and then back off: all ideas must fail. That's why we are in the business, you and I – we know what the conventions are, and how they cling on to reality. In the concrete world, we have no hope. All we have, is talent, so – we spin the wheel, just like you say, once in a while we win the prize, but mostly – not....'

> '*The sole and only work and deed accomplished by universal freedom is therefore death ...*'
>
> G.F. Hegel

'I believe in mystery,' says Anna. 'I believe that every story has a mystery, the creator, author, slips it in, knows exactly what it is, but buries it.... It's what people think they may reach, their end and purpose, when all they do is History; being present, doing things, then dying. Self-projection through action: – a process without a mystery. That is what we humans are. Dull and repetitious.

'No mystery. One thing follows another thing. The idea that what we do is *for* something other than its immediate purpose, a *beyond*: – that is art. Cinema. That's why only stories of a failure have traction with the critics. A happy end? No mystery. Failure, though – is infinite, and infinitely repeatable.'

'We could get the gangs to act it out,' I say. 'You don't need pros. In fact, actors would kill it all. People watch actors, as though they're real. A person, say. Even when it's been explained they act; not a person, but a version.... Gangsters are frightening – send up the tension.'

'Oh,' Anna says. 'You must believe there is a person there, on the stage and afterwards. Reality! Believe! You see it in the actor's pose. It's what you pay your ticket for.'

'You're right,' I say. 'I am your father. I pontificate.

'I can find you consolation for being Anna, having suffered from her failures, for her melancholy. Another throw of the dice is usually enough. Chance, hope – who will distinguish? But for myself – is there consolation? That Opposition that has dominated my life, and is *my* failure.

Where is my balance, my inner satisfaction for living it with honesty ... flying the flag, not ever gaining a centimetre of fresh ground...?'

'Oh, faddle,' Anna says. 'There is no consolation for what happens, not for anything. Failure is because you've not been good enough – and that is all. My melancholy is my cure, not the affliction: like all healers, you mistake the therapy for the disease. Your ideas, Osman, have had their day, they're thin and shaky, your fictions, padded with your quips and whimsies, droop. You suffer in this awful place because you think "this is not the end – it's too absurd to be my destiny, I shall arise...." It isn't so.'

She says, 'I have the power to leave. You don't. This, for you, is it. The End.'

Anna dresses well. It may be for interviews and cadging cash, but you can tell when woollen tops, long skirts, weren't made by grannies for the forest shop. There is insouciance, a lack of foresight, a worldliness, refusal to be cautious, that stands out in her....

However good your clothes, it's hard to sell them, make a profit when you have to buy yourself some more. Pants made by a tailor would be hard to shift. What fits too well won't go on anybody else. And somehow, you must find a substitute to wear.

Anna's a walking-stick – travelled, unvarnished. Full of character, as they say, but whittled down, straighter than a branch, a bough.

'Talking to you, Osman, is like talking to you twenty, thirty, years ago,' she says. 'Or to someone alive long before you were born, who uses your mouth to speak old words.... As if you've conquered time and death, and you're proud to ignore them now. To us – it is macabre.'

'You must remember, Anna,' I say. 'The *Bund*, the Workers' Party? Mensheviks? It's not trivial. It's been written up extensively.'

'I remember the history,' she says. 'Or – I remember reading the history. It's dead, and everyone is dead, and reading about it – you must escape, or you're dead too.'

'It's partly so,' I say. 'And yet – they had the vision. It is the seed, the cold season before the stinging frost that permits the germination, a new crop....'

'I might have helped you with a drama,' Anna says. 'But this obsession is out of order, out of credibility. That Opposition – suicidal!'

'People make stories out of stories,' I say. 'All invented, about much older magic and its gods – and people watch. All fantasy, all anomalies. I don't, and won't, follow: not for a fortune. But ancient wars, heroes and warriors – you see them strutting, banging, bleeding, everywhere. As film, as tattoos, on detergent boxes.... Such popularity, unquestioning....'

'And yet,' she says, 'you've no patience with the people here .... For you, they can't be masters of their destinies.'

'No,' I say. 'I'll change my side to deal with them. They're dolts, insentients, potatoes in the sack. They need telling everything – who they are, what's to be done, and what they must become. As it is – they think they're on the leading edge, the future of mankind. It must not be! Force! Discipline and guidance. The only way.'

'Pik is the boss. Get Denise to square it with the cops – they'll all help to make your gangster movie, Anna. Pik will take the lead....' I say.

'Don't be aggrieved, Osman,' she says. 'Your story's a disaster – maybe the gangster one is too.... We know the conventions – help me out, or go and find your paradise....'

'Pik,' I say, 'you have suffered. Living in a village where there is no imagination.... You're given an exemption from consequences by the police, for service to the state .... One of those postcolonial wars in Africa ... You organised the traffic, had the reward of escaping punishment....'

'Oh, the poor children,' Denise says, quite vague. 'Anna! Be careful with them, for they have no imagination. The paper mill, now ruined, had a brief life as a reformatory. All the village children were shut up there ....'

'The beds,' says Pik, 'so narrow, we could not explore each other, not mind, nor body.... We are stultified....'

'What you stole from Africa,' says Anna, suddenly enlightened. 'The tree, the plant of life. You set it up to grow on Osman's lodgings, then burnt it down.... Though avidity? Or remorse? Or nastiness ... fetishism, possibly....'

'Alas,' says Pik, 'a touch of all of those.'

'I have some doubts,' I say. 'Pik could be the villain of the story. He's sallow, must be forty, has a tic. Crimes infinite, even against humanity – a veritable *Jedermann*. We all will recognise ourselves in him – and yet....'

'Yes,' says Pik. 'There is a lack of true theatricality. I do not hover, cast dark shadows. It's how I was brought up. Good and evil – those terms mean nothing to me. Was I bad, or did I just conform? Analysing what is bad takes philosophers a while, and now they don't see it as their kind of question. I haven't made great profits yet, while they decide. And when they do – what then? There's slender pickings here, I fear. Since all here live in fear – I cannot terrify.... There's no reward for being good, for being bad, and so mere intimidation would pass unnoticed, unremarkable.'

'I'm a pro,' says Anna. 'I direct. I edit, too. I have the power to make you fill your gaps. That's what art's for. I'll make a monster of you, Pik; the Murderer amongst us.'

'I've done terrible things,' says Pik. 'That's what they might conclude. Myself – I'm unimpressed, unmoved. I feel nothing special, not for my excess, nor for my particular brutality. All's done, naturally, in self-defence. What I have done is what you do, if you are boss. It's so if you are president, or God, or smuggle drugs.

'And after all, here they geld pigs with bricks, eat turkeys, hang them up in chimneys to be smoked....'

'Now, now!' shouts Anna. 'None of your vegan rhetoric here. You should see our Polish sausages! We need feel no competition....'

'Peace, Anna,' Pik shouts back. 'Don't you want to see my fieldmarshals and lieutenants?'

'What are you going to conquer, Pik?' she asks, ready to be swept away – 'To energize this place, you need a continental plan.... A cocked hat helps....'

'I have all you could ever need, my dear,' says Pik.

It must be true – there's only ever one plan, and one person only, who has it cornered in their mind.

'You've started an avalanche, Denise,' I say. 'Or an eruption. Pik does hot and cold, a magma or a floe. Now, I have a tiny beef. Your house is full of stuff – and immense corsets, like tiny floorless bandstands, made of cast iron – I can't get in or out my room....'

'Oh,' she says. 'They're portable shrines. You get inside and then parade and whirl and dance....'

‘I thought you were a sceptic,’ I tell her, ‘Now you’ve all this paraphernalia, candle holders, whips and stuff ... even the faith....’

‘Those shrines,’ she says. ‘Are better than belief. You wear them. You show off, like in carnivals. Once you realise parades are a no man’s land, you find you can do anything at all in them: strip off, self-mutilate. Then, when you have had your strut, you make the rest adhere: proclaim yourself: bring in a host of priests, mount ceremonies with angels, the sick, the dead – and fireworks! Constellations of them! It will seem the end of all our worlds: it is. You can decree the universe starts over, with different rules. No one will trust you, but so what?

‘Your opponents? They must believe. If they don’t – it’s an apostasy. It means they’ve chosen the wrong side. Perversity. It means you’ve chosen evil, the wrong kind of sex, wrong comrades, wrong paradise....’

‘You keep on stabbing at religion. It should be dead by now,’ I say....

‘It’s all about belief,’ she says. ‘It’s about belief in anything at all – not spiritual, not mystery, not sociality and stick-together, not revelation. Belief that anything at all is why it seems: up, down, red, black. Get inside one of these shrines, and twirl with it. It’s better than expensive dope....’

‘Am I in the plot, Denise?’ I ask. ‘Is this the movie? Do I stand out against Pik’s plan somehow?’

‘You don’t have the balls, Osman,’ she says. ‘You hope and hope next time your wrong decision and your flops will gain you recognition. They will not. Pik does what comes naturally, and does it well. You are your losing side – you rush in, over and over, to defeat at your own hand. It’s ludicrous!’ She laughs.

‘This guy,’ says Pik, referring to me, and addressing no one and the world. ‘Where’s he from? Jail? A war? Anyway, a loser who thinks he’s won, who thinks surviving is a victory....’

‘Yes, Osman,’ Anna asks. ‘Which side are you on today? Who’s next? Russia? China? First it was Russia – they were so unlike you, and you admired them so. Then China. The same reasons.’

‘Reasons, for sure,’ I say, ‘They’re continents, the big tough areas. They’re not like us, don’t have a literature of cows in fields, foxgloves, love-lies-a-bleeding.... They’re a sack of mixed bonbons, sweet and sour: no parliaments, not like here, where there's a party of the workers and one of bosses, throwing compromises at each other, like kids playing marbles against a wall: – to see who edges who....

'Over there you have a boss, the nation, church or customs – and frontiers, history, and awkward types who'd do you down. There, it's different, but quite understandable. Everywhere is different, but it fits in the same small box, like chess pieces, or the rules of *Go*. My sentiments – they don't have similars elesewhere, but, instead, they have a way of making it all fit. Everyone has the same colours, seasons, deaths and births.... Some metaphors, some pictures hang on walls, others are scrolls or screens, or sequences of woodcuts. That's the materials, it's sentiments that's different. Liking life, fearing death – they exist quite otherwise than us....'

They stand around. The tale is wandering, naive, and yet beneath, there's something subversive, even treasonable.

'I never heard of flowers like those,' Denise says, breaking a shaky silence. 'You've always wanted to do great things, to understand how land-masses ride and mount on one another – and you must see it's hopeless. No one cares about you, no one wants your understanding, your analysis is finicky and right, but no one wants surrender to what is true. Understanding: it gets you nowhere, the truth is green, a field of grass, each blade is true, unique, and so's the whole – inedible and bland!'

'Is Osman in the film?' Pik asks. 'A boss? A cop? No one at all?'

'If he wants,' says Anna, quite reluctant. 'He could narrate. When the story rocks a little, he could be a bridge.'

'I can't do character,' I say. 'I don't care how I look – and you, you three – to me you look like someone tried to make a monster, and you're the bits he threw away....'

'No!' says Pik. 'It's a mistake to be frightened of the golem. He's you and yours. You're punished through the golem – he's like you quite a bit: can't feel, can't tell the difference between a win, a loss.'

'Oh, who can follow this?' Denise asks. 'We march on, there's nothing else. If you stand, it's good; fall in the ditch – your day is done. That's all. The rest is painted scenery.'

'This is a good start,' says Anna. 'There's a shape here. Contribute, guys – let's make the story-board! Even another person, a golem. I thought – there's this place, and there's like you say – Russia, China, and America. Which one will get to us, or – where shall we end up?'

'Where do I fit?' asks Pik.

'Oh, anywhere,' says Anna lightly. 'There's crooks get in everywhere. The shepherd disciplines the sheep with them ...' It makes an awkward pause. There's a big diff, Pik thinks, between a crook and someone who runs a gang, provides, makes rules and laws and lots of cash: an entrepreneur ... calculation, discipline....

'I love your tattooes, Anna,' Denise says.

'Oh, I shouldn't have them,' Anna says. 'It was a dare. My arms are rather scraggy, so the big picture is wrinkled over. You get the sense, though. They've faded rather – it looks like a psoriasis.'

Pik is fascinated by us, the process of making a film out of us all ... us into a film; a 'movie', if we move around, I guess: and it's just 'cinema' if we stand still and say the words.

'Those crates are full of guns,' says Anna, pointing. 'They're not for firing. I got them in a toyshop. None of us is free until the movie's made. We'll need a lot of others for the big scenes on the plains.... They are called "extras" – a racist tinge to that, Osman, if you ask me.... Especially seeing as they're Africans, Latinos, Ukrainians – that sort ... Pik must have friends....'

'Oh,' says Pik, 'I only work with guys I know.'

'These ones won't hang around,' says Anna, hugging him. 'They say that pawns are strategy, the queen, the knights, are power: the bishops and the king intrigue. These – the soldiers, the unspeaking hordes – they are the pawns. They don't involve us, not at all. We do our drama, they do manoeuvres on the plain.'

Anna's arms, all rose and violet inks! You scan them constantly – underneath, they're brown and wrinkled, like old nylon stockings, stuffed with crumpled paper – you could use them to stop a draught, or in the garden, somehow.

'I envy you,' Denise tells her. 'You tried to stay in shape. I just gave up. Shape's an internal thing, they say....'

'Hey, Denise,' says Anna, sharp and angry. 'I love you, but I want no Sapphic stuff. I'm a straight tree, a pine, an evergreen, although all else – the universe, for instance – is a curve.'

'You must emote, my dear,' Denise says. 'The public will walk out if we're not sniffing round each other's tail.'

'If it's like that,' I say, suddenly aroused and peevish. 'I'm out. I want no part of that, even if it's paid.'

'Cool off, my friend,' says Pik. 'It's all publicity and condescension. Let the people love you. That's a need. It's not about the olden days of gangs and dealers, selling dope and tarts. Investment! Opening the mine. No dirty stuff, except what might stick to spades....

'Security and order – that's our biz. For me, the camera's just a friendly eye, complacent witness....'

'This mine,' Denise says, quizzing him. 'I don't see a hole. Are you sure it's not a con...? One of yours, for sure....'

'It's not like that, Denise,' says Pik. 'Digging and carrying – what a fuss! You sell the estimates, that's all. They are resources – good as gold prised out. So – no hole, no digging, and no tailings. You sell the goods, and leave them there. Some day – up they will come, the gold and cobalt, lithium and mammoth bones ... loads of it – grubby stuff.'

'I see all that,' I say. 'But after all, you and your guys – you're squatting here, on top....'

'We've sold it once,' he says. 'The stuff down there. And naturally, if you want it excavated – we sell it to you once again with the percentage, naturally, and so and so ... and on, until....'

'You need to know and own what is invisible,' says Anna. 'The con must have been when you were buying land....'

'The con comes when you buy the law,' says Pik. He doesn't need to carry on – we all imagine how the story goes.

'We're all so creative,' says Denise. 'It seems a waste to throw it on a film. No one will see....'

'The mystery,' Anna finishes for her. 'And if anyone of us wants sex – we're stacked and scripted, limping and wrinkled, so there's no one of us would want to screw with anybody else. The arts are said to be a sexual free-for-all, a constant cage fight in the buff. Here – it is not so. We're all too proud and staid.... It just takes Pik to raise his bleat ... he'll change the genres, the rhythm of the dance.'

'It's true,' he says. 'I am not happy with my role. It ought to celebrate me, instead I'm cast as a sad idiot who corrupts the adolescents.... I want a starring role.... An impresario, an entrepreneur, a leading edge, an influencer – something of all of those.'

'You've nothing, Pik,' says Denise. 'Sausages, Anna! That's a start. Pik's a capitalist – he should be a risk, a terror: even a terrorist with operations that he'll finance. Too finicky to take the axe himself.

'None of us has a nation, a faith, a *dusha* – a soul. We have everything and it's too much – we're kids with too many toys – piled in a corner till we decide which one to play with. Our small bellies are full, there's no digestion. We're obsessed with getting away, but we've nowhere to go, nowhere we want to be. It's not that people don't want us – of course they don't. We don't want them, nor ourselves. We need a home, a place – one we shall never see again. It doesn't matter. We'll live and die unhappy – almost everybody does. But we are irrelevant to ourselves.'

'Back to the nineteenth century.' Anna says. 'Find people there who can paint a picture of something they can call a whole, with fire and smoke and lace and roulette wheels.'

'Yes!' says Denise. 'We should do something absolutely different. Be Angolans. Get a following in Burkina. Don't follow the tornadoes, don't let cute animals mislead you: join a people, follow what's in their head.... Seek people who count for nothing, dispossesed, exploited, confined, put in camps, in deserts, in armies, up for sale, abandoned, misnamed, friendless and resentful....'

'Yes,' says Anna. 'That is the way, the answer. But we won't take it, won't respond.'

'The fire? The kids in the reformatory?' Denise asks. Does she want to know, or is it obligatory to ask?

To aspire to a tragic end, an end you call a tragedy, other people must play along. Everything depends on them.

'We must pretend we know nothing,' I say. 'Nothing at all. Fires sleep when there is nothing left for them to eat. Kids disguise themselves as grown-ups, disappear.'

*

It ends in great distress. Best get it over quick. Trim the expectations. No one gets immortality by their merit. No hope in hoping, not for me. Denise smokes and falls to pieces. Distress becomes your shell, improvised, like a hermit crab's: a rusting can, pill bottle, to hold the shards.

It ends so; time. In a wild place.

Anna protests and leaves. Pik is killed by sword, or – no! moves higher up the pile so he can see better, further.

Smoke. *Dym.* This is a place for invalids incurable: a no-man's land, a purgatory. But, we wait for no *fidanzati, fidanzate:* we evaluate no city life, no culture. No similars, no comrades, no one worth hating. No confidences, no climbing magic mountains. We just wait.

Denise smokes and smokes. Thieves could kill us both, quite easily, and steal the fetishes. Or mash us, if they're high. The trick is to reach the end together, though we hate each other quietly, like two cats who share the single bowl.

It's done. Enough. It's mawkish, but distress is deep, a pit, your empty mine. You don't notice you're the last, and anyway, you aren't. There's not much left: – ash in a tiny box, a vase for violets – they're more than adequate for what is left of you or anyone.

The end, is coming, comes –

It's done:

The End

*

I expect a lot. Adventure: as I sit, on my own, in the bar down by the docks.

I'm very young. Perhaps some paedo'll try to pick me up....

'Drink this,' shouts Aqil, shoving a wickered bottle of maraschino at me. I swig it down – and grow large, very large. Clumsy. I see that Aqil, who looks enormous too, is really small, compressed within, but wears huge clothes – shagreen thigh-boots, an oilskin coverall ... it's very hot here, must be 40° at the least, scum everywhere, mouth, nose.... 'Let's hunt!' he says.

What can there be, to hunt? We're all sat down, nothing runs. It's a city, where there's everything except the chase.

'They're all gravediggers here,' he says, leaning close. 'That's the only job secure, and they're all into it. Shrouds. I know all about those – I've been wrapped in them for ever.... Climbing, climbing – till you see the sky.' And he laughs. 'My comrades have all gone free-lance,' he says, skittering through subjects, as if he fears I'll get bored with him and leave.

The maraschino's nauseating. 'We knew capitalism was finished, biting like a dying snake,' he says. 'Who heard of capitalism on a boat? Guiding it, directing it? We all thought the same, we sailors, the landless ones. Now, the great change, the revolt must come. We had a subject destined to transform the world. The working class! We saw it, waving, on the shore. Then, when we docked – it wasn't there. It melted. Machines? Robots? Should we wait for them, their consciousness, to arise, shake off their chains?

'Who will do the deed today? School kids and whitecoats and the bienpensants? The powerless and ephemeral.'

'I don't express myself,' I say. 'I think you're right. But if you say too much....'

'Yes, you're always starting over. Saying what everybody knows,' he says. 'Too much.'

'What will we hunt?' I ask. 'Not animals. I draw a line.... Fish? Birds? Ants? I have so many lines to draw, create ... hatching, it's called.' I laugh, pleased with myself.

'Listen,' says Aqil. 'The working class abandoned liberty, and worse, abandoned power. Even its parties did! They turned their coat. Sometimes, they're the worst – at least, the best of all the worst.... They even make it work in waltztime: capitalism!

'I had a mind to grow, to swell out in these clothes ... but I am small. Still, I'm hairier than you,

'I haven't lost my past. I don't believe we'll all grow large and loud by drinking maraschino....' And we laugh. He leans into my face. 'Frankly, I must ask ... you are a Turk, Osman? Now, is that good or bad? Does it put you on my side? Think very carefully....'

'Oh,' I say. 'That's easier than everything you've asked. Long long ago – we almost all were Turks....'

'And you let your parents hang the name on you, Osman?' Aqil mocks and laughs. 'What kind of babe is that? If you were unsure of what you were – you could shout out my name: 'Aqil'. That's me! – Aqil – '*Un tel: Tel quel*'. Just a guy. The wise! Seeker for justice!'

'I think I see, Aqil,' I say. 'We have to make it come out as we want ... all of it, everything.... Grasp reality, sculpt it.... It's too late, it always was. Do it anyway.'

'A holy fool like you,' he says. 'Even you, you see that is the easiest, the only way.'

He hunts.

The prey is me.

'This,' he shouts, 'this is how it feels, when you are pissed and out of shape, and full of fear and weak,' and now he's wrestled me down on to my back, I see the marlin-spike, my head's as tender as an aubergine – nothing to give him pause, his dark clothes flap like sails unfurled; he is a black storm.... 'No, no,' he shouts. 'Don't bleed out on me! I want you bowed and bloody, *al sangue,* ripe and red upon my plate, a scarlet fungus in your pretty mouth....'

What an adventure! What a lesson, what a teacher! How small the world is, how short our history, and the universe fitting over us, a glove without fingers....

'More maraschino?' asks Aqil, as we sit down again, and I've cleaned my face, the ears with crusts of blood ... Aqil, the Afghan matelot, from where there is no water and no sea. He slumps, in his sailcloth. Who wore it before he took it off them, I wonder, who had he found on the beach, washed up and crimped white with saltwater, wizened and wrinkled like a set of entrails?

'Now I know everything,' I say. 'So quick! What do I do with it, the knowledge?'

To answer that, you need another Aqil.

'Don't thank me,' says Aqil. 'I'm always here. I don't drink. Just ask for me if you don't see me – I have many names and any one will do.'

'That crew is always round,' the barman joins in. 'They wear the clothes, the canvas, sharkskin boots, but they've never left the shore. Look at his hands!'

It's true. They're soft: an architect's. 'So, it's another scam?' I ask.

'You drank his booze,' the barman says. 'He told you everything. You gave nothing, and weren't asked. Don't believe him, if you prefer. He's always here, always flush – he stole the money destined for the cause, and then stole the money destined for the cause again. You're innocent, he's not afraid of you.

'He's always round, better than God: he'll give you a drink, and pick you up when you fall down.'

'Oh,' I say, 'all I know, I've learned from him. Like – maraschino makes you vomit.'

'That's as should be,' the barman says. 'Everything's his speciality.'

I return, over and over, to the bar, for Aqil's lesson. He's seldom there, when he is – morose and taciturn.

Torn posters on the yellow walls – '*Caligari werden... Fantômas contre Scotland Yard*'.

'Ah,' says Aqil, 'the innocent joy in evil, in massacre! How they loved it, till they found they'd over-killed; and they themselves were on the list and in the wagon. Art flies at dusk, Osman, and then it's dark – quick! in your burrow or the hungry things'll eat you!' and he laughs.

No more booze, and sometimes he touches me, slyly, for cash: 'any forints, Osman?' 'those Lettonian banknotes – what a riot! Do show....'

'I'm a simple soul, an innocent among the analysts,' he says. 'Not science, not self-design: that's not the future. Not probity, and not decline: not survival, not virtuality.... It's euphoria: blind trance. You are untouchable, where the police can't go – corrupt, paternalist though they are – and people here and there find they can get away with anything, that their freedom is freedom from being caught. People suffer, we know; we love it, cause it, administer and conceal it. Me and you: victims and executioners. Colonists and colonised, exploited re-exploited.'

'I'm a libertarian myself,' I say, surprised. 'On and off. I thought at most – you had the faith, Aqil, or if you'd lost it, you had kept the memory, like we have of anything we lose. Instead – you're a moralist, a justice freak....'

'I see the world from both sides, Osman,' Aqil says. 'If you wander, you fall into the pit, that's all. I know the pit.'

'But you have scrambled out,' I say. 'You hop in and out of it, you show how shallow it's become....'

'Exactly so,' he says. 'Who is to save us now...?'

'Not the cops,' I say. 'When you've the taste for massacre and Armageddons – who's to stop you?'

'Not me, not you,' he says.

It's all a riddle.

He corrupts me, I love him, I hate myself, I am not worthy ... I don't understand.

One day the barman says – 'Aqil is dead. He fell downstairs. Those boots, the cape.... I told him – if you starve yourself, you grow unsteady, tiny, a pebble rolling at a touch. Your clothes take control ...and down you go.'

'It's terrible,' I say. 'But I confess – he was sounding quite confused and lost....'

'Oh,' says the barman. 'He couldn't get anywhere with you – the more he taught, the more you lost your innocence. Resisted. You grew reckless, a stampede like him – he couldn't stop you.... "Tell him, mind his step", he told me....'

'And was he beautiful?' I ask. 'He must have sought his golden rule, his modulor – his steady state, his destiny. People stare in the mirror hoping they're finished, perfect. I know you can renew your cells, take every course on offer, so that you know it all, a fully rounded person, let electronics do the rest, the work, the ageing.... What for? – you must decide alone.... Did Aqil find what we are looking for – or did he pass it on ... to me?'

'Oh Osman,' says the barman, laughing. 'I hear cheap cynicism on your part! Aqil planned nothing for the future – his own, or anyone's. He was one of millions of those Afghan sailors, strangers to the waves, who roam and starve, and have survived the worst. They know the search for purity is vain – vainglorious. Purity? – that means the faith, the faith in life, in waking up to more tomorrows. Salvation's been long lost. Now, like all of us, I wait for strangers to decide my life – strangers, brothers – a common father? Who is he?

'A mother, warned off cuddling ... where's she gone, indifferent to you? Aqil had the great fear, Osman – our future, his – closed to all us simple folk, barred and forbidden like the past....'

‘I hear,’ I say, closing my ears, ‘that when you die, you are an avatar for someone who will summon you and all your ancestors ... dead and the quick will have a picnic – like Etruscans on their family tombs.... The future is an album of the past: we’re all in it, everybody is, as kids, adults, and fading away.’

‘Think! Osman – have you seen him since his death?’ the barman asks. ‘Is Aqil ready for your call? Are you acquainted with his afterlife, do you see him, the bogeyman that haunts the stairs?’

He flicks his rag, and pours himself a tot.

I ponder. ‘No,’ I say. ‘He’s lying very low. It’s true – he taught me everything. And disappeared. His take, his cut – is gone with him. You’re right – the contemporaneous is all a ruse, painted up to make us pass the time, to keep us quiet and trivial.... This self-improvement, these fresh instructions all your life.... Engineering a perpetual change, a readiness for future victories ... on your toes! Even the legless, toeless, win, amass an immensity of human love; how they shine forth, rearing martial on their blades. Victory without an enemy. True, the last, they shall be first. Then, when they are the first, they’ll be the last again, and so, and so.... How to be good, not bored, follow the rules of each new hobby till you’re honed, refined?... And then you’re dead....

‘I ask myself – what’s to be gained from this obedience? Are you a contender, or a puppet? How do you win, and what is the prize we never see...? What do the powerful, the visionaries, want, that differs from what awaits the rest of us? What is *their* race?’

‘Aqil fell downstairs,’ the barman says. ‘Maybe he climbed too high, and knew too much. Perhaps – was pushed. Rushed, in the dark. Beware, my young and silly friend....’

‘I’d nothing of my own,’ I say. ‘Aqil made me swallow him. His experience, emotions, they are mine. How little do I know of them: – maybe there are warrants out, a gangster contract....’

‘Hush, then,’ the barman says. ‘If people know you’re rich within, they’ll cut you down, open you up – pull out your innards, scoff them like dampened pretzels.... Nothing is safe if it’s unique. Your own possessions ... uninsurable, unsafe ... your spirit, tasty and fragile as a plover’s egg....’

‘Why? I ask: ‘I’d never thought the others envied me....’

'Anyone with anything,' he says, 'is targeted. There is no limit to the nastiness....'

We should leave it there. But, 'Everything is coveted?' I ask. 'We're all desired, wanted, longed for...?'

'In a way,' he says, 'but put like that – it's sugary. Don't delude yourself – there's rough stuff everywhere. And – I know more than Aqil did, but don't believe a word I say...'

INSTRUCTIONS FOR LIVING ...

Here's what you do.

Check you have a valid passport, know where you're from, how much your face is worth.

You can do nothing, so – to live the easy and rewarding life you want, how much money do you need?

Is there something you like doing?

Don't expect help.

You're ready.

Don't worry – there's millions like you. You'll get bad sex. As much as you want.

*

'Stop calling me the barman,' says the barman. 'I'm Aziz. I get all Aqil's money. I was a son to him.'

'He had no money,' I say. 'He may have left a treasure map....'

'His teaching was his suffering,' says Aziz. 'When he's gone, you start again, but he'll have taught you not to linger, not waste your time.... That's good as money, gives you confidence.'

'Time? I think it's wasted anyway,' I say. 'It's an unlimited resource. Use it without charge. Yours is an easy life, Aziz. Routine, at least. You and I, we don't do science, don't invent. We're humble sorts, who fiddle with the language, and make our moods seem meaningful. We don't take space, when we're gone, there is no gap to fill, we've not discovered anything. We're tourists, transients. What we leave, after, goes in the skip.'

'He was a father to me,' says Aziz, without commenting. 'That's why I could disobey. He sought an heir, a companion possibly – someone empty, ignorant and willing. You, Osman. A Turk on the run, despoiling, assimilating, bold and a conformist, a lover who makes the rules so tight he never gets to fuck.'

'It's all true,' I say, 'but you've a mean lining. My name's no guide to bigotries.'

'It's not that Aqil valued you,' Aziz says. 'He used to say, "I take a bottle everywhere – people only listen when they're liquored up. Then they forget. It's pitiful."'

'That's as may be,' I say. 'He made the rules. I'm ready. I'll do what he wanted of me.'

'Oh,' says Aziz. 'I know what he wanted. To live! Do it all himself. Here's the map – all the places he wanted to go. And here's the parchment – all the beliefs, convictions, hobbies, he wanted to profess.

'Never did any of them. A life failed completely. Just a gap plugged between a birth and bottom of the stairs.'

'Show me!' I say. Then, 'I don't recognise all of these.... The Altai. The Tour d'Argent in Paris, possibly a restaurant. A *gouffre* with carvings by Neanderthals; a bridge somewhere: the Skyliner. Deserts – lots of those: the Chinese quarter in Moscow. Crocodiles in Malawi. Why these?'

'Oh, he'd be fascinated, and make a note. It costs,' Aziz says. 'I tell you, you gain nothing if you comply. See – here's the beliefs: a true socialist, an oppositionist, a liberal, a millionaire, a collector of Impressionists ... a mixture of what you think and what you are. It's hard work. I'd do the trips first. If you start with the beliefs, you could end up real bad, if you talk about it, spread it around.'

'I'm sure someone's done them all individually,' I say. 'Put them together, and you're a surrealist, or a butterfly.'

'It's an idea,' says Aziz. 'Put them together and you could be the person he desired to be. Find the place, the crocodiles, take a photo – and you're him!'

'Is that what he desired?' I ask. 'It seems inconclusive. Random, even. A case of *si j'étais vous* – if I were you, where would I be, and who are you?'

'You'd have choice,' says Aziz. 'It's not one of these fly-by-night romances, a boozy challenge – a tale with funny names, no place indicated, just hooch and pills and lots of talk. You can go deep and make the loving last.

'Aqil was straight, but that's not compulsory.'

'It's antiquated,' I say.

'It's things he wanted, never had and never would. His was as good a plan as any,' says Aziz. 'But I'm comfortable here. I can have all the travel, all the arguments, and I don't have to move.'

'I can do all these,' I say confidently, 'even if I don't know why. I guess we all seek to do what the fathers haven't managed. Seek universal peace, life beyond the milky way, create a wipe-out bomb, a brindled cat, a zip that doesn't jam.'

'You're second rate, that is the prob,' says Aziz, pouring himself another tot. 'You wander in, swig down a bottle of sweet stuff, and make a life's pledge to fulfil a stranger's plan.'

All true. Like in every criticism of others' lives, the barman sees through self-deceit, commitment to a project apparently unique – but really arbitrary, derivative.... Aqil's life plan. His life, my life – see through them in a second. Look through the hole in the seer's stone, see the future, and you're blinded? Don't believe it: not a word. It doesn't happen so. Instead, you're hooked.

I'd re-visited the life-plan in a month, done everything, stayed unenlightened, often bored....

The Altai was the most rewarding, took the longest: gave the most. The animals – at first you started to become them, you joined a herd, you lost your individual sensibility, you felt as if you were your daughter and your eaten fathers.... Then, you changed. You were a tormented herdsman: transhumance, forever packing of the tent, the search for pasture, the cold the heat; recalcitrance of beasts, counting them, their death, their heavy precariousness, short marginal existences, the knife, their blood in buckets ... a battle with the inert, the stubborn, and the ignorant – the desert, slopes and drops, the shale, the scree, the watercourses disappeared, the unpredictability and monotony of everything – the clouds the winds the dust the sand ... the bare grey mountains ... riding, your sore crotch ... the hot, the cold....

Most frightening was the bridge: the hump.... Surrounded by the long and clumsy autos, you hit the slope, the rise, nothing before you but the sky – nothing to orientate you but your motor's hood, pointing to heaven, and all the other cars that brush your feathers, like a swarm of starlings – one mistake? and down you'd go, farewell, one broken wingman, a comma on a dash – and all the rest swirl on ... or you must drive on up, up to an empty heaven you disbelieve in....

The rest I did in a weekend; then started on beliefs. Impressionism – you can collect the lot on postcards, still drunk from lunch. The cave will sober you: relatives!... Then, an hour in a *banlieue* and you will pass from group to group, through revolution, every shade of red, and all intensity, from action through indifference, alone or with your mates ... believer and multiple apostate, defender of the faith, scourge of the backsliders and infidels ... conned into carrying someone's parcel, you are a millionaire until delivery.

There is no barman assured, available to unroll a treasure map of quests that can involve you all your life. Can you avoid the pledge you made, to spend your life adventuring? No one will trust you and your bottle, as you go looking for an innocent: search as you will, history's too short and limited, geography is likewise, and getting tinier. Everywhere is reached in hours – except for warzones, camps, prisons, spynests. And networks, laboratories and barracks, movie sets and gangs.... Keep away from those: 'Armed Surveillance' – the notices are clear enough. Don't settle – you can be dispossessed or starved the longer you stay somewhere, have kids, have animals: keep moving. All exploration booked, prepaid and guided, sleep in a caravan, a hedge, or yurt, or five star, led by avatars and guardian angels half-answering all questions, speaking your language and many more, far better than you've ever heard.

What you can't do, you must convince strangers that you might; and hand the heavy torch to them to carry – enlightenment! discovery!

*

If you've no clue, no future – sit at the bar. A solution always comes along. If not – keep sitting there. You'll see...

'Let me help you,' Farnaz says. She dresses like this all her life: a tinselled sweater, raggedy jeans. Maybe she's trained to spot the dismasted, leaky hulks like me, who've tramped the Altai, collectors of bric-à-brac, not safe to know, not profitable.

Each for ever the other's shadow – no reflection, no adventure. We were out of fashion, time – satisfied to seek no further in each other.

'Farnaz.What a name!' I say. 'Mine was taken from a list.'

'Oh,' she says. 'Mine too. Opinions also.... True, I'm exotic, but not if I go where my name originates....'

'What help...?' I ask.

'Help to have you feel your life had not been wasted,' Farnaz says. 'Give it to others? You aren't the type. Children? If you bore them, they bore you. "Bear", then "bore" – it's in the grammar.

'Aqil? The world is full of Afghan sailors – all the other Afghans died, and these invented ships and sailed away – but since their boats are immaterial, there is no port, no merchandise. They're unquiet souls, who plant their insubstantiality in you, and you become the wanderer. You know too much, you wouldn't die, but live forever, if we weren't animals.... What good are you, what bad? You're not a scientist, you don't persuade, inspire, you can't spin yarns about the gods, you drink too much to go in space, too fickle and cowardly to fight in wars....'

'I know all that,' I say: 'I've been told. When you're told, it's like in school; going back a generation, learning to be unfashionable.

'What you must distinguish is between the bad you do to yourself, unavoidable; and what comes from being where you are, your group, your colour, your civilisation and being in the way.... Making the distinction – that's important. Then, there's what happens to everyone, from being human, a species, like felines that eat their cubs, insects that eat their husbands....'

'Whatever you do,' says Farnaz, 'Unless you're an idiot, you are a mediocrity who's never done enough, even if every seed you plant comes up and flowers.'

'This city,' I say, 'is hard. This country – very hard. Work....'

'Yes,' she says. 'Imagine the cemeteries underneath – a city with no métro – just dead priests lying down in catacombs, a pope of popes roaming above, chivvying, trafficking all sorts of stuff.... The past – all the dead, outnumbering us many times, with just a thin skin supporting and separating us, a crust.... And you're right – work is very hard, if you have it and keep doing it; very hard if you don't have it, or you have it and it slips away, over and over, like a dam bursting over and over, and you and your friends all drowned.'

'Lots of slave work,' I say, 'is not like it is here, in this city. Elsewhere, they stop slaves running away: they're worth keeping. Here, any work – you are enslaved, but can be fired. You're a piece of merchandise – but aren't worth anything. If you leave, you start from what you've always been – a zero. If you are taken on, you must join the family too. Love and duty – those are fetters added to those you already wear as bondage. When you're disinherited, thrown back among the worthless – whose only qualification is their need for work and food – you'll take all insults with a grin, humiliations with a snigger. You're beaten flat.

'Usually, slaves have a price: not here. No boss wants slaves, they say! – it must be goodness that makes him, her, take you on, untrustworthy and idle as you are, to live poor and insecure for ever and ever....'

'I see you suffered, Osman,' Farnaz says. 'All your fault. You went to the cruellest places! Only the Americans, the British and the French make slavery last all your life, and bind your kids.... There is no term, manumission is arbitrary, it's hard to be bought out – the contract's not with you, it's between your owner and the dealer.... In this country – there are no binding contracts anyway. Maybe a lawyer charges you big bucks and a document is written in invisible ink on mandrake leaves.

'You'll learn to prize your condition as a slave – without that, you would starve. If you starve, there's paradise. Or hell.'

'It's true,' I say. 'This country has everything – communism, fascism, latifundia, mafia, slavery and patriarchy, racism and religion, radicalism, submission ... but most of all – *imbrogli,* set-ups. Frauds and fiddles. You can be sure – you're being tricked.'

'Famous slaves in history,' she sings along, 'Write a list of them! You see? Not a soul, not even a dead soul.'

'What do I do, Farnaz?' I ask. 'I won't listen, of course, but give me the idea. I've waited for you all my life, I'll be loyal to you, for all of yours – just don't disappoint me....'

'You know death will come, wherever you are, whatever you think you did,' she says. 'So – don't wait for it. Do something, something else. Leave. Keep leaving. You're better off than where you are, always. Do it today.... Fail in another place....'

'Where shall we go?' asks Farnaz.

'Together?' I ask.

'Why not?' she asks. 'I don't mind you. We've nothing better. Two's a gang.'

'Sharing?' I ask, with foreboding. 'I'm not sure about that. It's academic for now. But – there's not much to share except bodies, and having been to the same places.'

'Bodies?' she says. 'If you really want to. I'm not religious, and to do exercise, you need a special building: I'm fit, but not for everything.'

'It's nothing,' I say. 'No apologies. Just like they say, liking comes from what you want: I don't want – no offence.'

*

'Finding the right place takes longer than you want,' says Farnaz.

'We didn't find a place,' I say. 'We came back where we didn't want. And some places – left a mark....'

'Oh, the bridge!' she says. 'Your panic, your great fear. That will have been its mechanism – it's a shark! It takes your arm off if you let it dangle out. At any rate – you have your riches, still intact.... Your ju-ju....'

'I know it's old,' I say. 'It must be valuable.'

'My family had lots,' she says. 'A thousand years ago, they made them all in moulds. It still surprises us – there's so much detail in the mould ... and there were sacrifices, everybody had to have a following, some heads, some dolls, some masks – the festa meant something then, not just a holiday you had to have – to spend in, and you didn't earn. Reflect – this city's old. I don't think it's valuable. If you visit it, and then you leave – you've paid, but that's not value, it's just revenue ... like a tax.'

'It's hot,' I say. 'You need a fan, but the guys that do that cost a lot ... it ought to be mechanical – the ostrich has its fans built in....' We laugh.

There is a plague of ostriches, they run around the suburbs, they peck and shriek – if you're lucky, you can find an egg, and even paint it – a procession, guys in silver-gilt corselets, pantaloons of velveteen, wide hats, riding on elephants ... slaves on camels fanning the boss with fronds....

'Yes,' she says. 'It's very hot. It always will be. There's the miasma – comes from the sewers, the *cloaca maxima;* the river's very low, there is perpetual mist out in the countryside. What can you plant? Mangroves, perhaps: you can't eat them, and the oysters taste of shit.... The sea is mostly weed, and there's those pink and purple blooms: can you eat those? Put them in a bowl and grow them, enormous ones, they're enviable, there's a magazine that shows arrangements, they are fashionable....'

'Enough, Farnaz,' I say. 'The mist, the steam – and now there's smoke, I swear.'

'No one would set a fire,' she says. 'It all comes from what's underground – the villas, temples, all those ossuaries, the marrow streams, there's flesh to bake and dry ... it's cooking, seething, broiling, but not stuff you'd want to eat....'

'It could be mafia,' I say. 'They burn the stones to make the powder ... cement? Or is it lime? Or whitewash, to paint more temples and more stones ... or passed off, shipped out, as dope, as coca....?'

'I bet it's priests,' she says. 'There's hell, just a handspan down, there's vents, volcanoes – the old guys used to go down in the fire, bring back the easterners, Romanians I'll bet – the prostitutes who work the alleyways where it is blistering all night.... The priests must burn the hay down there....'

'You said it's mafia, Farnaz,' I say, irritated. 'Hell is mafia property. Do the priests do mafia deals?'

'Of course they do,' she says. 'It's a sideline for them. Mainly, they deal with devils, visit the circles of infernal life, the celebrated dead, illustrious spooks. Hobnob with old Hob, quaff bull's blood with the Satanic ghosts....

'Mafia's just greedy guys who run some tarts and sell some pills, and fix the games....'

'Why burn the hay?' I ask, intrigued.

'There's several crops a year,' she says. 'You have to store it, and camels prefer the fresher stuff....'

'You don't know the minimum of how to farm,' I say. 'It's taradiddles, what you say. I bet there's archives to be burnt, all the legal stuff and casting horoscopes and things you're not supposed to do if you're an expert in the Book ... if you're a librarian, you have to scrub your traces, cancel spoors.... There's bandits round, horse-thieves, people who'll cut out a sheep and brand it theirs with their own iron, their die ... Remember, I was in the Altai, helping muster herds....'

'It all gets muddled up,' she says. 'Especially with you, Osman. There is one Book now, but you stick to your ju-ju – we're all free to think what comes to mind, but there you stand, out on left field ... it's crude, phased out, looks like an owl, chalcedony, once it had ruby eyes, got sold or gouged....'

'It's art, Farnaz,' I say: 'It's not belief.'

There's fire. Maybe below there's always been. In nature – fire is certain, for eternity. It powers the crazy mechanism. Bang! The universe! Behold!...

The old imperial buildings – temples, churches, hippodromes, the fountains – those are held together by lead joints. If they melt, down comes the whole, the enormous shooting match ... if there's lead letters, words and dedications – those flow too, the columns and the *stelae* lose identities, their provenance, the arches their victories, panoplies; the obelisks crumble, crack....

'It means new labels must be found for everything,' she says. 'I'm sure it's all been done before – the Pantheon – the dome, the hole – it was to let the smoke out from the sacrifices.... We must invent new great men, and women too, new triumphs, strings of captives ... new ceremonies and songs. And if you're right, the smoke will hide it all, give it a sexy twist.... The gods love the smell of cooking – since they don't eat, smouldering hay must make them drool ... better than rhinocerus, for sure.'

'Should it concern us?' I ask Farnaz. 'All the big cities – agglomerations – have a pall above them. Activity, dust, ash – just overheating, the guys who sweat, guys who fan, guys who cool down, cool guys ... guys unlike me....'

It seems too large for me, I've no measure or perspective ... why does it take this turn...?

'Well,' she says. 'We've travelled, lived close, never in intimacy. Everything that's happened to me, has happened late, very late. For you, everything was early, you knew it all, you'd been told, you only had to do what someone else had laid down for you to do. We were ideal for one another. Neither had this passion for finding out about the others' lives: you don't wonder about the cow, her inner life, when you eat her backside or her calf, don't wonder what the chicken felt about the cock when you have her stuffed and roast. And then, one day, you – it happened to be me this time – find the little something ... like a bulb, hot pepper, a fatal comma, a full-stop – maybe where you've often looked, or never even thought. Like a spare appendix – a serious addition: ... like Appendix One. Something for scholars to discuss. An after-thought, late style, a spare that grows and then drops off, like a buck's horns, makes you ready for the battle, the rutt – fascinating, how they cluster round.... professors. The photos! "stretch out and spread your legs, hold still, very very still ... it's just a test, to see if you have what we think you do...."'

'I'm so so sorry,' I tell her. 'They say it happens to one of two.... That lets me out.... The statistic's you!'

'There is no consolation – just don't try. I know exactly how you feel,' she says. 'You'll never know me now. You gain yourself, but lose a person to rejoice to. I am a text that's finishing – you'll roam around, unfinishable, no challenge faced, no Turandot scene, no "*Vincerò*". It will not happen. No drama, no emotion, and no theatre.

'I have them all! Don't envy me....'

I don't. I shan't.

'I must confess,' she says. 'I've always done you down. Sold you short, fiddled, cheated, lied, deceived, two-timed. Withheld myself, withheld.... Stole all your cash and reputation, documents as well, all shredded, or sold on.... Your life I envied, so I trashed it all. Maybe you are a genius – an explorer – better still, a finder! Instead, I cut you down....'

'You thrust me down,' I say. 'And here we are, in separateness. Back where neither wants to be, a place where we've accomplished nothing, lives trudged through and wasted....'

'It takes you so much time,' she says. 'You plod! Your tasks brought no conclusion, ended up stacked in the woodpile, and your old ghost, Aqil, weighty in your bundle. Your ju-ju ... a heavy blob ... weighs you down....'

'Everybody carries one quite similar around,' I say. 'Stolen from the past – it winds around you, mistletoe, or ivy, and if you let it – it will throttle you. My statuette, my other self: a gangly semi-precious ape – a shape adored, chipped out by some near-*sapiens* band, a clan whose diety never quite took off, unable to bear its followers aloft, their hope for an integrity unachieved ... purity defiled and thrown down in the sand. That tribe, its gods, engineered no holy war, no mountain levelled, no forests burned, no oracles, no pyramids, no Book: no history and no transcendance. Extinction.

'The universe – those guys left it quiet and sightless. The world undisturbed, as yet another prototype of "us", we, trial hominids, filed past and into incoherence; no planets visited, and none destroyed. A failure? Hollow bones, a mound of them piled up ... Ready for science, blowing through them, merry tunes.

'I had my chance. Ignored it. I didn't start to make the whole, *Gestalt*. The picture always eluded me, I knew it lay there in the box of colours – you stopped me painting it....'

'You thought blank canvas was so beautiful,' she says. 'You thought it poetry. I told you what I think is true: – it is a void.'

'And now you're proud,' I say. 'You have a growth. A cancer. A fixed term, completion. Genius? It turned out you're the creative one. Something new, inside. You cheated me – it's quite unpardonable....'

'Oh,' she says, 'pardon is something I have never sought. You lived with me, and never saw me, never spoke to me, I hid and changed my shape, howled like a wolf and bleated like a goat.... I've won. And all you see is smoke, like the idiots who paid to hear the oracle, and thought they saw a beauty, stoned, sat in a cave. They saw smoke, her smoke. A quantity immense, that seemed to have no source, beguiling, concealing, coiling out in runes and code.... Just smoke. As you'd expect, never a whisper of your destiny....

'And you're wrong, quite wrong. You believe as if you have a religion – you assume there's progression, doing good that leads to doing better, science that tells you what there is, and so it must be better than just being, being what it is. Evolution – you've got it going the wrong way! Evolution is all about decline, a necessary adaptation to a desperate dying world, ageing, diminshed. Your ju-ju should have shown you.... Evolution's all downhill....'

'I understand your anger, Farnaz.... I have causes too....' I say.

I don't feel resentment, though I should. Whole lives, sliding by.

'Yes,' she says. 'I'm furious. I am banal, an animal, a mortal. Disbeliever. It all flows, no continuity, nothing fixed and steady. Certainly not time – it stops and starts, like it will stop for me.... Don't fret – it's not a tragedy. Tragedies are where a naive, or innocent, or idealistic, person comes to grief, and we all see it happening, slow, deliberate. Or two, more, people, driven by some ideal, a love, a hope – conflict disastrously. That's tragedy: we see it coming and they don't, and when they go, they leave a perfume – withered innocence....

'We two, we never got off the ground, Osman, never gained height. It's what they call a tragedy. It's not. And anyway – it would be of no consequence.'

*

'Hold my hand,' she says. 'It's nothing. Nothing, it has always been. I shall be nothing. I've always been nearly that – I recognise it, nothing, for ever: a walk down the corridor, with the pictures either side. Was it "nothing"? If not, then what? A matter of opinion? You'll say opinions aren't nothing. I know people are angry now because we, all humanity, we suffer and nothing is resolved, the questions and the difficulties, limitations and the ultimata, they remain, are added to, forgotten. People are right to be irritated, unappeased. Nothing is resolved and it all becomes more complicated, we are not asked anything, not even for opinions.

'I see it this way – you can be angry, or indifferent. I've always been indifferent. If I say I've always been quite angry – is the difference so so great?'

'Put like that,' I say. 'I can't find fault. We two didn't sculpt or build – nothing is left, nothing of you or I or we. Nothing preserved, nothing destroyed. Just things we say, a rite, a rote, we're used to it, it's general, it's like breathing or digesting: it's intimacy, or not being capable of it, and – apologising.'

'Rome burns,' she says. 'It always has. Burns and burns. Is not consumed: unhappy people have to live in it.'

'All I remember is the steppe,' I say. 'The desert, the pastures, the mountains. And, of course, the bridge. The fear. Seeing the sky, and going very fast in crowds, up and up, faster, faster.

'The politics, the history the other tasks, infantile or causes lost – all over, done, all compromised, things we should have done, or not. Become irrelevant, not to be confessed, admitted ... all you might have wanted, born in your grannie's shoes, a failure ... happenstance that wasn't: didn't happen. Beliefs that wither, winning cards you find the pips have fallen off....

'And you, Farnaz?'

'My family,' she says, starting to cry, 'never saw them, in a country I have never seen, nostalgia like a thorn – in my throat, and jiggled down, it lodges in my heart.... Alas, what never was and will not be. How sad. How useless – memory, regret, the tight-wound spring of time. Just the one trick learned – to create what never is or ever will be, and it's on our shoulder, massive, one dark wing that cannot fly us anywhere....'

I had been down the *gouffre*. Now, Farnaz enters the cave called *Riesending*: the Enormous Thing. The life, adventure, she had wanted, she will never live? Now – the endless dark.

I'll never mention her – that is my tribute, my gift.

My adventures – they are me, and they're done, it's over. I'm not ready, not at all, but what's been done to Farnaz will be done to me. It happens to everybody, but that doesn't sweeten it at all. Forgetting, being forgotten.

My quests took longer than I'd thought. They were oddities that seemed a revelation. My messenger, my angel – Aqil; no one remembers him, whoever set him up and planted in his head the things he would not do. Now, the people are all new, things fall down, get demolished, set up in another place – but 'Justice' – 'Aqil', the significance of his name – who remembers now the country that he came from, there on the maps, but nowhere else?

And Justice – the idea, once contrived, was placed in a lexicon and abandoned there.

I'm glad Aqil did not set the search for it, for justice, among my tasks.

Aqil and Farnaz – what does it mean, my obligation to do justice to them?

*

Three old men are singing, under the window: one plays a prelude on a *duduk,* a wooden pipe... Here, we all jostle on together – all the faiths and loyalties. The hatters sell the different local hats – the Serbian forage caps, the white skull coverings made of pounded felt, tall shapkas in fake astrakhan ... to each his hat, to each her foulard, her bold hair.... I look down on them, the three old men – oh no! they are a radio. They've been canned, and as I close the window I see in the pane – myself. I've been canned too! My voice, were I to let it out, would creak and whine like theirs.

It must have taken years to tramp my road – I thought it's been just months, or even weeks. There must have been much more along the way I didn't see and don't recall....

It's time to pass it on, to a novice, acolyte; the map where all the boundaries have been rubbed out, the rivers dried, the mountains flat.

As for Rome: can it be sin, excess, or rubbish, makes it burn? It's what they said – the ancients, not loved by anyone. As they foretold, the whole world fries and steams, it roasts....

The smoke ... Paris too has its cap of obscurity, like Cairo, Istanbul. The coal that's under India – it's acrid as it burns ... Beijing – they say the pall is dust, or sand.

Volcanoes – they're a display, not set off all at once. The universal flame would spark up from an accident: a Roman candle dropped on a short fuse.

What next? A strike from space? Another dum-dum like what cut down the dinosaurs? A hundred years of ash and rock, and we'll all be white, and lose our sight – the sun eclipsed, the cold preserves another band of geniuses, fresh contenders waddling forth, a horde of penguin types who'll rule the world and in turn stumble to extinction. All animals, line after line, each new model believing it's invented intelligence and love, extinguishing the other species, then itself.

Farnaz is burnt with white flames – the ceremony is ignored, our eyes are on the doors that for a moment hide the fire, and as you leave, the chimney sends her, flakes and scraps, into the sky.

Life. It's been a repetition, academic. But – happiness! That, my story does not seem to tell. Even with Farnaz, her delicacy, her scorn, her discontent, indifferences and humiliations scattered round – even with her, unexpected ripe moments – of euphoria, of joy.

The world in flight – some to the cities, others as far as it is safe to go.... It's never safe, the further you can run, the more your spirit fails, your breath as well, and when you get to where you have to make a pause – you're evidently alien....

The far East of Turkey, far South of Chile, deserted zones of Argentina, you search and search for your rebirth, the distant place, clean and uncontaminated, where you slip in silently, with no history, no colour and no faith – and you're born again as someone quite quite different. New life!

One trade I have never practised – counsellor to the Prince. To do that, you need to know all people very well – and it's a fraud, because what you know is only useful to the Prince, and useless, ultimately dangerous, to you.

I can't stay here, not since the war: the camps, the killings; suspecting everyone, their recent past, their distant history. Religion, ethnicity – what trivial stuff is that? What lies we live by....

The Prince? Life in jail for all that sort, if they can't be executed quick....

I'll end up where once I started off with Farnaz. Now we see she is a dear departed.

With my respect, she'll be unmentionable ... as though she never was.

I'll go where I can see the smoke, far off.

About the author

John Fraser lives near Rome. Previously, he worked in England and Canada.

www.ingramcontent.com/pod-product-compliance
Lightning Source LLC
Chambersburg PA
CBHW020553310726
48979CB00008B/1194/J

* 9 7 8 1 9 1 4 9 3 8 0 4 7 *